THE Raven's Heart

Jesse Blackadder

T0125777

Bywater
BOOKS

Ann Arbor
2012

Bywater Books First Edition: September 2012

The Raven's Heart was first published in Australia in 2011
by HarperCollins*Publishers* Australia Pty Limited

Cover designer: Bonnie Liss (Phoenix Graphics)

Printed in the United States of America
on acid-free paper.

Bywater Books
PO Box 3671
Ann Arbor MI 48106-3671
www.bywaterbooks.com

PRINT ISBN: 978-1-61294-027-4
EBOOK ISBN: 978-1-61294-028-1

For Andi

I'll sacrifice the lamb that I do love,
To spite a raven's heart within a dove

William Shakespeare, *Twelfth Night*

Foreword

A sixth-generation Australian intrigued by the origins of my family name, I traveled to Scotland in 2004 and drove to a place in Berwickshire marked on the map as "Blackadder." The name turned out to signify the original Blackadder Estate and the remains of Blackadder House, built on the foundations of the much older Blackadder Castle.

The first sight of those stone ruins, rising through the mist on the banks of Blackadder Water, was haunting. That day was the first time I heard the story of how Blackadder Castle was taken by the Holme family in the sixteenth century through the forced marriage of Robert Blackadder's widow, Alison Douglas, to David Holme, the Baron of Wedderburn.

The name of Captain William Blackadder turned up in the history books a few decades after the theft of Blackadder Castle. William was appointed the Crown's Seeker of Pirates, worked for Lord Bothwell, and ferried the Queen of Scots to Alloa after the birth of her son. The Blackadder family history records are unclear on whether he came from the Berwickshire or Tulliallan branches of the family. John and Edmund Blackadder were both known as notorious pirates during the reign of the Queen of Scots, and another John Blackadder, head of the Tulliallan branch of the Blackadder family, was one of many nobles called up to support the Queen against rebel factions.

Mary, the tall and charismatic Queen of Scots, loved to disguise herself as a man and wander the streets of Edinburgh in secret. She held numerous balls and parties in which she and her ladies-in-waiting appeared dressed as men. She wasn't the only woman who passed as a man: after a battle between Sweden and Denmark in August 1567, of the 1500 Swedes left dead on the battlefield, 500 were found to be women. They had worn their hair knotted under their helmets and their clothes and arms were the same as the men's. They had fought with great valor and strength.

This novel is based on many of these real events and characters. Unlike William and the other Blackadder men, Alison Blackadder is fictional, inspired by references to courageous female servants and companions who helped the Queen.

The Raven's Heart

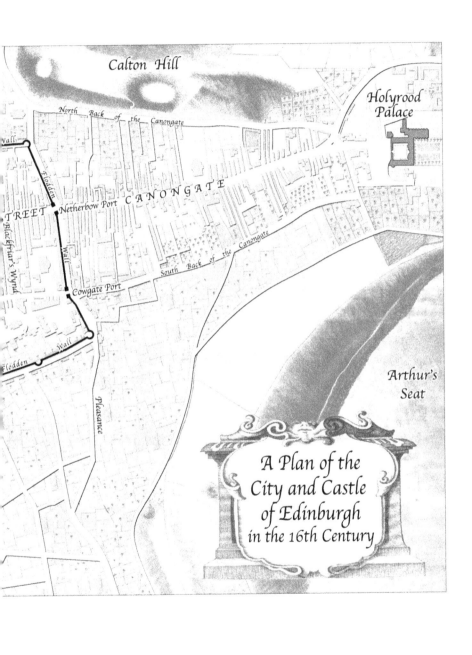

THE HIGHLANDS

Inverness
Inverness Castle

Loch Ness

BADENOCK

Battle of Corrichie

Aberdeen

Ruthven Castle

Dundee

Drummond Castle

Perth

Saint Andrews
Falkland Palace

Loch Leven Castle

Tulliallan Castle
Rossend Castle

Leith and Newhaven

Stirling

Alloa

River Forth

Callendar House

Linlithgow

Seton Palace

Haddington Abbey

Dunbar

Glasgow

Edinburgh

Craigmillar

Crichton Castle

Hills

Lammermuir

Wedderburn

Whiteadder Water

Eyemouth

Berwick

Langton Castle

Hume Castle

Blackadder Castle
Blackadder Water

Peebles

THE BORDERS

Jedburgh House

A Map of

SCOTLAND

in the 16th Century

Hermitage Castle

ENGLAND

Dumfries

Carlisle

Prologue

Scotland, 1519, twenty-six years before I was born.

It was deep in winter and the sound of rushing water penetrated even the stone walls of the tower room. Black running water, down below where the castle foundations cleaved to rock on the side of the river bed. Black running water, carrying our cursed family name in every drop. Black running water, carrying our downfall from the west, where our enemies, so close, were paused.

My grandmother Alison was born a Douglas and by the light in her chamber her hair fell down her back in a streak the color of blood. The man in front of her carried a streak of real blood down the side of his trouser, and his hair was lank and wet. A girl on her knees pushed and shoved at the fire, pumped the bellows, heaved in another log.

"You are certain?" Alison asked him.

"He is on his way now." The man looked down at his boots. "He comes to woo you, he says."

"Leading an army!"

"Aye."

She stood tall. "I would rather die."

The man looked up at her. "He will not waste a tender moment on you. If you had rather die, you shall. His brothers will simply marry your daughters."

"They are babes! Is he such a monster as to marry those oafs to children?"

"Children grow. All he has to do is betroth them. But he would prefer to seal the bargain with you."

Alison was silent for a moment. "And William?"

The man's voice was curt. "There can be no male heir."

Alison's face was etched deeply. She was a strong woman, tall, and not yet thirty. Six years a widow, alone in that cold castle bearing the weight of a name that had come to her by marriage. Six years of listening for the sound of hooves in the night, like some soft-furred creature with the predator's stink ever in its nostrils. She crossed the room and stood in front of the armaments hanging dusty on the wall.

"I could join those wretches downstairs and fight," she said softly.

He watched her back until she turned around. "Don't be a fool. This is an army coming."

"Well, what then?" she snapped. "Should I invite them in? Should I cut the children's throats and my own right now? Or should we run like cowards and let them have the place?"

"You must order the garrison to keep the castle secure. They are bound to fail, but you must put up a fight so it is known you resisted. When Hume comes, agree to marry him."

"What about William?"

"I will take William tonight to his cousins. They will see Hume brought to justice and you restored. Marry Hume and protect the girls until the marriage can be annulled. William will live to inherit."

This is the moment when I wish I could reach back through the years and warn her somehow, stop her putting in place the train of events that will lead to our ruin. Better to cut William off without his name, or find a place for him in the church, where any man of this family not skilled in warfare has been sent. My grandmother had known love with Robert Blackadder, who died on the Flodden Field six years earlier. She would have been better to cut all of their throats and her own while she had the chance rather than submit to this marriage with David Hume, Baron of Wedderburn.

She straightened herself and tossed back the red coils of her hair.

"Perhaps he has heard of our beauty?" she said. She turned to the serving girl, still kneeling motionless on the hearth. "Wake the children and bring them. Dress William to ride. Bring scissors."

The girl stood, curtsied, and backed out of the room.

"She will warn them," the man said. "Men will desert."

"Let them. I would not keep them here to fight to their death. Enough will stay." She put a hand out and her fingertips found his cheek, brushed its harsh stubble, and then fell to her side.

"Take William," she said. "Hume will find his pretty prizes shorn like nuns, and perhaps that will keep us safe a little while. If I were braver I would take a brand from the fire and draw it across all our faces to sully his victory."

Down deep in the castle the whisper spread like a licking flame and the smell of fear began to rise. Some took whatever was at hand and slipped out into the night, heading through four miles of darkness to Allanton village. A third of the fighting men stationed at Blackadder Castle were gone by the time the man threw six-year-old William up in front of him on a fresh horse, wrapped a cloak around him, cuffed him when he began to cry, and galloped into the night.

The two girls, still flat-chested and narrow-hipped, wept as Alison hacked off their curls close to their heads. Weapons were issued, heavy doors bolted and reinforced, look-outs stationed. It had rained heavily in recent weeks and the swollen river rushing past the castle's foot made it impossible to hear any approach.

I have never been in that castle, but the memory of it has been handed down to me with my name, the same name as the stones and the river. It came to me in dreams, from the whispering of William, my father, night after night as my eyelids sagged and my breathing slowed, the whispering of theft and murder and revenge. A story I know so well that it is as if I were in the castle that night, waiting with Alison and her daughters, Beatrice and Margaret Blackadder, in the bedchamber. As if I were fleeing with young William, clutching the horse's mane in terror. No sound except the roar of the river, and not a single soul asleep.

Part I
1561

One

Scotland, 1561.

We come across the North Sea, bearing the face of heaven in our hold.

A fleet of ships brings such a treasure, our galley speeding ahead and the rest following slowly with her horses and fineries, her tapestries and clothes. She returns from thirteen years in the French court to take up the reins of power.

She has been gone since she was five. Does she remember that she returns to a city of stone? Stone is too old to care what human hands press against it, what blood spills in its crevices. Even the palace, Holyrood, with its French architecture, is made of stone and, looming above it, Edinburgh Castle is hewn from the cliff so that none may attack it and none may escape. She sails to a stone city, an icy country, and a cold people.

As we draw close to the coast, heavy fog envelops us. Bass Rock materializes through the mist like something enchanted, its sides steep and forbidding, and the gulls scream and wrack and sweep around it in circles. The sea is brown and heaving; the outpour of the Forth River is a scum of Edinburgh's rot slapping at the side of the ship. She waits on the deck to set eyes on the land, but it refuses to reveal itself through the mist.

August nineteenth, five of the morning, and the ship lies becalmed. The wind has driven us at a furious pace all the way from France before abandoning us at the last mile. All I can hear is the sound of the gulls and my father calling orders to trim this sail, haul in that rope, edge the wheel around to catch whatever hint of breeze will come.

When finally we edge our way into the port at Leith, there is no fanfare, no welcoming party, no nobles lining the dock. Bothwell frowns until I can see the crease like a slash between his eyes. The Queen, standing next to him, is silent, her face composed. Her four Marys, in a colorful circle behind, look crestfallen. I am ashamed. She has come from the light and color of France, she has come from fireworks and flowers and an exquisite court, and her only greeting is the gulls.

Bothwell strides down the deck, anger in every footfall, and halts by my father at the wheel. They speak in low voices for a moment, then my father looks up and orders me over with a sharp movement of his head.

"The fools have not been watching the wind to know we are early," Bothwell says to me. "When we dock, you must run to the house of the merchant Andrew Lamb and find if Lord James is on his way. If there is no word, take a horse and ride to Edinburgh to rouse them."

"He will ride," my father says. "None faster."

Bothwell swings around and marches back to the Queen, and we busy ourselves so that none of us look upon her as the ship comes alongside the dock. Ropes fly down and men jump from sea to land; all is activity. The air smells of brine as though the mist around us is really a pale ocean and we a panicked school of fish.

A single fisherman on the dock limps over to see the commotion and stares up at the ship. "Who goes there?" he calls.

"It is Mary Queen of Scots," Bothwell calls back in a voice raised to carry across a crowd of hundreds. "Returned at last. Long live the Queen!"

The fisherman sinks to his knees and bows his head. The first Scot to greet the Queen in her own land, stinking of gut, his hands bloody, a royal scatter of silver scales glinting on his tattered jumper.

Then the Queen's laugh rings out like a bell on the morning air, a laugh as if she has no care, as if being met by a fisherman is entirely right and good. We all turn to look at her and the fisherman raises his head too, and it seems at that moment the fog begins to lift a little and our hearts, so used to being in fear, lighten. We are to be ruled by a woman with such a laugh, even if she can barely speak our native tongue any longer.

She and Bothwell turn to come down the ship and I stand by my father, hungry for a close look at her, until he nudges me sharply and says, "Go!"

Do I imagine or do her eyes follow as I swing over the ship's side and climb hand over nimble hand down through the ropes, leap lightly to the ground, and break into a run, swift over the wet cobblestones and into the mist?

When I pound my fists on the merchant Lamb's door, he leans out the window in his nightshirt to take my message. Within minutes a servant has brought a pony and I set off for the city, barely four miles away, my legs hard around his shaggy hide, spurring him to a gallop with boots and reins.

In Edinburgh nothing is ready for the Queen either; she is not expected for three days. I gallop up the deserted High Street as fast as the pony can manage, calling out so that the ordinary people will hear it too: "The Queen is coming! She has landed at Leith! The Queen is coming!"

By the time I reach the castle gate, a crowd is coming up the High Street behind me. My throat hurts, my voice is rough, the pony is steaming and heaving. The guards step out to halt me and far off in the fog I hear the soft boom of a cannon, the sound traveling all the way from Leith.

Lord James Stewart himself comes to the gate to take my message and his jaw tightens as he learns his half-sister comes three days early to take back her reign from his bastard regency.

"Go and tell them a party will come down to meet her," he says.

I ride to Bothwell's stable and trade the exhausted pony for my own mare before galloping out toward Leith again. People are beginning to gather by the roadside with expectant faces as I thunder by and disappear into the fog.

Lord Bothwell takes my horse by the reins as soon as we pull up in Lamb's yard. "Your mare will do nicely for the Queen, Robbie." He gestures to a servant. "Get the side-saddle."

The rest of the ship's men have been begging for horses to carry the royal party and they have assembled a herd of sorry creatures with muddy hides. Few have the saddles that a queen's party will expect— such is a luxury for commoners. John Knox the preacher, who has declared his implacable hatred for the Queen from the pulpit of Saint Giles, will no doubt be gleeful at this batch of evil omens and take it as further proof that heaven frowns on the monstrous sight of a woman ruling over men.

We wait in the courtyard and when Bothwell comes out of Lamb's house with the Queen, I am close enough to see her face as she looks around at the beasts we have gathered. Her expression stays impassive, but I see her swallow. I put my face close to my mare's, whispering into her ear that she will carry a queen and to do her proud.

Bothwell brings the Queen toward me. She steps to the front of the horse and strokes her nose with her gloved hand. "Does this creature have a name?" she asks in French.

"Artemis, Your Grace," I stammer.

She walks around to the mounting block.

"What is this?" she asks, looking up at the side-saddle.

Bothwell looks confused. "Madam?"

She gestures at the saddle. "In France a queen rides astride. Even Catherine de Médici does so."

He hesitates. "Shall I find another saddle, Your Grace?"

She shrugs. "Today I will ride the Scottish way. It is not so far. When my own horses and saddles arrive, you shall see how a woman can ride, Lord Bothwell. I'll wager I can outride even you."

He takes her boot to lift her into the saddle. Under her brocade riding dress I see the flash of breeks and I have to stop myself staring like a cabin boy.

She swings up lightly and I can see from the way she takes the reins that she knows how to ride. She smiles down at me for a moment and nods. My eyes hurt looking up at her, as if I am staring into the sun. She turns the mare's head and rides her in small prancing circles.

Another cannon booms. The lords have arrived to meet the Queen and accompany her to Edinburgh. Bothwell leads the royal party out of the courtyard and the first cheers rise from the crowd in the street of Leith. I let the party pass and fall back to mingle with the stragglers. I need a moment to catch my breath.

This whole country is starving in the gray, dour winter, though the reformers would never let us admit it. It is less than two years since we lost the Catholic Church and Parliament outlawed the May revelry. We are starving for life, for a brief, fierce moment of joy. We are starved from the lack of something more than toil, cold, violence and the bitter struggle for power.

Until I saw her, I believed I hungered only for the lost castle of Blackadder. If I were a court poet I would scribe a verse praising her as the first stream of sunlight to strike the slate-gray stone of the castle on the rock. I am no poet, so it is only my imagination's parchment where I scratch down that she has exploded into me like a gunpowder flash and I am still half-blinded, ears ringing.

Two

Edinburgh, the fortress. At its highest point, Edinburgh Castle broods over the city, dark and ancient. It crowns the Flodden Wall, which was built to keep the citizens safe but now encircles the streets so tightly there is nowhere to go except up. Some of the tenements rise twelve floors from the ground and waste is thrown down past the windows day and night. Edinburgh is sprouting upward like a crop of mushrooms in a bed of slop.

Holyrood Palace, built in the French style by the Queen's own father, lies far away from the tenements at the city's lowest point by the rocky rise of Arthur's Seat. Set into green gardens, it is wantonly decorative with its round towers, wide windows, and the soaring spires of its abbey. The Queen will live here as if there is no danger in the land, while the rest of the city huddles inside the wall with guarded gates and night-watch patrols.

She returns to the country of her birth speaking French, married, orphaned, and widowed by the age of eighteen, and the nobles do not know how to greet her. We have spent much of her life under a regent elect where the real business of majesty was the redistribution of wealth and power among the nobility, and there have been no pageants to draw attention to that.

But while the lords and nobles prevaricate, the ordinary people light bonfires every night and sing in the streets in their hundreds. It is not so long since they were Catholics like the Queen and just three months past they rioted against the reformers and held the May revelry in defiance. Robin Hood and Little John walked the streets as of old. The reformers condemned one of them to hanging but the crowds rose in fury and rescued him from the gibbet. The people do not want such joyless lives and the Queen brings with her the promise of delight.

Almost a fortnight after she rides into Edinburgh, the Lord Provost finally holds the first formal reception to welcome her home. My father and I manage to be included, dressed in the finest garb we possess, almost blending in among the lesser nobles. Once our name would have put us closer to the monarch but now it is by Lord Bothwell's grace we are here at all, included only as men in his service. We stand at the rear of the room with him, while the other nobles jostle close to the door where she will enter.

The musicians strike up a welcome, there is a ripple of excitement, and I crane my neck to see her. She appears: we drop our heads and sink low and then she bids us rise in her clear voice. As she begins to move, a hum of chatter breaks out.

"She needs a man," Bothwell says from the side of his mouth. "Look at her. Ripe."

For this evening she is dressed in a gloriously embroidered gown of simple white, while her ladies are her foil, garbed in shades that hurt my eyes. In reformist Scotland we have forgotten such colors exist.

"Those French idiots married her to a child." Bothwell gives a sly grin and drops his voice. "She's a beauty. I could give her an education."

"She's a girl." William almost spits the words. "Better for Scotland if she carried a sow's face. What good will it do us to have a pretty child Queen and a coterie of giggling maidens? We need a strong ruler."

The Lord Provost has set a raised chair for the Queen in the middle of one wall and she moves past us, making her roundabout way to it so that she may greet the guests. She favors Bothwell with a nod and when she catches sight of me she smiles. I smile back at her until William jabs my back and I drop to one knee and bend my neck. I stare at the stone, my knee hurting and my face burning, until she is seated to receive her nobles.

Bothwell winks at me as I rise to my feet again. "Another one to fall under Robbie's spell. You can even charm a queen, lad."

"You'd better learn some manners," William says.

Bothwell shrugs. "I'll bet the Queen is sick of manners. You should send Robbie to plead your family's cause."

"Robert is too young."

I straighten. "I'm not. I could persuade her, William."

He turns to look at me as though he has only just noticed I'm no longer a child.

Bothwell claps a hand on William's shoulder. "Our sailing days are over, my man. I'll be here in the city, serving her, and your cousins will have to run your ship for now. Why not try getting Robbie into the royal household and see what favor he can find?"

My father narrows his eyes but before he can answer, Bothwell nudges him and jerks his head. "See? Already he honeys her ear."

William clenches his fists when he sees who is addressing the Queen, and I ease away from him.

"Look well, young Robbie," Bothwell says, his voice dropping so none can overhear. "There is your foe."

I turn to take my mark of Lord Hume, chief of the Hume clan with its rich estates and castles. His cursed cousin forced William's mother, my grandmother, into marriage and his cursed clan has held fast to Blackadder Castle for more than forty years. He is one of Scotland's leading nobles. William is but a sea captain and I thought by all to be his lowly nephew.

As Hume and his wife bow and step away from the Queen, William hisses, "Do not stare," and I lower my eyes. But this is the first time I have seen the head of the clan that stole our birthright and I tilt my head to observe him.

He is born of men who have fought for their wealth and, unlike some of the Queen's lords, he is strong and battle-scarred. He smiles at the Queen, but it is the smile of a warrior, not a flatterer. With his fortress, Hume Castle, providing early warning of English invasions, Lord Hume controls much of the lower corner of the country where it abuts England and the sea, and he has not gained such lands and men by fawning.

"How will you win her favor?" Bothwell asks, so quietly I can hardly hear him. "Hume is already making himself popular. You must act quickly."

"Let me try," I say to William. "She has noticed me."

William says nothing and I turn my gaze back to the Queen. All around, the faces turned toward her are hungry. Not only the men, whose desire is more naked, but the women too. She is a fire roaring in a hearth that has been ashes for all our living memory.

There is a shift and a stir down the length of the hall. The musicians play a few notes and then strike up a galliard. Men and women shuffle and move into long lines, and the Queen rises to her feet to join in. In a few moments the floor is a swirl of color. I put aside thought of Hume, step up, and partner a pretty noblewoman, taking her by the waist and swinging her around in a practiced sweep. She smiles at me.

I glance up to see the Queen dancing her way toward me. She is easy to see, being a good head above the women and many of the men too, and none of us can keep our gazes where they should be. Under its bindings, my heart starts pounding. By the time she has progressed down the line and come to face me, my cheeks are hot.

"Welcome to Scotland, Your Grace," I greet her in French, my mother tongue. At its familiar tones, her half-smile becomes a full one.

"My Edinburgh messenger. I thank you for your hard ride and your fine mare." She looks me over unashamedly until my cheeks are even hotter. I concentrate hard on my step and skip, step and skip.

Our eyes meet as the final turn comes. I put my hand on her waist and spin her around. She moves easily. "I do not know your name," she says.

I lean in as close as I dare. "I am Robert, from the family of Blackadder."

She wrinkles her forehead. "I have heard that name," she says, before moving to the next man.

After the dance, I steal away to hold the words we have shared close to my breast. But no sooner have I settled back against a pillar than a hand falls heavily on my shoulder.

"I have it now," my father says, leaning close. "Bothwell was right, though he knows not why. It's time to put your sword away, my lad. A boy will never get close enough. But a lady-in-waiting could become a confidante. Such a girl could win the Queen to her cause."

I try to pull away, but he has me firmly by the shoulder. "She already has girls," I protest. "The four Marys never leave her side."

"The Marys have been away as long as she," William says. "She needs a woman who knows how Scotland works. I don't see that person here, Robert. You could make her need you. It's time to unbind yourself and return to womanly ways."

Since I was eight years old I have known how to use a dagger and sword, how to pitch my words low and cock my hips forward. For half my life I have pulled on my boots and walked or ridden as a boy.

It is so simple for him to turn my world in a moment. *Unbind yourself and return to womanly ways,* he says, as though it is simply a matter of loosening the bands of fabric that have constricted my breasts for so long they are part of me. As simple as unlearning the wide-legged stance, the turned-out walk, the set of the jaw, the lift of the eyes when challenged.

"She already knows me as Robert," I say. "Anyway, I have no courtly ways. I will stammer and faint in those choking frocks. I will forget myself and spit, or look upon her too boldly."

William drops his hand from my shoulder to my arm and closes his powerful fingers until I wince and grit my teeth. "You are getting too old for this disguise," he says. "Did you think you would run about as a stripling forever?"

"Even if a captain's child could come to court, Hume will find out that your daughter lives," I say.

"A Tulliallan Blackadder is noble enough for such rank. You will come as John and Margaret's daughter and pose no threat to Hume." William's fingers grind deeper into my arm.

"If you would have me a woman, then unhand me," I say.

He stares down at me for a moment, then abruptly loosens his grip. There will be a band of bruising around my arm, and not for the first time.

"Get home," he hisses. "Tomorrow you ride to Tulliallan."

≈　≈　≈

I remember the cold touch of the Blackadder Water, the black running river that carries my name, the river that holds our fate. I have never laid eyes on Blackadder Castle, but I have traced that river to its source, gone on horseback and foot through the Lammermuir Hills, pushed through gorse and bracken and come to the place where the water gently rises. There, at that soft moment in the heather, it is not black at all, but clear across my hand and as cold as death on my fingers. It burns like ice, water that doesn't know its own history yet, water that knows nothing but having fallen as rain on the hills, water that has been floating as mist, water insubstantial.

William is nearing half a century of years and he has lived all of those he can remember without walking on the land that carries his name. When he was carried on horseback for two nights to the safety of his relatives, the clan chief Sir John Blackadder did not want the might of Hume hammering at the defenses of Tulliallan. He kept William only a few days before sending him away to the west in secret. A poorer branch of the family took him in and for a time he disappeared among a rabble of brawling cousins, another dirty boy in a tiny holding.

The powerful men of the family set about winning back the castle and freeing William's mother and sisters from David Hume and his brothers. But the Humes were not known as the Spears of Wedderburn for nothing. Robert Blackadder, Prior of Coldingham, was slaughtered along with his entire hunting party by Hume men on the Lammerton Moor, shouting his curse on the Hume family as he died. Patrick Blackadder, Archdeacon of Glasgow, was ambushed on the way to meet Lord Hume in Edinburgh and killed in the swamp of Nor Loch. Sir John of Tulliallan, father to my foster father, the current Sir John, was beheaded, ostensibly in punishment for a crime, but the family believed Hume had a hand in it.

We believed the land would protect us as we protected it, that the very river itself would rise against those who stole it from us. This land was granted to us by a king, and is not a king second only to God? King James II stood by the riverbank and a battle-weary man knelt in front of him, head bowed, hands resting on the hilt of his sword, its tip buried in the dark earth. And when that man rose again, the name of the river was his name: Blackadder. He nicked his arm and let his blood drip into the water to signify his bond to it.

But as the Humes continue to prosper, Blackadder Castle stands strong. The river has not washed them away and the stones do not dislodge themselves in outrage.

When William was old enough, John Blackadder the younger, by then the family's head, bought him a small ship, a livelihood that would keep him far from Tulliallan. William lived a sailing life, taking his ruffian cousins Edmund and John (known as Jock) on board the *Avenger* as crew. He found himself a French wife on one of his voyages and brought her back to Edinburgh. They were a captain's well-to-do family on the middle floor of a tenement in the Grass Market. He carried goods for some of Edinburgh's greatest merchants and his cousins plied a fruitful trade in piracy.

But William never forgot what was his. To his wife, and to me his daughter, he whispered night after night of the castle so that I fell asleep with the stories of it echoing in my head. His words painted a picture of our lost home, its turrets rising from the bank of Blackadder Water. He whispered of his plan to petition the young Queen of Scots when she returned to Scotland from France, where she'd been sent for safety. He whispered that she would be our salvation.

Somehow those whispers reached the ears of the Hume family.

My mother, large-bellied with her next child, was murdered on Christmas Eve when I was eight years old. William had taken my hand and walked me to market to buy me a ribbon. I remember that day, the feeling of his big hand engulfing mine, the sound that came from his lips when we returned home and found the door swinging and the blood on the floor. He pushed my face into his belly so I would not see what they had done to her. And then, when a sound revealed an assassin still waiting, he swept me onto his shoulder and we fled, twisting through the secret ways of Edinburgh that he had made it his business to know.

≈　≈　≈

I run through the dark streets, slipping down the wynds and lanes, keeping my footfalls soft on the cobbles, my breath a mist on the air. A woman's voice rises in invitation from a doorway. A cur snarls at my heels until I kick out and hit soft, yelping flesh. Men spill out of a tavern. It is the Queen's welcome after all, and the whole city will dance and drink around such an event.

I slip into the darkness of the wynd, glancing around to make sure no one sees. I unlock the heavy door set low into the stone wall and step inside, locking it behind me. I know the long fall of these steps, down, down below the level of the city streets. Another locked door in the pitch-blackness, which I open by feel and pull closed behind me. I take out my tinder and flint and strike until I can light a candle, the light flaring in my eyes.

We have come from noble blood, but now we live in the city like rats, without daylight, knowing every escape route. We have made fast our own corner of it to keep out the drunks and condemned men who live in this subterranean world, and we can escape by the network of tunnels that crisscrosses beneath the city. Thus far, our enemies have never found us here.

I climb into my bed but my heart refuses to slow. I cannot sleep. The Queen has noticed me. She has danced with me; she has heard my name. After a life spent waiting for her return, at last I have the chance to regain our castle. Perhaps it will be I who wins back our lands and the family honor. If I can befriend the Queen and win her to our cause, it will not be long before I sleep in a castle of my own, without fearing that my enemies will find me in the dark.

I have seen the Queen through the eyes of a young man, wide-stanced, scabbard strapped to my waist, loose shirt over my small, bound breasts. I long to see her again, but to do so I must give up the life I know and take again the name that has always meant danger: Alison Blackadder.

Three

To make me as a woman, I must be unmade as a man.

There is one perfectly suited to this task. Margaret Halkerstone, the wife of Sir John of the Tulliallan Blackadders, who has railed against my disguise since the day my father first put me into it and she was forced to foster me.

"Who in God's name is this?" John had said, all those years ago when we stumbled into his great hall, William dressed as a serving woman and me a ragged-haired boy.

William pulled his rough cloak back and tore off his wig. "Someone betrayed us," he said. "Hume has murdered my wife in my own house. We barely escaped."

Margaret came across to me. "What have you done to the child?" she asked, running her hand over my close-cropped head.

"She's alive, at least," William said. "My customer Sophie disguised us so we could flee."

John shook his head. "I am sorry for it, but you cannot stay here. If this is true, you bring too much danger."

William's hand gripped mine as though he would crush it. "I will go to sea," he answered, his voice tight. "Word has gone to my cousins to bring the ship to Saint Andrews. But I cannot take the child and Hume will kill her if he finds her."

"It's not killing her that Hume wants," John said. "She's the youngest heir. If he gets your daughter, he'll marry her to one of his spawn and then the theft is complete."

They stared at each other in silence. I looked at the floor. In the days since my mother had been killed, I had already learned not to cry.

"Keep her in disguise," William said. "You have enough sons here. She won't be noticed."

"You can't!" Margaret said. "She's a girl, for God's sake."

"Then what?" William snapped.

"Let us have her," Margaret said. "Not as yours, but as our own. A Tulliallan Blackadder. I have longed for a daughter. She'll be safe as one of us."

William pulled me closer and I could feel his hand shaking. "I have nothing left," he said, and I heard the anguish in his voice. Then it hardened. "I won't give her up. You must foster her as my nephew, Robert Blackadder. Her life depends on you teaching her well."

"Not the name of your father," said Margaret. "And not Blackadder. It's too dangerous."

"You cannot make us relinquish our very name!" William roared.

"All right!" John stood tall. "We will do it. William, I will get you into service with Lord Bothwell, who will have need of a ship and a captain and is the sworn enemy of Lord Hume. Sail to France and I will send word."

I stayed at Tulliallan, learning the skills of a boy from John and Margaret's resentful sons, who delighted in having a girl they could torment like a brother. I learned fast how to twist out of a cruel hold and where to strike to hurt them most. I was tutored in the manners of a noble heir in case I should ever need them. Margaret never managed to give birth to her own daughter and in time she came to hate me for being dressed as a boy and not being her own.

But it was John who took the final step in my protection. Without William's knowledge, he sent a message to Hume that the family would desist in pursuing the castle in return for an end to the bloodshed. Word came that Lord Hume agreed, though it was never written down.

It was a relief when William came back after three years and took me with him to sea as his nephew, in the service of Lord Bothwell. I learned never to call him "Father" and how to live as a sailor. Each night, just like when I was a child, he whispered about the castle. "No matter what false promise John has made to Hume, it means nothing," he told me. "We will get it back. The Queen will return it to us. When the Queen returns, justice will be done."

Tulliallan Castle lies two days to the north and William sends me out before daybreak with my instructions. I must convince John Blackadder to present me as his own daughter when he comes to pay fealty at the Queen's welcome pageant. I have ten days to un-learn the habits of half a lifetime and become a young woman fit for noble service.

By day's end I come to Stirling, to the Stag's Rack Inn where my father and I are accustomed to overnighting between Tulliallan and Edinburgh. I take a table in the corner where I can watch the room. The innkeeper's daughter brings me roasted meats, dripping and dark and what my body longs for. My blood time must be due, with all the extra subterfuge it requires, and I am tired to the bone.

She has looked at me on other visits, the daughter. Smiled across the room, brushed my shoulder with her upper arm as she put down the ale. But she has never spoken and under William's iron gaze I have never even returned her glance. But now, as my bones loosen and the ale warms my belly, I watch her. Her dress is low and her bosom creamy, and the next time I pass this way, I will not be able to look at her in such a way, the way a young man looks at a woman.

She feels my eyes on her and in a moment she is at the table with the ale jug to top me up. She's so close I can smell her skin and see the pale hairs on her arm. She turns her head slightly so that her eyes meet mine.

"Alone this time?" she asks.

Her breath is warm on my cheek. Men and women both notice me, for I inherited my mother's fine French features and dark eyes. William has instructed me how to fight off those men who like their boys young and smooth of cheek, but he has taught me nothing of women. I have put my body out of reach of all.

"Yes," I say at last and I cannot help but turn. She is still leaning down and my movement brings our faces even closer. Suddenly I feel the desire to join our lips, as though the space between them is nothing so much as a distance to be extinguished.

When a yell comes from a man wanting his cup refilled, she steps back and I slump in relief. I look around carefully, but her father has his back to the room and he has not seen us. She finishes pouring ale and returns to the kitchen.

I finish my meal and drink more ale from a jug wielded by her father, until my eyes start to blur and the room begins to empty. She does not appear again and I walk out slowly, regret colored with relief.

But she is waiting by a corner outside my room as I weave upstairs. She steps out in front of me in the dim light and I grasp my dagger instinctively. She reaches out, covers my hand with her own, and leans in, her face tilted to catch me in a kiss.

The brush of her lips flares through me. In a day I will be a woman, but tonight I am a lad still. Her lips part under my own in invitation and in a second I understand the meaning of desire. My body moves forward against her, pressing her back against the stone wall. Her tongue is urgent. She reaches her hand along my thigh and the feeling between my legs is a new continent. I do not know if I am man, woman, or beast. Then her fingers brush my codpiece and, in the shock of it, sanity returns. I pull my lips away from hers and step backward. I turn away from her and stand trembling, my nipples aching underneath their prison, my breath ragged. She is silent for a moment, then puts her hand on my shoulder, leans in again, and closes her teeth on my earlobe in a nip that races down my body. And then she is gone.

I stand still for long minutes, my hand against the cold stone wall supporting me. A sound on the stairwell startles me and I gather myself and stride quickly to my room. The tavern is busy with travelers to Edinburgh and another man is already rolled in the bed, snoring lightly. I put my dagger under the pillow in close reach and lay my head down on top of it.

But I cannot sleep easily that long night. I burn as if fevered. It is many hours later that I finally calm myself enough to fall into a fitful doze.

William was right, though I have not known it till this night. I cannot stay hidden as a boy. There are dangers in it I had not imagined.

≈   ≈   ≈

It is another day's ride to Tulliallan and dusk is falling by the time I reach it. The castle's tall, sheer face rises from the ground on the top of a small rise, circled by a moat.

A servant opens the portcullis and ushers me up the small staircase to the first floor, where John and Margaret are in their chambers. They stand to greet me. John puts a hand on my shoulder and claps me stiffly. He can never forget what I am underneath. Margaret shudders when I reach for her hand. In public I would kiss it, but in private she keeps herself drawn away from me. Her gaze rakes my travel-stained clothes, my muddy boots, and the horse hair on my cloak.

I turn away slightly from her scrutiny. "You will be pleased, madam, to hear this news," I say, handing William's letter to her husband.

John reads the letter thoughtfully and passes it to Margaret. He considers me as she reads.

"Your father will never give this up, will he?" he says.

I stare at him. "Why should he? It is his birthright, and mine."

Margaret looks up from the parchment. "This is too dangerous. You will never pass as a noblewoman. And what will Hume do when he finds a Blackadder at court?"

I sit, keeping my back straight. "I'm a quick learner. I could bring honor to the family. Hume will believe I am a Tulliallan Blackadder and no threat to him. And what safer place in the country than in the Queen's presence?"

"One of our own boys should go to court," Margaret says to John. "Alison has no training to be a woman, let alone a lady-in-waiting."

"When I am high in her favor, I will reveal who I am and petition the Queen myself for the castle," I say. "Then the Tulliallan Blackadders can send a son to court."

John rubs his beard and turns to Margaret. "It could be to our advantage to have a Blackadder close to the Queen."

"She does not even own a gown."

"You have gowns aplenty she can pick from. The girl could bring honor to us, if she does well." He waves for a servant to begin ladling out the food. "I've made up my mind. Our sons can go to court later, when this has been done. You have ten days to make sure she knows how to act."

"Indeed." Margaret glares at me across the table as the servants lay out the food. "We'll start right now, then. Hold your knife this way. No—turn your hand. Like that."

So begins my unmaking.

≈   ≈   ≈

When the maid wakes me the next morning, I can scarcely believe that such an extent of fabric laid out can be a single outfit. To begin, a petticoat of soft linen against my skin, embroidered in tiny stitches, and silk stockings that slide up the length of my thigh, as soft as the touch of the innkeeper's daughter. The maid helps me into the Spanish farthingale, with its wooden hoops to hold out my underskirts. Then the bodice, the sleeves, the dress of blue damask, the gloves to cover my rough hands, the velvet hat, the rings, the necklaces, the velvet slippers, and the long cloak for when I step out of doors.

For the first time in years I have not bound my chest, but instead wrestled it into a stiff bodice a hundred times more constraining. It is cut low and my breasts are pushed up to swell at the top of the dress. The feel of air on my collarbones is shocking, as if I am naked.

It takes the maid more than an hour to dress me, paint my face, settle a wig over my cropped hair and braid it. By the end, I cannot recognize the person staring back at me from the hand mirror.

It takes all my strength to keep myself straight and upright when I walk into Margaret's chamber. She surveys me coldly, then rises and circles me. The maid stands, head lowered, while her handiwork is inspected.

"You have done well," Margaret says. "I wouldn't have recognized her." She dismisses the servant and I relax a little, letting out a tightly held breath.

"You," she turns to me, "look like a yokel. The clothes are nothing if you cannot carry them. Stand straight."

She places one hand on my belly and the other between my shoulder blades. She pushes and I try to follow her directions. Eventually, when

I am in such a position that it seems my bones will snap, she nods.

"Better. Now stay like that."

She crosses to the fire, seats herself, and resumes her sewing without another glance.

"It is a beautiful dress," I say.

"You will have another four such." She does not raise her eyes from her sewing. "Only the best, so you do not shame the family in front of the Queen. My husband says I cannot possibly need such finery down here in the country and that I shall hardly miss them."

I am silent. I hold the pose for as long as I can. At last I move slightly and the dress rustles.

"You think you will be allowed to slouch and fiddle while waiting on the Queen?" she snaps, looking up. "You have but a few days to learn to stand still. If you are such a quick learner, you will have no trouble with it."

I glare at her.

"Do not look at the Queen thus," she says. "Keep your eyes down unless she speaks to you."

"How am I to befriend her without looking at her?"

She laughs. "You will not befriend her. Do you think for a moment your father's plan can succeed? You will never get your castle, Alison. It is long since lost."

"She has noticed me already." My voice rises. "She has favored me. Our cause is just."

"She has noticed a boy, you fool." She stands and strides across the room until the hoops of our dresses touch. "I give you this advice for nothing. Find a husband, or you will spend your life in Edinburgh's sewers. Become a woman and make yourself a match."

I raise my chin. "I thank you for the advice. But I will win our castle, whatever you think."

She shakes her head and returns to her seat. "You think you know what it is to be strong, like a man," she says in a low voice. "That won't help you now. It's time to learn a woman's endurance."

≈ ≈ ≈

I win a single victory.

"The Queen herself rides astride," I say to Margaret when she comes to teach me side-saddle.

"The Queen comes from France, where all manner of wickedness takes place," she says. "A Blackadder woman does not ride astride."

I seek out John and appeal to him. "Something must make her notice me. She is a very great horsewoman. It is one way I can gain her attention."

He scratches his head and at last nods. "Ride side-saddle with us to Edinburgh. I will arrange that we carry another saddle for you. Once you are at court, the choice is yours. Do not cause a scandal, mind."

"Thank you." I hesitate. "There's one more thing. I will need an allowance. A lady in court must buy fripperies and new clothes and bribe servants. The family is expected to provide."

He shrugs. "Very well. I will make arrangements with the Queen's household."

If I were a boy I would have shaken his hand, but I do not know what to do and we stare at each other for a moment and then both drop our eyes.

"What does she wear for such a thing?" he asks, as I turn to leave.

"Breeks, under her riding habit."

He grins. "You will want some, I suppose. I will speak to the tailor and have them made." He glances sideways at me. "You had best pack them where Margaret doesn't see."

Four

When our party sets out for Edinburgh eight days later to welcome the Queen, a new Blackadder daughter rides by Margaret in unaccustomed side-saddle, voluminous skirts hanging down. Even Artemis still snorts and spooks when I come near, not recognizing me, and the stableboy has to hold her while I mount.

Bewigged, bepowdered, befrocked, starched, ruffed, pinned, primped, primed, head spinning with a million nuances of what to remember and what to forget. But pride keeps me stiff in the saddle, my slippered feet in the stirrups, my hands light on the reins as befits a woman of my standing. Pride reminds me to drop my gaze when men stare or wink at me.

We ride into Edinburgh in the afternoon, the day before the Queen's pageant. My legs ache and my head pounds but I will not let Margaret see a second of weakness. I hold my head high and smile as if we have just mounted up to ride out on an autumn day.

Edinburgh is in a frenzy. The trumpets herald the arrival of another noble family into the city. We clatter under the archway of Netherbow Port, led by John and flanked by servants and followers.

Above our heads a huge canvas dragon is being hoisted into place with ropes. Black-painted moors, dressed in yellow taffeta, march up the High Street before us. A choir of children raise their voices as we pass, piercing the babble of the street with the beauty of their rehearsal. Men roll barrels across the cobblestones to the High Cross fountain, which will flow with wine during the Queen's pageant. At the Salt Tron, they are building a bonfire that could burn a dozen heretics.

My father, pressed against the side of the road, is looking out for us. John stops to speak briefly to him and passes on. William's gaze turns to me and it is as if I am some magical creature. For a moment he looks afraid.

"Witchcraft," he mutters.

I open my mouth to tell him it is nonsense, and then close it again. He has never looked at me with awe before and I would not turn it away so fast. Then, strangely, he bows to me. I look up to see John and Margaret waiting, and Margaret inclines her head for me to follow. I look back at William.

"You are their daughter now," he says. "A Tulliallan Blackadder. Go."

≈   ≈   ≈

Her eyes flicker over me in an instant. They are politely attentive, no more. Her presence chamber is crowded with ladies-in-waiting, the unmarried daughters and cousins and eligibles of her nobility.

"We are honored to offer our daughter, Mistress Alison Blackadder, into your service," John says, bowing so low that his beard droops toward the floor. There is a titter among the finely dressed ladies standing behind the Queen and I hear them whispering in French. I keep my eyes lowered.

"What are her accomplishments?" asks a man seated by the Queen.

"She sews and sings and is fluent in French," John says.

"How does she worship?"

John hesitates. It is now against the law to be a Catholic, but the Queen herself is one. William has judged it best that I serve her as a Catholic, but it is risky to mention it openly. The Queen's first private mass in the chapel royal at Holyrood was disrupted by rioters until Lord James himself called them off.

"She is very devout in her prayers to the Virgin," he says at last.

The Queen looks away, fanning herself, and someone leans over to whisper something into her ear. I make a small cough, praying that only John will hear it.

"She is an excellent horse rider," he adds.

The man looks my way again. "Does she bring her own horse?"

"Of course, and a fine beast it is."

The Queen glances up. "Do you hunt?"

As Robert I could speak to her. As Alison I do not know what to say. I take a shallow breath, restricted by the dress. "My preference is deer, Your Grace, but I have hunted small game many times."

Her eyes could be glass. The silence lasts so long that I wonder if she expects me to say something else.

"I have heard that Your Grace will hunt the Caledonian bulls in the park at Stirling. I would be honored to be included in such a hunt," I add.

There is a sharp intake of breath from somewhere and her eyes suddenly focus on me terrifyingly. John clears his throat to make some excuse for my foolishness, but she waves a hand to silence him. The man who has been asking the questions leans over and confers with her. After a moment he sits back.

"Thank you, we shall take your daughter into our service for the winter and see how she learns the manners of court," the man says.

Another giggle comes from somewhere in the crowd of women. The Queen looks around in annoyance.

"There are several who require lessons in the manners of court," she says, and silence falls instantly.

"You will be seen to outside." The man gestures for us to leave.

≈　≈　≈

The man by the Queen's side is George Seton, brother of one of the Queen's Marys and the head of the new royal household.

"Come away to your room, then," he says, when at last he comes out of her presence chamber. "A servant will bring your trunks."

He takes me to a tiny windowless room with a bed, a chair, and a small fireplace. The servant squeezes my two trunks next to another already in residence. The largest holds my five dresses, my new jewels, my tiny shoes. The smaller, which Margaret does not know about, contains my riding breeks, my male clothes, my boots, and my dagger.

"You will share with Angelique Lambert, one of the Queen's French party," he says. "Put your things away and return to the antechamber."

He leaves and I sit on the bed and wrap my arms around myself. Compared with the French, we are peasants. John knows little of a royal court and William knows nothing. We have not had an adult monarch living in this country since the Queen's father died nineteen years ago.

I must put our case to the Queen before the Hume family ingratiates itself with her. But Lord Hume is one of her leading nobles and I am now one of the lowest members of her household. As Robert, I had a small chance of capturing her attention. As Alison, none.

≈ ≈ ≈

The ribbon is made from silk and it slides through my fingers, heavy with the weight of its own importance. It is a deep crimson, a fine offset to the white gown the Queen wore yesterday, which is now ready to be examined for damage, carefully arranged, hung, and aired. The ribbon is to be rolled free of creases and stored in a perfumed drawer, the embroidered slippers placed close—but not too close— to the fire so they are perfectly dry before being put away. There are dozens of such outfits that make up the Queen's wardrobe and the care of them is an exacting task requiring many hands.

The Queen's household contains several hundred servants, nobles, musicians, valets, ladies-in-waiting, and friends who seem to have no specific role. The four Marys, her companions since birth, are the apex of the court pyramid. They traveled to France with her when she was five and have not left her since. They share everything—even her name. Mary Beaton, Mary Seton, Mary Fleming, and Mary Livingstone. They are known by nicknames: Beaton, Seton, La Flamina, and Lusty.

The court of our new Queen is more French than Scot. More than half her three hundred household members are French and they carry an air of contempt for their new country and its inhabitants. They have helped me understand that my French is passable at best, my manners rough, my wardrobe of Margaret's best dresses laughably out of date, and my knowledge of the daily power-play of a royal court nonexistent.

I had imagined I might brush her hair or warm her nightgown by the fire. But for countless hours I sit or stand in the antechamber of the Queen's apartments, where all who wish to see her must begin their journey. I observe who comes to pay homage and the expressions on their faces as they emerge from her presence, searching for clues to how I might plead the Blackadder cause.

At night, when my jaw aches, I return to the tiny quarters I share with Angelique, another lowly ranked lady-in-waiting who sees no more of the Queen than I do. We barely speak during the tedious business of undressing. We say our prayers separately, bid each other good night, and roll on our sides to keep a space between us in bed. She falls asleep quickly and leaves me to my nightly planning.

Since I was presented to the Queen I have barely met her eyes. William has waited forty-two years for justice and I have waited the sixteen years of my own life. Every day has become interminable; I must fasten the words down inside me, lace them into place, and keep them there, lest they spill out at the wrong time and ruin our cause.

On my tenth day in court, a group of nobles arrives in the antechamber to see the Queen. Dark with resentment, I watch them being announced. At the rear of the group is Lord Hume.

I take a sharp breath at the sight of him and swiftly drop my eyes so that he does not see me. It was not so difficult to lead the Queen to believe I am the daughter of a lesser noble family. But we have never known for certain if the Hume clan realizes William still has a living heir. If Lord Hume hears the name Blackadder and believes our family is reviving the old claim, I might be conveniently murdered like my relatives.

When I look up again, he and the other nobles have passed through to the presence chamber. It takes all my strength to stand still, half smiling, when I wish to run or stamp and clench my fists with fury. He has the Queen's ear already.

I run through my useless plans again, but I can think of nothing new to attract her attention. My female accomplishments are unremarkable at best and my masculine ones inappropriate. William's plan is a failure. He would have done better to simply bring me as Robert every day with the other petitioners and wait in the hope of gaining an audience.

At last the nobles emerge, striding through the antechamber with the air of men well pleased. Lord Hume claps the shoulder of Lord

James and laughs out loud. Then, without warning, his gaze swings around and catches me before I can wipe the fury from my face. For a second his eyes fix on me and then he is past and I am left with the color high in my cheeks and my heart thudding with shock. Have I revealed myself?

George Seton follows the nobles out and announces that the Queen will ride to Stirling in the morning and any of the household with their own mounts may join the party.

My heart thuds again. There has been more excitement in a few minutes than in the whole of my ten days at court. I have a chance, at last, to ride with the Queen.

Five

The autumn weather is cold and gray, but I would not care if it was a tempest. I enter the courtyard dressed in my riding habit with my new breeks underneath. A stableboy holds my mare and I cup her velvet nose in my gloved hands and inhale her honest smell.

The French courtiers grumble about the icy cut of the wind but I turn my face toward it with delight, and my mare, sensing my desire, stamps and jerks her head. She has been confined too, in the royal stables, and she pricks her ears.

The Queen's horses have arrived at last from France. Milk-white palfreys: large-boned, shiny-eyed creatures with impossibly glossed coats. Even an autumn day such as this is enough to make them snort and swivel their ears at the breeze—they will suffer through a Scottish winter. My mare, with her coat already well thickened for the season, looks small and shaggy beside them, and her Spanish breeding is nowhere evident.

The Queen and her Marys all ride astride, though I notice that her French courtiers do not and my heart begins to pound. Am I violating some court protocol? Will she notice me not with favor but anger?

The Queen climbs her mounting block. She gracefully steps into the stirrup held by George Seton, though there is no missing the sight of her breeks as her leg rises over the horse's back and she settles into the saddle. I glance around. Some from her new Scots household have forgotten themselves and are staring in fascination.

The stableboy comes around to help me mount and I must remember to do so like a woman, relying on his strength to boost me to the horse's back. I can feel eyes upon me as I take my leg across. Head bent, I arrange my reins, my cheeks burning. Standing out in a court is a dangerous thing.

Some four dozen of us move in a clatter out of the courtyard through the front gates. Once we are away from the city outskirts, the Queen and her Marys push their horses into a smooth, fast pace. George Seton urges the rest of us to greater speed so that we are not left behind.

I am the only other woman astride, but I am surrounded and jostled, invisible as always. I take a breath, pick up the reins, and urge my horse through the scuffle of riders to the fore of the party. The Queen is some way ahead but the ground is rough, and while the palfreys hesitate and slow their stride, I catch up. Their horses plunge into a gallop and I press forward to join them.

I lean low over the horse's neck and she responds, her muscles bunching and stretching underneath me. The rest of the party falls away behind us and, when at last the Queen slows her horse, the countryside around us is deserted and our companions a blur of color far back along the road.

At the sound of my mare's hooves approaching, the Queen turns around. The Marys merely glance and return to their chatter, but I feel the Queen gaze intently at my horse. I halt a reverent distance away and she gestures me to come closer.

"I know this creature, do I not?" she asks. "She is like to Artemis, who carried me into Edinburgh."

I bow my head, unpracticed at the angle and depth of the movement on horseback. "Your Grace, she is the same horse."

"Belonging to a lad," she says musingly.

"Robert Blackadder, my cousin. He loaned her to me so I would have a worthy mount to ride in your service."

She smiles slightly. "Horsemanship must run in your family."

"Let's gallop up the hill," says Lusty, her horse recovered and prancing to be gone. "We'll see for miles from up there."

The Queen glances back to our party, still far behind.

"They'll catch us," Lusty says. "Come on!"

They even ride in unison, these five, like sisters. No sooner does the Queen smile and raise her reins than their horses break into a gallop together. This time I ride alongside, but as we veer off the road and onto a winding track leading up the hill, Lusty hesitates. Tracks branch out in all directions, worn by sheep and cattle searching for feed. I have traveled this road between Stirling and the capital countless times and explored its back tracks and byways. William has taught me every escape route. If my uncle Patrick had known such tracks when he was ambushed outside Edinburgh by the Humes, he might have lived.

"Lead us," the Queen says.

I urge my mare to the front and onto the summit track.

We canter to the top and pull up to survey the land. Their palfreys are blowing, coats wet with sweat, and the Queen watches my mare appraisingly for a moment before turning her attention to the countryside. I gulp the autumn air like a tonic and follow her gaze.

Edinburgh Castle looms up on its rocky outcrop, embraced by the Flodden Wall. Outside the wall, the strips of small holdings farmed by the city's inhabitants stretch out into fields and grazing lands. The harvest is almost done, the fields lie stubbled. In the distance, heavy clouds are dropping rain. A coil of smoke rises from the roof of a cottage below us.

"Why, look," La Flamina points. "They have grass on the roof. How quaint."

They all peer and then the Queen turns to me. "Is it some manner of shelter for beasts?"

"Beasts and men together," I answer. "In winter the beasts shelter inside and keep people warm."

"Let us look," Lusty says. When the other three make noises of disapproval, she persists. "Mary should know what manner of people she rules."

This time the Queen moves to the lead and they fall behind her without a word. I pause for a moment before following. Our followers could miss the track we have taken up the hill and pass us by. Does a lady-in-waiting dare to remind the Queen of such a thing?

As we approach the cottage, children stare open-mouthed. "What a hovel!" one of the Marys exclaims.

As the Queen rides up close, a man pushes aside the hide door and comes out. His red hair and ruddy skin are in high contrast to the dull gray of his clothes. He is bearded, hands and feet earth-stained, his blue eyes wary. The Marys come to a halt. There is a moment of silence and then the Queen rides forward.

"Good man, please forgive our intrusion," she says, and I can hear the warmth in her voice. "It seems we have strayed foolishly from the road and our traveling party. Would you be so kind as to point out how we might return to it?"

He takes a step toward her. She will smell the reek of him, the honest stink of earth and animal and sweat. I suddenly want him to show her that peasants in Scotland have pride and strength the equal of any in France.

"Dangerous riding alone," he says. "I'll take ye to road."

"You're too kind," she says.

He begins to walk and after a moment she realizes she is meant to follow, and turns her horse around. The children have crept outside the door and a woman tries to gather them back in, but she cannot help staring either at such gaudy finery.

He swings down the path in long strides, his bare feet unhesitating so we must keep our horses at a good step to keep up with him. I can feel the first spits of rain as he brings us around the hill to the road. Our party is halted some way farther back. Someone catches sight of us, a shout goes up, and they start to move in our direction.

The Queen smiles down at him. "I thank you."

He nods, his face expressionless. So close to Edinburgh, surely even such a family will have heard that the Queen has returned?

George Seton pulls up with a clatter of hooves, his face red. "Your Grace," he pants. "It is most dangerous to stray alone from the road. Scotland is full of wild men. I must insist you stay with the party."

"I have been well protected by one of my subjects," she says. "Pray see that he is rewarded."

She gathers her Marys with a gesture of her head and they break into a canter again. She has not looked at me and I hesitate. Can I still ride with her close circle, or am I relegated to the crowd of followers?

I glance down at the peasant, incongruous amid the glittering courtiers. George has pressed a coin into his hand and he clutches it, staring after the Queen. I cannot see the expression on his face under his wild beard, but his eyes are glowing like my own eyes must look on this day when at last I have ridden close to her and she has spoken to me.

Six

The small town of Stirling, with its steep cobblestone streets twisting and winding up the hillside, does not seem grand enough for a queen. But its castle is magnificent. Rebuilt by the Queen's father for his French wife, it rivals both Holyrood Palace and Edinburgh Castle and outshines the other royal castles of Linlithgow and Falkland. It is said its great hall rivals some of those in Europe. Presence chambers for queen and king are opulent and, without the crowd of Edinburgh courtiers, diplomats, and nobles, the Queen's rooms here seem spacious and bright.

The absence of Lord James, her bastard half-brother, lightens our lives also. In his Protestant black, he has brooded over the Queen's court at Holyrood. He can chill the laughter from a room simply by entering. This separation must be to their mutual relief. He can continue with the business of running Scotland, while she may play at being its glorious figurehead.

And I continue as one of her unremarkable ladies. I thought once we had spoken and ridden together that I might be admitted to her inner circle. But for three days she and the Marys walk past me in the antechamber as if I am a creature embroidered into one of the tapestries, and I am left again clenching my fists behind my back.

Four days after we arrive, Lord Bothwell comes to Stirling and strides into the antechamber. William follows. He nods to me and turns away, though from the prickle at the base of my neck I surmise he is trying to spy on me.

Bothwell shakes his head at the offer of wine and a tray of dainty food, and he refuses to sit but stands like a soldier, his legs apart while his presence is relayed to the Queen. He has found himself a position where he can observe the room, his back to the wall. I keep my eyes averted and half turn away from him.

Bothwell has believed I am William's nephew these past five years and he thinks Robert has some lowly position in the Queen's household. I have played my new role of lady-in-waiting well until now. But with William and Bothwell in the room, I panic. I feel like an oaf in my court-fine dress and I do not know how to stand or arrange myself. I fear Bothwell will see beneath all my layers of disguise.

When Bothwell and William are called to enter the Queen's presence chamber, I watch their backs disappear and wait for my color to subside.

"Do you know the Lord Bothwell?"

I swing around. It is Angelique, who sleeps by my side each night but is still a stranger.

"By reputation," I say, affecting a slightly bored tone. "A relative of mine serves him."

She nods. Like me, she spends much time in this antechamber. I have not mastered the idle conversation of courtiers yet, but this day, exposed, I need a companion.

"He does not look like a lord," she says.

I bristle. "He may not be such a courtier, but he is the most loyal of the Queen's nobles."

She shrugs and we lapse into silence. At last we hear the door to the presence chamber open and she turns. "Here they are. Your Lord Bothwell must be dining with the Queen."

I glimpse the Queen talking animatedly to Bothwell as they lead the way from the presence chamber. William waits behind and as I straighten from my curtsy he is standing in front of me.

"Why, cousin," I say, holding out a hand for him to kiss. "What brings you and Lord Bothwell to Stirling?"

"My Lord has business with the Queen," he says gruffly.

"Are you staying long?"

"No. Lord Bothwell is going to the Borders and I will go too."

I blink in surprise. "I thought Bothwell was staying in Edinburgh."

"Lord Bothwell goes where the Queen wishes," he says. "And what of you? Do you spend much time with the Queen?"

Angelique laughs beside me and fans herself.

"A little," I say. "I rode with her on the way from Edinburgh."

"Then you are not—close?" He stares at me, his face beginning to work.

"Cousin, you flatter me." I give a courtier's laugh. "You had best catch up with Lord Bothwell. Or are you going to your usual lodgings?"

He catches himself. "My lodgings. Good day." He turns abruptly and hurries away.

Angelique smiles at his back. "Your cousin has been little in court, either. In France, if a lord and his men arrived in such clothing they would be sent away to prepare themselves properly."

I glare at her. "Lord Bothwell is known in this land for having never wavered in his allegiance to the Queen, not even when offered inducements. You know nothing of Scottish lords and their loyalty."

She laughs. "And you know nothing of being in court." A moment later she walks away.

I unfold my fan and wave it while I think. In the Borders, William will be in the heart of Hume territory, with spies everywhere. I remember Lord Hume catching sight of my furious face. I may have exposed us already.

≈   ≈   ≈

I do not know Stirling the way I know Edinburgh; the places where I might don a disguise, the street boys and girls who will lead me safely for the payment of a coin. I do not know how a lady-in-waiting may leave the castle dressed as a boy without any seeing her, or how she may return again at night. But I must speak to William before he walks into such danger. I will step into the freedom of that disguise, the one that has become me, which is no disguise at all. I will slip out into the night and find him at the Stag's Rack.

I have drawn my first allowance and I make my way to the guard-house to bribe a guard. I affect a casual air and in an undertone ask for the use of the guardroom in which to change, and permission to return. He keeps his hand steady and his face expressionless while I press the coins into it, more and more, until my coins are gone and I whisper urgently that I have no more. He glances down once, briefly, nods his head, and gestures to dismiss me. I return to the antechamber with flaming cheeks. As a boy I can bribe my way anywhere, but as a woman I do not know how to drive the bargain.

After dinner I slip away from the antechamber. I step out into the courtyard, my head high and my step swift as if on an errand for the Queen, Robert's clothes bundled under my cloak.

The guard nods at me and stands aside to let me into the guardhouse. I smile in the new coquettish way I am learning and shut the door. When I am safely inside, it is all I can do not to rip myself free of the constraints of the dress. My hands are trembling with eagerness as I unlace and unpin, take off the wig, and wipe the powder from my cheeks. I step into my breeks and jerkin and boots as if they are old friends. I stand for a moment in the sheer delight of it before I open the door, leaving brocade and wig heaped like a carcass.

The guard jumps to see me and takes a step backward. "You are more man than woman," he says suspiciously. I wink at him and step out onto the street.

It is like stepping out of prison and I stride down the hill to the Stag's Rack like a young man who goes to court his sweetheart. In the tavern is the woman who kissed me. Has she been watching the door through the weeks ever since? As I shoulder my way inside through the warm bodies and the swell of noise, I see her eyes upon me and I cannot stop my smile. She turns away, but I see the smile forming on her lips and her quick glance in my direction a moment later.

I squeeze through the press of bodies. William is seated alone at a small table, an ale and a bowl of stew in front of him, his face grim.

"Uncle." I put my hand on his shoulder.

He turns in a flash. "What are you doing here?"

"We must speak." I sit down opposite, spreading my elbows wide across the table and parting my knees, my body relaxing into its familiar stances. I have been ruined for ever being comfortable as a woman.

A soft voice at my shoulder. "An ale for you?" she says, and her arm presses against me as she pours. I dare not look at her in front of William, but mutter thanks as she moves away.

William grunts. "Do you have news from the Queen, then?"

I pick up the cup and take a long swallow. "She knows my face and my name. But she keeps her special ladies by her side and I am not there yet."

He puts both his hands flat on the table and leans forward. "I do not want the castle when I'm too old to ride there and too blind to see it!"

"Then take me out of her service," I say. "Let me come back to you and Bothwell and petition the Queen as Robert. Bothwell will speak for us too. She has barely noticed me and I cannot get close to her like this."

William shakes his head. "Bothwell has no special favor. Today she appointed him keeper of the Borders, but it is the doing of Lord James, to keep him away from court."

"Lord Hume saw me in Edinburgh," I say. "You may be in danger going there."

He lowers his voice. "Hume will have heard by now that the Blackadders have a daughter in court. Even if he knows you are from Tulliallan, he may be suspicious. We are both in danger. It is safer for you to stay with the Queen."

I sit back in my seat, a sudden chill between my shoulder blades. I have always been protected, by William, by Bothwell, by Tulliallan's high walls. Now I am alone in the court, reliant on the Queen's good-will for my safety. She has no reason to care for me yet.

"I must go," I say at last. "I can't risk being missed."

He grips my arm. "Don't do this again. Your days as Robert are finished."

I stand, nod to him, and slip away between the drinking men. I can feel the eyes of the innkeeper's daughter on me. My desire for her is a clutch in my belly, but I am not Robert any more and, even if I was, how could I take anything more than a kiss?

Outside in the cool air, the moon has risen. I run up the steep, twisting streets to the castle.

The guard is keeping a look-out for me, and nods when I call softly from the shadows. I slip by him and into the dark corner where my clothes wait.

A woman of my new rank cannot dress unaided and this is the danger in my escapade. I wrap my long cloak over my clothes and tuck my cropped hair under the wig. If any catch sight of me, I hope I will pass as a woman cloaked to go outside.

I hear his step behind me. "You need help, I think?"

I turn quickly. "I am fine." I keep my voice level.

He is standing so close I can feel his breath.

"So are you man or woman?" he asks. His hand gropes at my waist and grips it.

"Please," I say. "I have paid you well this night."

"It does not cost so much to leave the castle," he says. "But it costs a great deal more to return. Now what are you?" He jerks me closer, pulling me against his body. I hunch my shoulders so that he won't feel my breasts. His lips meet my neck, forcing my head back, and his tongue is a sickening wet against my skin.

"I am a boy," I hiss, low in his ear.

He jumps back, pushing me so hard that I stagger. "Witch," he spits, crossing himself.

It is a dangerous accusation and I cannot allow it to stand. I snatch my dagger and swing around so its point is at his throat in a heartbeat.

"I am on the Queen's secret business and she will be most displeased if I am harmed." I reach down and pick up the bundle of my female clothes, pulling them under my cloak.

He says nothing, standing aside as I pass. I turn at the door. "Do we have an understanding?"

He makes a disgusted sound.

"I know where to find you," I say. "Not a word to anyone, or the Queen will hear of it."

I keep the dagger outstretched and back away until I reach a corner. "We will do business again," I say as I step out of his sight.

As I flee on silent feet across the cobblestones, my breath comes in gasps. I must cross the lion's garden, enclosed and unguarded in the center of the castle, and creep to my quarters unobserved. I reach the gate, wrench it open, and stumble through into the open square.

A rabble of voices meets me and I skid to a halt. The square is full of men, their voices upraised.

"Here! The Queen's woman," a voice calls and a guard is by my side, grasping my arm through the cloak.

"Quickly, we may not touch her." He breaks into a run, dragging me across the courtyard. I smell smoke and then I see the Queen on the ground, hunched over, eerily lit by flickering torchlight. For a moment my fevered mind thinks they are attacking her and I begin to struggle with the guard. Then she goes into a spasm of coughing.

"Help her," the guard says, thrusting me forward. I can feel my wig coming askew and I struggle to pull my cloak around me before I kneel down at the Queen's side. She is gasping and choking, her eyes streaming, and she clutches frantically at my cloak. The stink of smoke rises from her and I can smell wine on her breath.

"What happened?" I demand of them.

"Candle too close to the bed," a guard says. "The hangings caught fire. We just got her in time."

"A flask, does someone have a flask?" I put my arm around her shoulder. She clings to me, coughing. I unstopper the flask that a guard has pushed into my hands and hold it to her lips. "Just a sip," I say. "Hush. You're safe."

She sips, chokes, coughs again, and sags into my arms. I rock her.

A high-pitched cry comes from across the courtyard: her Marys in full voice. The Queen lifts her head, her eyes still streaming, and for a moment she looks at me with no recognition in her eyes.

You shall not touch a queen. I have forgotten this.

I pull my hands away from her and draw back as her eyes widen and she stares at me. My wig has fallen off, my cloak is askew, I am revealed.

I jump to my feet as the Marys come tumbling toward us. In the confusion I step backward through the guards and melt away into the shadows.

It's not till I reach my bed that I realize I have left behind my bundled dress.

Seven

My quarters are far from the Queen's chambers and the distant sounds of the hubbub have not woken Angelique. I undress in the dark, roll my boy's clothes into a ball, and stuff them into my trunk.

I spend the night tossing in dread. By the time I wake from fitful sleep, there are guards outside my door with orders to keep me there. Angelique looks at me round-eyed for an explanation, but when I shake my head, she silently helps me dress and leaves for her own duties. I pace the room, preparing an explanation. I cannot tell the Queen the truth, not before I have gained more favor.

The Queen keeps me waiting and it is afternoon before I am escorted into her presence chamber. A few servants are in attendance and the Marys are not with her. I cross the length of the room feeling her stare upon me and drop into a deep curtsy.

"It seems I have you to thank for helping me last night," she says, when I am seated opposite her and my cup is full. "The guards tell me you were the first to come to my aid."

I bow my head and say nothing. She looks at me for a long moment, then stands up and crosses to the window.

"But they cannot tell me how you arrived so quickly, when your bedchamber is so far away," she says, looking out.

I do not answer and my heart begins to pound. She turns in my direction but I keep my gaze on the floor.

"One of the guards swears that you had short hair and were wearing breeks."

I lift my head and she holds up her hand.

"I told him that could not be, but then he showed me your dress, bundled up and dropped in the courtyard. They say perhaps you are a spy and had something to do with the fire in my room. What say you to that, Mistress Blackadder?"

Though she is but eighteen years of age she has learned the look of a queen from her foster mother, Catherine de Médici of France, the look of a queen who holds your life in her hands and is turning it over and over like a bauble while she decides what to do with it. It is a look that sends me to my knees.

"I did not know of any fire. I was outside my rooms last night and came through the lion's garden on the way back," I say.

"Outside your rooms for what reason?"

This much I know from living in disguise. A half-truth is better than a complete lie. I take a deep breath.

"Your Grace, your people love to play and dress other than they really are. But lately the reformers have prevented it. They have forbidden the May games, and they punish any who play at Robin Hood and the Abbot of Unreason. They crush the pleasure of the ordinary men and women, who live hard lives and have little joy. Your people cannot even attend mass any more."

"So I am aware, but what is this to do with you?"

"Your Grace, I have seen that you like to ride astride and be the equal of a man. You may think it strange, but I have always loved to play in the May games as a man. I have done so since I was a child at Tulliallan, with the families on my father's estate, when we raised the maypole and the procession ran through the fields. I promised our people I would ask you to lift this cruel ban. I thought the best way was to show you myself the enjoyment that could be had from such dressing up. Last night I was rehearsing in a private place in the garden so none could see me. I planned to surprise you."

She regards me silently. I stay on my knees, head down. She only has to lift her finger and my life will end.

"When you dress this way, do others mistake you for a man?" she asks.

"Why yes, Your Grace."

"Do you dress so other than during the May games?"

I keep my eyes lowered. "I do, Your Grace. I do not like the restraint of being a woman all the time."

51

She reaches out as if she will stroke my hair, but then twists her fingers in my wig and tugs at it. The shock makes me gasp. It is too tightly pinned to come off, but she must feel that it is not my own hair she holds. She uses it to lever my head back until I am forced to look into her eyes.

"You will have to show me if I am to believe you."

The guard takes me out through the chambers, past the curious eyes of the courtiers, to my room. I am panting like a creature pursued as I take out my rolled-up clothes from the trunk. We retrace our steps through the stares of those in the presence chamber to the Queen's bedchamber.

She dismisses the guards and servants and watches me, her face impassive. I realize she will not turn away. With shaking fingers I peel off the dress, the sleeves, the ruff, the bodice, the farthingale, the dozens of pins, down to my under-shift. Off comes the wig to show my black, cropped hair. I unroll my clothes and pull on the breeks with their codpiece. I quickly bind my breasts and don the jerkin, the soft shirt, the boots. I lift my cloak, throw it around my shoulders, and raise my eyes to her again.

She walks around me. "I wouldn't know you," she says. "But can you be a man? The illusion is good, but there is more to a man than his clothes."

Our future rests upon me in this moment and the promise of the castle looms. I take a deep, trembling breath, and raise my head. I stride across the room, straddle the gilt chair, and cross my arms over its back.

"Madam," I say, dropping my voice to its accustomed timbre. "It's an autumn day out there and the weather is blooming. What say you we take the hawks and ride into the hills? We might flush a coney or two, or a pheasant whose feathers would seem richer in your hair."

There is a moment's shocked silence and then she claps her hands and laughs the delicious laugh I remember from the ship.

"Extraordinary!" she says, and comes and sits by me. "No, stay where you are. I like you better as this cocky fellow than another simpering lady-in-waiting. Alison? And what name do you go by as a man?"

"Robert Blackadder, Your Grace."

Her eyes widen. "Robert the Edinburgh messenger?" she says. "With the chestnut horse?"

I bow my head. "At your service."

"You dared to fool me. You even ride the same horse. You are a master in this."

She falls silent for a long moment. "What a slippery skill it is and what end might it be turned to? Can you be trusted?"

I drop to my knee in front of her. "Give my loyalty any test."

She considers me. "A woman may learn many things, disguised like this. Things that will never otherwise come to the eyes and ears of a queen. Is that not so?"

"I have gone unnoticed in worlds you can barely imagine, Your Grace."

She leans close. "Then you will teach me this. I want to learn to dress and walk and talk as a man. I can already ride and hunt and even fight a little, but all as a woman. I want you to teach me, and then you and I will creep out at night in disguise and explore the streets and drink in the taverns. Will you do this?"

She is a queen and she asks me such a thing as if it is a request.

"I will see what can be done about the May games," she says, before she sends me away.

≈ ≈ ≈

She has watched men die in any number of ways. She sat with the merciless de Guises as the French rebels were punished brutally and publicly, execution after execution in the courtyard by the Loire River until the water ran red and she was thoroughly schooled in the princely art of swift revenge. She sat by the bedside of her child-husband, the young French King, as the brain abscess led him to a slow and excruciating death. None of the French were surprised that the sickly Francis did not survive his seventeenth year, but the accounts tell of her weeping and lamentation at the loss of a boy more brother than husband. It is whispered that he was too young or too ill or in some way deformed and that their marriage was never consummated.

She has come from the most extravagant court in Europe, but though she has been a queen since she was six days old, she has never in truth ruled. She does not know the hidden struggles for power, the ancient lines of enmity and loyalty within the clans. She greets her half-brother with joy and does not perceive—or ignores—what I can see from his eyes: that his heart is full of rage at her return and his loss of the regency.

It does not take a prophet to see that as power shifts and hangs in the balance, danger is everywhere. She is always guarded and always at risk. It was so when Elizabeth came to the English throne and faced attempt after attempt on her life.

But in spite of the dangers around her, our Queen has brought laughter into the court. She orders her musicians and poets to perform, and calls for feasts and dancing each night. The serious business of ruling happens elsewhere in the realm of men, while the Queen has become its glorious public face. The men are well satisfied with this and they smile at their Queen and compare her favorably to wilful Elizabeth, who knows about every matter in her lands. How could our Queen know? She has been cloistered in the French court, the child Queen of Scotland married to the child King of France and both of them kept delightfully amused at every moment lest they notice the business of ruling taking place around them.

She smiles at these lords like a girl and I see them falter and the glaze come across their eyes and sometimes the swell into their trousers, and it happens to man after man, their cheeks hot, their speech faster, their hearts pounding. Men with wives, mistresses, servants, boys, girls, and whores. None seem immune. From my place I watch how she speaks to each, gravely and with intelligence, and realize these men know nothing of her power. She is content to wait and listen and dazzle them with her court. What does she plan to do?

≈ ≈ ≈

We leave Stirling and ride back to Edinburgh, and this time I ride close to her and the Marys at the head of the procession. I can hear her conversation and I am included in it once or twice.

I ride like a noblewoman whose family owns a castle. There are stares and whispers from other members of the court. Suddenly I have risen. Those who ignored me before now observe with interest, assessing how best to accommodate this shift.

The day after our return to Edinburgh, I come to the Queen's bedchamber to start the lessons. I have dressed in the womanly way, but I have made sure I will be able to disrobe easily, with fewer pins and laces, and I have brought my boy's clothes in a bag.

It is a cold day: the streets miserably wet, the rain drumming on the windows, the castle dark and damp already, and still two months until winter proper. But the Queen's bedchamber is comfortable, fire stoked, candles burning, the stone walls covered by heavy tapestries.

At my entry she dismisses the servants, keeping only La Flamina and Seton.

"Now we will see a marvelous thing," she tells them. She opens the door to the supper room and gestures me inside.

I strip out of my dress, bind my breasts, and put on my male attire. Then I open the door and step back into the bedchamber.

La Flamina does not have the Queen's training in impassivity and she gives a small squeal when I emerge. "Who is this?" she demands.

"Why, it is Alison. Don't you recognize her?" The Queen takes me by the shoulder and spins me around to show me off. "You see? Young Robert here could step out on the street and not draw a second glance. I think even in my court he would not be recognized."

"Extraordinary," La Flamina says. "It's witchcraft."

"Not witchcraft," the Queen says. "Skill and practice." She looks and smiles. "A skill she will share with me."

Seton stares at me. "It cannot be natural."

The Queen can order any clothes she desires and she has several male outfits laid out in her bedchamber. I look through them with a practiced eye and choose the least decorative.

"That's so dull!" she complains.

"Your Grace, it is better we look like merchants, not nobles, if we go out into the city. We will attract fewer stares."

She nods her assent and then La Flamina undresses her, undoing a good hour's work. When the Queen is standing in her petticoat, I instruct La Flamina on wrapping a bandage of fine French linen around the Queen's chest. I keep my gaze averted, though I glimpse enough to know that she, too, is naturally small in the bosom.

La Flamina helps her put on the shirt, the bodice, the doublet, the breeks, the boots, and the short cloak as I instruct. Seton unpins the Queen's hair and struggles to tuck its length under the short auburn wig. Then she wipes off the Queen's makeup.

"What now?" La Flamina asks me.

"Darken her chin," I say.

"I do not know how. You do it."

I step to the Queen's side, take the kohl from La Flamina's hand, and hesitate.

"You may touch me," the Queen says.

I try to keep my hands steady as I smudge a slight shadow around her chin and upper lip, to suggest that she has facial hair. Her skin is smooth and pale, flawless.

We turn her around to face the mirror and she studies herself carefully. Her height and slender hips help give her a masculine bearing and she has the stance of someone with power. She walks across the room with a long, firm stride, swings around, comes back.

"Well?" she demands.

"Very clever," La Flamina says. "This is a good game. Perhaps we could have a masque where we all come dressed as gentlemen and the men all come in dresses."

"That would be fun," the Queen says. "But La Flamina, do not mistake. This is no game."

She sits down again in front of the mirror. "A woman needs every device she can call upon and a queen more than most. The nobles still run Scotland, but one day I will in truth rule this country—and wider. I need every weapon at my disposal, and now I am filling the armory. I must know the hearts of men and women all over this land, from those wild men in the Highlands to the smallest babe on Edinburgh's streets."

She holds out her hand to me and I step forward and take it. "We have no urgent business today, Robert, save this. You will teach me your lifetime's learning before the sun sets. Tonight, in the dark, we will leave the castle and roam."

"Not yet!" In my surprise I answer sharply and then her face reminds me of whom I am talking to. "Your Grace, the streets are not safe and you have not practiced. Let us start here, let us walk, perhaps let us ride out in the park first. Let me show you how to turn aside a fight, lest a dozen come your way on the first night. It will not help your cause to be murdered in a tavern brawl."

"Very well," she says. "But I am impatient, Robert. I would see what job these men do running the country while I am cloistered in my rooms. They smile and pat my hand and tell me not to worry. But I will know what goes on in the streets and the taverns and what Edinburgh's citizens think of their Queen."

La Flamina and Seton sew and watch us while I school the Queen in the manners of a man. She takes the name of her dead husband, but while I am Robert and she is Francis, the power subtly changes. She looks at me for instruction. I choose what we do. I tell her to walk across the room again and again. I tell her how to relieve herself without causing suspicion. I am the more experienced companion. It is a heady feeling.

Darkness falls outside, the fire sinks down and is restored. At last a servant knocks to call the Queen for dinner. La Flamina goes to the door. "We shall come directly," she says.

The Queen nods and suddenly it is all back to normal.

"You have done well, Robert," she says. "On the next clear day we will hunt in the park like this."

"Yes, Your Grace." I bow again.

I am her plaything and she is tired of me for the day.

Eight

The Queen came to Scotland in summer, now we are in winter and still the right moment does not come to petition her. Each day there is someone she must talk to, or some meeting with the Lords of the Congregation that she must attend, or there is ice or sleet and we stay indoors. I strive for a chance to speak to her alone, but it never arrives. I did not understand how hard it would be.

She forms her Privy Council, some dozen lords of both religions, though in practice it is Lord James and her wily secretary of state, Sir William Maitland, who make the decisions. As the days pass, men come to see her and bend their knees to ask for this or that. The food is fine and we drink the best French clarets. Her tiny dogs are dressed in blue velvet to keep them warm, and fed titbits from her table. New fancies are paraded for her entertainment. A lion arrives in a cage from Africa and is released into a special enclosure in the garden. An acrobat juggles fire. A bear dances on a chain. One of her French servants, Sebastian Pages, devises exotic masques retelling the great myths. The valets of her bedchamber play viola and lute and sing to her. We play cards and dice, and each night there is music and dancing to keep away the chill of her first winter.

It seems in France the court is always a spectacle, but our Protestant Scotland is a drab place, our churches stripped of finery, our lives stripped of pleasure. Every Sunday, Edinburgh's citizens—under pain of punishment—gather at Saint Giles to listen to the impassioned voice of John Knox. We hear that he openly insults the Queen.

At last a day comes when the sun shows its face. The Queen appears in the presence chamber more plainly frocked than usual and there are lines of strain at the point where her eyebrows meet. She paces a little, pauses by the window, then turns back and beckons me over.

"I would like us to ride in the hills today," she says. "But first I must debate theology with John Knox, who has answered my summons at last. I pray I have the wit for it and that I may convince him his anointed Queen is worthy of some small respect at least."

I watch her leave the room. Today I will have my chance, I am sure of it. My whole body quivers like a hound straining to the hunt. Today, when we ride together, I will speak to her of the castle at last.

Two hours pass; the sun's light shifts from one window across to the next. The French do not know the rarity of a cloudless winter day, or they would never let it pass thus.

At last there is a stir. The outer door flies open and the Queen strides into the presence chamber. Her face is hard, lips pressed together. The Marys rise to their feet as one and everyone else sinks into a deep curtsy.

"Come," she says, gesturing at her Marys. I catch sight of her face as she leads them to the bedchamber. She looks like a young girl, her lip trembling.

An hour later, when the sun is slanting its low path toward the southwest, Lusty appears at the door and calls me.

The Queen has composed herself. When I enter she gives me a tight smile.

"While Knox stirs the entire kingdom against me, I at least will ride out and look over his God's lands. But I wish for a small party only. Can you lead us up Arthur's Seat?"

"Yes, Your Grace."

"Then let us go at once," she says, rising.

The six of us take the narrow stone staircase that winds from her bedchamber down into the empty king's chambers below, and from there make our way to the courtyard where the horses are waiting. We mount and I take my mare to the front of our small party. They fall in behind me and a knot of guards follows at a distance.

Afternoon clouds are threatening at the horizon and there is already a chill in the air. I have not ridden far when there is a clatter of hooves behind me and the Queen canters past into the lead.

"Come on," she calls. "The day is short and I would make it to the top."

I drive my heels into my horse's flanks and in moments we are galloping at full stretch across the park. The Queen leans over her horse's neck and urges him on. I am pressed to keep up, until the ground gets rougher and starts to rise at the base of the crag and we slow to a trot. The others are well behind us, cantering more sedately.

"That man would turn the whole country against me!" she says, and her horse tosses his head at the frustration in her words. "He sets himself level with God!"

The ground begins to rise and the horses throw their shoulders into the climb.

"The Protestants do not care for pleasure," she says, "or to sing or dance. But I cannot believe God Himself to be so set against beauty, or why would He have created it?"

There is no one else to answer her. "I do not know, Your Grace."

"So many of Scotland's people were forced to change their religion. Why did you remain a Catholic, Alison?"

Having been schooled by my shrewd relatives in both religions, now I see it is a thing that may be picked up and dropped at will, in spite of what the priests tell us. The whole country has changed religion and as yet we have not been punished for the heresy of it. But I cannot say this to the Queen.

"My family believes in the old ways," I say. "The auld religion, the auld alliance, the Queen of the May, the Lords of Misrule. Life must have some delight."

She smiles. "It pains me that people have been forced to relinquish it. Knox would have the Catholics burned. That is why he hates Elizabeth and me, who each tolerate the other's religion. He thinks it is the weakness of a female ruler."

We ride in silence, winding around the contours of the mountain, circling our way toward the top.

"I do not know what he would say to women dressing as men," she says. Then she laughs. "I am being foolish. Of course I know. He would call it an abomination in the sight of God."

Her face grows serious. We come to the last part of the climb, a steep scramble. I dismount, find a rock that will suit as a step, and take the Queen's hand to help her from her horse. When I let go, my skin burns underneath my glove.

We clamber up the final rise and, when we emerge at the top, she gasps. Scotland's capital lies below us. Holyrood looks insignificant down at the lowest point in the valley. It is Edinburgh Castle, high on its crag, which dominates the city. Beyond the Flodden Wall the land spreads out, winter-bare, the fields in their neat squares, the dark earth ready to receive the next crop of oats, the sheep dotting the pastures. Tiny wreaths of smoke coil up from the cottages and holdings outside the city, and, over the sea, storm clouds are piling. The wind cuts at us, smelling of rain.

"It is not like France," she says. "Some of my French companions think it a mean and barren place." She turns a full circle and smiles at me. "But its blood is in my veins. I will come to love it, as I have loved France."

She is standing by my side, so close, just the two of us and her kingdom spread out at our feet. I need only to turn her around and she will be facing the distant shape of the Lammermuir Hills where the Blackadder Water rises. On the southern side of the hills, the Blackadder Castle calls to me.

A voice comes up from below—the Marys have reached where our horses are tethered. If I am to ask her, it must be now.

I turn my head to face her, but before I can open my mouth, she speaks.

"Mister Knox would be outraged if he thought that I—or even you, Alison—played at dressing as men. I must give him no cause to attack me further. There must be no hint of scandal in my household."

My throat tightens. She stares across the valley and up at the castle.

"Your Grace—" I begin.

"If I am to do such a thing, no one must know. Only you and my four dear ones. Do you understand?"

Her eyes are burning into me. I am favored, like the Marys, and the feeling of it is a draft of hot wine on a cold night.

"You have my word." I try to keep my voice steady.

"Good," she says. Then the Marys are upon us and the moment is gone.

61

On Christmas Eve the Queen allows those of her household with family in Edinburgh to visit them. Lord Hume is one of the Queen's guests and I am glad for a chance to avoid him. I have learned how to bribe the guards of Holyrood successfully, with money and stolen wine from the Queen's cellars. I leave the castle dressed as Robert. I have heard that Bothwell and William are lodged in Bothwell's house in the Canongate and I want to report to William on my progress in winning the Queen's favor.

One of Bothwell's servants answers my knock. I wait in the hall until William comes down the stairs, carrying his weapons. He halts.

"I told you not to come like this," he says.

"How else could I see you?"

He shrugs. "Be swift. Bothwell is about to ride out against that madman Arran, who is busy telling everyone he will marry the Queen. We tried to trap him when he went to a whore last night but he escaped and now he's come to avenge his honor."

"Everyone knows Lord Arran is mad," I say. "Why does his father not just tie him to the bedposts when he raves thus?"

"The son is mad and the father is a fool. But tell me, are you close to the Queen yet?"

"I have made much progress," I say. "I am one of her favorites. Any day I will have the chance to ask her."

William leans close to me, even though there is no one to hear. "I learned in the Borders that Hume's spies are making inquiries. There is no time to lose."

"If I'm too hasty, I risk everything."

"Hume will find us out. You must act." William buckles on his sword and I watch him enviously. After the endless manipulation of the court, a simple street brawl would be a relief.

"Can't I come?"

"No," William says. "It's dangerous to be out. There'll be fighting all over Edinburgh tonight. Bothwell's got four hundred men waiting and Arran the same."

I follow William outside. Bothwell's men are gathering and the street is crowded with horses. Torches and lanterns flicker, the breath of man and beast turns into white clouds, the air smells of sweat and snow and ale. The city is throbbing and alive, with a thousand fighting men contained in its walls and no chance that the night watch can enforce the silent hours.

As a roar rises from Bothwell's amassed men, I leave them and wind through the streets back to Holyrood. The bribed guard refuses to let me in with so many people still around and sends me to climb the wall near the graveyard and slip into the Abbey. I creep through a servant's entrance into the kitchen and find a maid I can send to Angelique with a whispered message to bring clothes so I can return to our chamber without scandal. She does not know of my disguises, but I will have to enlist her help.

When the servant brings her to where I am hiding, she stares at my male dress, her mouth agape. I put a finger to my lips.

"The Queen wishes me to dress thus," I say. "She has asked me to be discreet."

She hands me a bundled-up dress and a wig as requested, and turns her back while I step into a storeroom, divest myself of Robert, and emerge as a disheveled Alison.

"It is only a game of the Queen's." I take Angelique's arm so that we may walk back to our quarters. "But no one else must know."

"It is a dangerous game," is all she says.

Nine

The Queen's first Christmas is feasting and drinking, dancing and masques, music, life, and color. The celebrations continue for three days until no one can face another meal laid out in the great hall, or raise themselves to dance another jig. The palace is quiet for one exhausted day, and the next morning she summons me to attend her.

Angelique helps me to finish dressing, and the guard escorts me, knocking firmly on the door of the Queen's bedchamber.

Her voice comes from within: "*Entrez.*"

She is standing at the far end of the room and with a jolt of pleasure I see that she is sumptuously set out as a man. She is wearing a satin doublet and a cloak of damask edged with fur. Her long legs are shapely in velvet hose. She has selected a wig in the same russet tone as her hair and her green eyes seem to glow. She offers her arm to me.

"Mistress Blackadder, shall we dance?"

Such questions from a prince are not questions. She leads me to the center of the room. I realize we are for once alone. No guard or servant attends us in the bedchamber. There is no one to see as she puts her arm around my waist and spins me quickly into position.

"Play!" she commands. Music starts in the supper room, and I realize she has hidden the musicians so they cannot see us, nor we them. She fixes her gaze upon mine and leads me into a pavane.

She strides into each step as if she has danced the man's part always, turning me with a restrained power, her eyes never leaving mine, burning into me. I, for the first time a woman under such a gaze, begin breathing faster, my heart drumming. Her gaze pinions me, as fierce as the wild stare of a hawk.

We are alone, we are dancing together. I am high in her favor. My moment has come.

But I look at her and, though she is dressed as a man and I a woman, I am Robert again, staring up at the Queen as she mounts my horse to ride into Edinburgh. My fortressed heart hungers for the life and color of her, for her laughter and her power. I feel everything that has ever been hidden under my breast bindings, every hour of my life I have been alone and unseen.

The last step of the dance presses us together and I wonder if she can hear my heart's thunder. She is so close I can feel her breath. The kingdom stops to wait for us. She lifts her hand and her fingers touch my cheek. For a moment she looks so deeply into me that I feel every secret I am carrying is revealed.

She steps back and the blood rushes to my face. What did she see in my eyes?

"Go behind the screen and change," she says to me, her voice amused. "There are clothes laid out."

As I step out of view, she calls on the musicians to leave by the spiral staircase. My hands are trembling as I fumble with my pins and laces. I thought I carried the secret of the barmaid's kiss buried deep, but I feel utterly exposed. What dangerous game have I stepped into?

The outfit laid out for me is a nobleman's plaything of gorgeous fabrics, ruffled and furred. In the time it takes me to divest myself of the feminine and garb myself in the masculine, my heart does not slow nor my color reduce. When I am dressed, I stand for a long moment trying to gather myself.

She has her back to me when I emerge from behind the screen and as I draw close she turns suddenly. There is a flash and she is in fighting stance, a sword held high.

"Today you will teach me the art of swordplay." She gestures to where another sword lies waiting.

The sword is not my strength. I am better at defending myself with a dagger when the element of surprise can be all. But I know enough to teach the Queen some basic craft. Not trusting my voice, I bow, pick up the sword, and face her. As I open my mouth to give the first instruction, she springs to the attack.

It is apparent in a moment that she knows plenty of swordcraft and there is something deadly in her eyes as she comes for me. At the first clash of our swords, the guards hammer on the door. Without a flicker of distraction, she orders them to stay outside. She makes a thrust, which I parry, swiveling the blade so that the flat of it clashes against hers. She attacks again and I keep the sword close to my body and my feet firm on the ground, the very moves I was about to teach her. I make a feint and when she blocks I try to dodge under her blade. She is fast enough to parry the thrust and I feel the strength of her arm.

With the rush of desire and fear coursing in my veins, I almost forget I am fighting the Queen and I attack with all the skill I possess. The metallic clash of blade upon blade is loud in my ears. Then she comes fast and low for a strike and the tip of her sword licks its hot tongue across my arm. The fabric in my sleeve parts and I gasp as a trickle of blood begins to run. Something passes across her face. For an instant I think it is regret. Then she comes at me again, hard, and I realize she means to show me no mercy.

To defend myself, to touch her flesh with a sword, would be instant death. But I could not strike her anyway, even if it would save my life. She has looked into my soul.

I lower my sword. She catches it with her blade and flicks it away with a clatter. She advances, sword tip to my chest, and I back away until the stone wall halts me. She raises the point of the sword to my throat.

"It appears you have not been completely frank with me," she says. "It appears that the Tulliallan Blackadders have no daughter by the name of Alison. It appears you have made secret reports to men who work for Lord Bothwell. It appears you are a spy and perhaps you know of some plot to bring down my rule. Perhaps you are the very core around which the plot turns? It appears there are more reasons you dress as a man than those you told me."

I can hear my own breath rushing in and out and the tiny splash as the stream of blood snakes down my arm, twists around my fingers, and drips to the floor. The point of her sword burns my skin.

"Before I slay you as a traitor, explain yourself."

She is prepared to kill me. But in this moment I am the sole focus of her attention. Every cell of her being is turned toward me, her will at the sword's point and my white skin pressed beneath it. Our eyes are still locked together and for an exquisite moment I cannot speak.

She presses the sword tip harder and at last my body responds like an animal to the threat of death.

"Your Grace, I am the daughter of Captain William Blackadder, the living heir to our family's lands stolen by Lord Hume. I have come into your service to beg you to intercede in this injustice."

She presses again, till surely the end of her sword will pierce my throat. "Why do you dress as a man?"

"My father believed the Hume family would capture me and force me into marriage," I say, my throat tight. "He disguised me as his nephew when I was eight. I lived as a boy until I came into your service."

She backs the point of the sword off slightly and I become aware of the slice of pain in my upper arm.

"Who is it you met on Christmas Eve?"

"My father. Lord Bothwell will speak on his behalf. We are not part of any plot against you. My only charge is to ask for your help."

She stares at me another moment, then straightens and lays her sword down on the table. She takes up a cup of wine.

"Lord Hume himself warned me I was hosting a viper within my own nest," she says. "He told me the Tulliallan Blackadders had no daughter called Alison."

The next droplet of blood falls in a crimson splash and outside the window a robin twitters as though this was a winter day like any other. My breath is frosted on the air between us. Lord Hume has seen me. He has asked questions and he knows I am not whom I claim to be. If I cannot win over the Queen, I am in danger the moment I leave this room.

"Lord Hume has reason to undermine me," I say at last. "A Hume took Blackadder Castle by force. He forced my grandmother to marry with his steel at her throat, and forced her two children to wed his brothers. Hume men have murdered every Blackadder who tried to help them. Hume men murdered my own mother."

"How can I believe you?"

"Your Grace, if my family petitioned you publicly, we risked my father's life," I say. "We have lost our birthright. This is the only way we could reach you."

The Queen puts down her wine. "I know what it is to have lost your birthright. I have lost my own. Do you know what it is?"

I shake my head.

She gestures around the room. "In France a woman may not inherit the throne, nor rule in her own right. When my husband died, the throne went to his brother. But it is the English throne that is my real birthright denied. Elizabeth refuses to name her successor, though in law it is I. She confounds her court and infuriates her advisers, but in this matter she is as mysterious as in her playing with suitors."

She begins to stride, agitated. "There are many who believe I should rule England and Scotland both, a Catholic queen again, uniting the two countries in the auld religion. I have powerful supporters in England and on the continent, and I have yet to choose where I shall marry. Believe it, Robert, I shall rule England."

I nod. "I believe you will, Your Grace."

She turns to me. "But before then I should cast you from my service in disgrace," she says, her voice cold. "You have lied to me and I require loyalty before all else."

I drop to my knees on the bloody floor. "Please, Your Grace. I am loyal. I swear it on my own birthright. I came to you like this only to protect my family from Hume's fury."

"Hume is one of my great and loyal lords," she says. "I will send for him and we will have the truth of this story."

The fear that rushes through me threatens to loosen my bowels. I want to lie my face on the ground at her feet and beg for her mercy. Yet I sense the Queen wants a different response from me. I raise my eyes.

"Reveal me to Lord Hume and you sign my death warrant, and my father's. But if it will prove to you that I am your loyal servant, then do so. I put our lives in your hands."

I hear another soft splash as the blood drips from my fingertips to the stones.

Suddenly she steps forward and takes my chin. She tilts my face up. "I am not finished with you yet, Robert." A smile creeps over her face. She releases me. "I will think on this further. Perhaps I can help you, but you will have to prove your loyalty to me."

I sway on my knees and her expression changes. "You are hurt. Go and have your wound tended."

She walks behind the screen and gathers my cloak. "Lord Hume will not learn who you are, not yet."

She wraps the cloak around me and pulls the hood over my head so I am obscured.

"I will have a guard accompany you to your room," she says. "Don't let any see you like this."

Alone in my room, the energy runs out of me and my head spins. The cut in my arm throbs. I wipe the blood away and bind it awkwardly with a piece of cloth before I undress and kick the nobleman's finery beneath the bed, crawl under the covers, and draw them up to my chin. My teeth chatter.

Putting our case to the Queen has nearly cost me my life. But she will consider helping me. For the first time in my life I have taken a real step toward the castle.

She has asked me to serve her and love her, to prove my loyalty. She does not know that today she has taken my heart for her kingdom.

≈ ≈ ≈

I wake to the sound of Angelique's voice repeating my name like a chant or a spell. The room is cold, the fire dead. She is staring down at me, her forehead creased. She puts her hand on my arm and the pain of it makes me cry out.

There are noises, lights, I can hear the crackle of the fire being stirred up. I am supported by strong hands, lifted, someone gasps, "The blood!" and I look down to see my rough bandage soaked in it. There is a bitter smell of herbs, pain as they place a compress around my wound. Angelique holds my head and helps me swallow a warm broth.

The fire is roaring now and I can hear the whispers through the door and from the hallway outside.

I am still shivering. There are more voices and then Angelique climbs into the bed with me. "Let me warm you," she says. Someone pulls the covers up over us and a delicious warmth steals across the bed and envelops me.

In the morning I am alone in the bed, but the warmth of two sharing still clings to the sheets and Angelique is moving around the room. When she sees my eyes open, she comes and sits on the side of the bed and cups her hand against my cheek, exactly where the Queen's fingers touched me.

"Rest today, *chérie*," she says. "Too much blood from that wound. Are you in pain?"

I shift my body and every muscle hurts, as though I have fought an entire battle and not simply cavorted in swordplay in the Queen's bedchamber.

"The Queen's apothecary will come again today to speed your healing," she says, rising. She has found my clothes and now inspects them. The tunic is stained with blood, the sleeve torn and hanging. It will take many hours of work to repair this nobleman's suit.

"You are good at disguise," she says. "When you dress as Robert, no one would know you are Alison. But you must learn to disguise your heart."

I look at her sharply. She leans down to speak beside my ear. "If it is love you want," she says, "at least go seeking where you have a chance of finding it."

Ten

The Queen is a new language that I must study, observing until I understand the subtleties of nuance and expression, the shades of meaning, the spaces between the words.

I have tasted one kiss, with the daughter of an innkeeper, and it has awoken desire in me. But a kiss is not love, is it? My groin aches when I think of it, but not my heart.

Now suddenly I know love. I love the Queen, who is more truly my master than any other, even William. The Queen, who holds my life in her fine-boned fingers.

I'm not alone in this love. It is whispered that someone has laid a spell over Holyrood Palace, that the Queen herself is an enchantress. Even her enemies' hearts are struck when they step into her presence. In this country, clan loyalty has always run deeper than the love of king or queen. But our Queen's court is full of nobles who are implacable enemies, whose blood feuds are almost forgotten as she enters the room.

It has never occurred to me to feel joy, not until we have our castle again. But while I wait for the Queen's help, while I serve her, my heart swells.

≈ ≈ ≈

Many of the Queen's French party returned to France before the worst of the winter set in, and the evenings are quiet. But I delight in this falling-away of her companions, for she stays in her chambers with the Marys and sends the servants away, and we spend our time dressing as men. It is a game for the Marys and often as not they would rather sew and gossip, but the Queen has become fascinated with it. We walk around her chamber, talking like two noblemen and practicing how to stand and sit, turn away an attack, drop our voices.

In the middle of January, Beaton and La Flamina fall prey to the mild illness that has swept Holyrood, leaving only Lusty and Seton—and me—to keep the Queen company.

"Tonight we shall go out," she says, one evening when there is no snow falling. "I am bored with these rooms. We have practiced enough."

Lusty claps, but Seton looks dismayed. "Not I," she says.

"Come on!" Lusty urges, taking her hands.

"It frightens me. Do not make me do it."

"But what an adventure! We'll be disguised. No one will bother us."

"Leave her alone, Lusty." The Queen crosses to them and pats Seton on the shoulder. "Stay here if it frightens you so."

"You should be frightened also," Seton says. "What if there's some tavern fight? What if you're discovered? At least take a guard to watch over you."

"How can I go among my people trailed by guards?" The Queen lets her hand drop. "No, tonight I will be an ordinary man."

Sworn to secrecy, two of the Queen's loyal French seamstresses are creating a growing collection of men's clothes and now we begin to look through them. Lusty selects a gaudy outfit in richly colored velvets and silks and holds it up against herself, giggling. They all look to me.

"Your pocket will be picked before the first ale," I say. "Pick out black or blue, no embroidery or slashing."

It takes us as long to get ready as it would for three noblewomen to prepare for a fine evening, but at last it is done. Lusty has a female air about her that is difficult to cover, but she will pass if no one examines her too closely. The Queen has mastered the art of looking masculine and it will not occur to many that such a tall creature could possibly be a woman. A look in her mirror is enough to show me what I know already—I am more myself as Robert than ever as Alison. I will not attract a second glance.

"How long will you be gone?" Seton asks as we stand by the door of the staircase.

"If we've not returned in three hours, you may send guards to look for us—but discreetly," the Queen replies.

"Where are you going?"

"Katy's Tams in Needris Wynd," I say.

We clatter down the stairs, wrap our cloaks close, and cross the courtyard, the air cold on our cheeks. I consult briefly with the guard to ensure that three young men of the Queen's household shall be allowed back inside the gates later, and we step outside of Holyrood, the high gate clanging shut behind us.

Lusty giggles and the Queen hushes her. "You will have to keep silent if you can't sound more manly," she admonishes. Lusty smothers her laughter until the effort of walking up the Canongate to Netherbow Port takes her breath. By the time we present ourselves at the city gates, she is silent.

Katy's Tams is owned by that rare creature, a merchant woman. Sophie Duncan took over her husband's affairs after his early death and proved far more astute in business than he had been, becoming one of Edinburgh's most wealthy merchants. William's ship carried her hides and wool and salted fish across the seas and returned with Roman satins, woollens from Flanders, swords from Germany, and spices from Turkey.

It was Sophie who sheltered William and me when we fled from my mother's murderers, hiding us above her tavern for two days until it was safer to ride to Tulliallan. She taught us the art of disguise, cutting my hair and dressing me as a boy and transforming William into a serving woman. Two of her men rode with us for protection right to the gates of Tulliallan.

I was too young then to wonder why Sophie knew so much of hiding and disguise and why she kept armed guards around her. Later I found out she was a Jewess, who had fled brutal persecution on the continent and sailed in William's ship to the relative safety of Scotland. There began a relationship of mutual assistance. When Sophie married and became a merchant's wife and then a merchant, William carried her goods and sometimes other Jews. In return, she gave us a haven in Edinburgh. Under the protection of her sharp-eyed guards, we have always been safe from Hume in her tavern, Katy's Tams.

We push the door open and walk inside. There are small knots of merchants, guildsmen, some apprentices, drinking and talking. I lead the way to a booth near the rear where we shall be less on show. We slide onto the benches and I wave to a barmaid with a gesture for three tankards of ale. She brings them across on a tray, places them on the table, and takes my coins.

I reach for mine, take a deep gulp, and belch loudly. The Queen and Lusty both look at me with rising alarm and then the Queen picks up her own tankard and follows suit. Lusty hesitates, then takes such a huge swallow that she chokes and must splutter and cough until she regains her breath.

"Stop sitting like a woman," I say under my breath to her. I catch the eye of a young whore across the room. I raise my tankard to her and wink, and she begins to make her way over.

"What are you doing?" Lusty squeaks, and I kick her ankle under the table.

"Why, gents, it is a cold night to be out," the whore says, sliding next to Lusty on the bench seat. "Is it company you seek?"

"My friend here has just come out of a monastery down in the Borders," I say, sitting back and stretching out my legs. "He is a young fool with no money, but I promised a glimpse of the beauty of Edinburgh's women, lest he think I've been lying to him."

She turns to Lusty and draws a finger down her cheek. "So smooth," she says with a smile. "How old are you, lad?"

"He's only a boy; don't tease him too much," I say. "He's barely seen a woman these two years."

She winks. "He'll want educating then."

I grin back at her. "We'll have to get him drunker than this first, for he is a pious lad and knows nothing of love. But keep an eye on him—he may call for you later."

"Very well. You gents should try a whisky instead. Does wonders for keeping out the cold. Shall I send some over?"

"Please." As she slides out, I press a few coins into her hand. I turn back to find the Queen and Lusty both staring at me. I raise my tankard to them both. "Come on, lads! You're both very dull tonight. Is our city so frightening that two country boys cannot raise a toast to it?"

The whiskies arrive and through cajolery, jokes, and toasts I make sure they both down a dram quickly before their wide-eyed silence draws more attention. I wave for the barmaid to bring us more drinks.

The tavern is filling up and the whisky is having an effect. The Queen's pale skin shows a pleasant flush and her eyes are bright. But they both are still staring around the room with wonder and I must keep up an unbroken stream of chatter.

"Let's have another whisky," Lusty says. "This is fun, Robert."

I cannot attract the barmaid now, for the floor is full. "Stay here," I say. "Don't look at anyone."

When I gather our drinks and return, a man has slid into my seat. The Queen and Lusty are regarding him like two startled deer.

"Where are you from, then?" he asks as I come up to the table.

"Good sir, my cousins are newly from the country," I say. "They are both church men and know little of Edinburgh. Thank you for making their acquaintance and I bid you good night."

"I would like to bid you good night," he says, his eyes on Lusty, ignoring me. "The church, eh? Tell me, are the reformers less likely than the Catholics to take the altar boys for their pleasure?"

"Sir, my cousin will be most offended. I must ask you not to speak to him thus."

"And who are you?" he demands, turning his eyes to me with an unpleasant look.

"None of your concern." Alone, I would wriggle away through the crowd while he blinked, or flash a dagger near his groin to discourage him, but Lusty and the Queen are pinned to their seats and their fear goads him on.

"I'll make it my concern, cocky lad. What are you going to do about it?"

"Are you bothering these gentlemen?" The voice at my shoulder is deep and I turn to see Red, Sophie's own bodyguard, looming above us. He is a massive man with an auburn beard and thick arms. He grips the interloper's neck and I see our harasser's eyes widen when he feels the strength of it. He rises without a word and disappears into the crowd.

Red raises an eyebrow at me.

"Thank you, good sir," I say, with a slight frown.

He nods almost imperceptibly. "You'd best come away. You seem to be attracting attention down here."

I nod to the Queen and Lusty and we follow Red through a small doorway, up some stairs, along a wide corridor, and into a sumptuous drawing room, hung with tapestries. A blaze worthy of Holyrood roars in the fireplace. Sophie, elegantly dressed to offset her black hair and dark eyes, is seated by its warmth.

"I thank you and your guard, madam," I say, before she can show she knows me. "Your man helped us out of a tricky spot down there. My young friends were worried."

She stands and smiles. "Please, sit down," she says, waving us across to the fire.

She looks at us, first the Queen, then Lusty, and then me. I drop her a wink that no one else sees.

"May I get you gentlemen a drink?" she asks.

"You are most kind to relieve us from the attentions of that lout, but we were about to leave," I say.

"At least have a dram." She starts pouring out whisky into small silver cups. "It is a cold night and you will need it if you have far to walk home."

She hands out the drinks. "I am Sophie Duncan, the owner of this tavern."

"I'm Robert," I say. "This is Francis and John. They are country lads and not confident of themselves."

The Queen and Lusty take their drinks. They have all but given up their act now. I half expect Lusty to burst into tears.

"Their mothers will have me drawn and quartered for sneaking them to a tavern this night," I say. "I must take them home before they are missed." I swig the whisky and get to my feet. "Come, lads."

Sophie stands too. "I shall have Red show you to the rear entrance so you don't run into your admirer again. When you come again, ask for me. I think you gentlemen might prefer to drink in our private rooms."

The Queen and Lusty walk past me and I turn to follow them out of the room. Sophie is close behind me and she puts her hand on my arm.

"You must come back and tell me about your new friends," she whispers.

Seton is half hysterical when we return. Lusty becomes boastful, marching about the room as she should have in the tavern, forgetting what a fool she became. The Queen says little and when I ask if she is all right, she nods and says she is ready to retire. I wrap my cloak about me and pull the hood over my head before creeping through the darkened palace and into my quarters. Angelique is asleep and I slide into bed silently. I listen to her even breathing for a long time.

≈   ≈   ≈

The next night, I answer the Queen's summons, but when I enter the bedchamber I find it empty. I can see candles burning in the supper room around the edge of the door. She has left me a noble's finery, a richly embroidered tunic, dark leggings, soft boots, and a velvet cap. When I am ready, I tap on the door of the supper room and she bids me enter.

She is sitting alone at a tiny inlaid table. It is January and the night set in hours ago. The doors have long since been bolted, the guards posted, the gates to the palace made fast. A fire is crackling in the hearth, hot and bright enough to keep the cold buried in the stone walls. The plates are covered with pewter tops to keep the dinner warm.

"Robert," she says, in her resonant voice, lifting a glass of deep red wine in my direction. In the candlelight, her skin is porcelain licked by fire. I expected her to be dressed as a man but she is the Queen in magnificence, her gown taut around her tiny waist, her hair pulled up in a French plait. She inclines her head to direct me to the place opposite hers. I lift the pewter lid to find a roasted quail.

The Queen begins to eat hers daintily, using a small, jeweled knife to cut it. I bring out my own larger knife, hack the bird into chunks, and pick one up. I eat it, lick the grease off my fingers, drop a bone to her dog, and take another mouthful of wine.

"Tell me about your castle," she says.

She catches me unawares and I straighten myself at once. "I have never seen it, Your Grace."

"Never?" she asks, surprised.

"It lies in the Borders, not far from Berwick. I know only that it is artfully built on the riverbank itself and that from its turrets you can see for many miles. My father believes that one of his sisters still survives there today, but he has never been able to contact her."

She puts her glass down and regards me. "I have decided I will help you. But it will take me some time to find out about the legal ownership, and I wish to be discreet. I cannot offend one of the lords of my Privy Council without cause."

I fiddle with the stem of my cup.

She smiles at me. "If your story is true and your castle was taken unjustly, I will return it to you."

In spite of myself, I draw in my breath sharply.

She holds up a hand. "I will have something in return from you. Our fates will entwine. Your castle shall be returned when I sit upon the English throne. Until then you will stay with me, serve me, prove your loyalty."

I sit back in my chair. She stands and walks to the window, giving me a moment to gather my thoughts. She has promised me the castle and snatched it back again in the same breath. The shock of it leaves my heart pounding.

"Know you the legend of Hugin and Munin, the ravens belonging to Odin?" she asks, peering into the darkness. "He sent them out each dawn to gather information and return in the evening to whisper the news into his ears."

"I do not know that story," I manage to say.

"But of course you know the Bible story that Noah himself sent forth a raven to find out if the floods had receded and the world was safe."

"Of course," I say.

She swings around. "I have a new role for you. Be my raven. Go out into the city and listen to its mood. What do the people think of their Queen? What do they think of Knox and his raving? Be my ears on Edinburgh's streets."

I bow my head to show my assent and to hide my turmoil. She binds me to her with such an uncertain promise. I don't know if I should dance in delight, or despair at the time it may take her to redeem it.

"There are clothes you may take," she says. "The outfit you wear, and others in my bedchamber that I have ordered for you. Keep it secret, Alison."

There is a knock at the door. "Your Grace, the Earl of Morton is in the presence chamber to see you," a servant announces from outside.

"I will be out momentarily," the Queen calls. She turns back to me. "Do not fear. I am England's rightful ruler under the law. That is why Elizabeth fears me so. I shall have its throne before long and then you will have your castle. All you must do is be loyal."

I rise to my feet and she walks to the door and turns. "Go down the back staircase," she says. "I cannot dine alone with a gentleman in my chambers." She smiles and closes the door behind her.

I make my way to her bedchamber and pause at the entrance to the back stairwell. I am alone in this place at once intimate and public. The place where she sleeps and dreams.

William will hate her for this promise.

I stretch out my hand and stroke her pillow, just once.

Eleven

The winter is so cold the streets freeze. I step into Saint Giles to listen to the sermons of John Knox and memorize his words. I drink in the taverns and join the conversations of men. I stroll around the market days and listen to the gossip of women. I store away information, divulging it to her later in private meetings.

Now that I come in and out of the palace alone, I do not dress in the Queen's bedchamber. I enlist Angelique to help me with clothes, and to watch until the corridor is empty and I may pull my cloak over my head and creep to the servants' passageways. I pay much of my allowance into the hands of guards to let me pass and, I hope, keep their mouths closed.

"Does she not fear a scandal?" Angelique asks as she helps me dress one night before I go to meet the Queen in her private supper room.

I shrug. "There's no harm in it. Few know what we do, and none of them will tell. And what if they did? It is a game."

"A game?" she says. "What would John Knox make of our Queen dining alone with you, dressed as a man?"

I pull away from her assistance. "Nothing. Don't be a fool."

"A queen may not act in such a way without consequences. Our Queen had best take care of her reputation, or they will be singing ditties in the street about how manly she is, and how will she marry then?"

"She has care enough for it that she does not need her servants to concern themselves on her behalf."

She stands back. "She is a queen and you are nothing, Alison. Don't give her your heart."

"I have given the Queen my service and in return she will restore my family's honor. My heart is my own concern. You do not know where it lies."

"Anyone who cares to notice can see where it lies," she says, turning away. "You have not seen what happens when a queen is angered. Or when she tires of you."

≈   ≈   ≈

I am awaiting my castle and the Queen is waiting for love.

In the question of her marriage lies my fate, for her choice of husband will be critical in moving her closer to the English throne. The courts of Europe and the unmarried kings and princes jostle for position. Elizabeth of England is the greater prize of the two queens, but she is Protestant and delights in keeping foreign kings and her own advisers guessing about her marriage intentions. She understands what will happen as soon as a powerful male enters the political picture. Her nobles are longing to deal with a man, just as they are in Scotland and, while Elizabeth would retain power in name, she knows it would be eroded in reality.

Our Queen is looking for love but a ruler is not free to follow her heart. She must marry where politics and power dictate. She needs a man who will take her part, who will add his power to her own and make both of them greater for it. He should have a prize of his own to offer—such as the crown of Spain. But the men who hold such prizes are busily wooing Elizabeth, who keeps them dangling. Without confirmation from Elizabeth of her right of succession to the English throne, our tall, beautiful Queen comes a pale second. Elizabeth holds the trump card in this royal game.

≈   ≈   ≈

The English envoy, Randolph, comes to Scotland to talk to the Queen of marriage and matters of state and she arranges a night of dancing and singing in the palace to ward off the winter and make him welcome. She has poached an Italian bass singer, David Rizzio, from another visiting ambassador, and delights in the chance to show him off.

"We shall go tonight dressed as noblemen," she announces during the afternoon.

The Marys and I stare at her. "I thought you wanted to impress the ambassador," says Beaton.

The Queen shrugs. "I will impress him with a game, to match the games my cousin plays in the matter of marriage. We will show him that we are not Elizabeth's pawns."

The Marys are downcast. They would prefer to don their finest dresses for such a night. But it is no light matter to me. My secret disguise will be revealed to the court.

"What if John Knox hears of it?" I ask.

"This is politics, not religion. Such games are often used in court to make a difficult point."

"Not in Scotland," I say, desperate. "It will be a scandal."

She laughs. "You have told me yourself how the Scots love to dress up and play-act. What would be a scandal in secret is clever diplomacy in public." She pats my hand. "It will be fun. You'll see."

"Your Grace, I dare not be revealed," I say in a low voice. "Is not Lord Hume among the guests this night?"

"But you are my finest actor," she says. "I know. You will wear a mask and speak only French. My nobles will be too busy staring at me to notice you."

I have no choice, only to nod and help them don the most extravagant male outfits. The Queen is gay and laughing, and eventually the Marys cheer up. But as we come to the great hall together, a gaggle of noble young men, I look at her and it hurts my heart. Our secret game, our private delight, is finished the moment we walk through the door. It is policy and politics now.

The hall is packed with guests and a collective gasp rises as we enter. Amid the shocked pause, the musicians strike up a merry note and there is a smattering of applause. Every eye is upon the Queen as she walks across the room to Randolph, followed by her boyish entourage. He bows low, hiding the consternation on his face. When he rises again, he is smiling.

"A very cunning disguise, Your Grace," he says. "You could teach some of Europe's royal blood how a man should dress."

"Tell me, does Elizabeth ever do the same?" the Queen asks, smiling.

"Why no, I have not seen it," says Randolph. "Though she often says she has the heart of a man."

"If only she had more than the heart of a man, then she might solve the pressing problem of both our marriages in one stroke!"

There is a ripple of laughter from the court.

"Why, Elizabeth has the heart of a man and you have the bearing of a man," La Jardiniere, the Queen's Fool, calls out. "Surely between you, you may make one man!"

I draw in my breath sharply but our Queen only smiles. "Perhaps I should come to England with you, Randolph, and see if I can win the Queen's hand as a young man and then unite our kingdoms. Do you think she would see through my disguise?"

More laughter as Randolph inspects her clothing carefully, buying himself some time.

"I am sure she could not fail to be entranced by you," he says at last.

The Queen acknowledges his footwork with a nod. "Then I shall send my cousin one of my own rings to show her the regard in which I hold her."

She claps her hands for the dancing to begin and takes one of her ladies-in-waiting as a partner. There is laughter around the room and those lords who are scandalized do their best to hide it.

The Queen is the center of attention tonight, but I feel exposed. I spy out Lord Hume and move as far away from him as possible. He is surrounded by men in the colors of his livery and my mouth dries as I watch them through my mask.

Lord Bothwell is standing alone and I make my way to his side.

"It is I," I say in a low voice.

He lifts his drink and toasts me. "You must be high in the Queen's favor, Robbie boy. You arrived in her own party. William will be pleased."

"Who are the men with Lord Hume?"

"David Hume, sixth Baron of Wedderburn, his son George, who will be the seventh Baron, their wives, and some younger brothers."

"Which of them holds Blackadder?"

He turns to me. "Alexander Hume. But he has never come to court."

I press myself back into the shadows. "Why are they here?"

"A show of strength." Bothwell drinks again. "It's better if they don't see you talking with me. Any enemy of Hume is in danger. I have been dodging his spies all over the Borders these past weeks."

"I will take my leave." I begin to move.

"Whatever your plans are, act soon," Bothwell says. "I may not be able to protect William much longer. Just the name of Blackadder is enough to put you in danger."

"I have news for William," I say.

"He is at Katy's Tams, and in sore need of good news."

I slip away through the crowd and flee the curious stares. I take the chance to leave the castle, draping a plain cloak over my finery. I make my way up the Canongate, through Netherbow Port, and along the High Street to Katy's Tams, the place between my shoulder blades tingling all the way.

William is sitting in one of the booths toward the rear, with his back to the door. I cross the floor, keeping my head low, and slide onto the bench. My palms are sweating. A barmaid comes over with jug and ale and pours me a cup. I take a gulp and look at William.

"I told you never to dress as Robert again," he says.

"The Queen herself dresses me like this for her amusement." I lean forward. "I have succeeded. She has promised to help us."

There is a flash of hope in his eyes as he raises his head. "Help us?"

"She has promised if I continue to serve her faithfully, our castle will be restored to us when she succeeds to the English throne."

His eyelid begins to twitch.

"Before this we had nothing," I say.

"Do you know," he says quietly, "how old Queen Elizabeth is?"

"She is older than our Queen, and England's last three rulers have all died young. The life of a ruler is never secure. Our Queen could succeed any day."

"She could die any day too," William says through gritted teeth. "It was a mistake to send a woman to do a man's work. You'll come back with me. We'll both work for Bothwell. The castle will be won back only through blood."

"I am committed to the Queen's service," I say. "John and Margaret have placed me there until the Queen gives me permission to go."

He clenches his fists. "I shall have them ask her to release you."

"No!" I say. My vehemence startles me. The prospect of leaving the Queen is a physical pain in my chest.

He starts to rise from his chair. I have never defied him before.

"I have a royal promise, and the protection of the Queen," I say urgently. "Even Bothwell cannot stand up to the might of Lord Hume and it may be he cannot protect you either. We cannot win it back by force, William."

His fists are still clenched. Will he strike me, here in the tavern? My body tenses, ready to dodge him. He stares at me another moment and then lowers himself back into his chair.

"Get me a drink," he says, and I am off the bench and halfway through the crowd before he can blink. I order him a full cup of whisky and take a small one for myself. My hands are shaking as I carry them back to the booth.

William takes the drink. "You must fight the way a woman does. Serve the Queen till she cannot do without you. Do her most secret tasks. Make her need you. Put her in your debt. Then use all your persuasion until she says yes. One of us will prevail."

I toss back my whisky and place the empty cup on the table. "I must go, or I shall be missed. I will do as you ask."

"I know," he says.

≈ ≈ ≈

The Queen calls for another masque to fight off the winter.

"Wear that outfit again," she says to me. "Put on the mask. Speak French. Lord Hume has gone back to the Borders, so you need not worry."

It is dangerous, but my heart thrills at the secret between us and the way she looks at me when I emerge from behind her dressing screen in my hose and doublet.

The Queen's Scottish poet, George Buchanan, has scripted a story for the masque where Apollo and the Muses throw themselves on the mercy of the Queen after fleeing their homes during war.

The actors declaim their parts dramatically, the music heightens the intensity. The wine flows freely and though the rest of the country will be chewing on salted meat this late in the winter, the Queen has ordered a slaughter so we may feast on fresh flesh.

I am her private favorite, but on such a night I do not come near the Queen. I stand back in the crowd and content myself with watching her. She is gracious to her guests, to her foreign dignitaries, to her Marys. I hug her secret affection for me to my chest and speak to no one.

It is late, after dinner, when he comes, sweeping into a courtly bow, sinking to one knee before her. He does not rise at once, but looks up, holds his cap to his richly decorated breast, and recites a poem to her. I edge through the crowd. As I come closer and hear his French, I recognize Chastelard, the poet who arrived in Scotland with the Queen and then returned to France.

I am no poet, but to me his words are sweetmeats: thick on the tongue, quickly gone, leaving my belly sour afterward. But French is the language of such poetry and already I can see that the court—and the Queen—are enchanted by his manner.

"Pierre de Chastelard," she says when he is finished, "It is a pleasure to hear your voice again. I have missed a true French poet."

"Ah, but you have the incomparable Buchanan, who is known even in France," he says, still on his knees. "My words are but a humble imitation of what he can compose."

"True, Buchanan has no equal. But I would fill my court with musicians and poets like a feast, and there are fewer of them here in Scotland. I pray you will delight me with your presence until the winter ends, at least."

He bows low again. "I would be honored."

"Come, sit by me, tell me of France."

Buchanan may be the Queen's favorite poet, but he would never sit so close to her side, leaning right across her to whisper into her ear. She does not rebuke Chastelard, but lets him stay there and then leans across him in the same manner to whisper some private thing, and they both laugh, faces close together.

The heart is a measuring device, able to detect the tiniest nuance of distance. I have seen her sit close to other men. I have seen her lean in to speak some private word. I have seen her laugh with them. But I feel a twisting in my chest looking upon the two of them.

The French ambassador is smirking, but Randolph, the English ambassador, is watching the Queen in alarm. She has asked me to warn her of danger, has she not? I move closer to them and cough to attract her attention.

"Robert?"

"Your Grace, the ambassadors look restless. Perhaps it is time you began a dance?"

She nods her head. "Come here."

I present myself before her.

"Pierre, this is my faithful servant, Robert," she says.

I rise in time to see her whispering in his ear and his eyes widen with interest. Suddenly I feel like an oddity for her amusement. With the shallowest of bows possible, I turn and walk away.

The musicians strike a chord to begin the dancing as I return to my place against the wall. When the Queen calls out for us all to stand and join in, I stay still, sullen.

Angelique crosses the room to my side. "Don't be a fool," she whispers. "Dance."

Somehow I put my hands on the parts of Angelique's body where they are required to go, enter the line of couples poised, and as the music starts, we dance.

I must help the Queen find a husband, but I have not, until tonight, known how it will feel.

Twelve

I have lived my lifetime with the bitter knowledge that something of mine has been taken, but I have not truly known what a vile thing jealousy is. I cannot bear to watch the Queen cavorting with Chastelard and I cannot bear to be away from her.

I must win back her fascination. I must find rumors and gossip and information that hold as much weight and color as Chastelard's poems.

Always the talk in the city is of her marriage, and much of what I hear will not be to her liking. Scotland is full of young nobles, come to power early after the bloody battles of Flodden and Pinkie Clough killed a generation of their fathers and grandfathers. They have time and money without maturity and they play the games of boys.

James Hamilton, the mad Earl of Arran, comes from the powerful Hamilton family which lies close to the throne. But he is not the only noble with the desire for royalty. I hear tavern gossip that John Gordon, a handsome son of Lord Huntly, thinks he has a chance at the Queen's hand too. Lord Huntly is chancellor of the Privy Council and a Catholic, high in the Queen's favor. But while he bows his head and makes fealty here in Edinburgh, it is said that he rules the northern corner of Scotland as if he were its king.

I listen and wait and watch for something more than gossip. The tale is repeated around the city, but I can never pin it down. Late at night I creep back into my room, strip off my clothes, pull a nightgown over my head, and slide into bed next to Angelique. She rolls her warmth toward me and breathes evenly and her eyes are closed. I do not know if she is asleep or only pretending.

≈　≈　≈

One morning in early spring I join the Queen's ladies in the presence chamber where the fire roars high. The Queen is an accomplished needleworker, but I am inadequate at best and have been assigned some mending where the quality of the stitching cannot be seen.

Chastelard is not with us and for once I can simply relax in the Queen's presence. I watch her, discreetly glancing up from my sewing. I have missed her.

The Queen jumps to her feet suddenly and strides across the room to the window. She peers outside restlessly while we watch, ready to move at her order. The room is warm and close; the windows have not been open since November. I am grateful that I may escape the feeling of suffocation, the inactivity, the always-cold fingers, toes, noses, the yearning for fresh air. Without my explorations I would sink into a half-stupor through the winter.

A guard knocks and enters the chamber. "The Earl of Arran," he announces.

The Queen nods. "Bring him in."

Lord Arran rushes across the room toward the Queen. By the time the guards have gathered their wits, he is on his knees, gripping her skirt and babbling incoherently. She draws back and as the guards haul him to his feet, some of his senses return.

"Forgive me, Your Grace, forgive me, but you are in wicked danger."

She considers him for a moment, then nods to the guards, who drop his arms.

"It was Bothwell, Madam, who made me do it. He wants to rule the country. He made me agree that he and I would kidnap you and take you to Dumbarton Castle."

"What?" Her voice is icy.

"Bothwell told me I must then use you for my pleasure until you agree to marry me."

There is a gasp around the room and the guards step forward again. The Queen holds up a hand.

"Then he and I would rule the country," Lord Arran continues. Spittle gathers at the sides of his mouth and his eyes wander strangely. "God told us to do this, but I cannot, and now I beg your forgiveness."

"You have confessed to treason, Lord Arran," the Queen says.

He sinks to his knees. "Yes. But it was Bothwell's suggestion, Your Grace, and he who put me up to it. I made him believe I agreed so I could reveal it to you."

She nods at the guards again and they seize him. His voice rises. "You must listen, Your Grace, you are in danger. He means to take the throne."

The guards drag him from the room and I breathe out in relief. But her face is grim. She says to another guard, "Bring Lord James at once."

It is eight months that she has reigned here on Scottish soil and her nobles are still jostling and vying for their own advantage. Lord James arrives within minutes and when he hears about Arran and Bothwell's plot, his lip curls almost imperceptibly. Statesman that he is, he has kept his loathing of Bothwell well hidden from the Queen.

"We will not tolerate any risk to you, my sister," he says. "They must both be arrested at once and thrown into the castle where we can keep them under watch."

She smiles at him. "Thank you, dear brother. It is a sensitive matter, as you can imagine."

Bothwell is a rogue, but in one way he stands apart from the rest of the nobility. His loyalty to the Queen cannot be bought off at any price. The other lords, with their complex networks of clan loyalty, religion, old hatreds and new feuds, do not like him for it, and now Lord James has his chance.

I must reason with her. Surely she knows the loyalty of Bothwell has never been found wanting? But she goes into her inner chamber. By the time she comes out, hours later, it is to hear from Lord James that Bothwell has been arrested.

≈　≈　≈

"I must speak to her!" I take my frustration out on Angelique in our tiny bedchamber, pacing up and down. "If she knows the truth, she will order his release."

Angelique is sitting on the bed, her hair loose over her shoulders. "Do you believe so?"

"How could she not?"

"No doubt she has seen your desire to speak to her and yet she has not permitted it," Angelique says. "I do not think she wishes to hear about Lord Bothwell."

"But only this night past I have heard the same rumor about Huntly's son John Gordon! Arran is deranged; he has likely mixed up the two men in his mind, even if any of it is true."

"Do you know that she secretly made her brother the Earl of Moray last week?" Angelique asks.

I spin around. "I have not heard this."

"You have been away from the palace much of the time," she says. "It is Lord James whom she favors now, and Lord James has imprisoned Bothwell. She does not wish to confront her brother. I fear your Bothwell shall stay in the castle dungeons for some time."

"But this charge cannot stand up in a trial on the word of a madman."

"If it goes to trial."

"How could it not go to trial? The Queen herself said she would examine Bothwell."

Angelique laughs, throwing up her hands. "Are you such an innocent, Alison?" I glare at her and her face becomes serious again. "It is not Bothwell you must think of. You cannot help him, but your anger endangers you."

"She has imprisoned a man wrongly."

"Is that it? Or is it because she favors another above you?" She stands up and comes close to me, dropping her voice. "I warned you. Do not think yourself safe for a moment. If you have heard rumor of another plot, then rebuild her favor by finding the details for her. Make sure you do not go down with Bothwell."

"You have been a courtier too long," I say, turning away.

"And you, not long enough," she says. "Courtiers die, just as noblemen and soldiers do, when their judgement is poor."

≈ ≈ ≈

On a normal night Angelique's eyes turn to me when I come in, dressed in whatever finery the Queen has ordered that day. She turns me with gentle hands, helps untruss me, peels back my disguise. She turns away when I'm down to my underwear and, when she looks again, I'm in my nightgown with no powder, no wig, no frock, no tunic, no clothes to delineate me as male or female. I help her with her clothes and brush her hair. We get into bed together like sisters.

She is asleep when she is meant to be and keeps her eyes always in the correct direction. So why do I wake to find us breathing in rhythm? Why do I let my gaze stray when she is undressing, in hope of catching sight of some sweep of skin?

I wake in the dark, the morning after Bothwell's arrest, to find her hand in my hair. Her palm curves around the shape of my skull. Our breathing is slow and in time. A warmth has spread from her sleeping hand and down into me.

Outside the first birds are thawing their frozen throats, ready to start the day. There is a different quality in the air this morning, some subtle scent or change in temperature. During the night, spring has arrived.

I allow myself a few moments to feel what it is like to be close to another body and then I draw myself away with a sudden movement.

"What is it?" she asks sleepily.

"I do not like the smell of your breath so close to me," I say.

She turns over, away from me, without a word.

Thirteen

I believed that William and I were allies of one of the Queen's leading lords. But Bothwell has fallen and all those aligned with him are now tainted by association.

Bothwell and Arran are imprisoned in cells gouged out of the stone-cold bowels of Edinburgh Castle. Lord James still rules much of the country with an iron fist, no matter who sits on the throne in Edinburgh, and his grip is nowhere tighter than on the lock of the cell where his enemy Bothwell paces.

I learn through the court gossip why Bothwell's trial will not be held. Lord Arran howls like a dog and shrieks of devils and witches from his cell below the castle. But though he is clearly insane, his family is so close to the throne that the Queen cannot risk the scandal of having to execute him for bearing false witness. For the moment it is simpler to hold him and Bothwell without trial.

I send word to William to meet me. With Bothwell imprisoned, he has returned to our underground rat hole for safety, coming and going through Edinburgh's hidden tunnels, creeping out to eat and drink at Katy's Tams.

I wait for him there and when he meets me, his face is winter-pale, his jaw set.

"It is Hume's doing," he says without preamble. "Hume and Lord James together. Can't you speak to the Queen?"

"The Queen will not hear of it," I say. "Bothwell made a bad enemy in Lord James. He has the Queen's ear and I can do nothing."

"I am bribing half of Edinburgh to get him out," William says.

"There is not enough money to grease the key to his cell." I lean across the table. "You must flee, William. It's too dangerous. Bothwell is an earl. If Hume has played a part in this, then dealing with you will be nothing."

"I have sent word to my cousins," he says. "They'll be here in a few days. It will take more than some henchman of Hume's to get past Edmund and Jock."

"Can't you sail with them? Wait in France until it's safe?"

He stares at me. "Bothwell would not leave me in prison without help."

"For once, listen to me!" My voice rises a little and William looks around. He leans forward.

"For once, listen to me," he says and his voice chills me. "I'm not leaving while Bothwell is in there. Don't speak of it again." He sits back. "What are you going to do?"

"I need to regain the Queen's favor. There are rumors that John Gordon, son of Lord Huntly, also boasts about taking the Queen by force and compelling her to marry him. Perhaps Arran mixed up Bothwell and Gordon in his mind and there lies the real plot," I say. "If I can find out more about it, get enough evidence to have Gordon arrested, it could clear Bothwell and help our cause all at once."

He looks at me with hope on his face. "I will find out what I can."

"Stay hidden," I say. "Leave it to me. When I have proof, I will go to the Queen."

"Very well. Leave word here with Sophie. It's too dangerous for us to meet again."

"Be careful," I say.

≈   ≈   ≈

"I have heard it with my own ears this night past, Your Grace."

I am close to her side in the presence chamber and I lean down to speak softly in her ear. It is the nearest I have been to her for many weeks, while spring has lengthened into summer and I have gone about Edinburgh as merchant, sailor, carpenter. I have missed her. I have ached for her, knowing that Chastelard has been ever at her side. But at last I have something to offer.

She waves away the women sitting nearby so we are alone. "He would ravish me and force me into marriage?" she asks, her hand on her throat. "Just like Lord Bothwell?"

"John Gordon said it himself last night in front of witnesses who will testify. Likely he will say it again tonight when he drinks at the White Hart."

"Treason," she says. "Again."

I nod. I will not mention Bothwell, not yet. Time enough when John Gordon is arrested to suggest that Arran has muddled the two men and there is only one plot.

She sends for Lord James and talks to him for some time in a low voice. He leaves the presence chamber, his mouth set. The Queen does not speak to me again during the evening, but as she rises to prepare for her sleep, she asks me to accompany her into the bedchamber. Seton, as always, comes to unbraid her hair and La Flamina helps ready her for bed.

"You have done well in this, Alison," she says as Seton releases the tight braids and her face relaxes. "I have missed your company here in court, but thanks to your devotion, another danger has been removed."

La Flamina finishes unlacing the stiff bodice and lifts it away. The Queen sighs. "What is it, do you think, that makes Scotland's nobles so disrespectful of their ruler? I cannot imagine such a thing happening in France."

"Most have not had a queen in their lifetime, Your Grace," I say. "They expect you to marry, and while you do not, they speculate."

"I do not believe Elizabeth is treated so," she says.

La Flamina laughs. "She cavorts openly with her master of horse."

"Hush," the Queen says. "Do not speak of my cousin so, even here. We have need of her goodwill."

"You must punish John Gordon without mercy," Seton says, her mouth tight.

"He shall be punished," she says. "My brother is firm on such matters."

"You should marry," La Flamina says, lifting the softly woven nightgown over the Queen's head. "That will be the end of such foolishness among your nobles."

"Don't you start on this too! The Privy Council reminds me at every opportunity. I'll be happy to marry a man to whom I can give my heart. Unfortunately there are few to choose from. My Marys will all find husbands before I do."

"Why, we have vowed not to marry before you." La Flamina smiles. "So you must hurry, lest we all become old maids."

"I have said I will not allow you to make such a promise," the Queen says.

"You cannot force us to break it," Seton replies, and draws the brush down the length of the Queen's auburn hair.

I have been away from the palace too much to step into the banter of her familiars. Too many hours wandering Edinburgh as a spy and too few as a lady-in-waiting in her dressing room. I have risen high as an informant but fallen away as a confidante. It is quite some time since I helped her prepare for bed and I have missed the closeness of it.

There is a knock at the door and La Flamina goes to it. The captain of the guards enters and kneels.

"We arrested John Gordon, Your Grace."

"Good. Lord James and I will discuss him in the morning."

He coughs. "Your Grace, we took him to the Tolbooth but he managed to escape."

She stands, agitated. "How?"

"I do not know." He hangs his head low.

She walks closer to him. "Have you searched his father's house?"

"We went straight there, but Lord Huntly has gone too. We believe they must be fleeing north. I have sent men in pursuit."

"Recall them," she says. "Go and tell Lord James what has happened and bid him come to me in the morning. My cousins the Gordons will find more than a posse of guards on their trail. I will go after them myself."

≈　≈　≈

I have never been into the Highlands. My heartland lies south, and the north of Scotland has no interest for me. But I have promised to serve the Queen and now it means turning my head away from the castle and riding with her in pursuit of the Huntlys.

She has said to her court and to her people that this is a progress; she would meet the people of the Highlands for the first time in her reign. But it is the Gordon family that she goes to challenge, riding down Lord Huntly and his son.

She carries a secret that the Gordons do not know. As Angelique told me, the Queen has made Lord James the Earl of Moray, handing over wide stretches of land in the north-east, thinking to tighten the bond with her half-brother through this great gift. But Lord Huntly has held that land for the Gordon clan for years and now she must find some queenly way to take it back from him.

The Queen has put on her dress armor, gold and exquisite, and let her long hair loose, and she rides astride like a warrior to show her strength to the northerners. Her glistening armor is in deadly earnest and hidden in her finery is a pistol, loaded and dangerous. This is not a disguise; it is the Queen showing her people that she is Diana the huntress and we are her handmaidens of war.

We travel into wild country, inhabited by rough men and ghosts, crisscrossed with bogs and sheep and mist and impassable mountains. The streams are so cold that our throats ache to drink from them and Lord James must ride with a guide by his side to pick out our path. We shiver through the nights and wolves howl in the hills around us.

The Queen comes alive in these rough conditions, like some contained creature finally set free. Instead of being trussed like a game bird each morning, she rises clear-eyed from her bed, dresses in leggings and breastplate like a man, and stamps around while the camp is dismantled, impatient to ride. I believe she would charge into battle like one of the ancient Amazons whose stories have carried across the world. When our spies ride back with the news that Lord Huntly waits with fifteen hundred soldiers, her eyes brighten and she laughs. She rides out with Lord James at the head of the army, ready for confrontation.

≋　≋　≋

"You must wait here, sister," Lord James says as we halt on a hill near Inverness Castle.

"I will come down with you," she says, pulling up her horse's head. "I have not ridden this far to watch you challenge the Gordons from a distance."

He spins his horse in a tight circle and brings it close to her side. "Lord Huntly has fled. He has left orders that you are not to be admitted here. Do you understand?"

"I understand he is a coward," she says. "And guilty of treason already. Why do we not pursue him at once?"

"Because then any lord in the country who holds a royal castle will think he can bolt the door on his Queen and act like its owner. We will take back this castle by force. Men will die, my sister. Your gold armor may glitter, but you are a woman and this is a battle."

He spurs his horse into a gallop, down to the castle to join his men. The Queen's horse won't stand still. She pulls the reins and it dances on its toes and tosses its head. Her eyes are alight, as if at any moment she will thunder down the hill to that windswept castle below and hack her way inside with a sword.

It takes three hours for the Queen's forces to fight their way into the castle. When it is done, Lord James comes for us. The Queen and her ladies and I ride behind him down the hill and into the courtyard entrance, which is littered with bodies.

"Lord Huntly's captain," Lord James says when the man is thrown to the ground before her, his wrists tied, his face bloody. The Queen looks at him and the soldiers fall silent.

"You held Inverness Castle against your anointed Queen," she says.

He knows better than to beg for mercy. He keeps his head bowed and says nothing.

"No lord is higher than your Queen." She surveys them all, her own soldiers and those of Huntly's who have survived the skirmish. "Do you hear me?"

They drop to their knees, all of them, and she looks at her half-brother and lifts her finger in a gesture toward the hapless captain.

Lord James nods in satisfaction. "I have let some of them escape."

They smile at each other. "Good," she says. "Huntly should know what comes his way. Send for more men from Edinburgh. We will show the Cock of the North who rules here."

≋ ≋ ≋

Lord Huntly, hearing that his castle is taken, his captain hanged, and another two hundred harquebusiers are on the way from Edinburgh, plays hide and seek in the mountains of Badenock. The Queen's scouts ride out each day searching for him and reinforcements arrive daily, uniformed harquebusiers with their harquebuses, shot, powder, and swords.

In the midst of it, the Queen rides out for pleasure, hunts, dines in the great houses of the north, and wins these men to her side. The enemies of the Gordon clan take their chance to emerge from the surrounding hills and join the battle against them, and thus reinforced she builds a small war.

I have learned to examine her without seeming to stare and I spend many hours watching her now. She did not touch Huntly's captain, but he died at her hand nonetheless, swinging and kicking at the end of a rope hung down from the castle battlement. The Queen's own men cheered when he stopped moving, as if they had forgotten any of us could die so easily, obeying an order that the Queen does not like.

She has been blooded in war—has she changed? She laughs and converses with the men around her as if she has not sent their comrades to their deaths. In the evenings, when we go to her chambers in whatever great house we are lodged and help her prepare for bed, she is tender with us. No one mentions the dead captain or the men killed in that skirmish.

But I cannot stop thinking of him when I lie down at night. My father is just such a captain, in service to a lord who has displeased the Queen.

≋ ≋ ≋

At last Lord Huntly sends a challenge. He will meet the Queen and her army at Corrichie.

The Queen does not argue with Lord James this time, but makes her preparations to watch the battle from the hillside. She and the Marys are mounted at the front, we lesser ladies behind. She has ordered all of us dressed in our female finest so that we decorate the hill above the bloody ground like iridescent game birds.

I cannot see the Queen's face, only the wiry tension in the set of her shoulders as the battle unfolds below us. The Marys gasp and turn away when it becomes too gruesome, but she never falters. I shut my eyes against the sight, but I cannot block out the sounds. Lord James and Maitland are experienced in battle and Lord Huntly's army cannot match them. The Queen's army forces Huntly's men down into a bog at the foot of the hill and hacks them to death.

When it is over, Lord James and Maitland begin picking their way back across the battlefield. They lead Lord Huntly, captured and tied to his horse. Halfway across he sways, falls from the saddle, and hits the ground heavily. Men gather around, talking and gesticulating. Eventually four of them manage to heave him across the horse's back but he lies there like a load of chaff, unmoving.

The Queen sits still and, though I have seen my share of convenient killing, it is I who sway and feel the cloud of blackness press in. I pitch forward in the saddle, dimly aware of my face against the horse's neck. A servant takes the reins as Lord James and his party approach, and I am taken away. I slide from the saddle into a darkness where I cannot hear the screams any more.

≈ ≈ ≈

Lord Huntly's heart failed at the moment of his defeat, but I do not witness the presentation of his unmarked body to the Queen. The Queen's French physician, Arnault, takes me back to our lodgings and, in the excitement of the Queen's victory, I am forgotten. I roll myself into a heavy sleep and by the time I awaken the next morning, Huntly's son John, he who boasted of marrying the Queen, has already been sent to Aberdeen for his punishment. Within a few days he is beheaded in the market square.

There is a feast to celebrate the Queen's victory over the Gordon family, but I do not attend. I stay in my bed, staring at the wall. I cannot drink to the beheading of John Gordon when I have played no small part in putting him on the block myself.

I have wanted our castle returned and justice done. But in striving for the Queen's favor, I set a trap for John Gordon that has seen dozens of men die, in a battle tracing back to a lad who drank too much and boasted too loudly one night in Edinburgh.

I hoped to show the Queen that Bothwell was innocent. But Bothwell's name has not been mentioned and it seems everyone has forgotten what set us on this progress in the first place.

≈ ≈ ≈

"Have you recovered?" the Queen asks me, as servants bustle around the room, packing her belongings to return to Edinburgh.

"Forgive me, Your Grace. I do not know what came over me."

"I thought I might faint too," says Beaton, giving me a sympathetic smile. "It was a grim sight."

"You thought the battle was grim," Lusty says. "Two strokes of the ax to sever John Gordon's head is something I will never forget."

"I closed my eyes," says Seton.

"I too," says La Flamina. "But the sound of it all. I still cannot get those battle screams out of my ears."

The Queen is standing by the window, looking out over the town of Inverness. "You can trust that I will never forget it," she says softly. "Elizabeth is right. A woman must have the heart of a man to be a ruler."

"But she should not forget she is a woman either," says Lusty.

The Queen turns. "You think I have been cruel, that it has not hurt me to act thus. But men understand the language of blood. They will treat me differently now. You will see."

She walks into the center of the room and holds out her hands. The Marys go to her and she nods for me to join them. We take hands, all of us, in a circle.

"This is a country where the ties of family and loyalty are stronger even than death," she says. "Having seen death, I pledge my loyalty and my life to you. And in return, I ask for yours. Do you make this same commitment to me? Do you become my family, as I have neither father nor mother, husband nor child? Will you stand by me?"

"You do not need to ask," Seton says. "We are already your family."

Her eyes fall upon me. "What of you, Alison? You warned me of the Gordons' disloyalty, but you could not watch their punishment. Do you still pledge your loyalty? If you cannot, speak now and I will release you freely from my service. I will not keep you against your will."

I want justice for Lord Bothwell and our castle returned. And there is the matter of my heart, which I have given to her and cannot easily take back.

"I am yours, as always," I say, and she squeezes my hand.

She looks around us all. "We are no longer girls. Scotland and I have taken the measure of each other now."

She releases our hands and we stand back. Before she returns to the window, she places the palm of her hand against my cheek for a moment. "You did well, my raven," she says.

I don't dare mention Bothwell.

≈ ≈ ≈

We will ride home to Edinburgh in full glory, victorious, dangerous, flanked by an army of thousands. The people will line the roadways and tracks and now there will be respect in their eyes as well as wonder.

Word comes just before we leave Inverness. Bothwell has escaped from the cells of Edinburgh Castle and fled the country.

Fourteen

It is close to winter by the time we return to Edinburgh. The smell of the city is like an old friend, rank but familiar. I breathe it in as if I'm starved for it.

Angelique waits till we are in our bedchamber to question me.

"Thank God you're back," she says. "Until Bothwell escaped we had nothing to speak of except speculation on the Queen's marriage and rumors from the north. Tell me if it is true she watched her enemies being slaughtered with a smile upon her lips?"

I force myself to laugh and concentrate on pulling off my boots. "She did not smile. She put down her enemies with the necessary force and earned all of Scotland's respect."

"She has harshly punished a lad who bragged in a tavern," Angelique says. "Even her loyal Bothwell has fled the country in fear of his life."

"We heard. But not how he escaped."

"No one knows. Perhaps he was able to bribe someone once Lord James had left Edinburgh."

I wonder if William has gone with him. "Enough of war. What is being said about the Queen's marriage?"

She smiles. "Talk was open while the Queen was away. Elizabeth grows ever more powerful and even the common people know she still refuses to acknowledge Mary as her heiress. There are suitors in Spain, France, and Norway. We hear rumors that Elizabeth is offering an English noble of her own. But none of those will put our Queen on the English throne, except through war."

"She has shown herself capable of war, don't you think?"

"A spat with the Cock of the North is not a war against the might of Elizabeth," Angelique says. "If your family's honor waits upon her holding the English throne, you could be waiting a lifetime."

"Do they say who Elizabeth will offer?"

"There are only two suitable men in her court. Lord Dudley or Lord Darnley. But they say that one is a traitor and the other is only a boy."

I stretch out my legs, my muscles aching after the two-week ride from Inverness.

"If you want your castle, I think you must encourage the Queen to marry in England," Angelique says.

"You think I have influence! Even if Dudley or Darnley were suitable and even if one of them were to bring her closer to the throne, what can I do about it? She will not marry without love."

"You can fan the fire of love. Find out what fascinates our Queen and then whisper to her about it. Make her suitor irresistible in the telling. A woman can be led to love."

I climb into bed and lie wakeful as Angelique rolls away from me and her breathing slows and deepens. Death lurks behind every corner, especially for a prince. If some ill befalls Elizabeth and our Queen is married to an English noble, she and her husband would rule England and Scotland uncontested. Angelique is right. It is my best chance at the castle.

I know nothing of Elizabeth's nobles and I do not think I will hear about them in the marketplace.

≈ ≈ ≈

"I expected you sooner," Sophie says, as Red ushers me into the upstairs room. She kisses me on both cheeks. "Your father has fled with Bothwell. They set out for France and will petition for Bothwell's pardon from there."

"How did Bothwell escape?" I ask, as her servant pours wine.

She smiles. "In true Bothwell fashion he prized the bars of his window and climbed down the side of Castle Rock. William waited for him in Nor Loch and they rode to Leith, where his ship was docked. No one has ever escaped from the castle before and they are trying to cover it up."

I raise my cup. "To safe escapes."

She touches her cup to mine. "Bothwell is bold, but he's a fool. He says he will never waver in his loyalty to the Queen, even though she had him imprisoned. What spell does she cast on men?"

"She casts it on everyone," I say. "Even Knox acknowledges her power."

She looks at me, taking in my merchant's clothing as if she has only just noticed my disguise. "Are you in thrall to her thus?"

I should reveal nothing. But I long for a confidante and Sophie can be trusted.

"She has my heart," I say.

Sophie is silent a long time, until I drop my gaze, feeling my cheeks redden. She takes my hand. "Be very careful, dear one. Keep this buried deep."

"Nobody knows." I draw my hand out of hers. "I would find out what manner of nobles Elizabeth may offer our Queen in marriage. Lord Darnley and Lord Dudley are both mentioned."

"Give me a week. Christmas Eve I shall have word."

I swallow the last of my wine and stand up. "Thank you."

She stands, kisses me on the cheeks, then leans in to whisper in my ear. "Look elsewhere for love, Robert."

≈　≈　≈

Back in court, as the Queen's second winter begins to set in, Chastelard has wasted no time since her return. He has written long, tedious poems about her victory in the north, all mists and crags and heather and deer bounding away at first light, no mention of the bogs and frozen fingers and the wind cutting through our clothes. According to Chastelard, Huntly was struck down by divine vengeance, a sign to the Queen's enemies that God is on her side.

I watch them each night. Chastelard sits by her side, laughing. He recites poetry, leaping to his feet when overcome by the urge to declare his love. He scribbles sweet words on pieces of paper and hands them to her, keeping his hand close to hers while she reads them. I see how her face lights up when he appears. They draw into dark corners of the room together and in the shadows I glimpse the Queen leaning in, her lips close to his neck. Do they touch? Does she kiss him, or just whisper in his ear? I cannot be sure. When I am close enough to see his eyes, they are shining and half mad.

"How can she bear him carrying on so?" I ask Angelique in the darkness of our bed. "He makes a fool of himself."

"He is in love with her," she says.

"Half the realm is in love with her."

"He believes she is taking his suit seriously."

I laugh. "But he's the court poet!"

Angelique says nothing in the dark, but she may as well shout the words into my ear. *You are a hundred times less than that, and look at you.*

She turns away from me and I slow down my breathing deliberately. We sleep back to back.

≈ ≈ ≈

When I come to Sophie's upstairs chambers on Christmas Eve, I am not the only visitor. The dimly lit room is crammed with bodies.

"Robert." Sophie comes to my side. She is dressed in finery befitting a noblewoman. "I have news for you." She draws me to a chair in the corner of the room.

"What I have learned about Robert Dudley is only what's widely known in England," she says. "It is no secret that he is Queen Elizabeth's paramour. It was even thought he might rise high enough to marry Elizabeth herself, but he cannot cast off the stain of his father's treason. He was married, but his wife died in strange circumstances and the suspicion of murder lurks. It is said Elizabeth does little without consulting him and they are together many hours of each day—and night too."

"Why would she offer him to her cousin, then?" I ask, frowning.

Sophie shrugs. "That I cannot find out. But our Queen would do well to be cautious of such an offer."

"What of the other?"

"I can tell you more about Lord Darnley," she says. "He is better known outside the English court, having recently returned from his education in France. His father is Matthew Stuart, Earl of Lennox,

106

who was banished to England some twenty years ago after he helped the English, and there married Henry VIII's niece, Margaret Douglas. The Stuarts are very powerful still in Glasgow, and the Earl has been asking Queen Elizabeth to let him return to Scotland and reclaim his estates. Now that his eldest son, Darnley, is of marriageable age, Lennox is ambitious for him, having lost six of his siblings. Darnley is Mary's own cousin and in line to the English throne."

"How old is he?"

"Seventeen a fortnight since. He is accomplished in Greek, Latin, Italian, and French, a musician, a poet, a man of letters. He is skilled in the physical arts and well versed in courtly manners. He has been groomed for royalty since he was born. The reports of his beauty and his height are not exaggerated."

I feel a knot of dislike for him already. "He sounds like the perfect husband for our Queen. Especially if he is tall."

Sophie lowers her voice. "I will tell you something not known in England. He has an appetite for younger boys and he likes to hurt them."

I stare at her. "Is it just a rumor?"

"The Queen should observe him with care. It is too early to see what manner of man he will become." She sits back and smiles. "Will you stay and celebrate the season with us?"

"I have an engagement elsewhere."

"A pity. I have friends here tonight you would be most interested to meet."

I stand. "Another time."

≈　≈　≈

I make my way to the lane where the entry to William's house is hidden. I let myself in and head down the stairs in the dark. When I light a candle, the room is cold and covered in dust, and I can see he has left hastily. I wrap a blanket around my shoulders and curl up on the floor while Edinburgh celebrates its Christmas above me.

William and I never speak of my mother, but on Christmas Eve, the day she was killed, William always drinks himself to insensibility.

I strain to remember her face, but I cannot conjure it. I strain to hear her voice, but it is lost to me.

I have lived my whole life hungry, yearning for the castle to fill the emptiness inside me. If I do not win it soon, it feels like I will starve.

Fifteen

The year 1563 begins with the coldest winter in memory. Food is in short supply already and even the great feasts of Holyrood are sparse.

It is in this deep winter that Chastelard plays his hand. You would think a poet would wait for spring and the softening of winter's cold grip. But madness has overtaken him and his poet's heart knows no meter or rhythm.

The Queen orders another night of music and dancing to take away the winter cold, and dresses us as young noblemen once more. When the dancing is finished after midnight, we climb the staircase, frosty-breathed, and pour into her presence chamber. The Marys are laughing and the room is warm after the iciness of the corridor. A serving girl has hot wine waiting and she pours it into silver cups.

As I sip my wine, I hear a soft, metallic sound from the bedchamber like the sound of a weapon.

I catch the Queen's eye, and I can see she has heard it too. Seton and La Flamina are still whispering and giggling, oblivious. Covered by their laughter, I rise, make my way to the door, and whisper urgently to the guard.

Four guards come quietly into the room. The Marys falter but the Queen gestures for them to continue their chatter and says in a bright voice, "Beaton, did you not think that Maitland was enchanted by your garb tonight? You should be careful; perhaps he would prefer a young man!"

Beaton gives an uncertain giggle and then the guards charge past us and into the bedchamber with a shout. Bumps and crashes issue from the room and a man's voice cries out. None of us recognize the melodic tones of the poet until the guards bring him into the outer chamber. When she sees Chastelard, the Queen turns white.

"Under the bed, Your Grace," the guard says. "Armed with these." Another guard holds up a sword and a dagger.

"Not to hurt you, Mary, you can't think that, you can't—" Chastelard's voice is cut off by a sharp jerk on some restrained body part.

"Put him somewhere cold and triple the guard." I can hear the rage in the Queen's measured tones.

"Just let me talk, let me explain." The guard twists on his arm and the poet's voice rises to a shriek.

The guards drag him from the room. The Marys babble in shock, and reach for their wine, and when the Queen stands, with a shuddering sigh, they stand too. Seton reaches for her and embraces her.

"We will all sleep here tonight," Lusty announces. "We will stoke up the fire and keep it burning, and bring quilts and pillows. You won't be alone."

"No," the Queen says. "But thank you. It's late. Seton will sleep with me in my bedchamber. The rest of you leave me."

I am the last to leave and I turn at the door. "Thank you, my raven," she says.

≈   ≈   ≈

The Queen calls me to her bedchamber early the next morning. Seton is already doing her hair.

"What did he intend?" she asks me without preamble.

"Your Grace, he is in love with you. He recites love poems to you every night."

"But he is the court poet." She frowns. "That is what court poets do. They do not come armed into the royal bedchamber."

"I do not believe it is courtly love he feels."

She is silent for a long time, then sighs. "What think you, Seton? Have I acted somehow improperly in this?"

Seton hesitates. "Perhaps you have been more familiar with him than you should."

The Queen stands impatiently. "Speak plainly!" she says to me. "What has been said?"

"You lean on his shoulder and whisper in his ear," I say, my heart

110

beating fast. "You kiss him, or so it appears. You keep him close by your side, you dance with him, you press his hand." I stop, lest the extent of my observation is revealed further. "There has been talk. The courtly love you speak of is not well known in Scotland. You are the Queen and marriageable. Chastelard, in his lust, perhaps truly thinks to woo you."

Her frown deepens while I speak and she walks to the window. Seton and I are silent. Eventually she swings around.

"We will go to Fife at once," she says. "Somewhere quiet for a few days. I will have Chastelard reprimanded and banished to France this day. No one else shall hear of this foolishness. You are not to speak of it."

≈ ≈ ≈

The Queen rides through the High Street in her elegant finery, flanked by the four Marys at their most gracious, smiling and feminine. Bringing up the rear is Lord James, now openly known as the Earl of Moray, in his grim Protestant black. His new name refuses to lodge in my mind.

I watch the shining faces turned toward us as she passes. Is it any wonder she cannot see the finer nuances of desire, when almost everyone who looks upon her is half helpless with it?

As we come out of the city to an area of open fields, she reins in her horse till I am beside her. "Ride with me," she says. We set off at a gallop across the heather, racing side by side, leaving the rest of the party behind. At last we draw up by a stream and let the heaving horses lower their heads to drink.

"You did not warn me of this," she says.

I feel a sudden pang of fear. "Your Grace?"

"You knew how he felt and what others were saying, but you did not speak." She pulls up the horse's head. "Chastelard is a fool, but a dangerous one. To be caught in my bedchamber could raise an evil scandal, and I can't have it, not when marriage and succession are undetermined. You must watch more closely." She swings the horse around. "Do not fail me again." She kicks him into a gallop.

I wait a beat before following her so that she will not see the blush on my face.

≈ ≈ ≈

At Rossend Castle we are given the best welcome that can be managed in such a foul season; the castle knew of our visit only when a hasty messenger arrived a few hours ahead of our party. We eat a plain meal of salted meats, listen to a somber recital by the Queen's musicians, and go to bed so early that many, used to the late nights of the court, grumble and find it hard to sleep. But the Queen promises that if the weather holds we shall go hawking.

The long February night finally comes to an end and in the morning we ride out to meet the hawking master. For some hours the fine birds swoop and scream and strike their prey and dig their talons into our leather gloves. They swivel their heads and watch us with their inhuman eyes until the hunting is done and they are masked again.

The evening draws in, bringing another gloomy night. The lord and lady of the castle do their best to make us comfortable. The musicians play once more in the cold hall, their breath frosty. But the Queen is fresh-cheeked from her day outside and goes to her bed with good humor. Seton and I accompany her to the bedchamber and she smiles as we begin to unhook her stays.

"It is good to be tired from doing something," she says. "I have breathed fresh air and felt the ground under my feet. I have left behind Edinburgh and my cares for a day. It is good to come out into the country."

As she speaks, I press my fingers against the stiff fabric of her dress, and loosen the lacings holding it tight. The soft fabric of her underthings is exposed when suddenly there is a clatter outside and the door bursts open. It is Chastelard. Where has he come from? His eyes are wild and he comes at the Queen in a headlong rush.

"Please hear me, my love, you must listen, you can't send me back to France. I love you, Mary. And you love me. You can't deny it."

He is raving and pushing at me to get to her. I shout his name—"Chastelard! Chastelard!"—to wake him from this madness. Seton is shrieking and then there is a crash at the door and the sound of steel. I have never been so glad to hear it.

It is Lord James, sword brandished, and he gives a roar that halts Chastelard long enough for the guards to rush in and take him. They push him face down on the floor, an arm twisted behind his back. Lord James pushes the point of his sword between the poet's shoulder blades.

"Kill him, my brother," the Queen says.

The room falls silent suddenly and a log cracks in the fire, making us jump. Chastelard's breath comes in sobs but he has the sense not to plead for his life. The sword tip quivers and I wait for it to plunge into his back.

But I have forgotten it is Lord James, the statesman, who has him pinned. He was regent for nine years and he knows how to choose the right moment for killing.

"No, Madam," he says, in a voice as cold as the castle. "Your honor hangs in the balance. Even I may not be able to retrieve it from this. He will be tried at Saint Andrews and, if he is found guilty in law, he will pay the price."

Chastelard moans in despair. As I look down at him, his face against the stone floor, I feel sorry for him. His passion for the Queen has made him mad.

I turn my head to look at her. I remember the morning before the battle at Corrichie and the way she set her jaw after she had watched the captain hanged and was preparing to send hundreds more to their deaths. She looks the same at this moment, her eyes like the Atlantic Sea, lips pale, knuckles white.

≈ ≈ ≈

Saint Andrews, the university town, prides itself on being an intellectual place, somehow above the veniality and mire of Edinburgh. But as if to make up for its high-mindedness, its citizens take an inordinate delight in torture and death. Chastelard's sentence—beheading—has barely been announced when people begin gathering in the square to watch it carried out.

Lord James comes to fetch the Queen from the chambers where we waited during the trial. When she would demur, he lays his hand on her arm. There is no more pressure in his touch than Seton might make while helping her undress, but it carries a menace that makes me shiver.

"Do you understand what he has done to your honor?" he asks.

"He has done nothing to my honor," she says, her measured tone matching his. "I have never been alone with him. He was apprehended by guards in my bedchamber, in front of witnesses. How can my honor be tarnished by his crime, when I am innocent?"

"This is Scotland, sister, not France where you may fawn over your courtiers and no one will blink. You have brought it on yourself with your encouragement of him. Now you will come and watch his punishment, and try to retrieve what little remains of your reputation."

He gives me a cold glance as he draws back. "Make your mistress ready. Do not let her swoon or weep. You women know how to turn such things on and off at will."

The people gather, jostling, grinning, elbowing to the front for a better view. The square is humming with the buzz of voices. When the Queen appears on the platform, the sound builds quickly to a roar. Her face is set, her expression hard. Gone is the shining Queen who beams upon her people. Come instead, the Queen of stone, who will send a man to his death rather than suffer a stain upon her reputation.

When Chastelard is brought out, the roar abruptly falls, and an eerie silence settles over the square. He listens when the charge and conviction are read out, then turns to look at the Queen across the crowd. Next to her, Lord James says without moving his lips, "Look at him; do not falter." But she does not need the reminder. I can sense from beside her that she has severed any kind feeling she held for him.

Poet to the last, he refuses priest or minister and falls to his knees to recite the poem "Hymn to death" by his countryman Ronsard. When it is done, he cries out, "Adieu, you most beautiful princess. Adieu, most cruel princess in the world," and lays down his head.

With a poet's calculation, perhaps he knows that even as the ax falls the words are being repeated in the hearts of the people in the square. They will ripple outward like a great tide, making their way surely across the land, reaching into every last corner of it. Ah, cruel Queen. Queen almighty, Queen worthy to rule us, Queen to be feared as well as loved.

When his head falls, a cry goes up from the crowd and the gathered gulls on the building tops all take fright and rise, wheeling across the square and out toward the sea, their mournful cries drifting back to us, their feathers light on the wind.

Sixteen

The rain pours down on our passage home from Fife. The sleet bites our faces, our fingers grow numb on the reins. The Queen rides in a litter, but the rest of us must continue on horseback. I do not care. I do not wish to ride close to her.

In life I hated Chastelard, but in death I feel a kinship with my rival for her affections. A wrong choice could see me laying my head on the block too. I have bound myself to her with ties of love and service and reward. I am trapped.

The Queen tries to make our arrival at Holyrood as ordinary as possible, with a plain meal and some music. I eat nothing and sip only a little wine. I can feel Angelique's gaze upon me, but I ignore her. As soon as it is late enough, I slip away from the great hall. I walk through the palace grounds in the moonlight, watching the frost glitter on the ground. The bare twigs and trunks poke from the earth, the beginnings of the Queen's French garden trying to survive the Scottish winter.

The moon is silver ice, and I can hear the lions that some dignitary has sent from Africa, grumbling and snarling in their winter house. Poor wretches, the cold will surely kill them before long, as it is killing the French roses and lilacs that the gardeners try to nurture in the shelter of the stone walls. But on a night like this, the frost's fingers reach into every corner and no French exotic is safe. Even the air smells metallic, like blood.

My chest hurts. When I can stand it no longer, I make my way inside and to my bedchamber. I open the door quietly so as not to wake Angelique, but her eyes are open wide. She has kept the fire burning and the room is warm. When she sees my face, she slides out of bed and comes toward me.

It is her touch that undoes me. I do not know what it feels like to cry, having not done so since my mother was murdered. It is only when she reaches her hand to my shoulder and I feel the weight of human comfort that my heart lurches like ice-melt. Something cracks. I take a breath and what comes out is a sob.

Angi draws me close and presses my face to her neck. When my body begins to heave, she knows how to muffle my sobs and hold me. The fact that I have never been held thus makes it all the more terrible.

When the sobs are wrung out of me and my breath has quietened, she takes my face in her hands and looks at me in the half-light. I flinch under her gaze, exposed.

She puts her lips against my forehead and her kiss speaks of everything my heart has longed for. There is no ownership and no power and no life-or-death in it, nothing but this moment, her neck wet with my weeping, the fire dying down, our bodies next to each other. Then she draws me into bed and I fall into an exhausted sleep, facing her. When I wake the next morning, she is gone.

≈   ≈   ≈

I have spent most of my life in disguise, never letting anyone close enough to touch me and find out the truth. I applied the strictures to myself as well. I have been as pious as any religious woman. I have never gone seeking what made me a woman, never discovered the source of that ache.

All day I am useless at my tasks. I ride out in a small party with the Queen, but even as we canter through the park, all I can sense is the longing in my body. I am both dreading the night when I must face Angi again, and desperate.

"You don't seem yourself today, Alison." The Queen rides close without me noticing.

I try to cover my start. "I feel a little strange, Your Grace."

"Are you ill, perhaps?"

"I think it is just my monthly time." I take a breath. "Perhaps I could be excused from your chambers this evening?"

"You may," she says. "It has been a tiring few days."

≋ ≋ ≋

While the rest of the palace attends dinner, I pile the fire in our tiny bedchamber with more than the usual allowance of peat and a few sticks of wood I have smuggled in. I take off my clothes, put on my nightgown, get into bed. I then get up and pace the room. I lie down again, force my eyes shut and wait, trembling.

I know nothing of love and eventually it is too much. I cannot remain here in such a state. I have misunderstood Angi's kiss. I don't even know what I want to do. I have seen couplings between men and women in the dark corners of taverns and laneways. I cannot do that to her and I do not know what else there may be.

I am half dressed again in my breeks with no clear idea of where to go when I hear her at the door and my heart is despair and hope. She steps inside and turns to me. I freeze, clothes in disarray and she must understand it all in a moment, for she closes the door behind her and comes to me and when she puts her hand on my arm, I start to tremble all over again.

Angi knows, somehow, about everything of which I am ignorant. She takes my face in her hands and brings our lips together. I am shaking so I can barely stand as she slides her lips against mine until they part and then it is like she has found some secret place inside me and set it alight.

She draws back so that I can unlace her. For the first time, undressing a woman from her layers of finery is not a task, but something delightful, and I have wit enough to draw it out and remove her garments slowly. She smiles and tilts her head for me to reach, and when my finger trails the bare skin of her shoulder her breath catches and she sighs. Then, somehow, I know what to do. I bend my lips to her skin, I follow her sighs to the parts of her I dare to touch—her arm, shoulder, neck, back.

When it is done and she is undressed, she slips me out of my half-fastened clothes and draws me to the bed before I can feel ashamed of my nakedness. For the first time there is skin pressed all the way along my body and I gasp with the exquisite shock of it. She smiles and then moves her hand down my neck and along my breastbone. Her mouth finds my breasts and strips them free of the years of hiding.

As my body arches, she catches my fingers and draws them down her body, to a place I have hardly let myself imagine. My fingertips touch moisture, slipperiness, and it is so unexpected I gasp and she laughs. Then she pants as my fingers become bold and the heat rises in my own body from the same place. Her hand moves to me; how is it I have never known this? I'm moving without plan, gasping, clutching her and then it moves through my body and I have never imagined such a feeling could exist.

I have no idea if three heartbeats have passed or an hour. She laughs, soft and low, and kisses me. "You learn fast," she whispers. She takes my hand again and brings it down to her and now I have some notion of what to do and her body tells me the rest, arching and moving as she makes soft cries. When she stiffens and clutches me, the feeling rises in me again without even her touch and I find myself pressing against her and she grabs me and rolls me on top, and then there's no careful touching but instead rocking and thrusting and sweating until the storm sweeps through me again and we muffle the sounds of our delight in each other's mouths.

≈ ≈ ≈

What a strange creature is the heart.

You think you have it tamed and obedient, like a horse, so that you may ride it when you please, urge it to gallop or rein it in and keep it stationary. You think you know its moods and longing, you think its needs are simple.

It had not occurred to me to love someone other than the Queen. But the stroke that killed Chastelard severed something inside me. It cut the reins keeping my heart in control and it bolted like a horse in panicked flight. And then, waiting with steady hands and soft words, was Angi. She brought me to a halt and calmed me, soothed me. When my heart thought it was safe, she kissed me and any safety I'd known was gone.

119

Without such a kiss, the Queen could have kept me as her own, for the promise of a lover's kiss, the desire for it without ever knowing it, is a powerful bond. But now that Angi's lips have been upon me, I can no longer be satisfied with my chaste longing for the Queen.

Thus I find love, in our tiny room in the cold of late winter, and I want to explode with it. I want to gallop up Arthur's Seat and stand at the top and breathe in the cold air. I want to run through Edinburgh's streets at night as a boy and skip and shout.

Instead I dress demurely. I keep my face down. I make sure I do not look at Angi in another's presence. I keep my breath shallow, I make myself invisible. I act as if there isn't a furnace inside me.

Angi says that in the French court, love between women and love between men is not so unusual. It is part of the courtly games. Kisses and tantalizing touches are everywhere, the only constant is surprise, half the court may be other than they appear. She tells me that when the Queen was tutored in the royal household of France, even she was taught to recite the poems of a lover of women, the Greek Sappho.

"Surely you know of her here?" she asks, and I shake my head, amazed.

She forbids me to speak any language other than French in our bed. "It is the language of love," she says. "Scots is the language of secret plots and bloodshed. Leave it outside."

"What would she do, if she knew?" I whisper.

"I do not know." Angi is thoughtful. "There were two women in King Henri's court who were lovers. I think it amused him. Once he ordered them to kiss in front of us all. His mistress Diane de Poitiers laughed while they were doing it, and he laughed too. Mary was there, but she was young. I do not know what she thought. This is Scotland and Knox is ever on the alert for ways to bring her down. No one must know."

I am used to secrets. When I dress in the winter darkness each morning, I bind my unruly love as firm and tight as I bind my breasts under my boy's clothes.

Late at night, when our passion is slaked, I hold Angi and I whisper to her of the fortress that will keep our love safe. I whisper of how I will bring her to Blackadder Castle and we will be free of the

Queen's court, with its strictures and demands. When she falls asleep, I lie awake and think of how I might persuade the Queen to speed her promise.

≈ ≈ ≈

Now that I am a lover, I listen intently when the conversations around me turn to love, as they inevitably do, from the kitchen to the great hall and everywhere in between. I listen to the jokes and sneers and laughter, trying to find some clues. Is it the same when men and women couple? Surely it must be, and yet some women roll their eyes and talk as if it were a chore like cleaning out the kitchen fire. Others blush, and as the color rises to their cheeks, I'm sure they know the feeling I am so curious about.

Angi says in France there is more care for the art of love between men and women, and she whispers of secret books with drawings of dozens of different ways a man may enter a woman to bring her pleasure. But she says in Scotland the men are more brutal and do not care so much for giving pleasure, while women know less of the pleasure to be had.

The Queen does not know about love of this kind, I can see now.

She orders a small morning concert by her court musicians, for her own pleasure and to try and speed up the wait for the season's change. Her best singer, David Rizzio, stands slightly to the front, his resonant bass swelling to fill the room. He has been rehearsing a new part and this is its first performance. He is not a beautiful man, with his hunched back and swarthy face, but his voice can drive an audience to tears.

Afterward, the Queen takes her inner circle through to the bedchamber and orders her best French wine to reward Rizzio. She calls a toast to him.

"To spring, to music, to love," she says, raising her glass. We drink.

"Randolph was watching you, Beaton," Lusty says.

A smile creeps across Beaton's face.

"He is too old for her," Seton says.

"Older men are more experienced." Lusty's smile is wicked. "Besides, it might be politic for Beaton to wed the English ambassador."

121

"You cannot trust an ambassador," La Flamina says. "I would be careful, Beaton."

"Perhaps a dalliance, then?" Lusty says. "Find out if an older man really does know more about women."

"Hush." Beaton glances at the Queen.

The Queen puts down her sewing with a sigh. "I wonder if I shall ever find a man to love as I loved Francis." She rises to her feet.

"Of course you will." Rizzio stands to join her. "Love blooms more fully the more adult you become. You have barely tasted it yet."

She looks down at him. "I did not know you were an expert, David."

He shrugs. "One does not need to be married to know this."

Lusty laughs. "What think you then, Rizzio, about older men? Do they know more of women?"

He looks from Lusty to the Queen and back again and then winks. "It has been said that learning to love a woman well is like learning to play an instrument. It takes years of application and practice but the noise you can draw out of it will show your proficiency."

They break into scandalized laughter. I see Rizzio glance at me and I join in to cover my sudden blush. The Queen is laughing too, but I can see beneath the smile she is perplexed.

"You and Francis were children," he says to the Queen. "Your next husband will be a man, and he will show you the joys of mature love."

"Unless she must marry Charles of France, who is but twelve," Lusty says.

"It was not such a terrible thing, to be married to a young man," the Queen says.

"But was it a pleasure for you?" Rizzio asks.

The room falls silent and I find myself studying the floor.

"It is time for our ride, and enough of this nonsense." For a second there is shame on the Queen's face. It is not the hot shame of lust. Shame instead, I surmise, that the rumors are true and that the young and sickly Francis did not have the strength or the knowledge to consummate their marriage.

She looks up to catch me watching. "What is wrong with you all?" she snaps. "You are like girls about to be wed. We will ride in a quarter-hour. Get my clothes ready."

As I turn, Rizzio grins at me. I can see that he knows pleasure all too well and in ways he will never divulge to the Queen.

≈ ≈ ≈

The winter of the dearth is so harsh that it leaves the country stripped bare. Storms dash ships against the rocks up and down the coast of England. Word comes to the court that one of them was carrying Lord Bothwell. He was shipwrecked upon the Northumbrian coast, captured, taken to London, and imprisoned in the Tower.

"But what of William?" I demand of Sophie, blundering into her chambers the evening I receive the news. "They left here on his ship, did they not? With his cousins?"

She takes my arm. "I have word he is with Bothwell."

I exhale in relief and sink into a chair by the fire. I gulp back the drink proffered by Sophie's servant.

She looks at me for a long moment and then touches my cheek. "What has happened to you?"

I pull away, but I cannot stop the heat rising to my cheeks.

"Ah," Sophie says. "You have taken my advice. Who?"

I hesitate. "Her name is Angelique and she shares my bedchamber," I say at last.

Sophie sighs. "I have seen this in you. But the danger! Under the Queen's very nose."

"I am a master at disguise," I say. "You taught me yourself! Nobody knows."

"In a court, there is always someone who knows. You are not the only spy. Be careful, my dear one."

≈ ≈ ≈

It is the beginning of the Queen's second spring in Scotland. Maitland, her secretary of state, arrives in the presence chamber still coughing with the last of his influenza. The Queen herself is pale and drawn from her own bout of the illness. The news came but a few days ago that not one, but two of her de Guise uncles in France have died in the past weeks—one of them shot in the back by a Huguenot assassin in the recent French uprising. She is grief-stricken.

"Chess?" Rizzio asks me, his eyebrow raised. He waves for me to join him and I cross to where he has laid out the board, in a quiet corner but still in earshot of the Queen's conversation. I sit down and he makes the first move.

"I wish you to travel to London with an offer to mediate between the English and the French in this uprising," the Queen says to Maitland.

"I think Elizabeth will feel you are too closely aligned to the French to take care of English interests," Maitland says.

"You will offer anyway. The real reason for your trip is to discover my cousin's mind in the matter of my marriage. I must be certain of what I may offer as a dowry to Spain."

Rizzio's eyes do not flicker from our game as I make my next move. "A bold play," he says, his singer's voice pitched low so it reaches my ears only. "You are careless, Alison."

"I am not certain of this approach," Maitland says. "The prospect of a Catholic union between you and Don Carlos will threaten Elizabeth's state."

"Then bargain with it," the Queen says. "Tell her I will consider her wishes in regard to my marriage once the succession has been agreed."

Maitland shakes his head. "Cecil will not like it."

"Cecil would have me a widow forever and barred from what is rightfully mine," she snaps. "He is Elizabeth's adviser, not her king."

I make a risky move with a rook, sliding it forward in a sneaking assault on Rizzio's queen. He examines the board, his brow furrowed. "Do you know how you are watched?" he asks.

I glance down at the board, then up at him. "What do you mean?"

"Confronting Elizabeth and Cecil with threats has never worked," Maitland says. "Let me go to London with an olive branch. I will press hard for your succession rights to be acknowledged and I will put it to them that you are willing to be guided in your choice of husband."

The Queen is silent. Rizzio takes my rook with his knight. "You must finish this dalliance, or you both will suffer," he whispers. "The

Queen may play at dressing as a man, but that does not make it safe for you to act as one."

I stare at him, my heart thudding. "You are mistaken."

"You will bargain with my heart," the Queen says to Maitland.

"With all respect, Madam, it is succession and dynasty being negotiated, not your heart."

"But it is my heart that will choose in the end."

The room seems to still at her utterance. Rizzio leans forward. "Hume is most interested in who you are and what you do," he murmurs. "Take heed, Alison. You are not as discreet as you believe."

I make a clumsy move with a knight, my hand shaking.

Across the room Maitland takes a deep breath. "Your Grace, it may be that there is a suitable English noble you can marry. One that will please Elizabeth and at the same time strengthen your own claim to that throne. Did you not meet Lord Darnley when you were in France?"

"He's a boy, Maitland. This time I must marry a man."

"He was a boy when you met him, but he is seventeen now, and by all accounts he is grown to a man. It is said he is tall and strong and fine-faced. Taller than even yourself, Your Grace."

Cunning Maitland knows how to woo our tall Queen, ruling a country of stocky men who reach her shoulder.

"Ride at once," the Queen says. "Find out who Elizabeth would have me marry and if there be any merit in it. Negotiate hard, Maitland, for I am weary of waiting."

She reaches for her cup and sips. "Without my cousin's knowledge, speak with the Spanish ambassador about the possibility of a marriage between Scotland and Spain."

"A dangerous game, Madam," he says.

"These are dangerous times," she replies. "And there is one more thing. Ask Elizabeth if she would be so kind as to release Bothwell from the Tower. He is pardoned of any wrongdoing here."

Maitland bows low to hide his furious face, and I look at the Queen in amazement, forgetting Rizzio for an instant. Could it be that Bothwell will rise in favor again?

"You must become a better player, Mistress Blackadder," Rizzio says. "It is no sport to finish you off so easily."

I turn back to the chessboard. Rizzio has made his move. "Check-mate," he says calmly. This time his singer's voice reaches every corner of the chamber.

≈ ≈ ≈

"How can he know?" Angi asks. "We never touch outside of this room."

I pace across the floor, running my hands through my hair. "Perhaps someone spies on us. Someone who can hear us."

She sits up. "Have you told anyone?"

I halt. "Only Sophie."

She strikes the covers with her fist. "We agreed—no one!"

"I have trusted Sophie with my life," I say. "It is not her who has spoken. I think Rizzio knows of such things himself and has guessed."

"If he has guessed, who else suspects?"

I take both her hands. "No one. It is a warning only, and we shall heed it."

She twists her hands out of mine. "We should ask to be roomed apart. Then no one can accuse us."

"You can't mean that."

Her eyes are full of tears. "If we are discovered, I could be sent back to France. There's nothing for me there, Alison. I would end up in a convent, or as a pauper."

I draw her to me and hold her hard, as if I can conjure up safety with the force of my grip.

"I will ask her again for my castle," I say at last, stroking her hair. "I will beg her to give it to me before she gains the English throne. We can live there more safely than here."

She lays her head on my shoulder and tightens her grip around me. "I'm afraid."

≈ ≈ ≈

After Maitland leaves, Lord James takes the Queen in a small party to the island of Loch Leven. The Queen invites John Knox to visit her there

126

and back in Holyrood we hear word that their debate is relatively friendly and that the Queen holds her own in their discussion. She returns to Edinburgh and asks me to attend Knox's services to find out if his opinion of her has softened.

I have already redoubled my efforts to gather intelligence on every aspect of the future marriage of the Queen and now I seat myself toward the back of the kirk each week, my head bent. I do not want to be where sharp-eyed Knox might come to know me.

It is a warm Sunday and the sun is shining in through the windows and falling upon the back of my neck. The memory of last night with Angi replays itself through my body and I struggle to concentrate on Knox's words. After some time I give up and surrender to the pleasure of memory instead.

A man creeps in late and makes his way across the pews to a space next to me. He seats himself uncomfortably close, jerking me from my reverie. I slide a little farther away but he follows, his knee pushing mine sharply.

I look sideways, scowling, to find myself staring at William.

The shock of it rushes through my body and I quickly turn my face away again and bend my head in prayer, my heart pounding.

As the service ends, he stands and gestures for me to precede him from the kirk. He follows so closely I can feel his breath upon my neck, and once outside he takes my arm and draws me across the High Street into the shadow of the Tolbooth.

"I heard your ship went down." My voice quavers.

"I wouldn't lose a ship so easily," he says. "We left my ship at Berwick and took passage on another. The captain was a fool and struck the rocks. Half his men drowned, but we made it to shore. The English took Bothwell but he made me leave without him."

He draws out a letter and hands it to me. As I take it, he pulls a ring off his finger and presses it into my palm. "The ring is Bothwell's token. He's been released from the Tower, but he dares not return to Scotland. He wants us to deliver his letters to the Queen."

"What sort of letters?"

"He has information that will help her choose a husband. He is with us, Robert. He has sworn to get revenge on Hume for having him imprisoned. Our causes are aligned. We will pass letters back and forth between him and the Queen."

I look at him in a moment of hope.

"Bring me her answer and I will carry it to him," he says. "I will be at Bothwell's house."

"No. It is safer to meet at Katy's Tams. I will come of an evening when I have a reply."

"At last you can be of some use in your position," he says.

≈ ≈ ≈

The Queen is busy and it is not until the evening that I am in her presence. I make the signal that I have intelligence to share and within a few minutes she has sent those around her on errands and nodded that I should come close.

I bow low and stretch my hand out. She offers hers and Bothwell's ring slips between us like two pickpockets.

"How did you come by this?" she asks.

"My father brought it with a letter."

She takes the parchment from me with eager hands, breaks the seal, and reads it swiftly. At the end she looks at me.

"He writes of whom I should marry," she says. "It seems every man in the kingdom has an opinion about my nuptials. And yet, I am inclined to trust Bothwell. He is a man, not a politician."

"He would have an answer of you."

"Would he now? Well, I shall think on it and decide if I will answer. That is all, Alison."

"Your Grace, I wonder—"

"What is it?"

I look down, lacing my fingers together. "I wonder if I could speak to you about the matter of Blackadder Castle," I say, my voice soft. "You promised you would help when you won the throne of England. It's just that my father is old and I fear he will not live that long."

She steps closer to me. "So you doubt me. You too think I will never marry, nor come to the English throne."

I bow my head low. "I do not doubt you."

She turns from me. "I have every noble in court pressing me to marry. I did not think to find such selfishness from you."

"I am sorry, Your Grace," I say, backing away.

"You should be. Do not speak of this again. I have made a promise and you insult me by doubting it. Do you think your castle is more important than my own marriage?"

"Of course not."

"Leave me," she says. "I have no stomach for this tonight."

Seventeen

Maitland returns from England with word that Elizabeth will not offer an opinion on our Queen's suitors, only an ultimatum that the friendship between Scotland and England will cease if the Queen marries one of the imperial sons of France or Spain.

It is typical of Elizabeth, I am coming to understand, but it brings our Queen no closer to a husband and no closer to the English throne. I am farther away from my castle than ever and the Queen is still angry with me. Rizzio's eyes seem to constantly burn into my back and the tension casts a shadow between Angi and me. We never speak together outside of the confines of our room, and inside it we converse only in whispers. The only place I forget my fear for a moment is in the blaze of our lovemaking.

The Queen orders her court packed up for a progress and, to show her continuing displeasure, she does not include me. She leaves Holyrood behind and rides to the west and southwest of the country to hunt and hawk with the nobles of the land, and takes her new bedchamber woman, Margaret Carwood, to attend to her needs.

Left alone with Angi, away from Rizzio's curiosity, I stamp my love across her body again and again, imprinting myself there to drive away our fears. I talk to her every night of how I shall win the Queen's favor again.

"You could leave," Angi says one night when we have fallen back against the pillows, flushed and sweaty from pleasure.

"What do you mean?" I coil her silver necklace around my finger.

"We could sail to France together. Make a life there, away from this danger."

I raise myself to an elbow. "As what, *chérie*? I have no prospects there."

She turns to me and grips my hand. "There is danger all around us here. While the Queen is away we could flee. By the time she comes back we will be long gone. Paris is not like Edinburgh. We could find work somewhere. Even living poor would be safer than this."

I stare at her. "You're serious."

"The Queen holds you with a promise that could take a lifetime to fruit," she says. "We court danger every day. Remember what happens to those who displease her?"

I sit up, pulling my knees to my chest and shaking my head. "I cannot."

"It's not worth dying for."

"But men of my family have died for the castle, and now I am charged with gaining it for my bloodline. If you think I can leave it, you don't understand."

She turns over to face the wall, her back stiff.

I sit, my chin resting on my knees. "You could go back to France," I say at last. "You will be safe and I will send for you as soon as she grants the castle to me."

She rolls toward me. "You would do so?"

"I would do anything to protect you."

She reaches out her arms and draws me down and I press my face into her neck. Then she turns my head and kisses me and the desire in it makes us both pant.

"I won't let you stay here alone," she whispers.

≈ ≈ ≈

The Queen and her party return to Edinburgh as the cold begins. Melancholy overtakes her almost at once and within days she begins to weep. Her physician, Arnault, prescribes diets and gentle exercise, but nothing helps for more than a few days. In December, after her twenty-first birthday, she takes to bed with a pain in her right side and it is not until January that she is well enough to rise again.

It is 1564 and still there is no husband. She is a widow, and even one who is as famed for her beauty as our Queen has no eternal hold on her looks. Time chips away at the promise of that porcelain skin;

131

the English succession is no closer. The winter is bitterly cold for the third year in a row and there are reports that children are starving in the countryside.

I bring a letter from Bothwell into the presence chamber one evening, when Rizzio and the musicians have put on another concert to try and raise her spirits. When they have finished playing, she beckons me to her.

"Do you bring any happy news?" she asks.

"Perhaps Lord Bothwell's letter carries some," I say.

She takes it. "I have missed you, Alison. It is a pity you did not come to the west with us. You would have liked the hunting."

I dare to look at her directly. "I missed you too, Your Grace."

She opens the letter. "Bothwell asks me to meet him at Dunbar."

"He wants to speak about your marriage. It's not safe for him to come to Edinburgh, but Dunbar is closer to the border and he can slip across from England."

"My advisers would prefer me not to see him." Then she smiles. "I am sick of my advisers, Alison. What say we take a small group and ride in disguise?"

I smile back at her, and it is like spring coming again. "When shall we go?"

≈　≈　≈

Just half a dozen of us accompany the Queen to Dunbar, and she leads us in a spirited gallop. As she and I thunder ahead she laughs.

"I needed this, not bed rest!"

"I too," I call back.

"Let's keep going," she says. "Two men seeking adventure and living rough. I am sick to death of this search for a husband."

"Willingly!" I say, and for a moment it is true. I would ride with her into the hills without a backward glance.

But instead we come around the coast to Dunbar, where the castle squats, a heavy fortress on the cliff over the ocean, the waves crashing on its very foundations. As we ride up with the smell of salt sharp in our nostrils, the Queen looks up at the battlements.

"I do not like this place," she says, shuddering.

The castle warden and his servants come out to greet us. As they open the gates, the Queen turns to me.

"Bothwell said he would wait in the town tavern until he had word. Go and find him. We must return to Edinburgh tonight."

I dismount and hand my horse to one of the servants. It is a cold afternoon, with rain sweeping toward us across the sea. When the gate closes, leaving me outside, I feel suddenly exposed.

I pull my cloak tightly around me and draw the hood over my head. The road into the village is empty, every door firmly closed. I soften my step so that my boots do not make a sound on the cobblestones.

A door opens behind me and I hear footsteps, measured and regular. The evening is closing in and the first raindrops spatter on my cloak. When the footsteps speed up, I break into a run, but I am not fast enough. Before I can reach the tavern, my pursuer drags me into a brutal hold.

"Where are you hurrying to, laddie?"

"I am on the Queen's business." I struggle, trying for a position where I can kick his groin.

"I don't doubt it." The cold of his dagger tips my throat. I freeze.

"What brings the Queen here to Dunbar in such secrecy? And who are you?"

"Her favored servant Robert."

"I will slit your throat if you don't speak." His breath is hot in my ear, his grip tight around my neck. "Who is the Queen here to see?"

"Bothwell," I choke.

Suddenly his entire body weight thrusts against me and he makes a guttural groan like a man in rut. His dagger clatters to the ground and he sags.

"Robert!" William's low voice comes from behind the man. He grabs my arm. The man crumples to the ground. I stagger away from him, coughing.

"Did you finish him?" It is Bothwell.

"Straight through the heart," William says.

Bothwell shoves the body with his foot and grunts his approval. In the faint light of the tavern lantern I can see his grin. "Come on then. We'll drop Hume's spy in the harbor on the way. Is your mistress ready to see us?"

"She's waiting," I rasp out.

≈ ≈ ≈

"How did Hume know we were coming?" William asks, as we wait for Bothwell to finish with the Queen.

"He has spies in court, like everyone," I say.

"You were all too ready to blurt Bothwell's name."

"He would have cut my throat!"

"Lucky I got to him before you betrayed me too." William glares at me. "You've forgotten what it's like to live in danger. Be careful, or Bothwell will guess you aren't a boy at all."

"You should tell him," I say, rubbing my throat. "It is better he hears from you than from the Queen."

"It's not time yet. What has she said about Bothwell's letters?"

I sip my wine to ease my throat. "She says Bothwell is championing Lord Darnley, but she thinks to marry straight to another throne. Don Carlos is her preference."

William stands and paces. "If the Queen marries Spain, do you think she will stay here in Scotland? Do you think she will care about some small estate on the border? Hume's spawn will multiply and you will end your days unmarried in the Spanish court."

I jump to my feet. "I tell you, William, I am doing everything I can!"

There is a knock at the door and Bothwell enters. He gulps down a cup of wine and looks at me. "Do you know anything of the Queen's mind in this matter?"

"She is not Elizabeth, with a man's heart." My voice is hoarse. "If you think Lord Darnley can win her love, you must contrive for them to meet."

"Sound advice," he says. "But Elizabeth will not let him travel here. We have an impasse."

I fix my gaze on Bothwell, ignoring William. "My Lord, all of Scotland knows your determination on the battlefield. Find a way to bring Darnley to Scotland."

The waning moon is a sliver in the sky as we leave Dunbar. My imagination fills the ride back to Edinburgh through the dark with menacing shapes looming by the roadside and hoofbeats ringing out behind us in pursuit. When we arrive at Holyrood I take my leave of the Queen and run to our quarters. Angi is under the covers, facing away from the door. I undress and climb in behind her, my arms moving around the curve of her waist to pull our bodies together. But for once she does not roll her head back and open her eyes with a smile.

"Angi?"

"It's nothing," she says. "Just my blood time."

Gradually her breathing slows and after a long time her body softens and twitches. Just before I drop off to sleep I remember the crescent of the waning moon. Angi and I have bled in tandem since we first shared the bed, long before we were lovers. But my own blood isn't due for another week, when the moon is dark.

≈ ≈ ≈

Angi is still distant when we wake. We must rise and dress early, for the Queen has arranged a riding party with a visiting noble and there is no time to talk. But she won't quite look at me and her face is drawn. For the first time I taste the fear of losing her, and by comparison the grip of one of Hume's spies on my throat is nothing.

The Queen calls me to lead the ride. I must turn my face into the north wind and take them in a gallop, finding the twisting pathway so her guest will see which way to ride and his horse will not stumble.

When at last we pull up, having left her noble trailing behind us, the Queen looks at me and furrows her brow. "Your lips are blue. Are you unwell?"

"No, Madam, only cold," I dissemble, as we wait to let him catch up.

When we ride back and meet up with the rest of the party, Angi gives me a tiny, tremulous smile that sweeps away my despair and makes me weak with relief. But when we return to the palace in the fading light of afternoon, she disappears in the hubbub of horses, riders, servants, and grooms in the courtyard. She is not at dinner, and when I retire, wild with panic to find her, the bed is empty.

When she creeps in, long hours later, with chattering teeth and icy fingers, and takes me in an iron grip, I break into wild sobs that she muffles against her neck, rocking me with soft murmurs. In moments, we're kissing, faces wet, bodies slick, and she slides down between my legs and brings me to a painful pleasure that is almost unbearable. I go to touch her but she draws my hand away and straddles my leg instead and her pleasure is as hard and desperate as mine.

Afterward, wet-faced, she murmurs, "It is nothing, don't worry, don't worry," and my raw heart is quietened.

But something has changed, and whatever Angi keeps secret lies between us at night, breathing in the dark. In the daytime my mind moves in wider and wider circles trying to find it, and there is no peace, only the fear that I will lose her. Each night in our bed, the unleashing of desire is as potent as the first time we touched each other. I sleep little, awake with terror or longing, and the cold seems more intense than ever.

Winter slowly loosens its grip. The Queen writes again to the Spanish King about marrying his son, but his reply, when it finally arrives, is evasive. There are no more letters from Lord Bothwell, and no word from William. Lord Darnley does not come to Scotland. The first daffodils sit in tight, hard buds waiting for warmer weather and the snowdrops nod their white heads.

Eighteen

The windows of the Queen's chamber are open to let in the spring sunshine. Rizzio has rejoined the musicians and sings in his angel's voice. Since the meeting with Bothwell I have had nothing to report to the Queen. The marriage stalemate has gone on for so long that no one is expecting a sudden move. When a messenger is admitted with news from Lord Darnley, the room comes to life.

"He has sent you something?" asks Lusty, peering around the Queen to see what the package contains. "What is it?"

"Patience," the Queen says.

"Patience!" Lusty nudges her. "You've been patient for three years! It's time for impatience. Open it quickly."

The Queen laughs and there is an air of anticipation in her voice. She pulls at the ribbon and takes the lid off the box.

"An engraving," says Lusty. "At last we can see what manner of man the young Darnley has grown into."

The Queen stares at the miniature closely, then puts her hand to her throat and passes it to Lusty. Once it is out of her hands, every courtier in the room clusters around to see the famous Darnley face.

The other ladies exclaim over his large, dark eyes, but it seems to me he has a weak chin and a thin mouth. I must see the Queen married, but I feel a hot knife of dislike for this lad.

It turns out that the gift is from Darnley's mother, the Countess of Lennox, under genteel house arrest in England at Elizabeth's order, a hostage to ensure that her husband returns to England.

"She urges me to consider marrying her son," the Queen says, reading the letter as the miniature is passed from hand to hand. "And here, she lists his qualities. He's outstanding at writing, hunting, hawking, dancing, music, golf, he is a learned scholar, a Catholic, in line to the English throne, and what's more, he's tall!"

A ripple of laughter runs through the room, although each of us can see the slight flush on the Queen's cheeks.

Rizzio's singer's voice cuts through the giggles. "Have a care, Madam," he says. "The way the Countess offers her Catholic son hides a treasonous idea, that England's Catholics may rally behind the two of you and challenge Elizabeth. It may be a snare."

The Queen sighs. "Ah, Rizzio, at the first hint of a suitable marriage partner you pour scorn upon him. Can you not permit me even a moment to dream of a husband who is accomplished, learned, of beauty, and here, she says it, utterly loyal?"

"Your court and your country contain plenty of men who are so, but they are not the husband for a queen," says Rizzio. "You, who are the prize of Europe, who may marry into any kingdom, should not lower yourself to one of your cousin's nobles."

My eyes widen to hear him speak to her thus, in front of all of us.

"Thank you for your opinion, good Rizzio," she says, tight in the jaw. "I will think upon it."

≈ ≈ ≈

That night the Queen summons me to her chambers and tells me we will roam the streets in disguise.

Now that it is spring, the night streets are busy, the taverns full, and for some time we simply roam like two young merchants. When we have wandered the length of Edinburgh, skirted the Tolbooth, peered into the castle gates, and walked all around Saint Giles, we step into the White Hart Inn and order ale. I elbow us through to a corner table where, under the hubbub of voices and laughter, we can talk unnoticed.

"It's been too long since I've done this," she says. "Too long where every word and deed must be watched and analyzed. I am sick of it. Rizzio advises that I marry Spain, and I would do it, but King Philip is a worse prevaricator than Elizabeth. She says I must marry where she tells me, but then she will not tell me!"

"There are rumors. You have heard them?" I ask.

She laughs, but bitterly. "I hear nothing but rumors; they are driving me mad. Is there anything new that you have heard?"

I have not mentioned this rumor before because of the insult implied in it. "It is possible that Elizabeth may offer Lord Dudley."

The Queen puts her tankard down with a thump, her brow creased in anger. "How widely whispered is that one? Where did you hear it?"

"First from my father, through Lord Bothwell, last winter. Did he not mention it to you? Since then, I have heard it even here in Edinburgh."

The Queen looks around the tavern at the red faces, the glow of the lanterns, the bare shoulders of the whores tucked into willing arms, laughing loud. She shudders.

"No, he did not mention it." She drops her head. "What will my people think of me? Elizabeth scarcely bothers to hide that her master of horse is her paramour. How is it she can behave so and yet still rule her court, while I, who am a truly good Catholic queen, am bullied and overridden day after day?"

"I have heard something else, about Spain." I lean forward. "They say King Philip keeps Don Carlos hidden because he is syphilitic. He's violent and unstable, and may not live."

She sits back. "I have heard he is ill, but not the cause."

"This is why King Philip evades you. He does not know if his son is fit to marry, let alone rule."

The Queen sips her drink and out of lifelong habit I scan the tavern. It is a merry night in Edinburgh and if anyone is spying on us, I cannot see them.

"Maitland says only that Don Carlos has had a fever and will soon be recovered," she says at last. "In this matter I trust him. Your rumors may be nothing more than that. Where did you come by them?"

"A merchant who has connections all over Europe and has given me much true intelligence. The Spanish ambassador will hardly reveal such a thing to Maitland."

She regards me for so long that I become uneasy and shift in my seat. "Do you wish to return?" I ask.

"I have a mind to see you married, even as I will be, God willing," she says. "When I asked you to dress thus and gather information, I thought it would be for a few seasons at most. But now it is time you stopped this and found a husband."

"I wish only to serve you," I say quietly.

"That is because you have not known love."

"I know the love of a loyal servant for her queen and that is enough for me. I have no wish to marry."

"And yet I wish it," she says, with steel in her smile. "I have a Catholic court, after all, and too many of my courtiers are unmarried. It gives Knox something to point the finger at. Rizzio agrees."

I lean close across the table. "I cannot marry until I have my birthright. My father will not permit it. Please, allow me to keep serving you as I have."

She considers me. "I will not force you. I know what it is to be told to marry for expedience. But you know my wishes now."

≈ ≈ ≈

I accompany the Queen back to her presence chamber, where La Flamina is waiting to undress her and sleep by her side. The Queen pats my cheek as she parts from me. "Don't look so stricken. Love is not to be feared."

The route back to my chamber through the darkened corridors of the palace leads me past Rizzio's quarters. So absorbed am I in the prospect of marriage—threat or promise—that I almost walk into the two dark figures holding a whispered conversation in the hallway. Rizzio's unmistakable twisted form and another cloaked silhouette. They draw apart at my approach.

"Angi?" I am bewildered.

"You are out late," she says. "I will be by presently."

Rizzio says nothing as I pass, but the hairs on the back of my neck rise.

It is another hour until Angi returns. She comes to the bed, cold-skinned, and turns her back.

I reach across, but she is unyielding to my touch. "What is his business with you?"

"Nothing."

She is the breadth of a kingdom away from me. I lie on my back, staring into the darkness.

"The Queen thinks I should marry," I whisper at last.

There is no response. Defeated, I roll on my side away from her.

≈   ≈   ≈

Now it is Angi I must spy on. She keeps her lips tight when I ask a question. She will not let me touch her. She says it is her blood time, but I know it is not. For three nights she turns away in bed, and she avoids me by day.

The Queen succumbs again to the pain in her right side and takes to her bed, and the whole of her court is called upon to try and lighten her cares. Her servants bring the most tempting pastries on trays from the kitchen. Her valets uncork the best wines. The fire is stoked and fresh rushes are laid on the ground.

Angi stands across the room from me. Our pact not to look at each other in public was once a delicious game, a promise broken a dozen times in an hour with fleeting glances. But now there is no game in the way she avoids my gaze.

"I am so sick of being confined," the Queen says, squirming under Seton's ministrations. "Where is my medicine? I need something to help me rise from the bed."

Rizzio steps forward. "I will send someone. While you wait, we have a song ready for you."

He turns to Angi. "Pray call upon the apothecary. He is late with the Queen's medicine."

Angi curtsies and leaves without a word.

Rizzio and the other musicians begin a soft song. As it swells around us, Seton supports the Queen into a half-sitting position and helps her sip a cup of wine.

The song finishes and we applaud politely. Rizzio looks across at me. "Alison, go and find out what is delaying Jean-Paul."

I can read nothing from his face. I curtsy and back out of the room.

The dispensary, with its bunches of dried herbs and potions in glass bottles, is below ground level, at the end of a twisting corridor. I must take a lantern to light my way, even during the day. As I approach it I expect to find Angi and the apothecary, Jean-Paul, returning to the presence chamber. But I make my way to the door without meeting a soul.

I raise my hand and bang loudly, then push the door open in a single movement. Jean-Paul has some creature down upon the floor, squirming, while his arse pumps up and down. Our eyes meet over his shoulder. It is Angi.

Some animal instinct propels me. I wrench myself away from the door and into the corridor and break into a run toward our chamber. I rip the hated dress and wig and jewels from my body, uncaring of the damage to them. I pull on my oldest clothes, the ones I wore as Robert before coming into the Queen's service. Thus dressed, I run down the back staircase, my breath coming in great gasps. I pelt across the courtyard to the stables, saddle my horse, and within twenty minutes of my betrayal I am galloping across the park toward the foot of Arthur's Seat.

The image of Angi underneath him is branded into me. By the time I have pushed the mare to the highest point that she can climb, steaming and snorting, I have still failed to outrun the pain. I throw myself from her back and run to the summit and it bursts from my mouth in a wild cry that sends the ravens up in flight.

I will kill them both and then, steeped in blood, I will ride like a madman to my father's castle and slaughter as many of the Hume clan as I can, until I am killed myself. At least I will have done William a small service in my agony.

≈　≈　≈

I wake to Rizzio's hateful angelic voice. "Robert."

I roll over and my head pounds. I can still taste the whisky that brought last night's oblivion. With awakening comes memory and I recall why I am asleep in the stables in the straw of my mare's bedding. I groan.

Rizzio nudges me with his foot. "The Queen has been looking for you. You disappeared without permission."

"You had a hand in this." I scramble to my feet.

"Do you know how much danger you were in? People are burned as witches for less. The Queen cannot afford such a scandal in her court."

"You have no right." I reach out and grab him. His twisted body is surprisingly light and how good it feels to shake him and drag him toward me. How good it feels to lift him so high that his feet are dangling and his breath choked in his throat.

"What future was there in it?" he gasps. "Angelique saw sense before you did. All I did was show you."

I drop him roughly to his feet.

He rubs his throat. "The Queen has not heard from Lord Bothwell and she wants his advice. I've told her you'll leave at once for London with a letter for him. There is a servant packing your bag."

"How dare you?" I spit at him.

"I've done much to protect you, but you are not above punishment," he says. "Be on the road to England within the hour."

"I do not trust you," I say, hating him.

"You shouldn't trust anyone, not in a court. You have spied enough yourself to know that. But I have explained away your disappearance to the Queen and got you out of here till you can see sense. You'll be grateful, in the end."

"I will pack my own things."

"No." For a deformed man, he orders like a king.

"Since when am I under your command?"

His look is knowing. "If you want to live, do not try to see Angelique. She has made her choice. Travel as a man and be as hard as one. It will take you several weeks to deliver the Queen's message and bring Lord Bothwell's reply. Don't rush back."

Before the sun is high in the sky, I am dressed, packed, and sent south into a terribly clear and sunny spring day without having stepped foot in the palace. Everything I have loved is back there and the lack of it is a hole inside me.

Nineteen

Queen Elizabeth says she has the heart of a man, the heart of her father Henry VIII, who was cruel even by the standards of princes. He wooed our own infant Queen Mary for his young son Edward by laying waste to the southern reaches of Scotland right up to Edinburgh when Mary's mother dared to reject such a match.

In Elizabeth's country I strive for such a hardness of heart myself. My mind constructs a wall of high stone around my treasonous heart to contain it the way the Flodden Wall contains Edinburgh and keeps it safe. When my heart tries to offer up a thousand excuses for Angi's behavior, a thousand reasons why she should be on the floor beneath the Queen's apothecary, my mind strikes them down as brutally as Henry smote the Scottish men and women in his way.

I find Bothwell and William, and stay with them a few days so that Bothwell may read the Queen's letter and respond to it. I speak little, eat little, and make my escape from them as swiftly as I can.

I use the gold coins that Rizzio gave me to stay in London taverns and try to forget my heart in drink and entertainment. There are bear fights and bull fights and cock fights, bowls and tennis, archery and shooting on the open grounds, and men throwing themselves into the Thames on the hottest days.

When the summer heat becomes unbearable, I take my stiff-legged mare from the stables and turn her head north, back to the land where my heart is imprisoned.

≈ ≈ ≈

In Edinburgh the summer days are so long the nights hardly exist. The streets stink; men walk bare-armed, women put on bonnets against the sun. At the gates of Holyrood, Rizzio comes to meet me and takes me himself to a new bedchamber close to his own quarters. I am to share with two unspeaking older women whom I barely know. They share one larger bed and I have a pallet in the corner.

I dress to meet the Queen, in the trappings of a lady-in-waiting again. Can I keep my heart hard, dressed thus? When I am shown into the Queen's chambers, Angi is among the party with her. I have rehearsed this moment. I fix my gaze on the Queen, approach, and curtsy.

She smiles. "It is good to see you again, Mistress Blackadder. Come to my rooms this evening, and you can tell me about your travels. I'm sure you have some interesting stories."

Dismissed, I curtsy again and move away. Rizzio is watching me, but I don't care. I find myself a seat and at last, after six weeks, raise my eyes to find Angi.

She is waiting for my gaze and when she meets it, her face pale, eyes dark, looking at me with entreaty, my manly heart lurches. Six weeks dissolve into nothing. I must go to her.

But there is something else. Not far away from her, the apothecary is watching me carefully. Angi raises a hand to her throat. My heart slams closed and my rage rises.

"Careful." Rizzio's voice is low at my shoulder.

I fight to breathe, hating all of them.

"Are your new quarters to your liking?" he asks.

"They are too close to yours."

"Consider yourself lucky. They face south, they catch winter warmth. You can stay in the Queen's favor if you are careful."

"Do you threaten me, Rizzio?"

He smiles and fans himself, covering the movement of his lips. "A warning only. The Queen knows nothing about you and your paramour. Keep it that way."

After lunch the Queen orders her courtiers to an afternoon ride in the park. The four Marys are gleeful, but I see a few glum expressions elsewhere. In spite of my resolve, I cannot help looking at Angelique. Her face is stricken, but when I see she is staring at Jean-Paul, I turn away abruptly. Rizzio, who has gained a permanent dispensation from riding on account of his twisted back, settles himself into a plush chair as we follow the Queen out.

"We will race around the foot of Arthur's Seat," she says as we mount in the courtyard. She looks across at me and smiles. "There is still no one here who rides as well as you."

Within moments she and I are ahead of the others, and by the time we reach the base of Arthur's Seat, they are far behind us. Normally the Queen can outride me too, but I have spent much of the past six weeks on horseback and my mare is road-hardened. I ride at the Queen's side easily, but keep from passing her, so that our horses gallop in tandem. When we come around the base of the rock, she pulls up, laughing and fresh-faced. She has never lost her delight at riding thus.

"With your gift for disguise, I should have left you here on the throne and gone myself, to see what the world is like these days," she says. "What is the mood in England?"

"All the talk is of marriage." I let the mare lower her head and catch her breath. "Yours and your cousin's. Among men there is great impatience, as if they are waiting to know who they really serve. The Catholics are afraid and many are converting. But some think that Elizabeth will never marry."

She nods thoughtfully. "And what of Bothwell?"

"I have a letter from him. He is still urging you to consider Lord Darnley. He writes to you of Don Carlos's accident."

"Accident?"

"The word is all over London that he fell down the castle stairs in a drunken rage and almost died. His father's surgeons have operated on his brain, and performed a near miracle, restoring his sight, but it seems he has lost what was left of his mind. He tried to strangle his father in a wild fit."

The only sound is the panting of the two horses, gradually easing. "The ambassador mentioned a small accident, that is all. He assured me Don Carlos had recovered," she says at last. "Why does Bothwell always pass me such troublesome information! If he had not been so loyal to my family, I would swear that he himself plots to make my life miserable."

The sound of hooves throbs behind us and both horses prick up their ears. The Queen lifts the reins and swings her horse around. "Bring me his letter tonight," she says.

The rider behind us is shouting as he pulls level with us. "One of the ladies has fallen from her horse. We need the Queen's surgeon quickly."

The Queen frowns. "I will go back to them," she says. "Ride for Arnault and bring Jean-Paul too."

I lean low over the mare's neck, urging her with boot and rein and voice, and she picks up her speed. We startle a flock of ravens, rising into the air cawing as we thunder past. My heart tells me which woman is in trouble.

I clatter into the courtyard, yelling at the stablehands to saddle more horses, and send servants running to find the Queen's physician, Arnault. He comes running out within minutes, followed by the apothecary, but I speak only to Arnault, refusing to look at Angi's lover. There are more instructions called, horses saddled, a litter made ready to follow us, and we set off again.

My mare gallops strongly, but I must slow down for the others over the rough ground and the ride feels eternal. At last the group comes into sight. The women are gathered around, while the men have drawn away to huddle by a rock nearby.

I ride close enough to see three things: Angi on the ground amid the women, her eyes closed, her face stripped of color. The splash of blood on her dress, shockingly red. And the Queen stepping forward to meet us.

I have seen that look of cold fury on her face before, her lips pressed hard together so they are almost bloodless.

"Gentlemen," she says, and at the tone of her voice they both stop in their tracks and bow low. "Your assistance is needed here urgently. Although it appears that you," and here she looks at the apothecary, "may have already had a hand in this matter."

Within an hour of Angi's slow return to the castle by litter, the news has spread from turret to cellar, kitchen to stable. The Queen's lady is pregnant and miscarrying. The father is the Queen's apothecary, who has given her herbs to cast out the child and hide their disgrace.

The Queen's fury knows no limits. She orders us all to leave her and spends the afternoon in the chapel with the door closed.

Now I have cause to curse my family for training me in both religions. I am loyal to neither of them, so I do not have a right to pray to God. If I did, what would I ask for? Mercy? Or retribution?

She sends for me at last, before dinner, with a request that I bring the letter from Bothwell. Rizzio opens the door to her bedchamber and shows me in, his face expressionless. The Marys are there, seated in a circle.

The Queen takes Bothwell's letter from my hands. She reads it swiftly, then hands it to Rizzio as if he were indeed her husband. He reads it while she paces.

"It is too much, this waiting and scheming for marriage," she says. "With so much intrigue, I cannot rule even my own court, let alone my country. While I am waiting on Elizabeth's pleasure, I cannot find a true word about the Prince of Spain or even meet Lord Darnley, and in the meantime there is scandal here right in my own palace."

No one speaks as she continues to pace, though Rizzio shoots me a warning look.

"It will not be suffered! I will not be humiliated by foreign princes and then by my own household," she bursts out. "I shall have an answer from Spain. I shall meet the young Lord Darnley, and I shall know my cousin's wishes once and for all so that I may make my decision."

Rizzio nods and I stand silently. The Queen stops her pacing and turns to face all of us. "This is a Catholic court, and if I let this matter today go unpunished, then it is proof to Knox that everything he accuses me of here is true. I must be as rigorous as the Protestants, as hard on wrongdoing as they. I have prayed for guidance in this matter. I must make an example of them. This will not be tolerated in my household."

"What about a trial?"

The Queen looks at me sharply. "There is no need of a trial, Alison. They have both confessed to their sin." She turns away. "They shall be punished. Some may think me too harsh, but a woman ruler must be harsher even than a man at times, to prove she is capable of it."

Rizzio's face is stricken and that, more than the Queen's words, sends a cold shiver through my body.

"Leave me now," she orders. "I thank you for the letter, Alison. La Flamina and Seton, ready me for bed."

I wait for Rizzio outside. "What punishment does she mean?" I ask when he comes out.

He is pale. "She means to have them executed."

It is as if he has punched me in the stomach. I stagger and he takes my arm to stop me falling and begins to hurry me along the corridor.

"Whatever hand you had in this, it will come back to you a thousandfold," I hiss at him. He half drags me into his room. I slump to a chair and he crosses to a low cupboard and splashes out two cups of whisky. He takes his in a single swallow and gestures for me to do the same.

"What did you tell the Queen?" I ask.

"I told her nothing of you and Angelique. It is unfortunate they were caught, or it simply would have blown over. I did not foresee this."

"I must see her."

"Listen to me." He pours out more whisky and his hands are shaking. "There's nothing you can do. If you interfere, you could end up on the gallows too. If you think this pregnancy is scandalous, imagine if the truth came out. All three of you would hang, or worse. At least a hanging is swift."

≈   ≈   ≈

It is raining on the day of the execution, the first hint of summer's end. The Queen has ordered me to attend her, finely dressed as a woman. "You must sit by me, lest I swoon," she says. "I cannot bear to put a woman to death, and yet I must."

I do not know how I can live through such a day, and yet I must.

When the two of them are brought out to the gallows and the charges read to a jeering crowd, Angi lifts her head to find me. Our eyes lock and she manages a tiny, ghastly smile that makes the crowd jeer even more.

Their heads are covered, and once her eyes are closed to me I can

149

close my own. The Queen takes my hand and holds it tightly and when the gallows crash, she squeezes and gives a soft moan. The crowd erupts in a cheer. Beside us, La Flamina falls in a swoon, and the Queen lets go of my hand as the ladies all turn to attend her.

I do not look at the gallows where two figures hang and I keep an iron fist closed inside me, lest the sound of my heart being torn apart finds a way to escape. I will run, after this. I will take my love for Angi and run as far from the court as I can with it.

I sit with my head down amid the flutter. And then there is a light touch on my shoulder.

The Queen is looking down at me, her face sorrowful. "You were friends with her, I know. I am sorry for it. I was fond of her too."

The Queen is pale but composed as she sweeps us all back into the carriage and down the High Street. We pass underneath the windows of John Knox's house where it juts out into the road, a spy hole where he may stand and keep his nasty eye on Edinburgh.

There is a moment in the courtyard when the Queen and I are standing together and the others have moved away, fussing with La Flamina as she is helped across the cobblestones. There is not even a servant with us.

The Queen turns to me. "I must have loyalty, Alison." She looks at me with such tenderness that I struggle not to weep. "Your loyalty has been steadfast. I have not forgotten your castle, or the struggle of your family. I have decided: you will not have to wait until I ascend the English throne for your reward. Only that I secure my succession. It is close. The English Parliament meets soon to discuss it, and it will be ratified in law. When it is done, I will grant you your castle."

≈ ≈ ≈

Autumn comes. The city swirls with red and gold leaves, falling in spirals of gorgeous color. Edinburgh's citizens venture out of the city's gates to look at them and speculate on what they portend for the coming winter.

My heart is curled up and dead within my chest. It crackles when I move and I know, dully, that soon it will simply crumble to dust and blow away. In the meantime my body acts as though it is still alive, waking in the mornings, arising from my bed, assisting my room companions with their dress, riding out with the Queen. I do not care for anything. I cannot summon the will to smile or converse. Every day has blackness at its core.

Even Rizzio leaves me alone. He daily rises in the Queen's favor. She takes his advice in decisions of state. I no longer care for any of it.

I have lost count of the days and weeks by the time the Queen calls me to her side.

"I have a task more suited to you than staying here in court," she says. "I am ordering Bothwell to France to lead my soldiers there. You will go with him in your old disguise and report to me on his activities. He says he is loyal to me, but I need more proof. You will find it for me. By the time you return, God willing, your castle will be yours again."

She takes my hand and presses it. In the early days of her rule she did such a thing often, but she has come to learn the dangers of touching her favorites. The last time she touched me thus was at Angi's hanging. This time my hand lies in hers, a dead thing. She releases me.

≈ ≈ ≈

The day of my departure arrives and I find myself standing on the port at Leith with salt wind in my face. I will leave this treacherous city, these bloody shores, these streets full of ghosts and dead leaves, and go to the milder shores of France instead. I have sold my mare, Artemis, blowing softly in her nostrils to say goodbye. I will not be coming back.

Just before I am about to step onto the ship there is a tap on my shoulder. It is one of Maitland's men. He draws me away from the ship to a quiet corner.

"I have something for you," he says. "A letter from your friend, the woman the Queen had hanged."

"How would such a letter have come to you?"

"She knew Rizzio could not be trusted. I have her token."

He opens his hand. Angelique's silver necklace lies on his palm. I reach for it, but he draws his hand back.

"In return, Maitland would have something from you." He withdraws two small leather pouches from inside his cloak and hands them to me.

"There are those who wish to ensure Bothwell never returns to Edinburgh and has no further influence on the Queen."

One pouch clinks with coin, and is heavy. The other is small, and from the feel of it, contains a bottle.

"A few drops in his food will do it. There is a payment there for you, and another much larger waiting if you are successful. Enough, perhaps, to free you from the Queen's service."

Rizzio was not the only one watching me to find a moment of weakness. How many others have been guessing at my thoughts?

He hands me the letter and the necklace, turns on his heel, and walks away. I stare after him until he disappears and then I crack the seal on Angi's note.

Alison, I must be brief. I fear Rizzio has told the Queen of the matter between us. You will think I betrayed you, but Rizzio promised if I went to Jean-Paul that you would be safe. In my heart I have been ever true to you. Leave her service, I beg you—you will never reach what it is you seek. Angi.

She has scrawled a date during my time away in London.

I look up at the ship, ready to carry me away. They are all full of treachery—Rizzio, who brought this about; Maitland, who held on to such a letter until it was of use to him; and the Queen most of all, who took my hand so tenderly and made me sweet promises, having murdered the person I loved.

The poison burns in my hand. Perhaps it will be useful to kill my traitorous body, which seems determined to live even without a beating heart at its center. I pocket the pouches, the necklace, and the letter, wrap my cloak about me, walk back to the gangplank, and step off Scottish soil.

Part II
1565

Twenty

February 1565, the coldest winter in living memory.

From London, word comes that the Thames has frozen over and Elizabeth's citizens can walk out on the ice, their children running and slipping around them.

In Scotland it is too dangerously cold for such frolicking. Its people live their lives with care, staying inside at night, wrapping warmly to leave the house, and never straying too far from shelter. A Scot respects the cold as a worthy adversary.

Edinburgh's citizens are tucked away in their beds, the only place holding a semblance of warmth, when the warriors come clattering down the deserted streets. Inside the Flodden Wall in the darkest hour of the night, hooves strike cobblestones, steel clashes against steel. Men jump up in spite of the cold and peer down from the tenement windows, but they cannot see anything in the darkness.

The next night the guard on the gates is doubled, but in the night's deepest hours the warriors come again. The sounds of fighting drift up from the wynds and closes and out onto the High Street. Again, the people come to their windows to see the source of such bloody screams, but they can see no one.

In the daytime, the Queen's soldiers roam, making inquiries. The town is full of talk, but there are no men with bloody wounds, and no clues.

On the third night, the fighting reaches a new pitch. There are dying shrieks, the sound of men cleaved by swords. The guards chase the sounds of battle through the streets but they cannot catch up with it. At last they pause in their pursuit, looking at each other uneasily. When the sound of fighting moves down the hill to the swampy moat of Nor Loch, the guards do not dare to follow. Edinburgh's people do not get up on this night, a night cold enough to freeze the air in their lungs. They lie awake listening as the last screams die away over the swamp. Still no one has laid eyes upon a single swordsman.

On the fourth day, Lord Darnley rides into Scotland to meet the Queen.

≈   ≈   ≈

When I arrived in France half a year earlier, I cared for nothing. In the country of my beloved, the language of our love on every tongue assaulted my ears. The poison throbbed at my breast. Every night I pressed my lips to it and Angi waited on the far side of that kiss. Every night I thought I would drink it, but each time my courage failed me.

William didn't seem to notice that all hope had left my world. He pressed me about the castle. At first I said nothing about the Queen's new promise. What did it matter? I never intended to return to Scotland. But one night William drank more than usual and came at me with his dagger, and I saw in his eyes that he had lost all reason. I found, to my dull surprise, that I was not ready to die and I stayed his hand with news of the Queen's word.

Once he understood what I was saying, he let his weapon fall. After that, he was content to leave me alone.

I had no heart for the task of judging Bothwell's loyalty, having none left of my own. I cared nothing for poisoning him and collecting a rich payment. I could not even bring myself to observe him. I barely spoke to him through the long months of winter.

He had sent for me to come to his chambers one night in late January. He had cups of fine French wine, as befitted his position of Captain of the Scottish Guard, and he pressed one upon me.

"Your blood is thin, lad," he said. "Drink."

After two cups I felt the relief of the wine start to steal through my veins. Bothwell, watching me, leaned over and put his hand on my shoulder.

"The very spirit has gone out of you. What has she done?"

I looked at the ground. "She has torn out my heart, Bothwell."

"Likely she will break all of our hearts before it is done," he said

156

softly. He slowly drew me toward him. I stiffened, then gradually relaxed until I was against his chest.

Holding Angi was like standing on the deck of a ship, in constant motion, but Bothwell's hold was solid as rock and stone, castle wall and keep. I could rest there, my head tucked under his chin and pressed to his chest.

"You have a secret," he said, above me.

I pulled back quickly, away from his touch. Did he know me a woman?

"What do you carry at your breast?"

My hand went to the hidden bottle of poison that I kept tucked against my chest. I drew it out and let it rest on my palm, such an innocent receptacle of glass, its evil tightly stoppered.

"One of Maitland's men gave it to me as I left, with a payment to poison you."

He laughed. "The lords do not like me overmuch. Are you planning to use it?"

I shook my head. "Not on you."

He smiled. "No. You are not a murderer. But I think you are not safe with that bottle either. Let me take it."

I was reluctant to hand it over. It had been a balm at my breast, a promise of release. But Bothwell held his hand out until I laid it in his palm and then he tucked it inside his own jerkin.

"Good," he said. "The Queen's spy should not carry poison."

"I am not much of a spy. I have sent no word back to her, of you or anything else. I will never return to Scotland."

Bothwell poured out more wine for both of us and gestured for me to sit. "But William has told me about her latest promise to you. Don't you trust it?"

I shook my head.

"Good," he said. "You should never trust the promises of princes. She may mean now to give you the castle back, but it depends only on the advantage to the throne when the time comes. Right now, Lord Hume is high in her favor, while William is only a captain."

"And I am only a lady-in-waiting." Was it because he held me that I wanted to stop lying and tell him at last?

He stared at me. "What do you mean?"

"You've walked past me, seen me, even talked with me as the Queen's woman Alison Blackadder. I am William's daughter. I have been disguised as his nephew half my life to keep me safe from Hume."

"I never thought William capable of such a lie." Bothwell got to his feet, shaking his head. He filled our cups again and downed his in a single swallow. "Does the Queen know this?"

"I went into her service as Alison, but was caught dressed as Robert within a few weeks. She had me teach her how to disguise herself. Do you not remember the masque when she and all her ladies came dressed as noblemen?"

He shook his head again and I put my hand on his arm. "Bothwell, do not doubt William. He is loyal to you until death. It was only for my safety that he told no one."

He was silent for a long moment. "No wonder she likes to use you for a spy."

"I am her spy no more," I took my hand away. "I will not serve her again. I don't care for the castle any longer."

"Now you are the fool," he said. "It is an evil thing to be impoverished and even more if you are a woman. I have lost most of my money, being imprisoned and on the run. My debtors hold my own castle. I will send you back to her myself before I will let you lose your birthright."

"She imprisoned you and banished you. Why do you serve her?"

"I have my honor," he said. "I have served Queen and country. For all her faults, she has been appointed by God as our ruler."

He refilled his cup, took another swig and winked at me. "And, by God, she is handsome and I never could resist a handsome woman." He laughed, then grew serious. "That is the truth, although you may report back to her what you wish."

"You need not fear what I will report."

"Good," he said. "For I need you to go back to her. Elizabeth has given permission for Darnley to come to Scotland. It can mean only that there is some advantage to England in a match between our Queen and him."

"I cannot go," I said, getting to my feet.

"I have pressed Mary to marry him and now I fear there is treachery in it after all. I cannot leave France without her permission. You must persuade her that I can serve her better in Scotland. I must return before it goes farther."

I made a grab, fast as a striking snake, to snatch the poison back from his breast, but he was faster and caught my wrist before I even touched him.

"I would rather die than go back to her," I said, trying to wrench myself free.

He shook me hard. "You may as well poison William and yourself if you give up like this."

"Give me the bottle and I will," I spat at him.

He laughed at me. I watched him, disbelieving for a moment, and then flew at him. I landed a punch on his face that split my knuckle before he held my hands down.

"Good," he said. "Don't let her defeat you like this. Go back and fight for your castle like a man. There's a ship leaving for Scotland tomorrow."

≋ ≋ ≋

I was sixteen when I made the journey carrying the Queen by sea from France to Scotland. This time I am near twenty. Three-and-a-half years in her service, drinking in the pleasure of love like a drunkard—the pleasure of my secret passion for the Queen and my real passion for Angelique.

On this rough winter passage back to Scotland I have no poison snuggled at my breast to comfort me. Without its promise of escape, I find that Bothwell is right. I want that damned castle after all. The Queen has torn my heart out and now I want the safety of high stone walls. I want to sit inside a fortress that cannot be taken. I will ride out and hunt stag, I will order feasts and music in my great hall. No one will tell me if I should dress as woman or man.

I have been the loyal servant of William's desire for the castle. By the time I arrive in Edinburgh, I know for the first time in my life what it is to want it for myself.

≈ ≈ ≈

The Queen is caught at the royal castle at Stirling in the freeze and Lord Darnley, who arrived in Edinburgh a week before me, has set out to meet her.

I stay with Sophie while I wait for their return and she fills me in on what is spoken in the streets. The city is ablaze with gossip. Lord Darnley and our Queen are in love. She has become his paramour without consideration for church or state. They have been secretly married. They will overthrow Elizabeth and rule the land. The French and the Spanish will send armies to further their cause. He has been sent by Rome to restore the Catholic religion. Sophie tells me that rumors of his secret vices have also reached Edinburgh.

Knox rants from his pulpit, blowing hot air on the coals of gossip. His two favorite words are *harlot* and *jezebel,* until in the minds of the ordinary people the Queen is already tried and damned for committing unspeakable acts with this English noble.

When finally the weather clears enough for them to make the journey back to Edinburgh, every inhabitant of the city risks the cold to come out on the street and see for themselves the scandal of our Queen and this boy who thinks he would be King. The gates at Netherbow Port are flung wide open and the crowds wait, muttering, pressing on either side of the road.

The Queen leads her procession up the High Street. They are bundled heavily against the cold, but the Queen and Darnley push back their hoods to show their faces. I crane my neck to see what is written there.

After my years in her service, I can read every nuance of her expression. It is true, what the gossips say. Our Queen rides with her head high and her feelings blazing like a war pennant in the breeze. It sears me like a brand—I too rode like this. Though I took more care to hide my heart, it blazed thus, until she cut it out.

She is in love. Perhaps, at last, I have a weapon of my own.

Twenty-one

I have left word at the palace of my return and I am summoned to meet the Queen the next day. It is still dark as I make my way down the High Street, muffled in heavy wraps. There are few people out and, though it is after eight in the morning, the gloom has barely lifted and the wind shrieks between the tenements.

The cold suits my purpose. I am ice inside and out. After six months in France, a man's clothes, a man's posture and swagger, and a man's confidence with weapons have become my protection. I am armored against softness as surely as I am clothed against this treacherous cold. I arrive in the palace, shake the ice off my boots and shoulders, leave my heavy coat and hood in an outer room, and step into the presence chamber to meet the Queen.

Rizzio, my betrayer, comes to the door to greet me. He is dressed in lordly magnificence, his fingers jeweled.

"It is good to see you back, Robert. You have nothing to fear here. It is all past now."

I say nothing, but incline my head. Did he betray Angi and me to the Queen in his efforts to avert a scandal? I doubt I will ever find out. His smile does not waver and he gestures for me to follow him to the Queen.

In front of her I bow down on one knee, keeping my eyes on the rich patterning of the carpet until her pleasant voice rings out.

"Robert. This is a surprise, and a happy one. Come and be seated by me."

She smiles at me the way she did when she first favored me and there was some girlish delight she wished to share. She holds out her hand and draws me to a chair by her side and calls for food and drink.

"Now, loyal Robert, tell me of France. Tell me of Bothwell. And you shall hear the news of Scotland."

Her attention is not completely with me. This is a woman infatuated; her pulse beating faster, her breath coming quickly, a flush on her cheeks.

I give her a public report of my activities, the one suitable for members of the court to hear. That Lord Bothwell is fit and well and representing Scotland with honor in France, though he sadly misses the Queen and yearns to see her. She gives me the public report of matters in Scotland—that there is no final word yet on her succession to the English throne, but relations between her and Elizabeth are warm.

"And our cousin Lord Darnley has come to Scotland at last to see his family's estates," she says, her smile widening. "However, the weather has been so dangerous that he has made his stay with the court for now. Perhaps you saw him in the procession yesterday?"

"I was not close enough to see his face. Is it true, then, he is as fair as they say?"

There is a titter from a couple of the ladies standing close by and the Queen's color becomes a little more heightened.

"You can see for yourself," she says. "He will be joining us for dinner."

The Queen may not be able to disguise her heart, but she is the mistress of conversation and she turns her attention upon me, asking about my father and the weather in France and inconsequentialities until Lord Darnley comes striding in the door.

He crosses the room in half a dozen strides, sweeps into a low bow, takes the Queen's hand and kisses it lingeringly. Seated next to her, I observe how he raises his eyes teasingly to hers and moves his lips softly against her skin, until she laughs and draws her hand away.

"My Lord, this is Robert who returns from Bothwell's service in France," she says.

His eyes flicker over me appraisingly and I can see something in him—something I've seen in other men who look at me as a boy. It is hunger.

≈ ≈ ≈

That night the Queen calls me to her bedchamber for a private meeting. I am wearing the uniform of the Scottish Guard from France, for the protection it offers. She rises while I am down on one knee and comes across to me. She stretches out a hand and runs her finger along my shoulder, feeling the thick fabric.

"You have become even more handsome as a boy. Does no one wonder, now, at your soft cheeks?"

"No one feels my soft cheeks, Your Grace."

She laughs. "Come and sit. Tell me of Bothwell." She waves at Rizzio and La Flamina. "You may play chess by the fire. I will speak to Robert alone."

"It is Bothwell who sent me back to you," I say, taking a seat close by her when they have moved. "He does not trust Elizabeth's motives in sending Lord Darnley to Scotland and now he is uncertain about the wisdom of the match. Bothwell says if Elizabeth has sent Darnley, she must have some secret reason."

The Queen tightens her lips. "It seems I can always rely on Bothwell to bring trouble. You have seen Darnley. Think you he has been sent by Elizabeth as part of some foul plot?"

I lower my eyes. "I cannot know that."

She laughs and puts her hand on my arm. "Come, forget diplomacy. Remember how many times we have talked as girls together? So tell me. What do you think of him?"

"There is no doubt he is as fair as they say, and as tall. But there are less complimentary things being said of him."

"Such as?"

"That he is not to be trusted, that he is a lover of boys, that he drinks to excess and is violent."

"Who says this?"

"It is common gossip in the taverns, Your Grace."

She looks away. "Being a soldier has made you hard. I thought you would have been happy for me. Would your gossips rather I marry some deformed foreign prince who will visit here once a year? I am

163

hounded by priest and nobleman alike to marry, but when finally one comes along who is suitable, they find fault with him."

I bow my head. "It is only foolish tavern talk."

"Talk that has reached across the seas to Bothwell's ears, and yet it was he who commended Darnley to me when all other advice lay with foreign princes."

"Bothwell begs your leave to return and speak with you of these matters himself."

"He does not have my leave," she says. "I have plenty of advisers here in Scotland."

"I shall tell him."

"You will send a message. I want you here. I need someone to counter this foolishness. You will speak of Lord Darnley's accomplishments and qualities. You will spread the word that he is worthy to be King of Scotland."

She looks at me. "It is as important for you as for me. Should I marry him, he strengthens my claim to the throne. Elizabeth herself has sent him here. Her parliament is debating succession right now and this can only help. As I promised you, once it is certain, you have your reward."

The twist of her hand and my life turns again. I nod, but don't answer.

She leans across and raises my chin with her fingers. "Ah, Robbie, what has happened to you? I should not have sent you away, not you who were so loyal to me back when I knew nothing of being a queen."

Her eyes hold me, and they are tender, as if she could never have sent Angelique to the gallows.

"I will have some new dresses made for you. You must be longing for something womanly after six months as a soldier."

"No, Your Grace." My answer comes out abruptly and she raises her eyebrows.

"I will serve you better as a man. I can be your eyes and ears in the world. It is safer in your court too. Alison was too closely watched by Lord Hume."

It is the first time I have refused an order, although both the order and its refusal have been couched in diplomatic terms. Not for nothing have I been a courtier for more than three years. She considers me for a moment. Is she completely blinded by Lord Darnley, or does she notice that she no longer holds my heart?

"You are right," she says, sitting back and reaching for her wine. "You can be a gentleman of my chamber. At any rate, Lord Hume is busy with his estates and little at court."

"Thank you," I say.

"If you are so suspicious of Lord Darnley, then I will not tell him you are a woman. You may keep an eye on him and let me know what you observe."

A burst of laughter comes from across the room and I look at Rizzio and La Flamina leaning over their chess game.

The Queen follows my gaze. "I have appointed Rizzio as my personal secretary. He is a most canny adviser."

"What does he think of Lord Darnley?"

"You know, I think he is rather taken with him," she says, with a sideways glance. "He pressed me for a long time to marry into Spain or France, but now he has come around to Darnley and, if anything, is the strongest advocate of this match."

"It sounds as though your mind is made up," I say.

"Not quite. He is charming, but there is much to consider. Elizabeth has not made her wishes clear yet and I would have her blessing first."

"We must pray that she sees sense."

She stretches out a hand and runs her finger down my cheek. "I have ordered a new room made up for you," she says. "I hope it will be to your liking. There is a large fire in there—this cold must be painful to you, after France. It is still painful to me even after four winters. Tomorrow, join us in court and you will see more of Darnley for yourself. When these evil storms pass, you may go out among the people again, but this time to speak instead of listen. I put my full trust in you."

"And Lord Bothwell?"

"I will write to him in the morning and tell him I have need of you here. When the weather clears, we shall go hunting. It will be like the old times. I think you will find Lord Darnley is a worthy companion."

Twenty-two

I no longer love the Queen, and now she finds me irresistible. The more aloof I become, the less I act like a servant, the more she likes it. She wants me as close as in our early days, her friend and confidante. She keeps me by her side, she confides in me, she rides out with me, she asks my opinions. And I, who do not care, come to enjoy this unexpected taste of power.

I see that when you keep your desires secret, the world is more likely to hand them to you. I decide I will not say a word about the castle. I will do what I can to bring her closer to the English throne, but I will let her believe I am indifferent to my reward.

Lord Darnley has used the bitter winter as his excuse for settling into the life of the court. It is he who woos the Queen with a ceaseless flow of flirtatious glances, kisses, light-footed dancing, poetry, discussion, hunting, and promises of sport when the weather clears. It is he whose desire is writ large, whose pursuit is soft but relentless.

≈　≈　≈

The Queen calls me to her chamber one night after I have been back for a week. The Marys, her shadows, are there, along with Rizzio and a couple of her other ladies. At their center Darnley holds the floor. He is reciting some long poem, with enough wit to keep them all entertained.

The Queen beckons me close, then stands and inclines her head, so that I follow her toward her bedchamber. She gestures for Seton to follow us. "Continue," she says to Darnley as he falters a moment. "We won't be long."

She is like a girl planning a party. Laid out on her bed is one of her male outfits, the plain dress of a merchant.

"I want to surprise him," she whispers. "Take him out on the streets in disguise. Help me dress."

It takes Seton a while to strip her of her garments and help her into the new clothes, while I, in deference to my persona of Robert, turn my back. I have not seen her do this for over a year, but she has lost none of her strong bearing once disguised. For a moment I glimpse what I once saw in her.

"Now, let us invite him to join us." Her smile is pure mischief, as if years of ruling have disappeared with her skirts.

I lead the way back into the chamber, and Darnley, ever attentive, halts mid-sentence. When the Queen steps out behind me and faces him, there is a moment of silence while everyone waits to see his reaction.

I am close enough to read what is in his eyes when he looks at her. Ah, clever Queen. Did she see how he looked at me and want the same for herself? He is undone for a moment, a flush comes to his cheeks, the hunger is naked in his eyes until he collects himself, claps his hands, and jumps to his feet.

"What a fine gentleman you make, Madam." He walks around her. "The illusion is extraordinary. Now that I see what you are capable of here, I shall doubt the sex of every person in this court."

She inclines her head, but not quickly enough to hide her smile. He stops, bows, and stretches out a hand. "Shall we dance?" he asks, and the ladies laugh.

"No," she says, and all fall silent. "Better than that. We will walk out and I will show you this city through the eyes of the ordinary man."

I stand back as he comes to her side, but she says, "Robert? You must accompany us and keep us from trouble. Let us show Lord Darnley the real Edinburgh."

She gives Darnley another merchant's outfit to change into and we cover ourselves in heavy cloaks and hoods and draw on leather gloves. Thus wrapped, the three of us cross the courtyard, pass the guard, and step out into the street.

The cobblestones are iced, so we must walk carefully and our slow movement is not enough to warm our bodies. In her fourth winter now, the Queen has started to adjust and does not feel it as keenly.

Being from a softer clime, Darnley is shivering by the time we reach Netherbow Port.

I steer them away from Sophie's tavern, for I would hear the mood of the rest of Edinburgh myself. In the White Hart the air is a soup of ale, smoke, food smells, wet clothing, and raucous laughs. I shoulder my way through, looking for a table. Those by the fire have been taken by the wealthy merchants who are regular clients. The Queen looks across and frowns. She is accustomed to having her desire the moment she thinks of it. I clap my hand on her shoulder and gesture toward a drafty table at the back, with a wink that is a warning.

Darnley is more at home than I expected. He knows what to order, how to joke with the barmaid, how to push his way to the bar without causing offense. The accent and pitch of his voice shift just enough that he sounds wellborn but not noble. I am not the only one who is good at disguises.

Within moments of him bringing the drinks back to our table, a woman approaches with a wide smile and a low neckline baring her cleavage.

"Cold night, gents," she says. "A body could freeze just walking to the tavern. What brings you here? Something special?"

I open my mouth to answer, but Darnley beats me. "Good madam, I am come all the way from London to see if it is true what they say about Scottish women."

"And what might that be, laddie?"

"Why, that you are so exquisite no king dares to rule you and only a queen of great beauty is fit to be above you."

The woman laughs loudly and pinches his cheek. "Of course it is true. Our Queen's beauty is famed. But if it is the Queen you are enamored of, why, we have our very own Mary upstairs here. Almost as tall as you, sir, red-haired, all dressed with a crown, and ready to grant you her royal favor. She doesn't come cheap, but why should she?"

Beside me the Queen stiffens.

"Really? How much is she?" Darnley asks.

"Thirty marks. But for all three of you, a better price. You must beware though, sirs. After an hour with the Queen, no ordinary woman will satisfy you again."

"That I can well imagine," he says. "Let us think on it. My friend here is waiting for his ship to come in and the foul weather has quite delayed it. It may be that we cannot afford any queenly services tonight."

She leans over, gives him a loud kiss on the cheek, and disappears into the crowd.

"It seems Scotland's Queen is well loved in the capital," he says, and takes a long swig of ale. I do not turn to look at the Queen, but I can feel her cold rage next to me.

"Indeed," she says. "It seems more of an insult to me."

He leans across the table. "But there, sir, you are quite wrong. The ordinary man of the city loves the Queen and dreams that she will grant him royal favors."

"You could say that the ordinary man of the city dreams of the Queen submitting to his base desires, when in reality he must serve her and can never hope for that reward," I say.

He turns to me curiously. "Have you spent much time with ordinary men, sir?"

"A good deal of my life, sir. And you?"

"Perhaps less, due to the accident of my birth. But I see no insult in a man desiring his Queen."

"You think good can come of every man thinking the Queen is a common whore?" the Queen asks.

"Not a common whore; she costs thirty marks, no less," he says. "But if you visit the taverns, you cannot expect to find a royal court. If you think this insults the Queen, then you have seen nothing of the insults the ordinary man makes when he is unhappy with his ruler. You have no idea, with respect, of the vile baseness that his insults will run to. I tell you, sir, this is a kingdom that is well satisfied with its ruler."

She exhales and takes a swig of her ale. "The Queen is well thought of in the whorehouses. It's in the church where you will hear the most vile insults and lies about her."

"Well, then, it is best you do not go there," he says. "I myself will go to hear this famous preacher of Edinburgh and the foolishness that comes from his lips. But for now, let's forget such matters and enjoy ourselves. I will get us more drinks."

He disappears into the crowd and she turns to me, a question in her eyes. It is time to play her desire with all the skill I am learning.

"He thinks as many men do, and that is no fault," I say. "But beware of a man with such a face, who converses as happily with whores as with queens."

"That is the very thing I like about him. A prince must be able to speak to all his subjects."

"He is not a prince," I say.

"Not yet." She turns to watch him coming back through the crowd. "Not a prince, yet."

He hands us the cups and sits down. I lift my drink, marveling at how easy it is to shape her longing.

Twenty-three

He has set himself to win her, but he makes the tactical error of playing his hand too soon.

The court is still confined by the bitter winter. The days are gloomy and short, the nights seem eternal. The cold creeps into my bones, no matter what fires burn in the palace. Everyone is sick of the taste of salted meat. Edinburgh is a city of hedgehogs and badgers, all of us curling into ourselves for the long winter, slow and groggy.

Except Lord Darnley. He sings to La Flamina, reads poetry to Beaton, plays skilful chess with Rizzio, discusses foreign policy with Maitland. He teaches us the latest dance from Elizabeth's court and shows the musicians how to accompany it. He teases Lusty about her forthcoming marriage to John Sempill and no one mentions the vow that the Marys have taken not to wed before the Queen. Even Rizzio has fallen under his spell and they are often seen together conversing in Italian, a tongue that few of us in the court can speak.

I am impervious to his charm. His sideways glances, his efforts to wheedle out my secrets, his knowing hints and winks, come to nothing. I invent reasons to absent myself from the Queen's chambers in the long, dark evenings. She thinks I am in the taverns spreading word of Darnley's qualities. Most of the time I am sleeping like a hibernating creature.

On one such night she sends for me, late. A servant pounds on my door and I have time only to clamber from my bed and pull a cloak over my nightgown before hurrying to her chambers.

The Queen herself is wearing gorgeous noblemen's finery and she is striding about her chamber in agitation when I step inside the door.

"I have need of your wisdom tonight as a woman," she says. "Come by the fire."

The Queen's fire burns the hottest of any in the palace and in my half-sleep I am grateful to stand with my back to it, its warmth licking through my heavy cloak. "What is it, Your Grace?" I ask, stifling a yawn.

She strides the length of the room again before answering. "Lord Darnley has asked me to marry him."

I am shocked, but only that he has misjudged his timing so much. He has taken the first step, of charming her, but he has not taken the necessary second step—moving back and letting her taste the fear of not having him. He is too young, this accomplished boy, to know that desire must have fear within it.

"It seems hasty," I say.

"I think it has gone to his head, knowing the Queen can be found in any whorehouse, and he thinks he might have what he wants just for the asking." She turns to stride again. "What arrogance! He believes I will simper and smile and hand him the kingdom after three weeks' acquaintance."

"What did you tell him?"

"I said do not think to buy the Queen for a handful of shillings, and I sent him away. I am of a mind to send him home to England."

The room is silent while she pours herself a cup of wine, then pours one for me too and brings it over to the fire. I am starting to shiver and I gulp it gratefully.

"What think you of this?" she says. "Speak plainly. I have no stomach for diplomacy tonight."

"Did something untoward happen?" I ask.

She blushes. "He came at me."

I look at her, dressed in her boy's playthings, and sigh. "Madam, it is two of the morning and he has been drinking."

"He forgets himself, and who I am," she snaps.

"No doubt he does. You dress as a boy and take him to taverns and whorehouses and then complain when he does not treat you as a queen."

She throws herself down in a chair, and her lip trembles. "Do you think I have encouraged his hasty behavior?"

"If you want to be treated as a queen, you need to act as one," I say. "He desires you, but it is equally clear you desire him and that marriage is the logical outcome. He has rushed you, but this proposal is surely not unexpected?"

She rubs her face with both hands. "He is my most likely suitor yet, but I did not expect he would be so clumsy. If he cannot handle this, how will he handle ruling a council of nobles with far more cunning and experience? Perhaps I should be like Elizabeth and rule my country alone."

Bothwell would take the chance to warn her off this marriage, but I will not be so selfless. I shrug as if it is no matter. "Madam, don't let a mistake determine his future, but watch now what is more important—how he deals with that mistake. Then make your choice."

"You are wise," she says, taking my hand. "And cold! I have kept you from your bed. I will take your advice on this. Darnley will be reprimanded and we will see if he is man enough to change his conduct."

As I shiver back to my room, I pass Rizzio's quarters. There is a glow of light under the door and I can hear a low mutter. Darnley's voice is unmistakable.

≋　≋　≋

At last the frost's iron grip loosens. The days lengthen and the country dares to dream of spring. But as soon as the seas are passable and the ships begin coming in and out of Leith, Lord Bothwell returns to Edinburgh without the Queen's permission. In the face of Darnley's arrogance and Edinburgh's restlessness after an ice-locked winter, the Queen is quick to perceive insult. Bothwell's enemies sense their advantage and move with lightning speed.

I have not even heard of Bothwell's arrival when I come to court that day, but Lord James is already speaking urgently into the Queen's ear when I arrive in her chambers, and there is a buzz of conversation in the rest of the room. Darnley, low down in her affection, stands by Rizzio looking glum.

"What has happened?" I ask the Italian, steeling myself to speak to him, looking at his twisted shoulder rather than his face.

"Your master has landed at Leith on a ship from France, un-announced and without permission," Rizzio says. "His timing could hardly be worse."

"What business is it of Lord James's?"

"He comes on behalf of the lords to report, before Bothwell can get here, that he is guilty of slandering both our Queen and Elizabeth in France," Rizzio says with a smile. "He has called them both whores, or some such."

"She surely won't believe it's true," I say, turning away impatiently.

"There are witnesses."

"It does not take much for a man to fall from favor here," says Darnley. "A word of accusation in her ear and her love is lost."

"All the more important, then, for a man to conduct himself im-peccably," says Rizzio. "Do not be petulant, my Lord. Stay true to her and you will win out."

"I have seen no man truer to her than Bothwell, but I am afraid of that expression upon her face," I say.

"Observe, my Lord," Rizzio says to Darnley. "In Scotland, when the Queen wears such a look, we whisper that heads will roll—often her suitors'. It may be to your advantage that a scandal with Bothwell takes her attention from you."

When Lord James finally leaves, the Queen beckons me to join her. She is white with rage.

"What do you know of this?" she asks.

"I know nothing except that some evil rumor comes about your loyal captain."

"It has been witnessed in France that these very words have come from Bothwell's lips: 'There is not between the two queens one honest woman.'"

"I have never heard him speak of you without love," I say. "Does Lord James say who these witnesses are?"

"He does, and furthermore they will testify against Bothwell."

"To what charge? Hearsay?"

"Treason."

"Your Grace, you surely can't believe this is anything more than Both-well's enemies plotting against him. He has never been untrue to you."

"How can I know that? He has been imprisoned for much of the time I have ruled. He escaped and ran away from Scotland. I have barely been able to have him here in court, he is so rough and uncouth."

"He has been defending your Borders with his life, while the other lords grow fat here in Edinburgh!"

"Enough. I am in no mood for this. Is there not one person left in this domain who respects me?"

I bow my head.

Later in the day, Bothwell's old friend Sir William Murray is given permission to speak to the Queen, though she refuses to see him privately. In front of the court he lowers himself to one knee.

"Your friend Lord Bothwell has abandoned his post in France and returned here without my permission," she says. "What excuse do you make for him?"

"Your Grace, Lord Bothwell begs your pardon for his presumption," says Sir William. "He says there are matters of grave importance he must discuss with you, which could not be entrusted to letter or messenger. His concern, as always, is for your well-being and the well-being of your kingdom. He begs that you grant him an urgent audience."

"Indeed. But I hear that Bothwell has committed treason and has come racing to Scotland to deny the charge."

Sir William blanches. "I do not know of this, Your Grace," he stammers. "Lord Bothwell has ever been your loyal servant. Surely you remember that he has served you all these years and your mother before you, often at great personal cost? Perhaps some rumor has been exaggerated or some action misreported?"

"Perhaps," she says. "But until I have further intelligence on this matter, I will not grant Lord Bothwell an audience. Keep him by you, Sir William, so that I know his whereabouts."

"Your Grace, it may be that an audience with him could lay this matter to rest."

"No!" Her voice is loud enough to reach every corner of the room. There is a shocked silence. Sir William bows his head lower.

"Lord Bothwell is to remain in your keeping, Sir William, until I am ready to speak to him. That is all."

≈ ≈ ≈

With Bothwell confined, she leads the riders of the court out on the first hunt of the season.

Both horses and riders are soft-muscled and out of condition after the winter, and the single deer that the beaters flush out of hiding in the park is a poor, wasted creature with hardly the strength to run. But we set off in pursuit, the dogs baying. It is a tonic to me to lean low over my mare's neck, to see the trees sprouting tiny buds and the spring flowers pushing through the soil.

The Queen and I draw ahead of the others, as always, but soon there is the sound of hooves behind us and Darnley gallops up. He strikes the horse a blow with his whip and it keeps pace with us, though at least he has the wit not to overtake the Queen. He has a strong seat, though by the look of his hand on the whip he would ride a horse into the ground without a second thought.

We gain on the deer, the three of us neck and neck, the horses blowing but excited now, the deer bounding for its very life. When we are almost upon it, the Queen calls out and swings her horse around. Darnley's charger rears back on its haunches when he pulls it to a halt. The deer crashes away into the woods, the dogs on its trail.

"You're letting it go?" Darnley asks her, smiling.

She smiles back. "It survived the worst winter in my lifetime. It would be cruel to kill it before it has its strength back."

"You are merciful. When we have all recovered from this winter, I hope I may join you in pursuing this one again."

They smile at each other before the rest of the riders gallop through the trees and pull up around us, the horses dark with sweat, riders with flushed faces.

We take the long way back to Holyrood. I drop to the rear of the party to get away from their glances and his smiles. How can she bear such sycophancy? But it seems his humility is working on her as they ride back side by side at the head of the party, conversing privately.

Rizzio is waiting in the courtyard when we return, his face alight as he comes running to meet the Queen. Never one to miss a theatrical moment, he makes his announcement loud enough for the whole party to hear.

"Your Grace, Nicholas Throckmorton has arrived from London with news from Queen Elizabeth."

The Queen's face lights up, and she swings her horse in a tight circle before the grooms help her dismount. Behind her back, Darnley looks at Rizzio, trying to gauge what the news might be. Within the hour he may have stepped closer to being the King of Scotland, or Lord Dudley might have snatched the prize from his grasp. Elizabeth is famed for being capricious and unpredictable and Throckmorton might bear any news.

"Give me time to dress, and I will see him in my chambers," she says to Rizzio.

Darnley and I are both left behind as she walks swiftly into the palace. He does not know that both of our lives hang in the balance here, on the word of the English Queen. My hope, just a small castle a day's ride away. His, a kingdom.

Twenty-four

An air of expectation fills the palace as the evening closes in and the riders of the hunting party change into evening wear. We gather in the great hall, where a seat of honor has been set for the English ambassador. But time passes and there is no sign of the Queen or Throckmorton. We stand in small groups drinking and talking. There will be headaches tomorrow from so much wine on empty bellies.

At last, long after darkness has fallen and the dinner has spoilt, Rizzio sends for me. I find the Queen seated on a chaise by the fire in her chamber, hands over her face, shoulders shaking. Seton and Lusty are trying to comfort her and Rizzio stands nearby.

The Queen rises to her feet, her face tear-streaked. "She dares to call me her sister, she dares to say she holds me in affection! All this time, she has kept me waiting on her favor and now—this!"

I turn to Rizzio, eyebrows raised, as the Queen begins pacing.

"Elizabeth has sent word that no matter who our Queen marries, she will not name her as successor to the English throne," he says.

At his words, the Queen gives a low, anguished cry, and weeps anew. Inside me, something freezes.

"Almost four years I have wasted, unmarried, to take her instruction," she says in a strangled voice. "I have become an old widow while she prevaricates, and all along she never intended to give me what is my right!" She collapses to the floor, sobbing. Seton rushes to her side and tries to hold her.

"Run for some laudanum, Robert, lest she do herself an injury," Rizzio says.

I push open the door and step into the corridor. I do not care if the Queen hurts herself with her hysterics. The same despair is flooding through me. She, at least, still has her Scottish kingdom. My castle has been snatched from me again.

It is a long way through the corridors to wake the new apothecary, an elderly grizzled man who looks to have been chosen for his inability to commit an indecent act. He answers the door in his nightshirt and quickly takes me to the dispensary. I wait while he prepares the laudanum. At last he hands me a vial. He shows me a portion between thumb and finger. "No more than this much at once."

I turn away from the sight of that room. As I run back down the corridor, Darnley steps out from a dark corner.

"Robert," he hisses, dragging me close. "For God's sake. Tell me what has happened." His breath stinks of wine and he is unsteady on his feet, but his grip on my arm is like iron.

"Surely you're not asking me to break the Queen's confidence?" I reply, catching my breath.

He twists my arm behind my back in a practiced move, wringing an exclamation of pain from me.

"Elizabeth has refused our Queen the succession, no matter who she marries," I say, and his grip slackens. I pull my arm free and step back.

He lets out a breath. "It is not Dudley, then."

"You are free to woo her now, with all your charms." I rub my wrenched shoulder. "She has lost what she longed for—she may as well find some comfort if you can offer it."

He laughs. "I can offer much more than comfort. My own claim to the throne is not far below hers. When the two are put together, they make one formidable claim in the place of two lesser ones. That is the comfort I can give her. More desirable than ever, wouldn't you say?"

He grins at me in the dim light of the corridor. He has a young lifetime of ambition burning in him, hotter than even the Queen's, as intense as my own. He knows that a throne is never easily won. For him this is a setback only.

The image of Blackadder Castle rises in my mind and I find myself clutching the vial so hard that it hurts. I have thought my chance to win it severed tonight, along with the Queen's English succession, but I could align myself with Darnley and put his ambition into the service of my own.

"I must take her the sleeping draft," I say at last. "She is in a terrible state. Let me go."

He pulls the vial from my fingers, opens it, takes a quick swig, kisses the lip, corks it, hands it back to me. "Let her know we will share this sweet sleep tonight, and tomorrow I will speak of strategy with her."

I say, "You've already lost her once through haste. Speak to Rizzio before you do anything."

The laudanum is already taking effect, and he sways on his feet as I turn away. "Kiss her for me, Robert," he calls, his voice slurring. I break into a run.

≈ ≈ ≈

When the Queen is drugged and calmed, Rizzio and I withdraw to the presence chamber, leaving the Marys to undress her. It is the first time I have been alone with him since my return and my gorge rises. But to succeed, I will need his help.

"This is grave news," he says, waving me to a chair. "It is true, Elizabeth cannot wipe out the Queen's succession rights, but refusing to name her is a serious threat. If Elizabeth dies unmarried and childless, which it appears is her intention, Parliament may find that another has a stronger claim. Especially if that other is a Protestant."

I take up the goblet of wine he has poured. "Darnley is roaming the corridor drunk, saying that the two of them have a better chance at the throne together than either alone."

"Foolish hothead," Rizzio says. Then he smiles. "Or not so foolish. He is right. Their children would have a powerful claim if Elizabeth died unmarried."

"She has not even agreed to marry him and you are planning what thrones their children might claim?"

Rizzio sits forward and fixes his gaze on me. "She will marry him, if he is not a fool, and you and I will see that he is not. He is our Queen's best hope, and yours too."

I shrug. "I do not care for the castle."

"You lie," he says. "You want it more than ever. And I will help you. I have made it my business to know more about Scottish lands and who has the care of them than any other in court. Lord Hume feels himself the ruler of the Borders. The Queen needs a way to assert her power over him. Your castle is the perfect tool."

I stand and go to the fire so he cannot read my face. I know what treachery lies in his breast. But aligning myself with him may now be my only hope. "Why should she marry Darnley if his hand does not guarantee her the succession?"

"There is no one else suitable and no one who could bring her any closer to the English throne than he," Rizzio says. "It will do her chances no harm, at least. Go and talk to Bothwell in the morning. Find out what he knows. We must decide if we shall put our weight behind this or not."

I laugh. "You and I? To decide the Queen's hand?"

He looks at me seriously. "You would be surprised what matters I may advise her in."

≈   ≈   ≈

Bothwell is pacing the room in Sir William Murray's house when I arrive the next morning.

"Has she come to her senses, then?" he asks.

"Not yet." I sit down and accept a hot drink from a servant. "The Italian sends me. Throckmorton brings news that Elizabeth will not name the Queen her heir, no matter whom she marries."

He slaps his knee. "Good. She can send Darnley back to England."

"It is too late for that," I say. "She's lonely. Darnley is handsome and attentive. He says their claim on the throne is stronger together than either alone. Once the Queen realizes this, how could she not marry him?"

"Her ambition will be her ruin!" he says. "God, I would have married her myself and we could have ruled Scotland better than it's been ruled since she was born!"

"If only you'd been taller, you might have wooed her."

"If only she'd been shorter," he snorts. "Perhaps these ruling women are half men, as Elizabeth likes to say. What else makes our Queen so freakishly tall?"

181

"Elizabeth said she had the heart of a man, not the legs," I say. "But have a care. You are already under the charge of treason."

"Treason," he grunts. "That liar, Lord James, who would bring his sister down in a moment if he could have power in his hands again, accuses me. Our old friend Hume has no doubt had a hand in it. I tell you this, if the Queen truly wishes to marry Darnley, I will support her with all means at my disposal. You should do the same."

I look at him in surprise and he shrugs. "If I were to speak freely, I would tell the Queen to send Darnley away at once. But I am in no position to say that. So you will tell her only that I am her faithful servant and I delight to hear that she will marry."

"What of the rumors about him?" I ask.

"If she has lost her heart to him, then you must never let a word against him pass your lips. Go back and pledge yourself to this marriage. I see no other path to your castle."

We both stand. "If the opportunity arises to put in a good word for me, please take it," he says with a grin. " I'd like to hold on to my head a little longer."

≈　≈　≈

I return to Holyrood in the dark of late afternoon. When I tap at Rizzio's door, it is some time before he answers. At last he lets me in and I find Darnley flung across his bed, snoring in a drunken sleep.

"Don't worry, I doubt he will stir until the morning," Rizzio says with a grin. "He has an appetite for liquor, this one, but no stomach for it. The Queen herself couldn't rouse him now."

I sit by the fire and warm my hands while he pours a whisky that sends fire down my throat. "Bothwell says he will support the Queen in her marriage if it is her will," I say.

Rizzio rubs his belly. "Very politic. She has already sent Maitland to London with a letter demanding permission for the union."

"I thought you wanted to gather information first?"

"She is beyond reason. She has gone to Leith with a small party, and we are to follow with Lord Darnley tomorrow. He does not know about the letter yet. It will not hurt for him to feel himself in our debt."

"I cannot see how he will be in my debt," I say, standing up to leave.

"She wants this marriage. She told Throckmorton today: "My heart is my own." She has had enough of waiting on Elizabeth's favor."

"Does he know her mind?" I look toward Darnley, his face flushed in the firelight, his mouth hanging open.

"He has not been allowed to see her this day," Rizzio says. "It's best for now he knows little and is kept occupied—he has too many ideas of his own and too little experience. Tomorrow we will take him to follow the Queen."

I cross the room, but he stops me by the door. "They will be married," he says. "Are you with me?"

In the silence, there is a roaring in my ears, the roaring of the river that runs below my castle. Drunken Lord Darnley, with his innocent boy's face and his lewd, knowing eyes, is my only means to get there.

"Yes," I say, and in that moment, condemn her to him.

Twenty-five

Spring, the season of love. The Queen orders the court to Stirling Castle. Lord Darnley devotes himself to winning her back and I devote myself to helping him.

Seton is never distracted from her love for the Queen, but the warm season is playing its magic on the rest of the courtiers. Lusty has married John Sempill and left the court, the first of the Marys to depart from the Queen's service. La Flamina pines for Maitland, sent with his letters to Elizabeth, caring not that he is near twenty years her senior and divorced. Beaton flirts openly with the English envoy, Randolph. Has the Queen directed her women to make love matches where it will do her the most good, counteracting the masculine play of power with a feminine web of liaison and desire, where words are whispered into pillows, and confidences made and broken?

Since hearing from Elizabeth, the Queen has been cool with Darnley. But at Stirling, under the force of his charm, she melts. She laughs like a girl and leans close to him. She is happy.

However, he still has not grasped one essential element of courtship, that of allowing her to long for him. He is by her side constantly, his suit unrelenting. He does not know about the dance of seduction, stepping forward, then moving back, the coming together, the drawing apart, the turning away. He is a boy and, when he wants something, all he knows is to put out his hand to take it.

≈ ≈ ≈

On a sunny April morning we are mounted in the courtyard, the horses' coats gleaming in the sun, the air so clear it hurts. We are waiting for Lord Darnley to appear for the hunt, but he is not an early riser and this is not the first time he has held up the party. This morning no one minds terribly. The horses arch their necks and prance, laughter rings out, the dogs sniff and wag around our mounts' legs.

At last Darnley's manservant appears and makes his way to the Queen. She bends in the saddle to hear him and straightens when he has finished.

"Lord Darnley is unwell and will not join us this morning," she announces. "Let us go, then." But her disappointment is plain.

When the deer pulls ahead of us in an overgrown part of the forest, instead of pursuing it even harder as she usually does, she reins in her horse and waves the party to a halt. The dogs disappear on its trail and a quietness falls.

"I have no heart for this today," she says. "Let us go back."

Rizzio comes to meet the Queen in the courtyard and whatever he says causes her to dismount swiftly and hurry inside. I swing to the ground and take his sleeve before he follows her. "What is it?"

"Lord Darnley is gravely ill," he answers. "I thought it best she go to him."

"This is good news." I hand the reins to a stableboy. "It may be just what is needed."

"Perhaps." He is uneasy.

"What? Is it some foul disease he has fallen to?"

Rizzio is pale. "I'm sure it is no more than measles."

"Strange for one of his age to have measles," I say. Rizzio's eyes slide away.

Quickly the rumor circulates around Stirling Castle that it is no ordinary rash affecting Darnley, but a virulent and agonizing outbreak across his entire body. Our refined Queen may not realize the significance of his symptoms, but even the stableboys know the marks of syphilis.

That evening I wait for Rizzio outside his room, startling him as he comes to the door.

"Is it true he has syphilis?"

Rizzio unlocks the door and pulls me inside. When the door is shut he turns to me, his face set. "The court physician says it could be measles. The cook's babe has it."

"She cannot marry him if he is syphilitic."

"Most of her other suitors probably are too."

I stare at him and he looks back, unflinching. "Nothing is safe in a royal court. You, of anyone, know it. We play deadly games every day."

"Could you send her into this, knowing the risk?" I ask.

He sits down. "I serve her, Robert. She wants two things: her right to the English throne and to marry for love. Darnley is her best chance for both."

I am surprised, in a dull way, what I am willing to do in the cause of my castle. I cannot resist the chance to taunt Rizzio. "Perhaps you should see the physician yourself. Darnley was in your bed only weeks ago."

"Get out," he says in a low voice.

≋   ≋   ≋

I do not know what happens in that sickroom, except that the Queen emerges with a flush on her cheeks and a tremor in her hands. Her kingdom has shrunk to this one room. Her divine service to the people has shrunk to serving one man.

She calls me to his chamber early on the fourth morning. Darnley is asleep and even at rest the change in him is shocking. The rash still patterns his body; I can see its livid trail running down his throat. The vital young man of just a week ago has disappeared.

"I did not realize he was so ill," I say.

She smiles at me and her face seems lit by some inner glow.

"Last night I thought I might lose him, like I lost Francis," she says. "But I bargained with death and pulled him through."

"When did you last sleep?"

"I take snatches here and there," she says, with a wave of her hand.

"He does not look well yet."

"The cook's infant has died of the measles. The physician has examined Henry this morning and said he should recover fully, as long as he has careful nursing."

I register her use of Darnley's first name silently. "No doubt you can leave the best nurses here with him when we go back to Edinburgh," I say.

"We're not going back to Edinburgh without him. I promised him that if he survived I would marry him."

≈ ≈ ≈

The Queen transfers her court to Darnley's room, justification perhaps for having housed him in the King's chambers when he is not a king. She conducts meetings and attends to correspondence. Men come and go, speaking to her awkwardly, glancing sideways at Darnley, who smirks at this demonstration of his place in her affections.

He shows no wish to recover too quickly. He rolls his head weakly, and the Queen places a compress on his brow. He lifts his limp hand and she is there with a sip of water. The musicians play and servants bring food. The fire crackles through the day and the night. He tosses his long legs when he is bored, and she strokes his head and devises some new entertainment to keep him happy.

She calls for Lord James. He comes to the bedchamber entrance, steps inside, and bows shallowly.

"Dear brother, come here." The Queen holds out her hand from the chair next to the bed.

"Thank you, sister, but I have a slight cold and the court physician has advised I should stay away from Lord Darnley, lest in his weakened state he succumb to another illness. If you can bear the inconvenience of raising your voice a little, we may converse from here."

"Certainly." She smiles. "Robert, pour my brother a glass of wine."

"Thank you, but not wine," he says. "Sister, it hardly seems private in here. Perhaps we should speak alone."

"Those here are my trusted companions."

He looks around briefly, his glance flickering over each of us. "What do you wish to discuss?"

"Brother, a matter of the highest importance concerning my state, my people, and my own happiness. I wish you to be the first among my lords to know that I will marry Lord Darnley, giving Scotland a king and, by God's will, heirs to the throne."

She has gambled that this unexpected announcement, in Darnley's presence, will force Lord James to give his blessing. But she underestimates him. He stands silent for a moment, his frown deepening.

"Madam, surely you do not take such an important step without the advice and opinion of your Privy Council? I shall call them together at once and advise that you wish to discuss the matter of your marriage."

"I shall certainly call them together, but my mind is made up," she says. "In this matter I will not be instructed by my Privy Council, nor any other."

He pauses. "Elizabeth has given her consent to this? I had not heard."

"Elizabeth has always suggested I marry an English noble, and there is no other so highly ranked, nor so suitable," says the Queen, her voice cold. "I am the Queen of my own kingdom, I do not need her permission to marry."

"But perhaps Darnley, who is her subject, does?" Lord James strides across the room. "Madam, there is a great deal to consider here, and not least the matter of religion. Scotland is a Protestant country now. You cannot marry a Catholic. I have it on good authority that Elizabeth will never approve of this marriage and that it will be the end of peace between our countries and the death of your hopes for succession. You must take advice on this."

The Queen tightens her lips and reaches across the bedcovers to take Darnley's hand. "I tell you once more, and I am your Queen, I will marry this man."

"As for the succession," Darnley pipes up, "once my claim and Mary's claim are joined, they become one claim so strong that it cannot be easily put aside. On the matter of religion: I am a pious man but I do not mind so much in which church God is worshipped. When I become Scotland's King, I am willing to worship in the manner that brings the greatest peace to the country. You need not fear."

Lord James looks over at the bed in contempt. "I see you have chosen yourself a man of principle. His moral code is stamped across his body for any to see."

He turns abruptly and strides to the door. When he reaches it, he turns. "I cannot countenance this union. I will call the Privy Council together to force you to see reason. You may be a queen, but where a queen marries is a matter of concern to every man in the country. You do not have the right to make this choice alone. I wonder you do not treasure your own health more highly, Madam."

He walks out into the hushed presence chamber, where even the musicians have fallen silent.

"I have the measles," Darnley calls out behind him. "Nothing more than the measles. Ask the court physician."

Rizzio looks through into the presence chamber and gestures at the musicians, who hastily strike up their instruments. "Let's call for some more wine and drink to your marriage. Your brother doesn't believe in celebrating, does he?"

The tension eases at his words and a murmur of conversation starts up. A servant begins pouring more wine. The Queen crosses the room to stand where Lord James himself stood, by the window.

"Don't worry, my beloved." Darnley holds out his goblet. "He cannot bear that his bastard birth has denied him a kingdom. Let him call the Privy Council. What can they say?"

"Better to call the Privy Council yourself." Rizzio joins her at the window and presses a goblet into her hand. "Here, drink. You are pale. Your brother forgets himself. There is no reason to think the rest of the lords share his views. Call them together yourself and give them the news."

"You are right," she says, and takes a swallow of wine. "We will convene the council at once."

She turns to Darnley and smiles, and he has already forgotten—if he ever realized—what he has said about religion, and she takes another sip of wine and perhaps she promises herself to forget too.

≈   ≈   ≈

She prepares for an Easter celebration the like of which Stirling has never seen before. She will hold a lavish feast at which Darnley is the guest of honor and, reviving an old tradition, she also orders preparations for a servants' feast at which she herself will wait on those who serve her. I have little heart for such celebration and I am relieved when she sends me to Edinburgh carrying messages for the Privy Council members, drafted in Rizzio's laborious hand.

He accompanies me to the courtyard to see me off.

"She asks that you come back for the feasts," he says. "But Lord Bothwell goes to trial in Edinburgh and I thought you would like to see him."

"What difference can I make?" I gather up the reins to mount. "She will probably have him beheaded, will she not?"

He puts a hand on my arm to speak for my ears only and I suppress a shudder at his touch. "She will need a soldier like Bothwell on her side if Lord James incites the other lords against her. We must make sure he survives this trial."

I laugh. "What do you expect me to do?"

"Do not let Lord James carry out his own vengeance," he says. "Send word at once if Bothwell is at risk."

Twenty-six

The trial of Lord Bothwell. There would barely be a man in the country who has held so loyally to the Queen, and barely one punished more for it. Likely that a hundred men will call the Queen a whore across Edinburgh's taverns this night—even John Knox does so—but they do not have Lord James Stewart, the Earl of Moray, as their enemy.

I do not realize how formidable a foe Lord James is until I arrive in the city. It is a spring evening in Edinburgh, long and warm and light, and the streets are crowded with men on horseback, thousands of them, wearing his colors, their armory clearly visible. Mothers pull their children close; men keep their backs to the stone walls and watch impassively. His soldiers do not go to their lodgings, but ride around the streets, grim-faced, so that any who may sit on the jury that judges Lord Bothwell tomorrow will feel the weight of the force against him.

Sir William Murray's house is outside the Flodden Wall in the Canongate, away from the city's stink. Armed harquebusiers challenge me before I reach the door and I must wait until a servant can fetch Murray himself to let me in.

"I am glad the Queen has seen fit to send someone," he says as he leads me inside.

Bothwell and William are sitting together and they rise to their feet as I walk in.

"Does the Queen send protection?" William asks.

"Only me." I can feel their disappointment. "But I have permission to send for help if it is needed."

William shakes his head and Bothwell sinks to his chair again. "Is it true the bastard has filled the city with soldiers?"

"There are thousands of them."

"Does he think I am an old woman, to be frightened by numbers? As if he would dare to have me struck down in the street!"

"It is the very kind of thing he would dare," Murray says. "Some soldier would carry the punishment and he would be rid of you."

Bothwell spits on the floor. "If he wants to be rid of me, let him come here in single combat and try his luck."

"Enough!" says Murray. "Listen to me. It is not safe for you to go to court tomorrow. He is intimidating the jury and stirring up the citizenry. If you are present and found guilty, the crowd might take the dispensing of justice into their own hands—there is no crime in killing a treasonous man."

"What do you suggest?" Bothwell asks. "There is not time to ride to Stirling and back tonight with reinforcements from the Queen."

"Your cousin and I will represent you in court," Murray says. "I will increase the guard and you must stay in the house. I do not believe they will drag you from here by force."

William's face is angry. "If the Queen is so concerned, why did she not at least send men?"

≈ ≈ ≈

There is little sleep for any of us that night. Murray retires to his room; Bothwell sits by the table, wide awake; William falls asleep in a chair. I doze on the floor. The clink of weapons, the low mutter of voices, and the clatter of horses' hooves move through my slumber.

When I open my eyes, the air is changing from black to gray. William and Bothwell are sitting at the table, their backs to me. The murmur of their voices has risen a little. I lie still.

"I am sick of it," Bothwell is saying. "All I want is to live my life and serve the Queen. A few more riches perhaps to pay my debts. Instead I spend my life dodging prison."

"The thing a man most desires is forever out of his reach," William says.

"If I survive this, I will ask the Queen to let me come home and marry. I will find some woman who likes her bed and make a brood of children on her. I do not like this feeling that if I am hanged tomorrow, there is nothing left of me."

"Offspring are not always as you would expect them to be," William says.

Bothwell drops his voice, but I can still hear him. "Ah, but your offspring is so fascinating. To live in disguise all this time! She fooled me utterly."

"Perhaps she is not even mine. You can never tell with women what lies they may tell you."

Bothwell laughs. "William, you fool, of course she's yours. Just look at her."

William grunts and I hear him shifting in his chair. I press my eyes shut and keep still.

"You have yourself a treasure there," Bothwell continues. "Have a care with her. If I had better prospects, I would half think to marry her myself."

"I have ruined her for marriage." William's voice is heavy. "She has no dowry, no lands, no title, and she is old now. I have done wrong by her and I do not know how to right it."

I cannot bear to hear any more and I stir loudly and roll over, yawning and stretching, silencing them.

≈ ≈ ≈

I thought Bothwell would be accustomed to confinement, with the time he has spent imprisoned, but he is restless all day, walking around, staring out of the window, giving sudden exclamations of annoyance. He leaves the room and roams the house, but he makes the servants nervous with his agitation, and soon he is back. In spite of his restlessness I am relieved. William and I have no words to say to each other and the silence between us is oppressive.

Late in the afternoon we hear the sound in the streets—a swell of voices, a faint but powerful roar like thunder rolling behind Arthur's Seat, portentous. We look at each other. The guards below stir and take a tighter grip on their weapons.

Murray and Bothwell's cousin Sir Alexander Hepburn come galloping down the Canongate. They stop and confer with the guards, then stride inside. In a few moments they are at the door and we are all on our feet.

"The jury was rigged, or bribed, or threatened," Murray says. "I'm sorry."

Bothwell takes up his whisky and downs it in a gulp. "Will I hang, then?"

"You have not been sentenced. They must now refer it to the Queen—and therein lies your hope," says Murray. "I asked for surety from Lord James that he and his men would leave you safe while he sent word to the Queen, and in front of the court he agreed."

"I will go." I stand up. "I will plead your cause."

"Take some of my men with you and make haste," says Murray.

I can count those who have lost their lives through displeasing the Queen. Chastelard, the beheaded poet. John Gordon, the beheaded rebel. The captain of the Gordon castle, kicking and swinging from the rope that hanged him. The Queen's apothecary, hanged in front of a jeering crowd. Angelique.

The thought of Bothwell joining them makes me push the horse faster and faster down the road in the dark to keep ahead of the feeling. Faster than Murray's men, whipping their horses to keep up with me. Faster than any messenger from Lord James carrying a request for a death sentence. Faster than my own thoughts. Faster than the whispered conversation between Bothwell and William when they thought I was asleep.

Only one thought catches up with me before I reach Stirling. Did Bothwell truly think I was asleep—or did he intend for me to hear?

≈ ≈ ≈

The Queen's banquet for her servants is underway when at last I force my groaning, lathered horse up the steep hill at Stirling and into the courtyard.

The great hall is crowded with those who invisibly keep the royal castle running. The kitchen hands, the cooks, the scullery maids, the gardeners. The higher ranked servants are seated around the tables that normally they serve. The lower ranked are crowded together at the rear, looking around this forbidden room with wide eyes. On the tables are foods they are rarely permitted to eat: the succulent freshly roasted meats and soft white manchet bread of the nobility.

I stand still, catching my breath, looking out for the Queen. Lord Darnley is sitting on the dais talking to Beaton and Seton. The Queen herself is carrying a tray of food. In the center of the room some of the servants have pulled back the chairs and are striking up a lively jig. She approaches them, lays down her tray, and joins hands with the baker to dance a polka. The rest of the kitchen servants surround them, stamping and clapping.

"When the Queen must woo her own servants, rebellion is brewing somewhere," Rizzio says from behind me.

"I must speak to her," I say. "They found Bothwell guilty."

"The wrong word here could hang him. She will send him to his death if she thinks he has besmirched her honor."

I watch her, laughing out loud as she takes another servant by the hands to swing around in a circle.

"There is one chance," he says. "Many of the lords do not want this marriage and she fears Lord James will rally them to oppose it. Freeing Bothwell will be a slap in the face for Lord James, and at the moment she longs to put him in his place."

"I will make sure she knows that," I say.

"No. Let me."

I hate that I must trust him with this task. An unbidden thought of Angi makes me shiver and I cannot maintain my usual indifferent semblance. I turn to him, my fists clenched.

"If you are untrue in this, Italian, I will come to you one night and carve such atrocities into your flesh that you will beg me to kill you more quickly."

The vehemence in my whisper causes him to blink and he walks away without a word.

The Queen has returned to the dais and Rizzio makes his way over to her. He speaks briefly to Beaton before sitting down by the Queen. He leans across and says something that makes her laugh. At the same moment, Beaton approaches Darnley and draws him to his feet and onto the dance floor.

Alone with her, Rizzio draws closer, and both their faces grow serious as he speaks. Then they draw apart, the Queen frowning. Darnley comes back from dancing and she turns to him and laughs as if the whole matter is nothing, her face moving from contemplative to delighted in an instant. She takes his hand and rises and they move onto the dance floor, so much taller than everyone else, like a queen and her consort from some glorious fable. When I meet Rizzio's eyes, he gives the tiniest shrug of his shoulders.

≈ ≈ ≈

I leave the feast, unable to stomach such merrymaking. I take to my chamber but do not sleep, and at first light I am up. I come into the hall as the last few servants are stirring and the musicians are stretching their tired arms and sucking their bleeding fingertips. I come across two figures curled up together in their grease-smeared clothes, and as they sleep I see it is the Queen's baker and a younger boy from the kitchen, probably the one who kills and plucks the birds with deft fingers. His fair hair falls across his pink cheeks, lying on the baker's chest, gently rising and falling. I stare at their soft faces and the sight hurts.

I make my way outside and through the garden to climb up on the parapet that runs along the castle wall so the monarch may stroll its edges and survey the kingdom in all directions. I feel a stirring in my blood that I had not thought to know again.

I stare down at the gardens on the plain below and then across to the forest blanketing the hills beyond, the hunting ground where she will go today after deer. She will have her huntsman strike one down for her and never give it another thought. Does she think of those men, and the woman, she has ordered killed? Or are they as the deer: sport, unmourned and unremembered?

Abruptly I turn away from the forest vista and stride the length of the parapet. I am damned if she will take one more thing from me. I will go to her at the start of today's hunt. I will go on my knees and beg.

The party is gathering in the courtyard, the dogs whining and anxious to be off in the spring sunshine. Servants are holding the horses but everyone is running late this morning after the evening before; riderless horses are everywhere and those who are dressed and ready stand about sipping hot spiced wine and blinking in the sunlight.

As the Queen emerges, fresh and untroubled as if she has slept long and deep, a rider arrives at the gates with a commotion of hooves. I hasten my step, but there are dogs and horses and servants and nobles between me and her and I must dodge and weave. As the messenger is being brought inside, Rizzio, with his faultless timing, steps out from behind a horse into my path.

"Let me pass!" I push him.

"If she has decided he will hang, do you think you will change her mind, here in front of her hunting party?"

I try to shoulder past, but his delay has worked. The messenger is down on one knee before the Queen, head bowed, parchment in his outstretched hands.

"The matter of Lord Bothwell?" She unfurls the message and reads it. "Rizzio?"

"Madam?" He steps through the horses and strides to her side.

"Pray attend to this message for me." She hands him the scroll. "Lord James wishes to know what sentence should be laid on Lord Bothwell for his misdemeanors. Draft an answer and see that the messenger returns at once with a good-sized escort. We would not like our instructions to be misunderstood."

Rizzio nods, and I edge closer. The Queen steps onto the mounting block and takes the reins in her hand.

"Lord Bothwell has caused me a bother once more, but he has ever been my loyal servant," she says loudly. "I impose a punishment of one thousand marks on him to be paid to the Crown, and I order him to return to France to his post of Captain of the Scottish Guard. Rizzio, arrange his passage. It would be expedient if he were to leave immediately."

My legs shudder and give way beneath me and I slump down till I am sitting on a mounting block.

The Queen swings onto her horse. The master blows his pipe,

the hounds burst into full tongue. All around me is a confusion of clattering hooves and wagging tails, and then they are gone, streaming out the gate and down the hill, leaving the courtyard silent. A stable-boy helps me to my shaky feet. Rizzio gives me an enigmatic Italian smile and disappears.

≈　≈　≈

There are weeks of meetings and discussions, and gatherings of the lords where the Queen cajoles, threatens, and makes promises to garner their support. She negotiates with ambassadors and sends letters to shore up support from Spain and France. A rift widens between those lords who would lend their weight to the marriage and those who implacably oppose it.

I come to the Queen's presence chamber one morning to find Lord Hume and some of his men among the crowd waiting to confer with the Queen. I have not seen him since I returned from France and even now, though I am disguised, the sight of him gives me a rush of fear.

I am wary of asking the Queen about him, but now that Rizzio and I have made an alliance—unholy though it is—I go to his secretary's desk of papers and maps.

"Is Lord Hume staying long at court?"

"For a while," Rizzio says, scribbling. "The Queen needs all her supporters close by. He's a Catholic, you know. He thinks the marriage is a good idea."

"Does he know of her promise to me?"

Rizzio lays down his quill, cracks his knuckles, and rubs his face. "As far as I know, he does not. But you should keep out of his way, lest he start asking questions once he hears the Blackadder name. I have something to keep you busy."

"Not Darnley."

"You have a knack with him. I need to help the Queen work out who to bribe and with what."

It is a natural division of labor. Rizzio, with his carefully garnered knowledge of power and title in Scotland, works with the Queen while she negotiates and pressures and bribes the reluctant lords. I keep Darnley's worst excesses under control until the deal is made and they are safely married.

Lord James, when he cannot change his sister's mind, withdraws from court. Once he is gone, rumors spread that he is plotting with the other lords who oppose the marriage. It is whispered that if the nuptials go ahead, a coalition of lords will rise up in arms against the Queen and Darnley. John Knox condemns the Queen and her proposed marriage from his pulpit and talks of taking up arms to defend the reformed faith.

Such a brutal whirl of diplomacy leaves the Queen with little time to register Lord Darnley's behavior. I have seen hints of his character flaws, but the ugliness of his transformation now that he has won the Queen's pledge is a shock.

Rizzio calls me to Darnley's rooms late one night, when most of the palace has retired from the presence chamber. I can hear banging and crashing issuing from the bedchamber, and Rizzio has lost his usual calm.

"He will ruin things for himself and all of us," he says in a low voice when I enter. "Drink is usually enough to stop him, but tonight it's made him worse. He's threatening to go to the Queen's bedchamber and take his husbandly rights, and the fool is in such a fury he might try it."

"What do you want me to do?" I ask.

He hesitates. "He needs to lie with someone."

"Finding a whore in Stirling shouldn't be too hard."

"Not a whore, Robert, a boy. One who can be paid enough to keep his mouth shut."

I will not let myself think of how it will be for the Queen in the marriage bed of such a man. "Where am I to find a boy at this hour of the night?"

"Surely there is some boy here in the castle who knows about such matters, and can be paid into silence?" He sees the look on my face change. "I thought you would know one." He presses a heavy pouch into my hands. "Pay whatever it takes. Hurry."

The door to the bedchamber flies open and Darnley stands there, clothes crumpled, cheeks flushed, hair wild. Rizzio jumps up and goes to him.

"Get away from me," Darnley says. "I'm going to the Queen. I'm sick of your crippled favors."

"The Queen is indisposed, but there are other pleasures in store for you." Rizzio leans closer to speak in Darnley's ear, while gesturing at me to go.

≈ ≈ ≈

They are sleeping near each other under a table in the kitchen. I put one hand on the boy's shoulder and clamp my other hand over his mouth to muffle his waking. The baker does not move and no one else stirs either as I lead the boy outside. I whisper in his ear and his eyes widen. I draw out the coins, the sort of money a kitchen boy will never see in his life. It takes only a moment for him to make a choice. Still believing he has one.

"Should you ever speak of it, you will die or wish you were dead. Not even to him." I jerk my head in the direction of the kitchen.

I have brought a cloak with a deep hood, large enough to cover him completely. I lead him past the guards, who know I am on Rizzio's business, all the way to the King's bedchamber. Rizzio has Darnley on the bed, talking to him quietly. He waves us over.

When the boy is close enough, Rizzio gestures at me to pull back his hood. In spite of the kitchen grime upon him, he is a handsome enough lad, broad-chested and fair with strong arms and blue eyes.

Rizzio stands and moves away from the bed, and he and I back out of the room. I draw the door closed.

"Let's hope he's tougher than he looks," says Rizzio, sinking to a chair. "When Darnley is aroused in rut, he's an animal."

"I will bid you good night, then."

"You will need to return the boy. It won't be long. Have a drink."

Indeed it is not long before a sharp cry issues from the room. Rizzio grins lewdly, but the cries rise in pitch and even he begins to look concerned. Sickened, I walk to the fireplace and crouch in front of it, poking at the logs.

200

"Let us hope he doesn't start screaming," Rizzio says.

The sounds reach a fevered pitch and abruptly cease. Rizzio waits a few minutes, head cocked, and stands. "I'll get him."

When he emerges from the King's bedchamber, the boy gives me one hunted look and lowers his face, streaked with tears. He is limping painfully, but when I put out a hand to assist him, he jerks away and pulls the cloak over his head.

"He's asleep, thank God," Rizzio says. "The boy has done well. Next time we'll have some eggs—the whites help to ease the passage."

The boy flinches, and I lead him out of the room. We walk slowly back around the courtyard, down the hill to the kitchen entrance. He turns to go inside and I stop him and hand over the bag of coins. He takes it without a word.

"I'm sorry," I say. "I didn't know it would be—"

He is gone, down the steps and into the darkness.

Twenty-seven

The Queen travels all over the countryside building support. We stay at Ruthven Castle, Seton Palace, Callendar House. All the time the threat of rebellion by the recalcitrant lords lies heavy upon us. The Queen changes our departure and arrival times at the last minute, alters our routes and destinations at short notice, and never travels without an armed guard. On Rizzio's advice she sends a letter recalling Bothwell from France.

In Stirling I returned the kitchen boy to Darnley's clutches several times, until he disappeared one night, leaving even the baker no word. At each new stop Rizzio sends me to find a boy to satisfy Darnley. Few of them can be prevailed upon to go to him a second time.

When we are back in Edinburgh, the Queen calls me into her chamber one evening after a long day of meetings. Rizzio is seated by her side and the Marys are playing cards with Darnley.

"Darnley has asked that we go out tonight, he and I and yourself, in disguise," she says.

Rizzio looks up, alarmed. "Madam, there is great unrest in the city. Pray find some other entertainment."

But the Queen sets her face. "I wish to see the mood of the people. The marriage will go ahead and I would know what will reconcile them to it. It will be good for Darnley too, to have some contact with the ordinary people he will rule."

"At least have Robert carry your pistolet," Rizzio says.

≈ ≈ ≈

The stones, having baked in the summer sun all day, hold the heat like a fireplace and I can feel it burning up through the soles of my shoes. The Queen's pistol lies hard against my side under my cloak.

"God, I had forgotten how it stinks here." Darnley wrinkles up his nose as we pass the dark entrance of a wynd.

I shoot him a warning look. "Shh!" When we are in disguise, I am their equal. For a short time they both follow my lead and, no matter how I have come to despise him, it is a heady feeling to have a queen and her betrothed treading in my footsteps.

"Let's go somewhere different this time," Darnley says. "What about that tavern down past Blackfriar's? The Siren?"

I shake my head. "It's full of sailors and thieves."

He shrugs and turns on his heel into Blackfriar's Wynd. The Queen smiles at me and follows him, and I have no choice but to trail behind. It is crowded and I keep a sharp watch for pickpockets.

We reach the Siren and push inside. It's stiflingly hot, packed with men, voices at a roar. It smells of sweat and ale and the street. I gesture to them to wait while I buy drinks. I will not have trouble finding them—they are both a good head taller than everyone else there. I elbow through the crowd to the bar.

The clamor of voices does not diminish, but there is something new and sinister in its tone. I notice sly glances at the two well-dressed merchants, too tall and too bright in spite of my care in disguise. This is a working-man's tavern, for laborers and seamen and those with a trade. Darnley and the Queen are too obviously ill at ease.

I push my way back to them with the ale and we drink, standing close together. No one strikes up a conversation with us.

"Let's go," I say. This time there is no argument. They both nod. I can see the Queen is afraid. The cups go to a passing servant and we jostle toward the door.

I am the first out on the street. I look back to check they are behind me and feel the sly creep of fingers along my thigh. In a flash I have caught an ear and the pickpocket gives a yelp. I twist his ear long enough to frighten him and then allow him to squirm out of my grip and scramble away.

When I turn back, I see he was only a diversion. Darnley is being held from behind by a man with arms like an executioner, and there is a gleam of steel at his throat. The Queen has her back to the wall, staring at a second man who is pointing his dagger at her.

"Bit grand for this kind of place, eh?" the one holding Darnley grunts. "No doubt you have a pretty purse, though, and if you give it to us you can get back to the High Street where you belong."

Darnley carries no purse. The Queen does not have one either. It is me who pays our way.

"I have our purse," I say loudly. I draw out the purse, shake it so that it clinks, and send it on an easy underarm throw to the ground near the Queen.

"Now get yours," says the man holding Darnley.

The dagger presses closer to Darnley's skin, making him gasp. He stares at me entreatingly, and a wet stain spreads on the front of his trousers. The other man starts patting at the Queen's clothes. His face changes suddenly. He drops the point of the dagger and grabs at her breast with his open hand.

"Jesus," he exclaims. "Quite a treasure hidden here."

The eyes of the other man dart toward them and in a moment it is all laid out before me. The man holding Darnley still has the dagger at his throat. The man facing the Queen has his back to me and his dagger down. I draw out the Queen's pistol. Who can I save?

I see, with a strange clarity, that he will break her heart and bring ruin down on this city. Rizzio says she is a grown woman making her own choices, but in this moment the choice is mine. I could save her from his cruelty and his disease, and give her a chance at joy. For a heartbeat I hold the future of all the country in my sweaty grip on the pistol. But with Darnley gone, the English succession crumbles and with it, my reward.

I make my choice. The Queen shall be wedded to him, Scotland shall have this boy as its King, and I shall have my castle. When the Queen flashes out a swift leg and catches the man facing her in the groin, I raise the pistol and fire upon Darnley's captor.

My aim is true. He takes the shot in the face and falls. Darnley staggers as the blood spatters him. The other man is still writhing on the cobblestones from the Queen's kick.

"Run!" I yell at them, as the door to the tavern starts to open.

Darnley hesitates. I grab the Queen's hand and pull her, calling him to follow.

I take us twisting and turning through the back alleys. With the roar of voices behind us, we weave and duck and turn and double back. I don't dare stop until we reach the gates of Holyrood, pull a hood over Darnley's face, and call for the guards to let us in.

When we reach the Queen's chamber, Rizzio leaps to his feet and Seton cries out at Darnley's bloody visage. Rizzio quickly calls servants to tend to him and the Queen, and draws me into a corner.

"We were attacked at the Siren," I tell him. "I had to kill one. The other lives."

He nods. "I will take care of it. You did well."

I lean close to him. "Rizzio, he is not only a bully and a fool, but a coward too. No good will come of this."

Rizzio shrugs. "It's out of our hands now. Nothing will stop this marriage."

"I should have let that ruffian slice his throat."

He looks across at the two of them, Darnley submitting to the ministrations of a servant, the Queen watching anxiously. "But you didn't," he says.

≈ ≈ ≈

The race is on for the royal marriage to take place before the rebellious lords raise an attack. The Queen is waiting for the Pope's permission for her to marry her cousin, and for the return of Bothwell at the word of a messenger. But when a spy arrives with reports of Lord James's army amassing, she decides to wait no longer and has the marriage banns read out at Saint Giles.

Rizzio calls me to the privacy of his own chambers. Away from the court's gaze, his arrogance has disappeared. He is pale with fear.

"The message she sent recalling Bothwell must have been intercepted," he says, twisting his fingers as he paces. "You must fetch him yourself from France. You will have to miss the royal wedding."

I give a bitter laugh. "You cannot think I will mind, Rizzio. When can I leave?"

"At once. I have your safe conduct, and money to buy you and Bothwell the fastest passage back."

I take the pouch from him and he grips my hand. "This is no minor spat among her lords. This is rebellion. What else could Lord James intend with an army but to murder his own sister?"

"Being the Queen's favorite will be no help to you then," I say.

He shudders. "Nor you. Hume's men are asking about you. I am deflecting them, but keep out of their way when you leave. You should travel in heavy disguise."

"That is my specialty, Rizzio." I wrap my cloak around me.

He takes my arm and I can feel terror in his clutch. "For God's sake, bring Bothwell with all haste."

Twenty-eight

It is a relief to sail away from Edinburgh. Every street in the city holds memories, while the sea promises nothing but waves. I long for the wind in my face, for the peace that comes with crossing the sea.

But all of my ghosts follow me. I judged the Queen a murderess, but it is I who have fired a pistol into living flesh and left a man dead. I do not know if she recalls those she has sent to their deaths, but I cannot stop thinking of the boys I have sent to Darnley to keep him busy and the thief who had his knife at Darnley's throat. Perhaps a woman waited somewhere for him; perhaps he had children who are now hungry.

The ship carves its steady course southward. The sailors scurry and scramble, never at rest, while I stand by the rail and watch the empty horizon, thankful I will be absent from the Queen's wedding. Since the night at the Siren, I have seen little of either the Queen or Darnley. I am not surprised he avoids me. I saw him piss himself in terror and he will not forgive me for it.

While I am rocked by the sea, my blood time comes. When the Queen first sent me to France as a soldier to spy on Bothwell, I went to a wise woman who gave me herbs to forestall it and I have not bled since Angi was still alive. I hide my bloody rags and throw them overboard in the dark. I do not want to become a woman – not yet.

≈   ≈   ≈

When William first takes me to Bothwell, I have to force myself to stand still and clench my jaw so that I will not weep at the sight of him.

"Robert says the Queen wants you back."

Bothwell half rises. "Is she in danger?"

"Grave peril," I say. I tell them the tale of Lord James and the other rebel lords, the armies amassing, the rumors of kidnap and assassination.

Bothwell interrupts me. "When was she to wed?"

"It will be done already, if all has gone well," I say. "The twenty-ninth of July."

"She might already be murdered." He pushes away the plate and stands, knocking food and pitcher, leaving the table a shambles. "I have known it. I did not want to leave her, and now it is a week at least till we can get back. Damn that greedy brother of hers. Surely the Earldom of Moray should have been enough for him."

William laughs bitterly. "Would it have been enough for you?"

Bothwell gives a soldier's dangerous grin. "We'll get the first passage."

"She has sent money," I say, jingling the purse.

≈   ≈   ≈

We sail on the *Medusa,* a small, sinister-looking vessel with a solid set of cannons on the deck. The captain takes us by an indirect route, keeping close to the French coast and spending much time peering through his spyglass.

The weather has changed. Sky and sea and wind are portentous with the uprising in Scotland, tasting of smoke and blood and steel. If we arrive to find the rebels have seized the throne and murdered the Queen, then Bothwell will have a price on his head, while my life and William's will be worthless.

Bothwell questions me about the past three months: which lords are loyal, which have rebelled, and any that are prevaricating still. He listens to what I know about forces and numbers, then screws up his forehead and makes his own calculations. He asks about locations and stares skyward to visualize them. My information is old now, but his soldier's mind takes it in, wrings out every detail, and examines the possibilities.

"And what of you?" he says at last, when we have exhausted matters of state.

I look out to sea. "I have been the Queen's loyal servant, doing everything in my power to help her marry where she desires."

"So have you discovered what is wrong with Scotland's new King, long may he live?" he asks.

"There is little right with him," I say. "He is cruel, vicious, cowardly, spoilt, and selfish. It's hard to imagine a worse man to rule Scotland."

"Yet she wants him."

"With a passion. And I have obeyed her will, though the things I have done make me sick."

"Such as?"

It is the kitchen boy I think of. Sending him to Darnley seems the worst act of all and I cannot bring myself to confess it. Instead I say: "I shot a man."

He is silent, but I sense him listening still, this soldier who has killed men in hot and cold blood, for revenge, punishment, and survival. Even, perhaps, for convenience.

"He set upon us when we were in disguise in the city. I would have done better to let him kill Darnley and rescue the Queen from this marriage."

"But you want your castle."

"I did not know the foul things I would do for it," I say.

"It was taken with bloodshed. There'll be bloodshed to get it back," he says. "Have you the heart for it?"

"I have no heart left." My voice is shaking.

He closes his big hand around my forearm and squeezes it. My chest heaves with a dry sob, so close to escaping that it's almost unbearable. He keeps his hand on me until I have myself under control again, and there is something so solid and steady about his grip that I ache when he lets go.

We stand in silence another few moments and then he stiffens, stares at the horizon, and lets out a shout. The captain lifts his spyglass in the direction Bothwell points. A moment is all he needs to confirm the sighting. The wheel spins and the deck tilts suddenly as the ship yaws to one side. Bothwell is gone, down in a few bounds to stand near the captain. In a moment I understand why he chose a small, fast vessel. His sharp eyes can pick a larger English ship on the horizon before our lower mast is visible to them, and we are able to flee before being seen.

We set a zigzag course and lose them by the afternoon, running ahead of them into a storm. Bothwell and William ride it out with all appearances of delight, but I feel wretched. I steal William's hip flask and tie myself to the railing, hunched into a tight ball against the wind and rain. By the time Bothwell comes out to find me, I am half insensible, my head nodding, body rolling with the ship's pitch.

He unties me and takes my weight easily as I stagger against him, slip, clutch, half-fall, recover. Everything is moving—sea, wind, deck, and the inside of my head; the whole world is rocking and pitching. There's rain running down my face and my mouth tastes of salt. He leads me to the tiny cabin the three of us share. William is not there.

"Take your clothes off, and get into bed," I seem to hear him say.

After that there is nothing I can recall with certainty. I dream I am still clutching his sleeve and that he must peel my fingers away. I dream that he presses his lips for one tender moment against my forehead. I dream that he strips my clothes off and wraps his huge body around mine like a blanket and that I fall asleep with my head on his broad chest.

When I wake in the morning with my head split in two, I am still in the sodden mess of my wet clothes in my tiny narrow bunk. There is no room for another body to have fitted beside me.

≈ ≈ ≈

In any spare hours, Bothwell drills me in swordplay. I lack a man's strength and though I am fast with a dagger, I have never had much practice with a sword. The first day that we train, Bothwell has no trouble pinning me, over and over.

"You're wasting your time, my Lord," William calls out sourly.

Bothwell smiles. "If the rebels are fighting, everyone who wants to live will need to know how to use a sword."

Under his tutelage I begin to improve. We chase each other around the ship, up and down the steps and across the decks. During one fight we both leap up and balance on the railing that runs across the middle of the ship, dividing the upper deck from the lower. We inch across it, swords clashing, while some of the crew watch us, cheering and whistling. At the end, Bothwell puts up his sword and bows low, and I do the same. When I straighten, he is smiling.

There is something in his eyes that stirs me and the moment lengthens. Our gazes are locked together and I cannot turn away from him.

The sound of running feet jolts me out of the moment. William is down on the deck below me, his sword raised.

"Let's see what you've learned," he says.

Bothwell laughs. "Show him, Robbie."

I jump down in front of William, hold my sword up straight in front of me, and we begin to fight. To my surprise we are evenly matched and I can see William did not expect it either. Around us the sailors fall silent and I can hear only the clash of steel on steel, the whistle of wind in the stays, and our harsh breathing. I was already panting from my duel with Bothwell but it is not long before William is panting too and the sweat begins to course down his face.

He comes for me hard, giving no quarter, but from somewhere I have found the grace of a sword fighter and he cannot find a way through my defenses.

"Have a care, William," Bothwell calls. My eyes flicker toward him and in that instant William flashes the point of his sword to my throat. I freeze.

"Ship!" the captain bellows.

William lowers his sword. The first boom of cannon fire comes across the water.

"Come and help me, old man!" Bothwell yells, running to the foredeck of the ship.

"You'll do," William says and runs after Bothwell.

≈ ≈ ≈

With capricious winds and dogged pursuers, it is twenty-one days after setting sail from France when we make a last dash for the closest port of Scotland. The ship puts in at Eyemouth just across the border, with the singing of cannon balls in our ears. The English warship pursuing us falls back. The captain sends a last cannon shot

211

in its direction in defiance, though it is out of range of our smaller weapons.

"They would pursue us only if our arrival will make a difference," Bothwell says, as we stand on the deck. "It is good news."

We take the first boat ashore. Bothwell goes in search of intelligence and William and I to a tavern for a meal that isn't salted. Bothwell is back by the time we are halfway through, and he tears into his own plate of meat, dark and juicy.

"The battle hasn't been fought, though there was a skirmish in Edinburgh when the rebels tried to take it over," he says. "The Queen is traveling around, gathering troops to fight them. We're in time."

William hits the table with his fist and grins. "Then let us get to Edinburgh!"

I look at him in surprise. Why is he so enthusiastic?

"No," says Bothwell. "She's called for my help, and it seems she's not yet in Edinburgh herself. We'll gather troops and weapons. In two days I can raise an army here and then we have something to offer when we arrive. I'm still guilty of treason, remember? I must go back with a show of strength and not creep into Edinburgh's gates like a dog."

William nods. When Bothwell goes to find another drink, William leans over the table to me. "It is good you've learned to fight. Lord Hume and his clan will be on that battlefield. You and I will find justice through the sword this time."

Twenty-nine

She has defied them all and married him and, when her own lords rebelled against it, she rode out to fight them.

I can feel the difference of it as soon as we step into Holyrood, bringing two thousand armed men with us from the Borders. When I left, the palace was preparing for a wedding but expecting bloodshed. Now the fear is gone and in its place is a reckless confidence. Even the servants are jaunty.

The Queen calls us to meet her in the great hall. She is seated on the dais, Darnley by her side, and she is dressed as a warrior queen, in gold-plated armor, her hair flowing loose. She is magnificent. My breath catches at the sight of her, no matter how I thought my heart was hardened.

Bothwell and I kneel before her. She offers him her hand.

"We have the rebels on the run." Her voice is strong and clear. "They are cowards and will not stand. We have chased them from Glasgow to Edinburgh and back again."

"We heard there was fighting in Edinburgh," Bothwell says.

She smiles. "When the forces of Lord James tried to take Edinburgh, the people themselves rose up and drove them out. Knox has fled, Lord James hides like a rat in Dumfries, and the rebels betray each other. My army is at Stirling now and I have gathered forces from all over Fife to meet me there. We shall rout the rebels for good, and Lord James shall see who rules this country."

"You will hardly need me, Your Grace." Bothwell smiles back at her. "I thought you a queen. I had no idea you were such a general." He looks up at Darnley, on his throne at last. "I congratulate both of you on your marriage. Together you are a force to be reckoned with."

The Queen laughs. "Come and eat. I'm sure we shall find some task for you."

As we dine, Bothwell listens, nodding and asking questions about strength and forces and location and weaponry. Darnley sits by the Queen's side, all affability and attention. I watch her. When I left, she was frightened and defiant, a child determined to have what she wanted, but afraid of the wrath of her brother and other lords. Now, she tells us, she has donned pistol and helmet and ridden out at the head of an army, into rain that the very devil could have sent. She has set the rebels to flight without a blow being struck. They are not defeated yet, but she has won the moral victory already. With a soldier like Bothwell on her side, there is not much chance the rebels will get the upper hand.

There is something else, too, in her face and her bearing. Our Queen has become a wife while I have been away, and I see it has not been displeasing to her. She has grown from a young, infatuated girl into a woman. Perhaps Darnley is capable of love?

"We should march at once on Dumfries," Bothwell says. "While the lords lead you in this merry dance, they tire your men and run down your supplies, and gain time to build up their own strength. We can leave today for Stirling and take all the men there."

"They have run like rats, and shown themselves cowards," Darnley says. "They have no spine to fight."

"A cornered rat is vicious and a rat's bite can kill," says Bothwell. "We must strike hard, and soon."

"I agree, Lord Bothwell," the Queen says. "I am reappointing you as Lieutenant General of the Borders to lead the army."

"My father is to lead the army, my dear," Darnley says. "It would be unseemly if someone other than the Lieutenant General of the Royal Army took the lead."

"I have not made that appointment yet." There is a chilly silence.

"I can make ready to ride to Stirling at once, while Your Graces discuss the details of the battle," says Bothwell.

The Queen dismisses us, saying she will send word. Rizzio is frowning and I have seen that look on Darnley's face before. There is a sullen cast to his pretty features.

≈ ≈ ≈

Rizzio meets with us again later in the day. "We will all ride for Stirling in the morning to meet with Lord Lennox, who will lead the army."

"The Earl of Lennox is not much of a soldier," says Bothwell.

Rizzio nods. "She wishes you to run this battle, but the King and his father will be at its head."

Bothwell shrugs wearily. "Very well."

I follow Rizzio outside. "How goes the marriage?"

"Until today, it has gone well," he says, checking to ensure we are alone. "But they have fought all afternoon over this matter. The Queen has conceded that Lennox can lead the army, though he's days away and will hold us up."

"What of the rest? Can she bear him?"

"I sent him a courtesan before the wedding to teach him some decent ways. It seems to have worked. She looks happy, does she not?"

I look at him closely. "It is hard to imagine the boy as King."

"He is the King consort only." Rizzio winks. "The Queen has sense enough not to give him the crown matrimonial until he proves himself."

"The crown matrimonial?"

"With it, he becomes her equal. His word carries the same force as hers, and if she dies he takes the crown himself."

"So he is not a real king yet?"

"Not quite."

"What of Queen Elizabeth and the succession?"

He claps his hand on my shoulder. "Darnley has won his prize, but the Queen and you are no closer to yours. Elizabeth is furious that Mary married an English subject without her permission. She has sent the Countess of Lennox to the Tower and ordered Darnley and his father to return to England. She is on the side of Lord James and the rebels."

≈ ≈ ≈

215

In the morning we ride for Stirling. The Queen and Darnley lead us through the High Street before leaving the city and I have never seen such love for her on the faces of Edinburgh's people. They cheer and wave and jump up and down as she passes.

At the Tolbooth the Queen halts. She thanks the people and pledges that we will drive the rebels out for good. She calls on the citizens to bravely defend Edinburgh in her absence. Even the soldiers are smiling and it seems impossible she could ever be defeated. The cheers rise and half deafen us. William, who so rarely smiles, is alight, and Bothwell is grinning too. We ride out through West Port and break into a canter down the hill to join the legions of fighting men.

Our reception in Stirling is less effusive, but still warm. The people crowd the streets to greet the Queen as we wind up toward the castle, having stationed our fighting men down on the plain with the armies of those lords who are loyal to the monarch. The younger Huntly, pardoned and given back his family lands, Fleming, Lindsay, Livingstone, Ruthven, Athol, Mar, and, of course, Hume and his clan.

John Blackadder of Tulliallan has gathered a small army from his estate and ridden to Stirling. William sends word for me to join them in the Blackadder pavilion for a council of war. When I arrive, I find the whole clan gathered. John and Margaret's two boys are there in the tent, along with other cousins I barely know. The Blackadders have not gathered often, lest the Hume clan hear of it and set an ambush.

William sits with his cousins Edmund and Jock, two of the boys from the disreputable branch of the family that raised him. Since the Queen's return to Scotland saw William all but give up sailing, they have taken over his ship, though I warrant it is a darker and meaner business under their leadership. I doubt they carry Sophie's Jews to safety any more.

John gestures for everyone to move closer. "There will be spies every-where. We must cleave to each other with all the honor we possess." He gestures. "Now William will speak."

William stands. "Thank you, brothers. We have the chance to be avenged. Lord Hume, though he is a known ally of Lord James, has judged he would be better to support the Queen this time. We believe he has brought his whole clan here. They will be concentrating on the rebels and not expecting an attack from the rear. This is our chance."

There is silence for a few moments.

"We fight on the same side," says John. "Are you suggesting an open attack?"

"We watch them carefully and maneuver to separate the Wedderburn Humes from Lord Hume," William says. "Then we must strike, all together and hard."

John stands. He is the head of the family and William, the disinherited son, slowly sits.

"Too dangerous," says John. "We'll fight near them. When the opportunity arises, we'll pick them off one at a time. You and I, William, shall aim for David Hume of Wedderburn and Alexander Hume of Blackadder, but we shall approach them like assassins."

William clenches his fists. "They will believe we are still afraid of them."

"Courage must be tempered with caution," John says. "I will not have more of this family slaughtered for no reason."

"What colors will you fight in?" I ask.

William turns to me. "You'll be fighting too. You've had lessons from Bothwell himself. Don't you want Hume blood on your sword?"

John looks from William back to me. I keep my face expressionless.

"Margaret would hate to hear this, but it is your own choice," he says at last. "We will dress as peasants. We could be fighting under any of the lords."

William scowls. "I want them to know who has killed them."

John turns to him sharply. "You must strike like a snake. Fast, invisible, unexpected. This is revenge and we have only the slimmest of chances."

I stand, my heart beating fast. "This endangers all our efforts. The Queen has promised the castle in return for my service as soon as she is named Elizabeth's heir. Would you risk that by murdering the kin of one of her loyal lords? You might strike David and Alexander down and even escape alive, but I tell you, the Queen will not be pleased. This could lose lives and our chance at the castle in a single stroke." I sit down again.

"You have nothing to contribute to a council of men," William says through gritted teeth. "You will have to prove yourself on the field if you want to make a suggestion here."

Every man in the room is watching me. "I am not afraid to fight with you," I say. "But it will get us nowhere. I beg you, don't throw our chance away like this."

John steps back into the middle of the pavilion. "This has been a bloody struggle for our family. Too many Blackadders have lost their lives for this castle and I will not add to the tally willingly. But we must act as one. We will spill Hume blood. *Vise a la fine.*"

See it through to the end, the words that twine around the snake on the family crest. There is a roar of assent from every man in the tent. William turns to look at me and I nod with the rest of them.

≈   ≈   ≈

At last Lennox arrives at Stirling, five days late, fat and flustered. Within two hours Bothwell has struck camp and the armies are ready to march under the standards of their lords.

Stirling's citizens are relieved to see the last of us. They line the streets and cheer our backs and wonder how they will feed themselves through winter without the food and drink that we have stripped from their stores. The men are just as relieved to be moving. It is harder for an army to wait than to fight once it is wound up for battle.

William and I are riding with Bothwell at the front of the armies and so we do not have the chance to watch Lord Hume and the different branches of his family march out under their banners.

Bothwell is so delighted to be riding out at last to do battle with Lord James that a grin is spread across his features. He winks when he catches me staring at him and claps his hand on the hilt of his sword. "Don't be afraid, Robbie. You're on the winning side. A good way to fight your first battle."

William is smiling too and the whole of the Queen's army is at my back. Perhaps it will be as John says: we will strike hard and invisibly at the might of Hume. Perhaps we shall find Alexander Hume, who holds Blackadder Castle, and cut him down.

My longing for the castle rises in me, hot and sharp, and I want to strike a blow for it that will make my family look at me with respect. Taking the life of a Hume is a possibility in my hands this day and my lifelong fear of them turns into blood-lust. I can feel it humming through my body as we canter south.

The great column marches for three days. The year has turned and the days are rapidly shortening, the temperature dropping. Our breath is mist in the mornings and the horses are growing in their winter coats.

A day out of Dumfries a messenger gallops to meet us and the leaders of the army stop to greet him. The Queen sends for Bothwell and, when they have all conferred, Darnley pulls his horse into a theatrical rear, wheels it around, and canters down the line.

"The rebels have fled in front of our strength," he calls loudly. "They have stolen away to England, showing themselves for the cowards they are. We are victorious. God save the Queen!"

The cheers roar out around us. I look at William. His face is bitter and he smashes his fist against his breastplate.

Thirty

The estates of the rebel lords, seized by the Crown, must be redistributed, and a new web of power woven that secures the allegiance of the loyal lords and binds them to the throne even more tightly. Rizzio, having studied the landholdings of Scotland, works with the Queen each day, discussing alliance and allegiance, power and persuasion. Scotland must also present a strong face to England, and the Queen must soothe Elizabeth's rage and petition to have Darnley's mother released from the Tower.

For the first week Darnley attends the meetings, but his interest quickly wanes. After a tantrum in which he spills wine across a valuable map, ruining it, the Queen appoints me to keep him entertained. I must take him riding and hawking while she and Rizzio decide the matters of state.

I take a perverse pleasure in my small cruelties to Darnley, riding far enough that I know he will complain on the way home, pushing our horses over rough ground to try and bruise his arse. For I came into the Queen's chamber one morning when she was not expecting me. She was sitting on a chaise in her nightgown, her hair in disarray. The fabric of her nightgown was torn, and beneath, on the pale skin of her upper arm, I saw a plum-colored bruise. When she followed my glance and saw it exposed, she hastily pulled the sleeve up to cover it.

"He is young," she said. "He does not know his strength sometimes."

But she had to face away from me to compose herself. I kept my head bowed until she spoke in a normal voice again.

Darnley has not changed with marriage. What a fool was I to think he might.

≈ ≈ ≈

She calls Bothwell to discuss matters of state, and the new structure of power and favor in the kingdom plays itself out at the dinner table. Rizzio, seated next to the Queen, has never stood so high. Bothwell, after his disgrace, is now her most valued military adviser. She seats him by her other side.

Darnley, coming in late with flushed cheeks from hunting, is forced to sit on Bothwell's far side. He drinks heavily. When the Queen tries to include him in the conversation with Bothwell, he snaps at her. Rizzio leans across to speak to him, and is rebuffed too.

But the Queen does not seem troubled. She and Rizzio converse with an easy intimacy, sprung from their many hours together. A stranger to the court could think Rizzio the King and Darnley a highly ranked noble.

After dinner, the Queen and Darnley take to the dance floor together and for a while they are simply a handsome couple again, tall and slender, moving gracefully. But he lifts her up and holds her in the air, and something changes in his smile as he stares up at her. He continues to hold her suspended until she says something in an urgent whisper. Then he brings her down none too gently. When they return to their seats, her hand strays to her waist where he has gripped it.

Bothwell makes his way to my side. "Perhaps the Queen's marriage does not go so well," he murmurs.

"Perhaps not," I say. "Lord Bothwell, how goes my father?"

He shrugs. "Bitter. Old. I think he has forgotten that you are his daughter, not his son."

"I have almost forgotten it myself."

"Do you not wish to marry?"

I laugh and gesture at my boy's clothes. "Who would marry me?"

"If I could give you freedom, I would marry you," he says. "But serving the Queen has been very expensive. My creditors are holding my own castle. I have nothing to offer you."

"You are kind to think of it," I say.

"It is not kindness," he says, his eyes fixed on mine. My body responds with a rush of heat, shocking me.

It is nothing like what I felt for Angi. How could it be? Then, I knew no better than to throw myself open to her. Now my heart is a hard and twisted thing. Nevertheless, I had not thought to feel anything again. The castle was to be my fortress.

"She comes," he says. The Queen is moving toward us. I bow my head so she does not see the expression on my face.

"Excuse us, Lord Bothwell," she says. "Robert, dance with me."

I follow her to the dance floor and we join the flow of couples. When she leans in close to speak, none can hear.

"I have not forgotten you," she says. "I have been considering your castle, but it shall have to wait a little. I am with child."

The last sentence is in a whisper and she draws back smiling. "I will announce it tomorrow, but I wanted you to know."

"I thank you." I drop my head. My hands are shaking and I try to still them so she does not feel it.

"You are so formal now," she laughs. "Do you remember when I first came to Scotland, just a girl? We had the leisure to ride all day and then dress up and roam the streets at night."

The dance finishes. I bow to her and then watch as she walks back to her seat. Rizzio shifts in his chair to let her pass easily and Bothwell does not take his eyes off her. The King, with his sulky face, looks like an overgrown child.

I will not think of what creature will be conceived from such a union. My castle is not lost, and that is all that matters now.

≈ ≈ ≈

The Queen invites her loyal lords to celebrate Christmas at Holyrood. The entertainments are lavish to celebrate her nuptials, her defeat of the rebels, and her pregnancy. No one mentions aloud the uneasy state of her marriage, or the fact that Darnley rode off in a temper to Linlithgow and then on to Peebles, staying away for three weeks before returning in time for Christmas.

On Christmas Eve she invites her intimates to her chamber. The musicians entertain us, there is more food and more drink, and she plays cards with Rizzio and the ladies. The lords lounge in their sumptuous outfits.

Rizzio, who is better than anyone at cards and loses only when it is politic to do so, wins another round. Beaton throws down her hand, pouts prettily, and refuses to play any longer. The party around the card table laughs. Rizzio bows low in apology. Lord Ogilvy takes his chance to step forward and invite Beaton to dance, and she blushes as she accepts. The musicians strike a lively air and several couples join the dance. The card players sit back to watch while Rizzio shuffles with a fast snap-snap, the cards blurring as they move between his hands.

"Pray, good Rizzio, where is my husband this Christmas Eve?" the Queen asks, her eyes on the dancers.

"He is in the chapel, Madam." Rizzio flicks the cards to each player.

"The chapel?"

He shrugs. "You are not the only one surprised. He has been on his knees these last three hours. He says he will spend the night there."

The Queen shakes her head, perplexed. "I wonder his knees can take the strain," she murmurs. Then louder, "I'm pleased to see his devotion."

The players study their cards intently. In the corner the musicians finish their tune with a flourish and the dancing couples bow to each other and clap.

"I wish you were a woman and I could dance with you tonight," Bothwell says, coming up beside me and speaking into my ear.

I jump, and laugh to cover the moment. "There are plenty of women who would dance with you. You could rescue Beaton from the advances of Lord Ogilvy."

"Beaton does not wish to be rescued. But perhaps you do? Or is there a secret love that you hide from the world?"

"Are you prying?"

"Yes," he says. "How do I know who is the real person inside there? Sometimes a boy, a girl, a woman, a soldier, a spy—which of them is you?"

There is another burst of clapping as the musicians strike a beginning note. Their next tune is a merry jig. The Queen claps her hands and says, "Dance!" Groaning in mock protest, the men push themselves to their feet and the ladies curtsy.

The dancing becomes hard and fast to keep out the cold. Bothwell is still standing close beside me. I inhale his scent, a soldier's smell of sweat and leather and horse, nothing like the scent of a woman. The way he looks at me makes me draw in my breath, and my cheeks feel as hot as Beaton's look. I do not think at this moment he cares if I am boy, girl, woman, or man.

"Lord Bothwell, you are needed." La Flamina emerges from the press of bodies to stand in front of us. "We are short of partners. Would you join me?"

"It would be a pleasure." He takes her outstretched hand. "Excuse me, Robert."

I stand with my back to the wall. When he has gone, I remember some of the tricks I knew as a boy. I slip out of that merry, jostling room like a cat, and no one sees.

≈ ≈ ≈

Fat snowflakes drop slowly to the ground in the courtyard and the sounds of merriment from the Queen's chambers drift down among them. I stand still. Soon the marks of my feet across the courtyard will be obliterated.

A glow shines from the Abbey where the King, if Rizzio is to be believed, is spending the night on his knees. I cross the white expanse of snow and step into the vestibule. The heavy door is ajar and I creep inside to spy on him.

Candles are burning near the altar. I walk up the aisle like a soldier, silent on the balls of my feet, peering to find him.

A rumble from the front pew startles me. Darnley is stretched out fast asleep, his cloak wrapped around him. His mouth is open and his cheeks are flushed. As I draw near, I can smell the wine on his breath and another snore rasps out.

I stare down at him. My hopes, the Queen's hopes, the hopes of a kingdom rest on this boy. I should slice his throat right now and put an end to it. But this snoring King brings the Queen closer to the English throne and me closer to my castle.

The snow is still falling as I step outside and shut the door behind me. I can see my tracks on the snow and beside them another, fresher pair.

"It is only I," Bothwell says softly and steps forward from where he's been waiting in the shadows. He wipes the melted snow from my cheek with his thumb, and takes my face in his hands.

Kissing him is nothing like kissing Angelique. He is not a tall man, but he is strong and thickset. He has a grip that could kill—and yet he kisses me tenderly. He draws his lips from mine and looks at me with a silent question.

I lead him out of the Abbey, around to the small gate into the cemetery, the snow falling on our cloaks. My feet follow the path through the graves of their own accord. The old gate creaks open and we slip out unseen.

We kiss against the wall. His cheek is rough against mine; he has hair where I have known only soft skin and there is nothing sweet in the taste of him, but I press against him as though we might become fused.

Voices and footsteps echo from up the street and he pulls his cloak around us both. I tuck my head down into his warmth as the revelers pass us, laughing and whistling. When they are gone, he moves me to his side, still under his cloak, and we run away from curious eyes, through the snow to his lodgings in the Canongate. He bars the door behind us.

≈　≈　≈

I am twenty years old and I have never known a man. I wish that he would blow out the candle, but instead he stokes the fire high and lights more candles while I stand in the middle of his chamber and melted snow runs off me. Then he stands in front of me, reaches out, and removes my cloak.

He takes a long time to undress me, as if he knows that I could take

225

flight. He removes my clothes item by item, stopping to peel off his own as well, so that by the time I am stripped to my skin, he is too.

My curiosity is no less than his. He steps closer to hold me when I start to shiver, and he is all hair and muscle, soft and hard at once. His member, that strange thing, is straining upward, pressed between our bodies, and at first I cannot even look at it, but pull him to the bed so we can hide under the covers. Then he pulls me on top of him and in a moment I am kissing him in earnest.

But when he rolls on top and penetrates me, it hurts. I stiffen and cry out and he holds me still and kisses my neck and strokes me and waits until I begin to move again. As his own pleasure mounts he moves faster, driving into me. I cannot tell if this feeling is pleasure or pain; it is both. He makes sounds like an animal and all I can do is hold on with arms and legs. I could not escape from him if I tried. At last, with a deep thrust, he groans and falls heavily across my body so I am pinned and can hardly breathe beneath him. We are both slick with sweat and I am sore, aroused, aching, awaiting release.

Another sound comes from his mouth and I realize he is snoring. I hold myself still, though I would like to batter his barrel chest with my fists. When I cannot bear the weight of him any longer, I squirm and push him, and he wakes enough to slither off me and murmur a half-question. I turn away from him and he rolls up behind me, pressing his body the length of mine. He is asleep again in an instant. I do not want his touch, but it is cold without it.

≈   ≈   ≈

I wake, slowly, with a headache from the wine. I can see by the light in the room that it is late on Christmas morning. I raise my head. Bothwell is crouching by the fire, blowing it into life. I watch him coax until it is crackling. When he sees I am awake, he strides back across the room as if he scarcely notices he is naked. He kneels by the bed. When he sees the look on my face, he sighs.

"I did not do well by you last night." He strokes my cheek. "Wine and anticipation—they make everything too fast. But let me make it up to you. I am not such a ruffian as you think."

I roll away from him, but he gets into the bed nevertheless and lies behind me. His warmth is comforting and he strokes my hair and kisses my neck and though I wish nothing more than to find my clothes and leave, my body has other ideas. Having been denied so long, my desire flares up. I lie still, fighting it, but when his hand reaches around to my breast, a sound escapes my lips and then our two bodies are speaking to each other, moving, sliding, pressing, and when he finally reaches his fingers between my legs, it is so hot and slippery there that we both gasp.

"There is a thing they do, in France," he says, breathing heavily, "For a woman's pleasure; let me show you."

He rolls me onto my back and moves down my body. I arch up to meet his tongue and grip his hair with both hands. He is not as deft as Angi was but my body does not care. I do not want tenderness. I find his hand and push his fingers inside me and the combination of tongue and fingers and need pushes me over the edge and I am crying out. Before I finish shuddering, he lifts himself up and slides inside me, and it doesn't hurt but wrings a groan from my lips. I wrap my legs around him and arch my back. Our cries are matched until he shudders and thrusts and collapses.

This time he doesn't fall asleep, but pulls me close till we are lying side by side, while our panting subsides and the sweat cools. I pull the covers up against the day's chill.

"Now I know you, but you are as much of a mystery as ever," he says, his hand on my hip. "Last night I could swear you were a virgin. This morning you know pleasure well."

When I will not be drawn, he smiles and kisses me. "I have found out some of your secrets, and I intend to find out more. But for that we need sustenance. Let's eat."

I sit up. "I need to get back. The Queen will be wondering—"

He laughs. "The Queen will live without you today. Half the palace will be sleeping off the wine. I will send a message that I have need of you."

Breakfast comes: hot, creamy porridge. Bothwell despatches a messenger to the Queen. We eat our fill and he draws me back down into his arms. This time he lies on his back and guides me to straddle

227

him and the shock of him inside again is still pleasure-pain-pleasure and I do not know which one makes me cry out. My pleasure does not peak this time but it is satisfying anyway. Afterward I fall asleep against him.

It continues for the rest of the day. I keep expecting that he will rise and get dressed and go about his business, but when he does rise it is to stoke the fire and bring me food and drink or use the privy. He comes back to the bed and uncovers me. He explores my body with his eyes, fingers, tongue, lips, looking for my secrets and finding them.

I become brave enough to explore him too, all the ways he is so different, and some not so different. The snow falls outside in big, soft flakes, muffling us from the world. The daylight hours are so short that we are soon back in the no-time of darkness again, with the luxury of warm lodgings and a seemingly endless supply of wood and coal.

Neither of us speaks of what is outside the room, but as the morning light seeps in for the second time, perhaps we somehow sense the footfalls of someone sent from the palace, for we take our pleasure urgently. We roll across the bed and snarl and bite like wolves. I rake his back, I wrap my legs around him and hold hard. Neither of us cares about making a sound, and this time it happens when I am on top, astride, pushing against him. He takes my hips and drives up into me and my head arches back and I forget everything.

Before our breath has quite subsided there is a soft knock at the door. He gets up, speaks to the servant, then comes back to the bed and strokes my face.

"Has she sent for us?" I ask, my hand on his chest.

He nods.

He helps me wash, and then helps me dress in my boy's clothes. When I am ready, he shakes his head.

"You still look like a boy when you are dressed. But you are more a woman than many who wear a skirt. I am confused."

I kiss him. "Perhaps that's what you like."

He grins and pulls me close. "You have been assisting me with some errands. I do not expect she will ask you about them."

In the Queen's presence chamber it's as if we never left. Even at this early hour of the morning, the musicians are playing, Rizzio is dealing cards, and there are courtiers and nobles dancing. Food and wine are laid out in abundance.

The Queen gestures for us to come before her and we both bow.

"I trust you did not work Robert too hard during the Christmas festivities," she says to Bothwell.

"No, Your Grace." He rises. "I needed help with one or two matters and Robert was good enough to assist."

I dare to glance up, having worked to set my face into its usual countenance. I can feel Rizzio watching, but I keep my attentive gaze on the Queen.

"Good," she says. "For I have need of him. The King is returning to Peebles for more hunting and I wish Robert to go in his party."

She is staring at me hard and it takes all my years of practice to stay impassive. My heart sinks at the prospect of the King's hunting party. But until I get my castle back, I still serve her and these are my orders.

"They are leaving before lunch," she says. "You will need to hasten to make ready. Bothwell, you and I will speak this afternoon."

Dismissed, I bow, rise, turn, and am out of the room without a backward glance. Within the hour I am mounted up in the courtyard with the rest of the party, waiting for the King. He emerges with a set face, mounts the latest horse with the misfortune to be assigned to him, and leads us out through the gate, clattering and slithering on the frozen snow. The Queen does not appear to bid us farewell. Neither does Bothwell.

Thirty-one

We arrive at Peebles half-frozen and the weather is so bad that even Darnley, in his rage, hesitates to take out a hunting party. Food is starting to run short already and every meal has the same salted flavor. We wash it down with ale, having exhausted the wine stocks of Traquair House.

It is snowing and time hangs heavily on us. There are two things that occupy my daydreams: Lord Bothwell and Blackadder Castle. I imagine myself riding up to the courtyard of Blackadder Castle, seeing its turrets above the trees from a distance. I imagine the clatter that my horse's hooves will make on the flagstones and how the heavy door will open to admit me. In my daydreams I am not alone there: Bothwell is by my side.

Darnley sits by the fire for hours with his distant cousin George Douglas, bastard son of the Earl of Angus, who talks into his ear late every night. George is young and lithe, with the leanness that comes from being illegitimate and hungering for the privileges his paternity should have brought. I watch their heads low together and the same expression on their pretty faces. George, for some reason of his own, feeds the fire of the King's wrath. At least he keeps him so drunk with whisky that by the end of each evening, Darnley can barely walk and there is no question of my finding someone for his bed.

One afternoon a group of riders canters into the courtyard, their cloaks covered in snow. Starved for news, we attendants crowd to the windows to watch their arrival. A tall figure dismounts with an easy swing and tosses the reins to one of his men.

"A visitor," says George, peering down through the snowflakes.

Darnley raises his head. "Who?"

George shrugs. "Someone most interested in seeing you, to ride in such filthy weather."

In a few minutes a servant taps on the door to Darnley's chamber. "David Hume, Baron of Wedderburn," he announces and the man pushes past him and strides into the room.

On hearing the name of Hume, I visibly start. Deep in the corner of Scotland dominated by Hume, I do not have the Queen's protection.

"Your Grace." David Hume bows. "What has brought you so far from court in this evil winter?"

Darnley scowls. "Court is not to my liking."

"You have chosen an unfortunate time to enjoy the Borders' hospitality. There is little good food and not much hunting to be had in such a season."

"It is a vile corner of the world indeed."

David bows his head. "Your Grace, I have taken the liberty of bringing some modest supplies from Wedderburn and one of my cooks. It is a meager offering, but I hoped to provide you with a meal more fitting for a king."

Darnley perks up. "Did you bring any wine, perchance?"

David smiles. "My man carries a haunch of venison that has been steeping in claret since yesterday. And we bring flagons of our finest French wine."

"Well, break them open. My blood's freezing on nothing but whisky and ale."

I shrink back against the wall although fortunately Darnley's manners do not extend to introducing David Hume to the members of his own party and I am able to melt farther into the background. By the time darkness falls and Hume's men are serving us a feast of Lorraine soup and succulent venison, Darnley is flushed in the face from drinking and beginning to slur his words.

After dinner Darnley, David Hume, and George Douglas draw close to the fire and stoke it till it roars. Their discussion is intent, of some secret matter I surmise. I would leave it be, but I see Darnley's expression change and an evil grin come to his face. The Queen has charged me with keeping watch on him.

I slide along the wall, gradually moving closer to them. The candles sway and gutter and the wind moans as it tries to claw its way inside. Eventually I am close enough to catch Rizzio's name in their mutterings.

"She prefers him," Darnley bursts out. "In her chamber, all hours."

"Hush." David puts a hand on Darnley's arm and leans in. I cannot hear his voice. George is nodding. There is something in their expressions that makes the hair rise on the back of my neck. I edge a little closer.

"We shall do it, then," Darnley says, "with Ruthven. Teach them a lesson."

David Hume catches sight of me and his eyes narrow. "Who is this listening so close to us?"

Darnley half turns to see me. "Robert. Another of the Queen's beloved pets."

I bob my head to hide my face. "Your Grace, shall I make your bed ready?"

"By God, yes." Darnley goes to rise, but staggers. David Hume jumps to his feet and catches him before he can fall.

"Warm my bed and put some whisky out," Darnley says, his words slurring even more.

"At once, Your Grace." I step back quickly. It seems I can feel David Hume's gaze burning into my back as I leave the room.

I reach Darnley's bedchamber and prepare his bed, my fear making my stomach lurch. There is a crash at the door and he stumbles into the room. I take his arm, giving silent thanks that David Hume did not accompany him, and lead him to the bed.

"Take my clothes off," he says as he sits on the edge.

He takes a deep swig from his flask as I kneel and pull off his boot.

"David Hume was very interested in you."

"I can't imagine why." I tug off the second boot.

"I told him nobody knows what you are underneath," Darnley says, as I start to unlace his jerkin. "I told him the Queen allows you all sorts of liberties."

I move to the other shoulder and pull at the leather laces till the jerkin comes loose. My hands are shaking.

"You and Rizzio!" he bursts out. "She lets you in her chambers at all hours, she whispers secrets to you. I bet she lets Rizzio into her very bed, where she will not allow me!"

"Your Grace." I put my hand on his shoulder. "I swear to you that the Queen is your faithful wife in every way. Rizzio amuses her, that is all. Do you not remember how he helped you to marry her?"

He stares at me and lets out a burp. His breath stinks of wine and whisky and I must school my features not to show my disgust.

"He is a misshapen devil," he mutters, and swigs his whisky again. "And you are too secretive."

"Are we to hunt tomorrow?"

Darnley climbs clumsily into the bed. "Very interested, he was," he murmurs as I draw the flask from his fingers.

I take a deep breath. "Did you tell him my family name?"

He mutters something I cannot understand and starts to snore. I breathe out and my body sags.

Any Blackadder to step into this territory has cause to fear for his life. David Hume, if he knows I am a Blackadder, may decide to find me in the night and cut my throat. I dare not leave Darnley's bedchamber. I pull one of his heavy cloaks over me and curl up in a chair by the fire. I pray that the guards outside the door will stand firm if anyone tries to enter.

I have dreamed of Bothwell like a young woman dreams of a lover, but now I come to think I should be like the Queen and marry with a firm eye on the advantage it will bring me. Bothwell is Hume's sworn enemy. If we were to fight for my castle together, what might we achieve?

≈ ≈ ≈

David Hume and his men leave at first light the next day. I watch them from the slitted window of Darnley's bedchamber and, once they have cantered off into the snow, I let myself out and leave him to sleep off the effects of the wine.

The days pass and the snow keeps falling. I keep my back against the wall and speak as little as possible. I lie in bed at night with my eyes open, clutching my dagger, listening for footsteps. I try to reassure and cajole Darnley. He does not mention Hume again, and I do not dare ask.

At last news comes from Holyrood that the French have sent a delegation to invest Darnley with the order of Saint Michael, the highest honor offered by the French King. Even Darnley is relieved to get an invitation so he can return to Edinburgh without losing face. By the time we set out on the freezing three-day ride, the spirits of the whole party have risen and my relief at returning to the safety of Holyrood goes unnoticed among the general air of anticipation.

In my imagination, Holyrood has become larger, brighter, warmer, and more colorful. I am surprised when we clatter into the courtyard that it is smaller than I recalled. But the Queen, waiting to receive her husband with a cautious smile, is as tall as she ever was. She stands to greet him and turns her cheek for his kiss. The musicians strike up and already the discomfort of Peebles is receding. The French party has arrived, the smell of fresh roasted meat is in the air, the winter dark is kept at bay by candles and lanterns and roaring fires. I am safe at Holyrood, as close to a home as I have had since I was eight years old.

There are so many guests at the feast to welcome the King and the French delegation that there is barely room for us all in the hall. I squeeze into a seat with some lower ranked courtiers in a far corner from which I can watch the dais. Who is high in her favor at this time? She seats the King by her side, so that all is in order under the careful eye of the French, who will be watching to see how the royal marriage progresses. Beaton, Seton, and La Flamina all sit at the Queen's table, as do Rizzio and Bothwell. I will him to look at me.

"It's been buzzing while you've been in Peebles," one of the courtiers says. "Madam Beaton is to wed at last."

"I thought Randolph was out of favor with the Queen," I say. "Surely she's not allowing Beaton to marry him?"

"Oh, you have been away a long time," she says. "Randolph is long gone. Beaton is to marry Lord Ogilvy."

At my blank expression she rolls her eyes. "Robert, Lord Ogilvy has forever been the prize of Lady Jean Gordon. She was hopelessly in love with him. But even her dowry couldn't entice him to marry her. She's heartbroken. The Queen has promised to find her a good match but she says she'd rather cut off her hair and go into a convent."

"The Queen has plenty of her own admirers to choose from; she'll find someone to settle on Lady Jean," says another from across the table. "Or one of those young men in the French party, that dark one. He could mend a broken heart!"

There is a ripple of laughter. The members of the French party are uncommonly handsome, especially the young man my neighbor has singled out. But I pay him little attention. My eyes follow Bothwell and there is a feeling in my chest that is half pleasure, half pain.

I sit quietly during the French speeches praising the King and Queen of Scotland and their union. The announcement of the marriage of Ogilvy and Beaton is made by the Queen herself. Beaton blushes like a virgin and not the woman who kept the English ambassador dancing to her tune as long as it was fortuitous. Then the Queen and King invite a select party to accompany them and the French delegation into the presence chamber for dancing and poetry. Bothwell leaves in the Queen's party and I spend the long night alone.

The next morning when I attend the Queen, her chambers are in a flurry, crammed with people and entertainments even before the winter sun has lifted its cold head over the horizon. She calls me into the supper room and when I rise from my knee, she offers a cup of wine. The tiny room is hot and close, the fire crackling in the grate, but after the cold of Peebles even this stuffiness is welcome and I let it seep into me. The French wine spreads fingers of warmth into my belly.

Carrying a child agrees with the Queen. Her face has filled out, her eyes are bright, her long fingers rest on her swelling belly. The visiting French delegation has cheered her.

"Speak to me of the King," she says. "What has his manner been?"

"Your Grace, he was in an unhappy temper at Peebles."

"Why?"

"The crown matrimonial."

"I cannot give it to him unless he shows himself ready for it," she says, with a frown.

I keep silent.

"What company does he keep?"

"There is one George Douglas, a cousin. He left with us for Peebles and was ever in the King's ear. David Hume of Wedderburn came one night and the three of them spoke for a long time."

235

She frowns. "Perhaps this investiture from France will raise his spirits, if he feels some honor is his due."

"I don't know," I say. "But their talk concerned me. They do not wish Rizzio well."

"Now my husband is back in Holyrood, I will keep a closer watch." She strokes her belly. "It is strange to me that our King was so agreeable and mild of manner before our marriage, and then became a changed man after it. Do you not think it odd, Robert, that there was no warning he would prove so difficult?"

"It is strange," I say.

"Perhaps you are not such an astute spy after all," she says, after a silence.

"I have been a poor judge of the King's character. Let me serve you some other way, I beg of you."

"He always asks for you, and there is no other I trust to keep a watch on him."

"I could serve Lord Bothwell, if it pleased you," I say, as if it matters not.

"Lord Bothwell," she muses. "He can scarcely afford any servants of his own. We shall have to do something about it. But that is a soldier's life. Don't you wish for something softer?"

"I will go wherever it pleases you, Madam."

"You will," she says. "I have need of you today. In our entertainment for the French tonight, we will all be appearing in male dress. You will help us get ready."

"Even you, Your Grace?"

She laughs and pats her belly. "Not me, this time. But all my women. We must keep the French delighted and they do enjoy such play."

Thirty-two

I glue moustaches to their upper lips and make sure their breasts are bound, though nothing will make Beaton flat there so I disguise her bosom with draped frills. By the end they are like a group of gorgeous peacocks, bright of face, slender of leg, smooth of skin, as handsome as the French delegation itself.

The Queen, radiant and big-bellied, is the perfect foil for them, their boyishness highlighting her womanhood and showing it off to perfection.

As everyone is going in disguise to the masque, I will too. I have not dressed as a woman since Angi's death more than a year and a half ago, but I am bent on my quarry now. Tonight I will approach Bothwell as a noblewoman, masked so that he does not recognize me. The Queen lends me one of her lesser gowns and sends a servant to help me get ready.

The musicians are playing a merry beat, the buzz of voices rises to the rafters and the hall is hot, lapped by the icy air outside. Already there is flirting and laughter; already every person in the room wants to drive away the winter cold. Some of the more pious of the lords look scandalized, but they do not leave, instead using stern faces as their own disguise.

The Queen and King enter the great hall to a blast of trumpets and the applause rises to a roar. The Queen inclines her head, smiles, and takes Darnley by the hand. His eyes are wide with anticipation and he gazes around the room in delight.

I have placed a half-mask across my eyes, which allows me to move in anonymity. But even with my disguise, the sight of the Hume party across the hall brings goose bumps to my flesh. Lord Hume's glance around the room seems filled with menace.

Just before the masque begins, I find Bothwell. I remember what a woman would do and pause nearby as though I have happened to come to rest. When he catches sight of me and gives a bow, I see from his smile he has no idea who is behind this finery. He turns away to continue his conversation, but when the trumpets blare again for the masque to begin and we all shuffle to clear a space in the center, it happens that we are next to each other as the actors begin the play.

I am acutely aware of the animal scent of him. The heat and un-accustomed tightness of the bodice around my ribs make me sway. He notices and puts out an arm to steady me. When I sag against it, he takes me around the waist, leads me out of the press of bodies to a chair, and finds a cup of wine for me. As I sip it, his eyes are on my breasts, swelling up at the top of my dress. When I catch him gazing, he lifts his eyes to mine with a smile. I thank him without giving myself away and send him back to watch the rest of the masque.

But whatever I set out to do has worked, for he is back by my side as soon as the masque is complete, inviting me to accompany him to dinner. The noise of the hall means he cannot hear my voice clearly, and I take care to speak softly with an accent. I begin to enjoy drawing him to me when he does not know who I am. I let him think I am part of the French delegation. I sit by his side at the table and my body of its own accord does those things that a woman does to attract a man—turning toward him and then slightly away, lips parting a little, looking into his eyes as he speaks and then lowering my gaze.

I am not acting. It is a revelation to find myself as a female animal hunting for a mate. It is as ruthless and bloodthirsty as anything I've known.

The wine flows freely around me. The dancing begins decorously enough but quickly becomes wild and fast, a blur of color and move-ment. I am in Bothwell's arms. It is not just the dancing that makes me pant. My cheeks feel hot, my whole body is charged and vital, the quarry is in my reach.

He leans close to my ear. "Take off your mask."

I smile and shake my head. I know how mystery inflames him.

Our bodies are pressed together and speaking their own language, one that passes through brocade and leather in a heartbeat. His hand tightens around my waist. I am half amused and half angry that I can draw him to me so easily in the guise of someone else.

At last the dance finishes and we come to a halt amid raucous cheering.

"You must be quite out of breath, madam," Bothwell says close to my ear. "Would you care to step outside?"

I nod.

We wind through the crowd just as the musicians strike up the next dance. In the courtyard the flakes of snow drift down, melting as soon as they touch the stone. We stand side by side, drawing in the cold air, but my cheeks won't seem to cool.

He leans in slowly, so that I may pull away, but I can no more pull away than I can catch my breath in the rib-crushing embrace of the dress. Our lips meet and I am so hungry for him it makes me dizzy again. He does not break from the kiss, but brings his arms around me to hold me steady and draws me closer.

This is no casual kiss between a French visitor and a Scottish noble before returning to the dancing. After some moments he pulls back and I reach behind my head and untie the ribbon holding the mask in place. It falls.

A soldier is never taken unawares. His eyes widen a little, but if he is shocked he conceals it well. "You must be an enchantress," he says, coming back for another kiss.

Now his kisses are demanding and his mouth moves down my neck and shoulders, his lips are on the swell of my breast, his mouth hot and the air freezing. The sound of the party drifts out, the snowflakes melting everywhere. No doubt the guard at the gate is watching but I don't care. I am wild and dangerous, my heart thudding, the call of my body insistent. I would have him here against the wall in the courtyard.

"I have rooms in the palace tonight," Bothwell says at last, his breath hoarse. He picks up my mask and ties it on again and then we find our way to his chamber. He dismisses his dozing servant and kicks the fire into crackling life.

I am gorgeously trussed in the Queen's dress, and when he turns me around to unfasten it, I shake my head. I cannot return it damaged, and I cannot get in and out of it unassisted.

We stand, my back hard against a tapestry, the Queen's skirts spread out around our hips and thighs while he finds his way to my pleasure. Once he is inside me, I wrap my legs around his waist. My desire is so great, and the constriction to my breathing so extreme that it feels I will die from them both. I am gasping, my eyelids flickering, lights dancing in front of my eyes, a roaring in my ears. He is in me, deeper and deeper. My whole weight is balanced on him, I am splitting in two, I am falling, the roar in my ears is the Blackadder Water, the stone against my back is my own castle wall. He is groaning in my ear and he drives through the center of me as the fire roars up into the room, as the snowflakes hiss and sizzle, as my body convulses and gasps, as I cannot breathe, as the lights swirl and swirl, as it all turns dark.

≈ ≈ ≈

When I wake, there is a pillow against my cheek. I am lying face down and there is blessed air flowing into my lungs, as cool and life-giving as water.

"Are you all right?" His hands are struggling with the lacing of the dress. I nod and feel him relax.

"I was worried I hurt you," he says, helping me roll over.

I take a deep, shuddering breath. "No," I say, and my voice sounds strange to my ears.

He pours whisky into a cup and brings it across to the bed. I sit and gulp a mouthful and gasp at its fiery taste.

"It's too dangerous for you to stay here tonight," he says. "When you are recovered you must go back to your rooms."

His eyes are dark in the firelight, his lust sated. In its absence I cannot see love there. It is a sobering moment.

He may not love me, but we desire one another. Very well, then. For the sake of the castle I would bind myself to him and forgo love. I like him well enough, and that will serve us when the lust of the body slackens. But now I must use lust to bring about this marriage.

≈ ≈ ≈

The next evening I dress myself carefully as Robert and go to Bothwell's chambers while he is dining with the Queen's party. He has a new manservant, a Scot nicknamed French Paris, whom I send out to the stables with a false order from his master to saddle the horse and wait.

It is late when Bothwell strides through the door. He stops when he finds me there, his hand moving at once to his dagger.

"You surely don't think I mean to harm you," I say.

He drops his hands. "You surprised me." He comes to me and brings his face down to mine for a kiss. I ignore the rush in my belly and draw back slightly.

"I have not had my blood time since you first brought me to your bed, at Christmas."

Our eyes meet. "Jesus." He draws back. "You said nothing last night."

"I meant to. I did not expect it to be so—wild—between us, and afterward there was no time to stay and talk. I thought it better to come to you tonight like this, rather than risking a scandal."

"With this news a scandal is upon you already."

"The scandal is on both of us." I look at him hard. "Remember the Queen's lady and her apothecary? Both were hanged, not just the lady. But perhaps you do not know, for you were in exile then. The Queen was merciless."

He sits, staring at the flames. "What do you want me to do?"

"We must marry. The child will be early and some may gossip, but by then we will be safe."

He jumps to his feet, his face working. "I cannot."

"Of course you can. You are high in the Queen's favor. If you ask, she will permit it."

"You don't understand," he says, pacing. "The state of my affairs is desperate. I cannot even afford my own lodgings in town, but must beg on the Queen's generosity and stay in the palace. I am a hair away from destitution."

"Destitution matters nothing if we are both hanged." There is no act in my anger.

"Let me finish." He halts. "My situation came to the Queen's attention and she has matched me with Huntly's sister Lady Jean Gordon, recently jilted by Lord Ogilvy. She is heartbroken and rich, while I am poor and in dire need of a wife. She announced it tonight, at dinner. We are formally betrothed."

I stare at him. Edinburgh's cold seems to claw its way through the castle walls and into my blood, tracing a path around my body and into my chest until it is a physical pain under my bindings.

He reaches a hand out, but I cannot go to him, or I will be lost and doubly lost. The promise of safety snatched. And worse—my secretive heart did not tell me it had given itself to him.

"It is not only I who did not speak up last night, it seems." I get to my feet. "You were content to take me to your bed knowing you were about to be betrothed."

He drops his hand. "A noblewoman of my acquaintance is much practiced in enchantment and knows how to cast out a child with herbs and spells."

I turn upon him. "You would rather murder your own child than offend Lady Jean?"

He puts up his hands to ward me off. "If you cannot face it, I have a man in my employ who needs a wife. He is a good man, and he would treat you well. If we arranged it fast, perchance not even he would know that the child is not his own."

The cold inside threatens to swallow me. "I am of noble birth, Lord Bothwell."

He spreads his hands. "What am I to do? The Queen has decided, Lady Jean has agreed, it has been announced. I will not be permitted to change my mind, not now. It is too late for us, Robbie. I'm sorry. More sorry than you know."

The few steps to the door feel like the distance across half the city. I reach for the latch and then something makes me swing around to face him.

"I say this to you, Lord Bothwell. Your only chance for a living son lies in my belly this night. Once he is cast out and I am left with that stain on my soul, you will sorrow for the rest of your life, for never will a child of yours live to birth."

He stares at me, shaken, and I am shaken myself by the intensity of my words, based on a lie. My final card has failed.

Thirty-three

It is a witch's creed, to beware of invoking a curse lest it return threefold.

I stumble into my chamber, lock my door, and wrap my bedding close around my shoulders. My teeth are chattering and I cannot warm myself. My enemies are coming closer, the Queen cannot help me till she gives birth, and my chance at safety with Bothwell is lost.

All night I believe I can hear the footsteps of one of the Humes outside my room. When the morning comes, I cannot rise from my bed. I try to move the covers back and the fear that engulfs me makes me whimper. I burrow down into the darkness like some winter creature, shivering, and press my eyes shut.

I feign sickness, hiding in my darkened room while the freezing winter days pass. Bothwell marries Lady Jean with great ceremony, reclaims Crichton Castle with her money, and takes her there to live. When I hear he is safely gone, and that Lord Hume has also returned to the Borders, I emerge back into the court.

While I was hiding, the Queen called Parliament to try and force her lords into drawing up a bill of attainder against Lord James, withdrawing his properties and privileges. She sent for Bothwell to lend his strength to her cause. And she called on her astrologer to cast the charts and examine the planetary aspects affecting her and her favorites.

"Damiot says you will triumph in winning your family's inheritance," Rizzio reports to me.

I shrug. "What does the Queen's horoscope say?"

Rizzio smiles. "No one is allowed to know that save the Queen herself."

"And yours?"

He waves his hand. "I think those who do not like me must have

244

bribed him. He told me I must go back to Italy at once. He said: 'Beware of the bastard.' I will take care that the Queen never allows Lord James into Scotland again."

"There are many bastards in Scotland," I say.

He laughs. "Indeed. But not so many castles. It is time to fight for yours."

The Queen is six months' pregnant and radiant. Though nothing can cover the parlous state of her marriage, I often see her in repose, her hand resting on her belly, her face calm. When the child kicks, she lets her closest ones lay their hands upon her dress and feel the drumming of his impatience to be out. "That is the footstep of a king," she says, laughing.

Back in the safety of her inner circle, my fear gradually recedes. Seton goes home to visit her family, Rizzio sings to the Queen each night before bed, the babe dances in her stomach, and I dare to think again that I might prevail.

≈　≈　≈

Bothwell comes into the presence chamber in smart new clothes, bowing to the Queen with a flourish. I have prepared myself for this moment and I look upon him coolly.

"Marriage suits you, Lord Bothwell," the Queen says. "Your wife knows how to garb you well."

He straightens. "Indeed, Your Grace. She says I dressed like a soldier."

"I pray it is good to be home."

He smiles. "Very good, but too far from your side. With your confinement approaching, I must stay here at Holyrood."

"A pleasure to have you nearby, as always. Does Lady Jean come too?"

His smile does not waver. "She is settling into Crichton, Your Grace. It needs all her attention."

"She is most generous to let you go so soon after wedding you," the Queen says. "Stay with us for supper. Tomorrow I will speak to you of Parliament."

He finds his way close to me when the chatter of the presence chamber has resumed. There is no room for privacy, for which I'm grateful.

"I heard you have been ill," he says. "I trust you were well nursed?"

"I am quite well now," I say stiffly. "There is nothing for you to concern yourself with, Lord Bothwell."

I can see the relief on his face and for a moment I hate him. He leans forward. "It is time you were married."

"If I could get my castle back simply by marrying, Lord Bothwell, no doubt it would be as attractive to me as it was to you. Good evening."

He backs away and I keep my face impassive. I will not show any weakness.

≈　≈　≈

Two nights after the first assembly of Parliament, the Queen invites a small group to share a meal in her supper room. We must squeeze our way inside and around the chairs, but the close quarters are warm in the flickering light of her fire. For the occasion, she has invited some of her other relatives—Lord Robert Stewart, her half-brother, and her half-sister Lady Argyll, as well as her apothecary, her equerry Arthur Erskine, and Anthony Standen, the page.

Rizzio, who has promised to sing a solo later in the evening, is magnificently dressed in a satin doublet and a gown of furred damask. He looks like a king himself and when he raises his cup to make a toast, everyone falls silent.

"To loyalty," he says. "And to the punishment of Lord James, who has shown none."

We raise our cups. "To loyalty!"

"Let that be the last mention of him this night," the Queen says. "I would dwell on happier times ahead and celebrate those who have been true to me."

A servant brings in a veal flory, for the Queen has a dispensation from the Lenten rules so that the babe is well nourished in the womb. He begins to ladle it out and the smell of herbs and mushrooms rises, rich and appetizing.

There is a thud outside the door from the back staircase that winds down into the King's quarters and Darnley appears at the door. The Queen looks up in surprise as he steps into the supper room.

"Red meat in Lent—a queen's feast indeed," he says. "And your favorites here to share it."

"I did not know you wished to join us this evening." The Queen tries to recover her composure. "But I will call for another plate if you wish."

"Don't bother." Darnley waves his hand. "I have eaten this night. As I was not invited to join you."

"You may join us," she says. "I am always pleased to have the King's company."

"But not as pleased as you are to have David Rizzio's company," Darnley says, staring at the Italian.

The Queen sighs. "Peace, my husband. Come, sit by me." She holds out her hand.

As Darnley comes to her side, another thump issues from the back staircase and Lord Ruthven, one of the nobles who supported the Queen's marriage, appears in the doorway. His face is deathly white, his eyes burning and dark. He is wearing a gown, but underneath it I can see armor.

The Queen puts her hand to her heart, as if shaken by his appearance. "You are ill, Lord Ruthven. You should not be so far from your bed."

"I am here to defend the King's honor," he says. "Send out Davy. He has been too long in your chambers and your favor."

All eyes turn to Rizzio, who stares at Ruthven in surprise.

"What offense has he done?" the Queen asks.

"Great offense to the honor of you and the King," Ruthven says. "He has stood between Lord Darnley and the crown matrimonial for his own profit and has made Your Grace banish the nobility, including your own half-brother. He is the destroyer of your kingdom and he tarnishes your own honor by being ever in your chamber."

The Queen stares at him. "Are you mad, Lord Ruthven? David Rizzio is here by my royal wish." She turns to Darnley. "How dare you allow Lord Ruthven to come to me with such accusations? These are my private chambers."

Darnley shrugs. "I know nothing of this."

She turns back to Ruthven. "Begone, my Lord, or I shall have you arrested for treason."

Ruthven ignores her, staring at Rizzio, who looks back at him with a hint of arrogance.

"Did you not hear the Queen?" Rizzio says. "Begone!"

"I will not."

A gasp runs around the room at his defiance. Lord Robert, Standen the apothecary, Arthur Erskine, and I rise to our feet as one. Lord Robert, who is the closest to Ruthven, seizes his arm.

Ruthven throws him off and draws out his pistol in a swift motion. "I will not be handled!" he snaps. "I have come for that man yonder."

Rizzio's bravado deserts him at the sight of the weapon. He shrinks back in his chair. When Ruthven begins advancing, Rizzio whimpers and makes a dash to the window recess behind the Queen.

"Stop this at once!" the Queen cries.

There is a crash in the stairway outside and in a moment men are shouldering into the room, so many of them I cannot count. The Queen screams and I have time to see daggers and pistols in their hands and to recognize George Douglas, the bastard, before the table crashes over and the candles are doused in the fall. Lady Argyll manages to snatch a single taper that lights up the hellish scene.

The room is full of men and in the flickering light I see Ruthven grab the Queen and thrust her at Darnley, who restrains her. Blocked by the bodies, I cannot come closer to her. I struggle and one of them pushes me back hard against the wall.

Rizzio is scrabbling on the floor, slippery with the spilled stew, reaching for the Queen's dress. When he finds it, he holds on as if it will save him. In his terror he shrieks, "*Sauvez ma vie, Madame!*" Then a dark shape lunges across the Queen toward Rizzio and I hear his scream of anguish.

They push past me to take him and his shrieks fill the confines of the supper room as they drag him to the door, until I want to clap my hands over my ears. I can hear his fingernails scrabbling across the bedchamber floor.

"Let go of me," the Queen says to Darnley. "Help him, for God's sake!"

"Don't move." The man in front of her pushes and I hear the Queen's gasp. I peer past his silhouette to see that he has a pistol pressed against her belly.

"Keep your sovereign and wife to you, Sir," Ruthven orders Darnley. "Don't be afraid, Madam. This is done with the King's consent."

From out in the hall, Rizzio's screams rise suddenly in intensity. I can hear the sounds of the struggle, unarmed Rizzio against the daggers of a dozen men. Despite his betrayal of Angi, despite the uneasiness of our alliance since, I could not wish such a slaughter for him.

"Oh God." The Queen clutches her throat. "I beg you, do not kill him."

Rizzio's voice trails off in one last, awful cry that seems to chill the very air, and then silence falls. It is broken by a battle yell from the outside staircase: "*A Douglas! A Douglas!*"

"Bring her into the bedchamber," Ruthven says to Darnley.

The Queen blanches, looking down at the pistol still pressed to her great belly.

"All is well," Darnley says, loosening his grip around her. "You are safe."

They push us into the bedchamber. A smear of Rizzio's blood streaks the length of the floor. The man holding the pistol puts it away and Ruthven disappears into the presence chamber. The Queen sinks to a chair.

"This is a wicked deed," she says to Darnley.

He walks to the bed and seats himself upon the covers. "Rizzio has enjoyed your company and—it is said—even your body. Why should I stand for it? I am a fool in my own kingdom. You promised me when we married I would be your equal in all things, but Rizzio has persuaded you to treat me cruelly. He deserved his punishment."

The Queen puts her hand to her belly and I cross to her side. She waves me away and looks up at Darnley.

"I tell you this, my Lord," she says. "You have known of this evil plan and now you will live with what it spawns. I will never lie with you again. I will be your wife no longer. One day I pray your heart will be torn out as mine is now."

Ruthven staggers back into the room and makes his way to a chair. "Take the counsel of your nobility and all will be well, Your Grace." He slumps over. "Bring me wine, for God's sake!"

Anthony Standen looks around the room. When no one moves, he goes to the sideboard, splashes wine into a cup, and puts it down in front of Ruthven.

"If I die in childbirth from this, then my friends will hold you responsible," the Queen says. "The King of Spain and the King of France, among others, will be revenged upon you if I perish. The very child in my womb will live to see you repaid."

A roar comes from outside, the sound of voices raised. I can hear footsteps and shouting. One of the henchmen peers out the window.

"It is the town watch," he says. "Calling for the Queen."

She goes to rise, but Ruthven gets to his feet. "If you speak to them, we will slice you into pieces and throw you over the wall."

She sinks back to her chair, stunned. Darnley crosses to the window.

"Good people, all is well," he calls down to them. "We have justly punished a papal agent who infiltrated the Queen's household. The Queen is safe. Do not be alarmed. Return to your beds."

He closes the window and comes back to the Queen's side.

"What was David's fault?" she asks.

"He is too Catholic for this kingdom," Ruthven says. "He plotted with Lord Bothwell and caused you to ban your brother from Scotland, which is an evil thing."

"Lord James, my half-brother, called his own army to rebel against me, do you not recall?"

"He is ever loyal to you," Ruthven says. "He will swear his fealty when he arrives tomorrow."

"What do you mean?" she asks. "He is banished in England."

"He is on his way to Edinburgh," Ruthven says. "Your own husband signed his safe conduct from England and Lord Hume and his men accompany him."

Thirty-four

The conspirators remove all of us from the Queen's presence as the night deepens. They take Darnley first and she turns her back on him as he leaves.

I walk to the door. She is fighting to keep her composure, but I can see her terror at being left thus in her chamber, unprotected.

"You cannot leave her alone," I say to Ruthven.

"Lady Huntly will stay with her," he says, pushing me outside.

Lady Huntly, the widow of the Earl of Huntly and the mother of John Gordon, who both died in the Huntly rebellion, has good cause to hate the Queen, even though her husband's clan has since regained its standing. She is waiting at the door and I have almost passed her when she drops one eyelid in a wink, keeping her face otherwise expressionless.

I descend the main staircase outside the Queen's presence chamber, expecting at any moment to be seized. Rizzio's enemies are my own; they have no reason to spare me. Rizzio's blood is on every step and the metallic smell of it hangs heavy in the air. Douglas men are milling around at the foot of the stairs and calling out to each other. I can see Lord Lindsay and the Earl of Morton in their midst.

As I reach the bottom of the staircase, I glimpse Rizzio's body. They have stripped him naked and thrown him face down across a large chest. There is more wound than skin upon him and the blood of his cuts and stabs is still dripping to the floor. The gorge rises in my throat.

"Do not tarry." Standen is waiting for me. "They have sealed the palace doors."

I walk past Rizzio without pausing. The men who were in the Queen's supper room follow Arthur Erskine to a silent corridor, white-faced with shock.

Erskine looks around at us. "We will be lucky to live through this night. But swear, all of you, that we shall help the Queen however we can."

We swear.

"We must find Bothwell," he says. "Pray he has not been murdered too."

With perhaps only hours until Hume and Lord James arrive, my own survival as well as the Queen's depends on finding Bothwell. But when we creep to his chambers, they are empty, the door swinging open. He has gone.

I clutch Standen's arm as my courage deserts me. "What shall we do?"

Erskine looks grim. "We will hide in the wine cellar tonight," he says to us softly. "There is a stout lock and the kitchen servants will keep watch for us. If there is any chance for the Queen to escape, that will be her route and we should know how it lies."

We creep through the servants' corridors, hands on our daggers until we come to the kitchen. The Queen's French servants, terrified at the noises that have drifted down to them, beg us for news of what has happened in the palace. When Erskine fills them in, there are cries of outrage.

"We will find a way to rescue her," he tells them. "There are too many guards tonight, but tomorrow we will make a plan. Will you keep watch if we shelter in the cellar?"

We descend the short, steep flight of stairs into the dark of the cellar and the servants push the heavy door closed. It is all I can do not to cry out with the horror of it, the walls pressing in on us, the cold air and the single flickering candle. We lie down on some sacks and pull up the rough blankets the servants have given us.

"Try to sleep," Erskine says. "We will need our wits tomorrow."

He blows out the candle, but I do not sleep in the thick darkness and I doubt the others do either. Sometime in the night's blackest hours I remember watching David Hume and George Douglas fanning the fire of Darnley's fury at Peebles with their whispers. Now I know what they planned. And David Hume knows I overheard them.

≈　≈　≈

In the morning we climb out of the cellar and make our way cautiously along the corridors until we emerge at the foot of the staircase leading to the Queen's chambers. Armed Douglas men are everywhere. My gut roils with fear as we cross the floor and join the Queen's ladies who wait there, staring at her captors defiantly.

At last the door to the presence chamber opens and Lady Huntly comes down the staircase, her chin high. "The Queen must have a midwife," she says loudly. "She is in danger of losing her child."

Lord Lindsay pushes his way to the front. "It is likely some French trick she plays. Just craft and policy. I will see for myself."

As he shoulders his way up the staircase, a guard seizes Lady Huntly and runs his hands over her. She slaps him away and comes down the rest of the staircase.

"You." She singles me out. "Take me to the Queen's physician at once."

She takes my arm and we hurry down the corridor. As we round the corner, she reaches into her chemise. Swift as a pickpocket she passes a folded note into the palm of my hand and murmurs, "To Bothwell at Dunbar." As we round the corner and come across another knot of Douglas men, she drops my arm. "Get the Queen some food from the kitchens, lest she faint away from the lack of it," she says and walks away.

In the kitchen the Queen's servants keep watch so that I am safe to unfold the square of parchment. In the Queen's looping script it says, *Stand by at Seton with horses tomorrow night.*

≈　≈　≈

I climb out the back of the wine cellar, creep through the cemetery, and emerge into Edinburgh. I make for Sophie's tavern, where I beg a horse. The city is heaving and straining like a ship riding its anchor rope in the storm. The streets are full of people talking and gesticulating in the direction of Holyrood. The road out of Edinburgh is already crowded with riders heading away from the capital. Those who have somewhere else to go—relatives living nearby or country estates—are fleeing, to wait until they know how the Queen's fortunes will turn out.

Darnley has betrayed the Queen and sided with Lord James. And Lord James is on his way to Edinburgh, protected by the might of Lord Hume. I ride as though the army of Hume pursues me, beating the horse when it falters till its hide is lathered with sweat and its breath comes in deep grunts from its chest. Every safety I have known has been torn down and my heart gallops in tandem with the horse's hooves. When I see the silhouette of the fortress of Dunbar against the sea, I almost sob in relief.

Already Dunbar is a soldier's camp. I gallop up to the gates to see a confusion of men coming and going, the clatter of hooves in the courtyard, shouts, weapons being prepared. A lookout calls news of my arrival and in a few moments Bothwell himself comes running out to meet me. Men drag the heavy gate open and slam it behind me, as Bothwell almost pulls me off the horse.

"Is she alive?" he demands.

"She lives." I pull out the note. "She sent this."

"How did you get it?" He almost tears it open in his hurry.

"Lady Huntly was the only one allowed to stay with her last night. But can she be trusted? It could be a trap."

He reads it for a second. "She is my mother-in-law now. Huntly and I left her word to take to the Queen. She can be trusted. Come."

"What happened to you?" I ask as we hurry inside the castle.

"Ruthven confronted me and Huntly after Rizzio was killed. We were armed, having heard the commotion, or he would have slayed us too. When he left us alone a moment, we escaped out the window. We rode here at all speed."

We enter the great hall of Dunbar. A group is sitting around the table and Bothwell leads me to them.

"Word from the Queen!" he cries. "From your mother."

I look at those seated more closely. Bothwell turns to me. "Lord Huntly," he says, gesturing. "His sister, my new wife, Lady Jean

Gordon. The Earl of Athol. This is Robert Blackadder, the Queen's close companion."

I take the measure of Bothwell's wife. Her face bears a look of unhappiness and she is not pretty, but her features are intelligent.

"Our mother is with the Queen?" Huntly asks. "Good."

"The Queen wants us to be ready at Seton with horses tomorrow night," says Bothwell. "She must have an escape planned. But how? Surely we must do more than wait with horses! We must take the palace back by force."

The other men are nodding at his words, but Lady Jean stands. "Read carefully. If the Queen has instructed you to wait, do you not think she has a plan for escape? Your arrival with an army will put the traitors on their guard. She has never shown herself short of courage or wit. Does anybody know how she might be able to leave the palace in secret?"

"Yes," I say and they all turn to look at me. "There is a secret way that I have taken her and the King before, and I left by that route today. Through the kitchens and the wine cellar, into a passage that emerges in the cemetery. It is not far from the King's quarters, but if he is involved in keeping her prisoner, it might be difficult for her to pass by his chambers."

She considers for a moment. "Perhaps she has won the King back over to her side."

"That is a womanish idea," Bothwell says.

"You must consider a womanish idea, my husband, for it is our Queen who is imprisoned and my mother who is our only contact with her, am I correct? They have the Queen as hostage, so force will be of no avail. If they threaten to kill her, you will have to back down. It is like to be the cunning of a woman's mind that will save the Queen this time."

"They will not threaten the Queen's life," says the Earl of Athol. "It is treason."

"This whole plot is treasonous," she says. "The Queen's servant is murdered and the Queen is held against her will. There is only one person in the realm who is above a charge of treason." She looks around in the silence. "What is the King's involvement?"

"When we came to see what the noise was, Ruthven forced your brother and me back into our rooms and told us that vengeance had been taken on Rizzio at the King's own command," says Bothwell.

Lady Jean sits back. "Therein lies the proof. The King is deep in the plot. Ruthven and Moray would never put themselves at risk of treason without the promise of some great advantage, and the only person who could imprison the Queen and not be guilty of treason is Darnley."

"I am sure Lord James has a hand in it too," I say. "He is riding for Edinburgh under the protection of Lord Hume's army. They are due today."

They all stare at me. "Lord James must have known of this," Bothwell says. "But I am surprised that Hume would stand against the Queen. It is treason to support a traitor."

"The King signed a safe conduct for Lord James. He returns to Scotland with royal permission, so Hume does nothing wrong under law. But the Queen knew nothing of such permission and would never have granted it."

I check the room to ensure no one can overhear. "David Hume was aware of this plot. I heard him and George Douglas talking to Darnley at Peebles, though I did not know then what they planned."

Bothwell sits back. "Let that go no farther than us for now. You would be foolhardy to accuse a Hume of such treason."

Thirty-five

It is a cold night, with a lonely wind keening around the towers of Seton. The only other sounds are the creaking of harnesses and the horses mouthing their bits. I warm my hands on the neck of my horse and count my breaths to try and keep track of how much time has passed. I cannot stop myself thinking of Hume and wondering if he has truly thrown in his lot with the traitors.

At last I hear the distant drum of hooves from the direction of Edinburgh. Our horses stir and stamp and prick their ears, and mine whinnies softly until I check him.

There is a moon out and I can see the small group approaching from some distance away. Four horses, some carrying pillion riders. But as they draw nearer, yells break out and the horses scatter.

It is the King's voice that rings out, high with panic. "Hurry! I don't care about the damned baby."

I feel such a surge of hatred for him that I reach for my dagger and kick the horse into life. Bothwell canters past me and calls, "Your Grace? Bothwell and your other loyal servants await you."

The first horse flashes by in the dark at a gallop, two figures mounted upon it.

The Queen's voice comes from the second horse. "Lord Bothwell, it is good indeed to hear you." She is under control but I can hear the strain.

"Madam, are you safe?" He pulls to a halt alongside her. She is mounted behind another rider. "Are you chased?"

"We have not heard a pursuit."

"We must ride at once for Dunbar. Can you manage it?"

"With a horse to myself, I will manage."

The horse that galloped past us returns at a trot.

"Lord Bothwell? I thought you were Ruthven and Morton." The King's voice is petulant in the dark. "They are probably after us now, ready to slit our throats."

There is silence for a moment. "Your Grace, let me help you to a fresh horse so we may make haste," Bothwell says, as though Darnley has not spoken.

"Thank God, it is most uncomfortable riding pillion," Darnley says. "Can someone assist us down?"

Bothwell helps the Queen down from her pillion ride, but no one approaches the King. Standen, who rode in front of Darnley, at last dismounts and gives him a hand. Men stand aside as though some foul creature has slunk past. The hair rises on the back of my neck and I tighten my fingers around my dagger.

Bothwell helps the big-bellied Queen into the saddle of a fresh horse. She has ridden pillion nine miles from Edinburgh, clinging to the waist of Arthur Erskine, but she does not complain.

"Let us ride, then," she says, taking up the reins.

"To Dunbar," says Bothwell and in a clatter of hooves we are off.

≈ ≈ ≈

Dunbar Castle, standing on a crag above the North Sea, is one of the country's most powerful fortresses. Its royal apartments rival those of Edinburgh Castle, and Scotland's store of weapons and gunpowder is under our feet.

"Darnley's door is guarded," Bothwell says, coming into the royal apartment where the Queen has been led. "Now, speak freely."

The Queen sits straight in her chair, her hands resting on her belly. Her face is white, her lips tinged with blue.

"I could not escape without him. If I had left him, the conspirators would have drawn him back into the plot. With both of us gone, they are revealed as common traitors."

"We heard that Rizzio died on the King's orders," says Huntly.

"He says the lords tricked him and he never intended that Rizzio would come to harm," she says.

There is a silence, and at last she bursts out: "I am wed to him. He is the father of Scotland's heir. When the child is born, the King must be at my side to acknowledge it. I won him back from the traitors and that must be enough for now."

"How in heaven's name did you escape?" Bothwell asks. "We planned to come with an army to free you."

She looks up at him. "I persuaded the King that the traitors would kill him too once they had my babe. I won him over and he helped me feign that the babe was coming early. I promised to pardon the traitors if they reduced the guard. They thought themselves safe with the King on their side, and left me with only a midwife. The King and I crept out of his apartments and escaped through the cellars. My loyal men had horses waiting for us outside."

Bothwell shakes his head. "You are extraordinary. It would be hard enough for a man to escape thus, let alone a woman breeding."

She smiles at him. "I am indebted to you for this night, but I must rest if the babe is to be safe. Leave me now."

When they are gone, she lies back on the chaise with a moan.

"I have great need of you, my Robbie," she says softly. "I am surrounded by enemies on all sides. I cannot trust my own husband with my safety. Thank God the child has hung on in my womb through these dreadful days, but I will not do anything else to risk him."

She holds out a hand to me and I go to her side. "I need you to be my lady-in-waiting again. Rizzio spoke to me about you and begged me to take you out of the King's service. Now I can see why and I am sorry I left you with him so long. I needed someone I could trust to keep an eye on him. But now I need you with me. I am not safe in my own chamber! Will you do that for me? Bid your male disguise goodbye and become Alison again?"

She reaches out and takes my other hand. She is the Queen, she is used to speaking calmly when inside she is afraid, but her fingers are tight and cold and I feel her terror. "I am begging you," she says, her lip trembling.

Whatever resolve I have made in the past to keep my heart hard against her melts in a second. I go down on my knees beside the chaise. "I will serve you in any way I can, Your Grace."

"Speak to me as a woman and a friend," she says. "Call me by my name. Will you be constant, Alison? Will you stay by me?"

I cannot refuse her. In her vulnerability, I love her as much as I ever have.

"I will, Mary." I do not think I have ever called her that before. She puts out her arms and I hesitate, and then, daring, come forward and take her into my embrace.

In my arms she feels so slight. Her shoulders are tiny, her belly huge, and she is shaking. The minutes that I hold her stretch out long, in this night of betrayal and danger. She clings to me and I stroke her hair and murmur words of reassurance. I am holding the future of the realm in my arms and it is such a small and vulnerable thing.

"Your loyalty means everything to me," she says. "After the child is born I will attend on the matter of your castle at once. I promise this solemnly."

"Do not think of it," I say. "Your safety is more important." But my pulse quickens at her words.

"I must rest and in the morning I must find the courage to face my husband again."

She draws back and stares into the fire. "I must not let him know I fear him." A grim smile crosses her features. "I think, Alison, that I shall cook breakfast for the men who have helped me this night."

"Your Grace?" I am dumbfounded.

"You will help me. When the King rises in the morning, he shall find that all is very merry here at Dunbar. I shall make a soldier's breakfast of eggs for Bothwell and Huntly and their men and then we shall hold a council of war."

≈ ≈ ≈

Bothwell's soldiers call for support in the surrounding districts and, before the end of the first day, men begin pouring into Dunbar from the Borders and surrounding districts. Within days we have eight thousand armed men at Dunbar, and Bothwell gives the order to march upon Edinburgh.

The Queen rides out proudly at the head of her loyal army. She dresses to show her belly to full advantage, reminding Scotland that she carries its heir and that he is yet safe. She is flanked by her now most loyal lords, Bothwell, Huntly, Athol, Seton. The King rides behind the Queen, his head low. Not one lord will bow to him. He has betrayed some of Scotland's most powerful men during an attempted coup and no one on either side will forget it easily.

In the midst of such danger I hope he does not notice another lady-in-waiting with the Queen. Nor wonder where Robert has gone.

A messenger meets us on the road outside the city with news that when the loyal Earl of Mar held Edinburgh Castle fast and the people of Edinburgh came out with weapons, the traitors panicked. Without Darnley to give their actions legitimacy they had nowhere to turn. When they heard of us advancing they fled, following the same tracks as the Queen's previous rebels, around winding back roads to the border and into England.

The cheering breaks out down the long ranks of men following the Queen and our ride to war becomes a victory march into the city. Edinburgh's people turn out to greet the Queen and their cheering makes my ears ring. Women and men weep openly and try to press forward to touch her stirrups or hand her flowers. The guards hold them back but she smiles and waves to them. It is unimaginable that her subjects would not lay down their lives for her. They would take her enemies with their bare hands and tear them apart rather than see her harmed.

She does not return to Holyrood Palace, but takes lodging in a manor house within the city's walls, guarded day and night, while once more the lines of property and power are redrawn to punish and reward.

It is rebellion over again, but with a different set of villains having stepped up from the ranks of the nobles. On the run across the border this time: the Lords Morton, Ruthven, Lindsay, with George Douglas the bastard and Fawdonside, who held a loaded pistol to the Queen's belly. Waiting away from Edinburgh until they see which way the wind blows: John Knox and Maitland.

Lord James, the wily politician, who indeed rode into Edinburgh the morning after the murder, manages to convince the Queen that he had no involvement in the plot to kill Rizzio and she pardons his earlier misdemeanors. She also sends out pardons to those lords she now needs, including the rebels from the last rebellion, the very men who were about to be attainted in Parliament. Postings are canceled and redistributed at dizzying speed. She grants Bothwell the wardship of the castle of Dunbar in reward for his role in her rescue.

I recount to her the meeting at Peebles between David Hume, George Douglas, and Darnley and she considers it carefully. "This is a weapon I shall keep for the right time," she says. "For now I will put Lord Hume on notice."

She summons Hume to her presence chamber. I beg her leave to absent myself but she shakes her head. "I want you to hear what I say. Sit with my ladies across the room. He will not notice you. Not while I am speaking to him."

Hume is all solemn humility, bowing low and staying on his knee, his head lowered, until she bids him rise.

"You accompanied the Earl of Moray to Edinburgh, even though he was outlawed and banished."

"I would never have done so if I thought it displeased you," he says. "When I saw the King's signature on the safe conduct, I naturally thought it was with your blessing. As it turned out, it was a blessing that your brother arrived when he did to assist you."

"Indeed," she says. "Though strange that his return coincided with the murder of my beloved servant. I am still looking into this evil plot, Lord Hume. My Privy Council is calling sixty-eight conspirators to answer for Rizzio's murder and some of them are known associates of your family."

"With respect, Your Grace, some of them are leading nobles and known associates of the men of the Privy Council themselves. It is a disgrace they should plot against you in such an evil manner, but association with them is no evidence of complicity. I joined your armies to ride against them as soon as I understood what had occurred."

"It is more than a disgrace to plot against me, Lord Hume. It is treason," she says, her voice chilly. He bows his head and waits.

"I am grateful you rode out in my support," she says at last. "Now go back to the Borders and take your clansmen. I shall come there on a progress in August, after the babe is born, and we shall meet again. I have matters to discuss with you. But for now I prefer you to stay away from court."

Lord Hume kneels and when he rises his eyes flicker around the room and he catches my gaze for a second. Does he remember Alison Blackadder from when I last appeared as the Queen's lady-in-waiting?

"Your Grace, I am your loyal servant as always," he says. "We will be honored by a visit from you. If there is anything you wish of me before then, it shall be done in an instant."

She meets his gaze without a smile. "You would be wise to make sure your nephew David Hume of Wedderburn does not associate with the Douglas family. That is all, Lord Hume."

He leaves the room without a backward glance and the Queen gives me a small smile. I smile back at her, but it takes an effort. Dressed as Robert, it was I who saw David Hume and George Douglas plotting with the King. Now I cannot be sure of my safety from Hume in either disguise.

The Queen has promised we will go to the Borders in four months. On that date I rest my hope. Until then I will keep my head down and my thoughts to myself. I will serve her loyally and accompany her in her confinement. I have lived nearly five years in her service. I am determined to survive four more months.

Thirty-six

The Queen announces she will move the court to Edinburgh Castle for her lying-in. The day before we are to leave the safe house in Edinburgh, a letter arrives from the traitors Lord Ruthven and the Earl of Morton. I am present when she opens it, for since Rizzio's death she has no private secretary and I have begun to assist her with these duties. The sound that comes out of her mouth as she reads it brings me hastening to her side.

"What is it?"

She hands it to me, her hand pressed to her mouth. Morton, with nothing left to lose, has sent the bond on which the conspirators set down their signatures in agreement to murder Rizzio.

"It is my husband's handwriting," she says. "Morton wishes me nothing but evil to have sent this."

I read the paper. It is written in Darnley's hand, setting down that he is the chief author of the plot to punish wicked, ungodly Rizzio in the presence of the Queen, and to protect his fellow plotters from any repercussions of the murder.

"Perhaps it is a forgery?" I say.

"No." She shakes her head. "Oh no, Alison, this is no forgery. I know his hand, and I know what a fool he is, and now I know the depths of his treachery."

She stands, slowly, hands on her ponderous belly. "Tomorrow we move to the safest fortress in all of Scotland." She walks to the window. "But how can I ever be safe with such a husband?"

"This is evidence of treason."

She wraps her arms around herself. "If I did not need him to confirm the babe's paternity, I would turn him over to the law at once. But all I can do now is let him think that I may soften toward him, and keep him close enough that he can be watched."

≈ ≈ ≈

The next day we ride in procession through Edinburgh to enter the castle. The citizens are still eager for any glimpse of the Queen and flock to the streets to see her and Darnley. But I am riding farther back in the party and I hear the mutters in the crowd once the King and Queen have passed. Why has the King sworn his innocence when it is all over Edinburgh that his dagger was left lodged in Rizzio's body? Is there any truth to the rumor that Rizzio fathered the Queen's child? Is that why he was murdered so violently?

The Queen rides next to her husband and together they wave at the crowd. But she never looks upon him and the cheers that come from the crowd are for her, not for him. He is forcing a smile—he has learned that much of statecraft at least—but he has lost his chance for the crown matrimonial. What will his next move be?

Entering the gateway and riding into the castle compound feels like preparing for a siege. It is a small group of lords that draws close to the Queen now, some who have always been steadfast, some allowed back on sufferance. Rizzio, the small man with the vast presence, gone. Darnley, slinking around like a cur, ignored.

The royal apartments have been cleared and decked out in sumptuous hangings and tapestries in honor of our arrival. The Queen's bedchamber has a small anteroom, like the supper room off her bedchamber at Holyrood. Here she will give birth. But until the child begins its passage, she avoids it. Since Rizzio's murder, she has a horror of tiny enclosures. She is never present with the King without a bodyguard—Anthony Standen, who has been assigned to be the King's manservant. There is no secret staircase for the King to come into the Queen's rooms.

Into this poisoned atmosphere, Scotland's heir is to be born.

≈ ≈ ≈

The nineteenth day of June, 1566, the dark hours of the morning. In the tiny birthing room, the Queen's screams bounce off the walls and back into my ears with piercing intensity, as shrill as Rizzio's shrieks

265

in the supper room. The force of her nails draws blood on the skin of my arms. Seton, on her other side, is scratched and bleeding too.

When the contraction passes, the Queen sags in our arms and her head lolls. She has been in labor since midday and I fear her strength is fading. The midwife's tone is encouraging as she wipes the Queen's brow but there is a furrow of worry on her face.

The next contraction follows quickly. The Queen's body twists, her screams ring out, her nails cut into my flesh again.

There is a light tap at the door and the midwife opens it, while Seton and I try to hold the Queen in place. After a whispered consultation, she comes back. When the Queen sags again, gasping, the midwife speaks.

"Your Grace?"

The Queen manages a nod as I wipe her skin.

"Margaret Fleming will use her craft to transfer your pain to Lady Reres, but she needs you to agree," the midwife says.

"You speak of sorcery," Seton says sternly. "The Queen is a Catholic!"

The Queen screams again, her voice hoarse, her body tight. When she can speak, she gasps, "Yes, tell her yes."

Outside the birthing room, the bedchamber is crowded with the Queen's ladies. Margaret Fleming opens the connecting door wide and then leans down over the prone figure of Lady Reres, lying on the royal bed. She mutters and waves a bundle of smoking herbs. She comes into the tiny birthing chamber and does the same to the Queen. In response, the Queen lurches forward and vomits, then goes into another contraction.

In the bedchamber, Lady Reres begins to moan and scream in tandem with the Queen's cries. Far from taking the Queen's pain, she seems to be adding to it. For an hour the two women moan and scream together; another fruitless hour when there is still no sign of the child's head.

The Queen can barely speak, but she gasps and I bend down close to her. "For God's sake, send that woman away."

I stand slowly, trying to ease my aching muscles, and cross stiffly to the bedchamber. Lady Reres looks disappointed.

"I tried," she whispers. "I am truly willing to take the Queen's pain. Are you certain she has had no relief?"

"I'm sure you tried," I say wearily. "Thank you."

The atmosphere in the bedchamber and the presence chamber, so jovial at lunchtime the previous day, is now thick with fear. So many hours and so much pain, and still no sign of the child. Every woman who steps into a birthing chamber confronts death, but what will happen to Scotland if the Queen cannot deliver the child and they both die?

There is hot spiced wine to help us stay awake and a tray of food arrives as I take a break. It is hard to eat with the Queen's screams echoing through the chamber every few minutes, but I manage a sip of wine and a few mouthfuls of bread. The midwife has been attending the Queen almost nonstop and I gesture for her to come out for sustenance. She sips the wine. Her face is deathly white and her hand trembles on the cup.

"What is it?"

She leans close. "I fear she cannot last much longer. I cannot feel what is wrong, except that the child is big and she is slim in the pelvis and too tired. I have told her to push and it seems she cannot."

No wonder the woman is trembling. It will be terrible for all of Scotland if the Queen and her child should die, but I do not care for the fate of the midwife charged with their safety.

"She is strong, and still not too old. What can be the problem?"

"She is losing her will. She is in so much pain, she does not care if she lives or dies. If you can say anything to rouse her, for God's sake, say it now."

If the Queen dies this night, then I truly have lost everything myself. At once I cannot stand it. I refuse to lose it all now because the Queen cannot summon the will to live.

I stride into the birthing chamber fast and hard, like a man would. "Mary!" I call. She is in the arms of her women, her eyes rolling back in her head, retreating from the world.

"Mary!" I shout it this time and everyone jumps in shock except the Queen. Whatever place she has retreated to, she can barely hear me.

For the third time: "Mary Stuart, Queen of Scotland! Listen to me!"

While the women look at me with open mouths, the Queen lifts her head and tries to focus.

"If you give up now, you will die." I grip her by the shoulders and lean in close so there is no way she can avoid my stare. Her eyes, slitted, meet mine.

"I do not care," she whispers.

"You have carried this child safely through the worst travail. You cannot forsake him now."

Her eyes start to roll back again. "Pray to God that I die quickly and you can cut him from my belly."

I shake her. Seton and La Flamina are too shocked to stop me.

"You are the Queen!" I say. "If you let yourself and the babe die, then all that is evil has indeed triumphed. Call on your God, call on your courage, call on what makes you a ruler. I will hold you, we will all breathe with you, and he will be born!"

I wave to one of the ladies and she brings over the brandy and trickles a little in the Queen's mouth. Another comes with the smelling salts and puts them under her nose. The Queen chokes and jerks her head back, but her eyes are open. Her will to live may be faltering, but my will has risen up strong enough to carry her. I will not unlock my gaze from hers till the child emerges.

Somehow she responds. She takes another gulp of brandy and a long swallow of water and then settles her body to wait, her eyes on mine. I can see the next wave of pain approaching. Somehow I know that if she is not to drown under the weight of the pain, she must find a way to ride its waves.

"You are a boat, Mary, a strong boat crossing from France to Scotland, the wind behind you. You can see land ahead. When the wave comes, it lifts you up on its back and you surge forward and it takes you closer to land. It's not far now."

My eyes never leave hers and so I see the moment when the pain ceases to swallow her. She still screams, but something has changed in the shrieks. Can the entire, wakeful castle hear the difference? The bedchamber and birthing room regain an air of expectation. The midwife is down between the Queen's legs and I can hear the relief in her voice. "That's it, Your Grace. Keep pushing."

In fact it is another four hours and toward the end I am holding her alive with my fingertips and the force of my will. At eight in the morning the midwife gives a glad shout when she glimpses the babe's head and an hour later the Prince inches his way out and into her arms.

The room erupts with cheering and in the midst of it the Queen and I look at one another and there are no secrets between us now. The cry of a healthy babe rings out and every woman in the room is weeping.

The midwife says, "What a lad, what a prince," and she wraps him and lays him in the Queen's arms. I see the delight on her face and then I stumble back from the bed on legs that have turned to water. I sink to the floor and lean against the wall, and when the first cannon fires its joyful message to the city, all of us laugh and cheer again.

"I shall call him James," she says, and the smile stretches across her face as if it is an independent thing. "The man who will grow up to unite Scotland and England."

Someone has distributed cups and we all lift them and say, "To James," but I am filled with foreboding. The name of the brother who has betrayed her twice and the father who turned his face to the wall and died when he heard of Mary's own birth.

Another roar of cannon fire rings out and James lifts up a wail at the assault of sound on his tender, new ears.

Thirty-seven

It is a hot summer and the streets of Edinburgh stink as if the smell of murder is rising from the deserted rooms of Holyrood Palace and creeping up the High Street. The Queen is so afraid for her life that she will not countenance setting up a separate household for the babe, as is the custom with princes. She keeps him in a cradle by her bed, lest he be snatched away by some conspirator.

Lord James, with his skill at playing upon the Queen's fears, worms his way back into her favor and builds his empire again. Within a fortnight of the birth of her son, he is the only one of her nobles living in the castle. Even her favorite, Bothwell, who is charged with the castle's defenses, must reside in the midst of Edinburgh's stench.

The King, shunned by those in power and barely tolerated by the Queen, gathers himself a band of sycophantic followers, younger sons of the noble lords and lesser hangers-on. They roam the streets in the long summer evenings like a pack of dogs, starting fights in the taverns and frightening women and children.

At least I do not have to face him. He spends little time visiting the Queen and so distracted and so drunk is he that he has not realized her lady-in-waiting, Alison, bears any resemblance to Robert.

The Queen is slow to recover from childbirth and spends many hours each day sleeping. Her fear infects the Prince so that he is fretful and noisy in her presence. When I take him away quietly, it seems to soothe him and soon it is I who pick him up when he screams and his wet nurse, Helena, who soothes him.

One afternoon it is so hot that all activity in the Queen's chambers ceases after lunch. The babe had a restless night, keeping us awake. Full bellies and the summer's heat make all of us sleepy. The Queen returns to her bed and her women doze around the presence chamber.

I am holding the Prince, but he stirs and begins to grizzle. I do not want to disturb the women around me, so I take him downstairs into a drawing room below. I sit on a chaise and rock him gently until he settles. The afternoon sun slants in and strikes the thin strands of his fair hair.

The door creaks open. "She is here, my Lord," a guard says, and Bothwell steps into the room. When he sees me holding the Prince, he halts.

"I came to see the Queen, but I am told she sleeps. I wish to speak to you too." He peers at the bundle in my arms, his face curious.

"The boy kept us awake many hours last night," I say.

He comes across and stoops to see the Prince's sleeping face. His own face softens. I have seen that gentleness on his face before, after lovemaking.

He reaches out a finger and softly touches the Prince's round cheek. "This suits you."

I feel a wave of anger so intense I am surprised the Prince does not jolt awake in my arms. "Don't dare speak to me of that."

He reaches his hand out and lays it on my arm. "I'm sorry how things turned out."

I glare at him. Word of his latest infidelity has made its way even here. "Sorry enough that your wife's serving maid must comfort you?"

He draws back as if stung, his face hard again. "Some gossip is spreading rumors."

"You were seen in the cloisters of Haddington Abbey with her," I say. "You should be more careful, my Lord."

He stands up. The babe stirs.

"You would do well to keep such baseless rumors to yourself, for they would bring unneeded pain to my wife."

"Lying does not suit you."

"But when it was you I trysted with, you did not mind our lies."

I keep my voice low. "You were not married then, my Lord. Some would say our liaison was wrong, but it was not adulterous."

"Was it wrong?" He backs away. "You worked some spell on me, and when I was powerless to help you, you cursed me. I went to my wife's woman because she too is an enchantress and I wished to have

271

your evil curse lifted. My wife has shown no sign of conceiving since we married. Her woman promised to break your spell with an enchanted tryst, but all that has happened is that Lady Jean heard of it and now refuses to let me in her bed. I come to beg you to lift this curse, and find you holding the Prince as if he were your own. You are a witch!"

To be called a witch by a man as powerful as Bothwell is dangerous. I sit up, startling the babe into full wakefulness.

"My Lord, listen to me," I say urgently. "You know yourself that some word of marriage had passed between us. It was not unreasonable for me to hope. I lashed out at you in disappointment, that's all. Angry words from a slighted woman cannot prevent you siring children!"

He looks at me with a mixture of hope and suspicion.

"When we dallied, you were almost bankrupt and in no special favor," I say. "Since then you have become one of the most powerful men in the country. Would this happen if you were cursed? Go home, beg your wife's forgiveness, show her your skill at pleasing a woman, and children will follow."

The Prince begins to make mewling noises and I shift him into an upright position against me. Bothwell comes and sits by me. His face is hungry as he looks at the boy.

"I am getting old," he says. "I am powerful, but what does it mean without heirs? I want a son. Can you wish that for me?"

"Come closer," I say. He shifts so that he is right beside me and I lift the Prince into his arms. "Close your eyes and smell him."

He does so and his face softens.

"I wish this for you with all my heart."

He opens his eyes and looks into mine. I am unguarded. It is only a moment and then my heart starts up in alarm at the danger of such a feeling.

"Go home to her," I say.

"After the Borders," he says, soldier-like again, standing. "I have come to convince the Queen to hasten our trip. She holds her brother in high favor again, but behind her back he and Lord Hume are stirring up trouble there."

He grins. "It is time for her to reclaim your castle. Hume walked a fine line by bringing Lord James to Edinburgh, but she needs to remind him of her power. I cannot wait to see his face when she orders him out of Blackadder."

The Prince squirms and starts to cry. Bothwell continues, "By the Christmas after this one, perhaps we might both have healthy children and I shall bring my family to visit yours and our children will play together. Perhaps one day, if we are fortunate, they might marry and our two families might be united."

I laugh a little. "I do not have a husband, Lord Bothwell. Do not wish children on me just yet!"

"I wish you might find happiness in marriage," he says seriously.

I busy myself fussing over the child. The door opens and Lady Reres comes in with the wet nurse. "Lord Bothwell, do you mind?" she says.

He bows low to both of us and walks out of the room. Everything inside me aches as I hand James over for the breast. I have to walk away while he feeds. I cannot watch the look of bliss on his face as his hunger is sated.

≈ ≈ ≈

While the Prince thrives, the Queen wilts in the summer heat. She has her child, but her kingdom is in disarray and she has not the strength to rule it again. This rebellion, with Rizzio's murder and Darnley's treason, has truly frightened her.

It is Bothwell who breaks the spell. "You are pale," he observes. "You must come out of your confinement, Your Grace. It is not healthy for you to spend all your time in your apartments."

"Where would you have me go?" she asks.

"I will make up a party and we will ride to Stirling with the Prince. It is time, is it not, for the Earl of Mar to meet his young charge?"

The Queen shudders. "I cannot let him be fostered yet."

"There is no fortress in the country safer than Stirling and few men more loyal than Mar," Bothwell says. "The country is full of unrest. You must take it back in hand, Madam. It is time to foster the Prince in the way of tradition and return to your duties. A progress to Stirling will let your people know you are returning to them."

She puts both hands up to her face for a moment and we are silent, watching her. She takes a breath and drops her hands back in her lap. "The King sends messages daily that he waits for me to end my confinement."

"You cannot avoid him forever."

The Queen straightens. "We shall go to Stirling. But not yet, Lord Bothwell. I cannot ride out to meet the people in this state. You must take me somewhere secret instead. Somewhere I can spend a few days in safety and enjoyment."

"An excellent idea," he says. "Mar waits at Alloa for word that you are to bring the Prince to Stirling. Why not ride there to visit him? His castle is said to be most pleasant in the summer."

"I do not feel safe to ride so far."

Bothwell stands in frustration and crosses to the window. Then he spins around. "You do not need to ride, Madam. It is only a few hours by boat. You may travel in secret. No one will know that you are not here in the castle with the Prince."

"A queen never seems to travel in secret."

Bothwell laughs. "This time you will. There is a ship at Newhaven that none would expect a queen to travel upon. Its captain is Alison's own father and one of my most trusted men. You can come down to the dock in disguise and no one will know you have sailed."

She looks up, a trace of hope upon her features. "But surely it is not safe to leave the Prince unattended?"

"I will attend to him myself. No harm will come to him and the break will do you good. Let me send word to Mar at once. I will take you to the dock and see you upon Captain Blackadder's ship."

"What about the King?"

For a long moment no one answers. Then Bothwell shrugs. "Perhaps he, too, will not even know you are gone."

Thirty-eight

When we dress as young men in the early light of the next morning, there is nothing of the playful air of old. She is so heavy of heart that I wonder if I shall have to draw her away from the side of the Prince's cradle by force.

But as we ride behind Bothwell through the streets at a gentle pace, out of Edinburgh and down toward the small port of Newhaven, it is William who is on my mind. William who has given up on his castle and returned to a life at sea, sailing with his pirate cousins, Edmund and Jock. I am still afraid of his rage.

It is a clear morning, with the promise of heat later in the day, and the familiar lines of the *Avenger* rise from the dock. Bothwell helps the Queen dismount. When her feet touch the ground she straightens and looks around her.

William comes down the gangplank of the ship and approaches us. His eyes rove across the party and rest upon the Queen, who stands taller and straighter than any of us, even in her disguise. He bows his head and it seems he might also go to kneel, until Bothwell coughs to remind him that she is in disguise.

"Captain Blackadder," she says in a low voice. "Is your ship ready to sail?"

"The tide is right to take us," he says. "The wind is in your favor."

She turns to Bothwell. "Guard the Prince," she says. She reaches out and lays her hand on his arm. "Thank you."

The moment lengthens beyond the proper time for such a touch and such a fixed gaze between them, until the Queen at last releases him. We follow William up the gangplank and he shows us to the captain's cabin, the only one large enough to accommodate her with any ease. We stand on the deck as the ship casts off, unfurling its sails to catch the morning wind up the Firth of Forth. The sails flap in the clear sunlight, the water is a deep blue, and the wind from the sea takes the smell of Edinburgh away so that it is only a memory.

For a while the Queen watches Edinburgh from the stern of the ship and her face is solemn. When the city has grown small, she turns to me with a wistful smile.

"Help me change my clothes," she says. "Dressing as a man is not play any longer."

When we come out of the cabin again, the Queen is transformed. Bearing a child has not made her less beautiful. Her dress is cut low, her bosom swelling and creamy, her waist small. She has left her hair loose to fall around her shoulders.

She takes my arm and we walk to the prow of the ship. The crew falls back to let her pass, open-mouthed. These are rough men and boys and they have never seen a woman like this at close quarters.

She stands at the railing, eyes closed, hair streaming out behind her. When she opens her eyes again, the men quickly busy themselves.

"Ask your father to join me," she says.

I pick my way down the ship to where William holds the wheel. "The Queen asks for you."

Edmund gives a low whistle.

"Take the wheel and bite your tongue," William says. He steps around me and I trail him along the deck to where the Queen stands, resting her hands on the railing. When he comes close to her, he stops and bows.

"You do not need to bow, sir. I am a visitor to your kingdom today, am I not? Alison, join us."

William and I both step to the railing beside her.

"How long has your daughter been in my service now?"

"Five years, Your Grace," William says.

"At first I did not know if I could trust her. When I found that she had been creeping out of the castle in secret dressed as a man, I believed she was a spy. I came close to having her killed."

William is silent.

"But she has served me most loyally. It is a long time now that I have wanted to reward her. You must have wondered if I would keep my word."

"No, Your Grace."

"Speak frankly, Captain. You doubted me, did you not?"

He drops his head. "Yes."

"Now I will redeem my promise, in spite of your doubts. However, I have my own concerns. Forgive me, Captain, but you are old. Blackadder Castle and its lands are a great holding and running such is no simple thing. How will you do so?"

William grips the rail. "I will learn. My sister, if she still lives, will show me. My cousins at Tulliallan know all about the running of a great estate."

"Lord Hume's lands will surround you. He may feel himself wronged when he loses a prize won so long ago by his ancestors. How will you protect yourselves?"

"The bondmen and peasants will still be loyal to the name of Blackadder," William says.

"Many years have passed and they have served another lord since then. I hope you can command their loyalty, Captain Blackadder."

William stares straight ahead and I clutch the railing myself, my knuckles white, willing her to stop speaking. But she continues.

"Your daughter has lived in court for five years and has learned much. I have made up my mind. I shall bestow the castle upon her. She will be its owner and do what she shall with it. I shall urge her to marry, but if she does not, you cannot compel her. You will advise her and protect her, but she shall be set down as the owner of the castle, for it is her efforts that have won it back."

William bobs his head in a downward movement that could be construed as a bow. I don't dare to catch his eye. When did she make such a decision?

The Queen tosses her hair out of her face. "To show my gratitude that you gave your daughter to my service, I appoint you the Crown's Seeker of Pirates. It is a position that gives you much authority on the sea."

William's expression is unreadable. She does not know, perhaps, that Edmund, standing at the wheel, is one of Scotland's most notorious pirates.

"When the Prince has been installed in his own household at Stirling,

I will be sending Bothwell to the Borders to settle that district," she continues. "I wish you to accompany him, for he tells me you are loyal in his service too. I shall follow Bothwell there and dispense justice. Authority is long overdue in that region."

She places her hand on my arm. "When that task is complete, I shall visit Lord Hume and his family and compel them to return your castle. You have waited a long time. By the end of summer this will happen. I give you my word."

Her hair is blowing back from her face, her skin unearthly, her eyes a deep ocean color. She looks infinitely young and at the same time old. Then a yell comes from the bridge and we all turn to see Edmund waving. We have come around the corner to Alloa. A bugle rings out from the shore.

"I must bring in the ship," William says.

She smiles. "I am glad to have spoken to you at last, Captain Blackadder." She turns to me. "Go and help your father."

I follow William down the deck and stand near him at the steering wheel. He says nothing as he brings the ship close to shore and begins angling it around to meet the dock. When we have made fast to the side, he glances around to ensure no one is standing near us, and then glares at me, his lips pressed together tightly. "You are as untrustworthy as the one you serve."

"I knew nothing of this," I say, reaching out to him. "It makes no difference who owns it in name. It belongs to our family."

He steps back so I cannot touch him. "I trust you will not speak of this to anyone," he says, his voice low.

I follow the Queen down the gangplank without looking back at William.

≈ ≈ ≈

After four days at Alloa we return to Edinburgh by horseback. The fresh air has brought color to the Queen's cheeks and, if she does not laugh, at least she does not look as if she will cry at any moment.

As soon as we arrive, she calls for the Prince. Lady Reres brings the babe into the presence chamber and the Queen's face softens as she reaches for him. He is used to being passed from arm to arm, but when he goes to his mother, he squirms. When she cannot soothe him, she hands him to Lady Reres so the wet nurse may suckle him. Afterward he is content, and then he falls asleep while the Queen holds him.

"It is time for him to move to Stirling," she says when his breathing is deep and even. "I have been selfish keeping him with me. There is no hand on the reins of the country. She is like a horse ready to bolt at any moment. There is no one to take back control except me, and I must do so."

"There may be no hands on the reins, but there are those willing to throw a stone at the horse's rump," says Bothwell, who has been waiting impatiently to speak to her. "The Borders are at breaking point. I am ready to march the moment you give your word. You must let me go at once, in force, before the whole region slides into anarchy."

"How many men will you take?" she asks.

"I have three hundred ready to ride today. You can follow us within the week and try those rebels we have captured. You have never visited this region—it is time they saw you."

"I have heard that the Elliots and the Armstrongs and Johnstones care for no one, including their Queen," she says.

"They will care by the time your progress is finished. I will not be soft in bringing them in, and you will dispense royal justice that will teach them a lesson. Then the innocent might know some peace again."

"Very well, you have leave to ride at once. We will take the Prince to Stirling and once he is safely installed, we will come."

I follow Bothwell out into the corridor. "Does my father ride with you?"

"He does."

"My Lord, have a care of his safety. He is not young, but still thinks he has the same strength. Do not let him be killed by some Border ruffian."

He smiles the smile of a restless man allowed to move at last. "I will appoint him keeper of those taken prisoner at Hermitage Castle. It is an honorable job and will keep him out of the field."

279

"Thank you," I say. "I would have him alive when the castle is returned."

His face changes. "You don't expect a life of peace, I hope. The Humes will look for revenge as ceaselessly as William has, and with far more strength. In the Borders you are a long way from the Queen's protection. It seems you will win your castle at last, but it may be you never sleep unafraid again."

Thirty-nine

The Queen appoints Joseph Rizzio as her new secretary, plucking him from the staff of a French diplomat as she earlier selected his brother. But Joseph, a quiet lad of barely eighteen, is no David Rizzio. Known by his first name for fear of the association, he helps the Queen with the routine tasks of a secretary so discreetly he is almost invisible.

Without the murdered Rizzio's canny knowledge of power and loyalty, the Queen must somehow bring the country together and control the lords. She orders Maitland to return to Edinburgh and resume his role as secretary of state, and installs the Prince in the stronghold of Stirling Castle. Then she calls together those of her nobles she can trust to ride with her to the Borders. More than a dozen of Scotland's noblemen ride in the train behind her, trailed by household officers, judges, lawyers, clerks, servants, and her ever-present armed guards. Among such exalted company, one face is missing. The King has left Edinburgh and ridden to Glasgow to complain to his father of his treatment at the hands of the Queen and her council. No one is sorry to see him go.

The people come out to cheer her, as always, but they observe the number of men-at-arms who must accompany her on this progress and they do not smile. The Queen is out of her confinement but all is not well in the kingdom and her people are afraid.

The progress winds its slow way south, stopping at the great houses and castles to meet the southern lords before arriving at Jedburgh for the trials of Bothwell's Border rebels. The Queen's party stays in Jedburgh House, a handsome building of modest proportions that can be easily guarded.

Bothwell has sent only a small number of prisoners across from Hermitage Castle, with word that he will bring the rest once he has captured a band of Elliots who has so far eluded him. The Queen, with Lord James at her side, begins hearing the charges.

I stay with her to attend to her needs as the prisoners are brought in one at a time to face justice. Bothwell, I am sure, envisaged hangings, but the Queen is in a merciful frame of mind and she dispenses fines, small punishments, and advice to the Border louts who come before her.

Lord James makes his disgust clear.

"For God's sake, you must hang some of them," he says to her in a low voice, as a released prisoner walks out, looking stunned at his good fortune.

"I have spoken to each about the wrongness of his actions. If they break the law again, they face death," she says.

"I can assure you that means nothing to such men," he says. "Except that their Queen has grown soft. Where is the woman who had John Gordon beheaded?"

She turns to him and pauses for a moment. "By the same reasoning, my brother, I should have punished you far more harshly."

He clenches his fists on the table in front of him. The next prisoner has been brought in and there is an expectant silence.

"You have known the power of my forgiveness, and it has brought you back to my side," she says quietly. "There has been enough killing. Let me dispense justice as I know how."

She looks across at the prisoner, a filthy, unshaven man, and settles her features into a disapproving expression. "What is the charge?"

Before the bailiff can answer, a commotion rises from the rear of the courtroom. At the sound of urgent voices from outside the door, everyone turns to see what is happening.

The Queen is pale. "Alison, see what disturbs us."

I make my way through the courtroom and squeeze through the door. The guards are keeping a messenger in Bothwell's livery outside and he is arguing loudly to be admitted. When he sees me he pushes forward. "My Lord has been mortally injured in battle. He lies near to death."

The shock is ice water in my veins. "What are his wounds?"

"He has taken a great cut to his thigh and smaller wounds to his arm and face. He lies like a dead man in Hermitage Castle and we have no one who knows how to tend to him."

"Wait." I push back through the heavy door, wind through the audience to the Queen's podium, and lean forward to whisper the news into her ear.

"We must go to him." The Queen goes to rise.

"There's nothing you can do, and we must continue the hearings," Lord James says. "If you leave now and rush to his side, these ruffians will have won a victory."

"I can't leave him to die," she says, twisting her fingers.

"Send your physician. You can follow in a few days, when we have finished here."

She turns to me and I can see the strain in the set of her lips. "Alison, send Arnault at once."

"Do you wish me to ride with him?"

She hesitates a moment. I keep my face expressionless.

"Yes, go," she says.

I have time to snatch a few items of clothing and pull on my riding clothes before I run to the courtyard. Bothwell's messenger is already mounted on a fresh horse and Arnault rushes out a few moments after me, clutching his bag of medicines.

It is twenty-five miles to Hermitage and we accomplish much of it at a gallop, slowing to a trot when the ground is too rough. Arnault, not accustomed to such riding, tries to keep up, and often Bothwell's man and I must slow down till he catches us, clinging to the mane of his horse, his bag thumping up and down beside the saddle.

We make it just before full darkness blankets us, clattering into the courtyard, our messenger yelling our identity to the guards. I help Arnault climb painfully from his horse. He winces, then straightens up slowly, his hand clutching the small of his back. The messenger unbuckles the medicine bag and leads us to a damp chamber on the lower floor.

My father, crouched by Bothwell's side on the floor, seems to have shrunk. His hair is almost completely gray and his eyes are haunted. It is a moment before I can wrench my gaze away to Bothwell's face. He looks like a corpse, his lips faintly blue, skin icy white, eyes closed.

"Does he live?" I ask.

"Just," William says. "Have you brought a physician?"

Arnault pushes past me and kneels down at Bothwell's side, forgetting his own discomfort in the manner of one who heals. The wound, when he unwraps it, is ugly and gaping. Its ragged edges are still oozing blood. I bite my lip and the physician's brow is a furrow. His eyes meet mine.

"What do you wait for?" William asks, bundling the bloody bandages. "Hurry, man!"

"He will need stitching," Arnault says. "We need hot water, something to wipe away the blood and fresh bandages." He looks over at me. "Can you help me stitch?"

"I have little expertise, but a strong stomach," I say.

We make the preparations and then Arnault picks up the needle and catgut, and gestures to me. I take Bothwell's torn flesh in my hands and draw it together. He does not wake as the needle passes through his skin.

It takes a long while to repair the wound and I am sweating and trembling from the strain of it by the time we are finished. All of us breathe more easily once his flesh is closed up as it should be and William gives a grunt of satisfaction when the fresh bandage is secured. The other gashes, on his hand and forehead, are deep but not mortal. Arnault washes and bandages them.

"Not too much damage," he says, when he is done. "But the bleeding could still kill him."

"What can we do?" I can hear the tremor in William's voice.

"Keep him warm, don't let him move. When he wakes, try to feed him broth," Arnault says, getting painfully to his feet. "We will rouse him from time to time to see that he still lives."

≈　≈　≈

Arnault dozes in a chair while William and I seat ourselves at either side of Bothwell. Every hour, servants bring in broth from the kitchen. William cradles Bothwell's head and I try to dribble it into his mouth. At times he seems to swallow, but mostly the fluid runs down his chin and I must stop lest he choke on it.

Some time in the small hours he swims up from the depths of his swoon and opens his eyes. William is there in a heartbeat.

"My Lord," he says softly.

"Captain," Bothwell's voice is a dry croak. "How bad is it?"

"Not bad at all," William says.

William lifts his head and I come closer with the broth. Bothwell catches sight of me, but cannot make out my features in the half-light. "Who is that?" he croaks.

"It's Alison," I say. "The Queen sent me with her best physician."

He blinks and attempts a grin. "That bad?"

The physician comes across and kneels by Bothwell's side. "I have stitched your wound," he says. "If you stay still, God willing you will recover."

"I must piss," Bothwell says.

"Your captain will hold a container. Afterward you may have a little laudanum. Is there much pain?"

"A little," he says. A soldier's answer.

I leave the room while they attend to his needs and come back with fresh broth. William and I take our accustomed positions and this time we are able to trickle more down his throat. When we have finished, the physician gives him the laudanum and after a few minutes his head rolls back in William's lap. William lowers him to the floor. I have never seen him so tender.

The physician listens to Bothwell's heart and then sits back on his heels. "We should pray."

He means this literally, but I do not pray, God having never saved anyone I loved. Someone in the castle brings a priest to mutter some Protestant prayer over Bothwell.

"Why don't you take some rest?" I ask William, who is still kneeling uncomfortably by the bed.

"Do you think I am too old to sit watch?" he snaps.

Arnault frowns at me and I try to think how I can placate William. "Next week the Queen's party is riding to meet Lord Hume," I say softly. "She is taking the castle back from him and returning it to us. She has all her lords with her to compel him."

The look on his face changes and I cannot fathom his expression.

"Come back with me to Jedburgh and ride to Blackadder in the Queen's party. We have nothing to fear from Hume now. The might of her kingdom is against him."

He still won't meet my eyes.

"William?"

"I have lost my honor," he says, so quietly I can barely hear him. "Do not talk to me of the castle. I must make amends before I can step foot in there."

"What do you mean?"

"I will not speak of it!" he snaps.

"If you will converse thus, you must go outside," Arnault interjects. "You may lead his men, Captain, but in the sickroom I have the authority."

If there was somewhere else to go, I would leave, but it is deep in the night and we are in a fortress full of fighting men. I stand and move to another part of the room where there is a chaise.

It's not till I am lying down that my exhaustion washes over me. My riding clothes are stained with Bothwell's blood, my body aches from the hard ride and the strain of crouching by the physician holding Bothwell's flesh steady for the stitches. I look across at William's face as he kneels on the ground by his lord. What has happened to his honor?

Forty

Hermitage Castle is a stronghold of Bothwell's family—a military base—well fortified, but with little in the way of comfort. I am the only woman there apart from the servants. While I crouch by Bothwell's side and will him to survive, a messenger is despatched to Jedburgh to inform the Queen that Bothwell still lives. I stay by Bothwell's side and ensure I am not left alone with William. We barely speak to each other.

For that whole night and the next day, Bothwell hangs in a twilight, drifting in and out of consciousness, awake, asleep, half-dead. We dare not move him from the rough bed on the floor. William, Arnault, and I are all stiff from kneeling beside him and taking only snatches of rest.

At last, after the second night, he wakes fully with the sun, and there is some color in his cheeks again.

The physician pushes himself painfully out of his chair, limps across, and lowers himself to Bothwell's side.

"It seems like you're the one in need of a doctor," Bothwell says, and the ghost of his booming voice is present again.

I smile and there is a lightening of William's exhausted features as we kneel on the floor by his bedding.

Bothwell looks at the three of us. "You're enough to give a man nightmares."

"Keeping death at bay is hard work, my Lord," Arnault says.

Bothwell snorts. "I kicked death in the arse and told him to leave me alone a while longer. But he'll be back if I don't get something to eat."

We call the servants and order food. I can almost feel the word flashing through the castle like a thaw. Bothwell lives! As he tears into a plate of roasted meats, the sound of cheering rises from the courtyard. He cocks his head and listens for a moment.

"Did that damned Jock Elliot get away after he stuck me?" he asks, chewing loudly.

"You killed him, they said," William says.

"Good," he grunts. "Treacherous dog." He wolfs down a few more mouthfuls and gulps a cup of ale. I have forgotten what a soldier he is underneath his court manners.

"Have the trials started?" he asks. "Has she hanged any yet?"

There's a pause. "The Queen is riding up from Jedburgh tomorrow," Arnault says. "You'll hear about the trials then."

"You'd better get me off the floor, then. And give me a wash and a shave."

His rush of energy doesn't last long. By the time he's finished eating, his eyelids are drooping. "William?" he says. "Get me a report on our prisoners."

"My Lord—"

"With your own eyes. I want to know exactly how cold and hungry they are."

"My Lord—" William struggles.

"William! Now!" Bothwell says. "I'm sick of the sight of you!"

William heads for the door.

"You too, good fellow," Bothwell says to the physician. "Go and stretch your legs. I am weary of being watched."

I get up too, to go with them, but Bothwell's gaze, not sleepy at all, pins me. "Wait. I would have a word with you about the Queen."

The door closes and we are alone. I come to his side. He reaches up a hand, clasps my fingers with what remains of his brute strength, and draws me down till I am kneeling on the floor at his side.

"I'm not out of danger," he says. "Just a kiss. A kiss to save my life."

The pull of his hand is inexorable. I should fight it, but I do not. I have seen him almost die. I want this kiss too.

He tastes like a soldier but he kisses like a king. My body remembers and I do not draw away. I breathe as much life back into him as I can, and then I forget about life and respond to him. My own body is on fire when at last I draw back.

He smiles. "At least Jock has left me with my manhood."

Feet approach from outside the door and I drop his hand. He

says nothing, but gives me a long look, breaking it only as Arnault comes in.

"You must rest, my Lord," the physician says, raising his hands in frustration. "Sleep, and in the morning we will move you to a proper bed, ready for the Queen."

"Ready for the Queen," he murmurs, his eyelids falling. I get up and walk away from him. I promise myself it is the last kiss.

≈　≈　≈

The next day Bothwell and I play cards. He is recovered enough to be chafing at his restriction and in need of activity that will keep him safely confined to his bed. His men wash and shave him, dress him in clean clothes, and move him into the largest chamber in the castle with a fire roaring in the grate. There's color in his cheeks again, but too much movement drains it away in an instant, and under the glow his cheeks are sunken and thin. He is recovering, but a sour wound could still kill him. The physician has instructed me to keep his spirits up and stay by his side. But I must glare at him warningly when his eyes stray to my breasts. At my look he grins, unrepentant.

Lunch has been served and I am helping Bothwell cut up his portion when there is a hammering at the door. "The Queen!" a servant calls through the slit. Before there is time to dissemble, the door flies open and she is there.

I can see in an instant what these past days have cost her. Her face is whiter than Bothwell's, and her eyes stare from dark sockets. There is nothing regal about the way she rushes into the room and the working of her face when she sees him. For a moment it seems she will weep openly, but she takes control, gathers herself, and crosses to his bedside. I stand and move aside.

"They told me you were near to death," she says, her voice unsteady.

"Madam." He bows his head, ridiculously, in the bed. "I am a tough old soldier. It will take a lot to kill me."

"It takes very little to kill any of us, Lord Bothwell. I am more grateful than you know to find you have survived."

There is an awkward silence and with a visible effort, she tears her gaze away from him and takes in the presence of the physician, and me, waiting by the bed. Her eyes narrow slightly.

Arnault steps forward. "Your Grace? We have a meal prepared for you and your party downstairs. Do you wish to eat?"

"Bring it up here," she says. "Lord Bothwell and I have much to discuss and little time, as I will ride back to Jedburgh tonight. You and Alison must go and make your preparations to return with us."

I drop into a curtsy at the hardness in her voice and, without daring to catch Bothwell's eye, I leave the room, my cheeks burning.

After all these years with the Queen, I have become a mistress at hiding my heart and my desire. I have covered up, meticulously, any hint of what is between Bothwell and me. But in one moment she has caught me unawares.

≈ ≈ ≈

I change into my riding habit, which a servant has labored to clean of its bloodstains, and go to find William.

He is in his room, a small, dark place where the chill of the castle seems especially concentrated. He is lying on his bed, staring at the ceiling and I'm struck again by the way he has become an old man so suddenly.

"William?"

Silence, and at last a soft grunt.

"I am riding with the Queen tonight. In a few days we will go to the castle. Will you come?"

He shakes his head and anger rises in me.

"All these years, and now it's in reach," I say. "Bothwell lives. Why do you mope like a woman?"

I expect this will drive him to his feet, his hands at my throat, but he turns his head away from me and his voice is flat.

"I was left in charge of the castle and the prisoners when he went after the Elliots. They broke out while I slept and took over the castle. When the garrison came back carrying Bothwell near to death, the prisoners demanded weapons and freedom. They got them, else he would have died at the gate."

I take a deep breath. "Border criminals are scum. You're not the first to be tricked by them."

He glares at me. "I'm disgraced and no womanly words will change it."

"For God's sake, you've been an honorable soldier all your life. Aren't you allowed to make one mistake?"

"Old men make such mistakes." He rolls away from me and faces the wall. "Even the Queen thinks me too old to take the castle."

I do not know what to do with him in such a state. I am used to his rages, but this black melancholy mystifies me.

"It is no crime to be old," I say, trying to sound gentler. "When we have the castle, you can rest. You don't need to be a soldier any more."

He says nothing and at last I rise. "In days, Hume will be brought to justice. If you wish to see it, make haste to Jedburgh and ride with me."

≈ ≈ ≈

The Queen spends several hours cloistered with Bothwell and the day grows short. The horses are saddled and waiting in the courtyard, the stableboys stamping and blowing on their hands, the sun slipping lower toward the hills. Lord James strides up and down impatiently, slapping his riding gloves on his thigh. He comes to a halt beside me.

"We will be riding all night," he says. "Go and tell my sister to come away. Bothwell might live, but that won't be much use if she is lost in the dark!"

I curtsy and hasten back into the castle, through corridors heavy with evening gloom. I knock on the heavy oak of Bothwell's door. There is a moment's silence, and then his voice: "Enter."

The Queen and Bothwell are alone and something about their studied positions feels odd. I look from one to the other.

"Lord James begs you to leave for Jedburgh, Your Grace," I say. "It is late and he fears for your safety."

"Indeed, he is right," she says and rises from her seat near the bed. "Lord Bothwell, you must excuse me, for we need to return this night."

"I am humbled you have traveled so far," he says.

They gaze at each other and she does not move. The silence grows until there is a small cough from the open door. Arthur Erskine, the equerry, has come up.

"Madam, the hour grows late."

The Queen lingers a moment more. "Very well," she says at last. "Lord Bothwell, your health. I will see you at Jedburgh when you can be moved."

Her tone is so formal that I drop my head as she sweeps out of the room. Bothwell's gaze is fixed on her departing figure.

"Alison, Arthur, do not tarry." Her voice is imperious, and I must follow her. I take one last glance at Bothwell, who gives me a crooked smile, and then I am hurrying after Erskine through the corridors. The sun slips behind the hills as we emerge into the courtyard and mount the horses.

A full moon is rising, moving in and out of the clouds. Erskine and Lord James lead the way in the moonlight and every shadow is full of menace. Where there is flat ground we canter, but when the track is pocked or boggy we must walk the horses painstakingly through the muck. The Queen wraps herself in her cloak and says nothing.

A few miles from Jedburgh, when her weary horse, eager to reach home, has cantered to the front of the party, the ground changes from firm to wet in a step. Erskine shouts a warning, but the Queen's palfrey slips, loses his footing, and falls to his shoulder with a splash. When he scrambles to his feet, the saddle is bare.

I wrench my horse to a halt and jump down. I wade through the muddy water, calling, "Your Grace, Your Grace!" I cannot see her in the dark and the confusion and the milling horses, and my riding clothes drag at my legs with the weight of the water. Then I hear her soft moan and the suck of the mud as she sits up. The sharp and most unroyal curse she gives fills me with relief.

"Madam? Madam?" Arnault's voice is frantic in the darkness.

"I am here, Arnault."

With a scrabble of arms and legs we reach for her, falling in the mud so we are as wet as she. Arnault finds her first and hauls her to her feet and we slosh our way back to firmer ground where the rest of the party has had the wit to wait with the horses. She is unharmed but already shivering.

Lord James takes charge.

"You and you," he points. "Ride as fast as you can and have them make ready for us. Sister, ride behind me and I will block the wind. Here, wrap my cloak around your shoulders. We will ride fast and you shall be back at Jedburgh before any harm comes to you."

But it is half an hour of cantering with the cold wind cutting at us and we are all shivering by the time we arrive. The torches blaze out in the dark from Jedburgh House and men come running with a litter to meet us.

"I hope you have built my fire high," the Queen greets them, and she manages a smile, as though she is not near to frozen. "I do not need a litter, pray just help me from my horse, and I shall walk inside."

"Your Grace, please use the litter." Arnault's voice is hard with worry. "We do not know what hurt you may have taken."

They help her into the litter, raise it, and break into a run. The rest of us slide from our saddles. I run inside in her wake and the chill in my belly is not just from my wet clothing and the cold wind as I rode.

The Queen's chambers are hectic with servants and ladies-in-waiting fussing around her. I am excused and find my way to my own bed and try to get myself warm. It is a long time before the feeling comes back into my toes and fingers.

To have my fate dangled thus is almost more than I can bear. I send a few words of thanks to the God I don't believe in before I fall asleep.

≋ ≋ ≋

Our Queen may be stronger than most women, but all her life she has been plagued with illnesses. The terrible pains in her belly, the fainting, the vomiting, the days when she takes to her bed with violent fits of weeping, until she is near hysteria and must be quietened with laudanum. It is only a few months since she almost died in childbirth. In the past few days she has suffered the shock of Bothwell's injury, the long ride in the dark, the fall, and getting chilled in her wet clothes.

By lunchtime she is shivering continuously. Arnault orders her back into bed and calls for a roaring fire in her room. By evening she is in the claws of illness, alternately burning and freezing, racked with coughs, doubled up with the pain in her gut that has dogged her since she was a child.

Seton, Arnault, and I try to ease her discomfort, moving the bed-clothes on and off when she calls for it, sponging her face when the fever grips her, rubbing her icy limbs when she shivers.

My fear is like ice in the pit of my belly. Seton looks panicked and Lord James and Maitland peer into the room to see how her illness progresses.

At last, late in the evening, the Queen recovers a little. The pain eases and her fever drops. Seton manages to trickle some broth into her mouth and the Queen gives a tiny, weak smile.

"Madam, that ride was too much for you," Arnault says, taking her hand. "I will not allow you to strain yourself again. Do you hear me?"

She gives a tiny nod. The terror on Seton's face subsides. She has never learned to conceal her feelings. I, a little more schooled in dissembling, exhale slowly and let relief flood my body.

"You must rest now, Madam," Arnault says. "In the morning you will feel better."

We eat a snatched meal downstairs and Seton insists on sleeping in the Queen's chambers. I return to my tiny room, exhausted.

≈ ≈ ≈

When I wake, Jedburgh House is quiet. It is early still; the sun has not risen. Outside a robin calls and another answers.

Tomorrow, or the next day or the one after, I will come home, for the first time in my life. Perhaps the restlessness that has lived inside me will subside. For the first time, I will not be under the rule of another. Not William, not Bothwell, not the Queen. Perhaps at Blackadder I will feel peace.

On this quiet morning, I see the Queen dispassionately. I know her faults and vanities, her need to be worshiped, her cruelty, her kindness, her jealousy. I know how it is to be a favorite one moment, forgotten the next. I know the danger of angering her or making her afraid. She is a queen, divinely appointed and set above the rest of us, but I have seen the woman behind the Queen.

I do not allow myself to think of Angi much, for the pain it brings, but this morning she comes back to me as clearly as if she had just stepped outside the room for a moment. Her eyes are full of mischief and she comes toward the bed, allowing her nightgown to slip slowly down from her shoulder. She pauses just out of my reach. I have forgotten the delight of this feeling, the anticipation of our skins meeting, the way she laughs and makes me wait, and wait.

Faintly, down the corridors of the house, comes a cry so despairing that the hair rises on my scalp. I throw back the covers, stumble from the bed, grab a cloak, and rush out of my room. I take the stairs in great leaps until I reach the hallway outside the Queen's apartments, where it seems that cry still lingers in the air. A servant rushes past me and I grab her.

"The Queen is dead," she gasps, and flees.

Forty-one

I push my way into the Queen's bedchamber. It is crowded with people, their voices an unintelligible wall of sound. The only thing I can hear clearly is Seton's despairing cries.

In the center of the chaos the Queen is a storm's eye of stillness. Her face is as cold as a snowdrift, her lips blue. I shoulder my way through the maelstrom to her side where Seton is kneeling, tears running down her face. I take the Queen's hand in mine. It is waxen, absent.

I am filled with a white-hot rage as I stare down at her closed eyes.

"Alison!" It is Arnault, standing by the Queen's feet. "We may yet save her. Help me!"

"She is past our help." Seton chokes on the words. "Pity, Arnault. At least let her body rest peacefully."

He ignores her. "We must bind her limbs."

Seton flies to her feet, crosses the room, and drags the window open. "Let her spirit be free," she cries. "Leave her, Arnault."

The priest is muttering and waving incense, and Lord James seems to be pawing through the Queen's jewels, while Maitland strides back and forth in consternation. La Flamina and the Queen's other ladies weep loudly.

I cast another look at the Queen's face. She is surely dead. I let go of her hand and move down the end of the bed to Arnault. "Close the window," I snap at Seton.

"I will hold the leg and you must bind it as tightly as you can," he says.

She is limp and cold to the touch; he has surely lost his mind.

"She's free now. Let her go to God." Seton stands by the window.

"You'll kill us all with the cold—close it!" My shriek so startles

Seton that she reaches out and shuts the window and then sinks to a chair and covers her face in her hands.

Arnault directs me with short, sharp orders. "Tight! Go faster. Move around the knee!"

Maitland and Lord James stand close together in a corner, talking urgently in low voices. Servants tear at their hair. Seton sobs as though her very heart is leaving her own body.

When all the Queen's limbs are bound, Arnault leans his ear down close over her mouth for a moment, though I do not know how he can hear anything in the hubbub. I follow his directions to rub and slap at her arms and legs.

"Harder!" he says, and I need no urging. I am as cold and cruel as her half-brother, standing by her deathbed counting her jewels. With every open-handed slap, I recall how she has dangled me, made me promises, taken away what I loved, and now left me. It is hard to keep my hand open and not beat her with my fists.

The hubbub dies down as people watch us. Even Seton's sobs quieten, and the priest's voice drops to a mutter.

Lord James crosses to the end of the bed. "Arnault! Pray leave my sister in peace. This is unseemly. You can see she has gone."

"The Queen yet lives. Look, there is a blush on her cheek," Arnault says, rubbing her limp hand.

There is a gasp throughout the room and Lord James hurries to the bedhead and bends over the Queen. Seton rushes to the other side.

"I can see nothing," Lord James declares, drawing back. "I order you, desist from treating her royal body in this manner."

Arnault ignores him. "Help me. We must get the emetic into her mouth."

Seton, La Flamina, and I take the Queen's shoulders and lift awkwardly, until her head is lolling more or less upright. I cannot see any sign of life, but I take her chin so he can force her lips open and dribble the dark, foul-smelling fluid into her mouth.

"Careful, careful," he mutters, allowing a few drops at a time. "Swallow, Madam, swallow it down."

He says she lives, but when she retches suddenly it's all I can do not to drop her and leap back, and the cry that runs around the room is half horror. She retches again, her eyes fly open, and she begins to vomit in earnest. Arnault leaps to her head and helps us lift her and lean her forward so she doesn't choke. The servants start screaming, the priest is back by the bedside calling on God, and black vomit sprays across the bed. The Queen gags and retches and coughs and still it comes.

At last she pauses and takes an agonized breath. Seton's face, opposite mine, is suffused with joy. Even I, who hated the Queen only moments ago, feel the tears on my cheeks at her return. It is not only the prospect of my future making me feel so.

Then I happen to catch sight of Lord James as he stares down at his half-sister. His mouth is working and his fists are clenched. When he realizes I am watching, he turns away. With his back to me, he calls out, "Thanks to the Lord, the Queen lives this day. We must all give thanks for this good fortune."

Over the doubled-up body of the Queen, Arnault meets my eyes. "The Lord always gets the credit."

≈ ≈ ≈

The Queen has survived, but she is like a wraith and I think something of her spirit must have escaped the horror of her life when Seton flung open the window, believing her dead.

For days, Seton, La Flamina, and I barely leave her side and Arnault, too, is in constant attendance. We watch her as though the force of our will can keep her fixed to the earth. We feed her the tastiest foods that the kitchen can produce, in tiny bites as if she were a child. We hold cups at her lips for her to sup at broths and spiced wines and thick soups. But she lies, thin and listless, her eyes dark circles in her face.

Secret word is sent out of her illness and near-death. A messenger rides to the King in Glasgow, but he makes no reply. Another messenger takes the news to Bothwell where he lies recovering from his wounds at Hermitage. By the evening of the next day, a party rides into Jedburgh carrying Bothwell on a litter like a woman.

But there is nothing womanly in the way he comes into her bedchamber. While we have stepped around her silently in slippered feet, spoken in whispers and moved slowly, I can hear the sound of his boots on the floor all the way up the corridor. He limps into her room, all size and bluster and noise, and crosses to her bedside. He snatches up her hand and kisses it hard, far longer than is seemly for a married man greeting a married woman.

"Lord Bothwell." The Queen's voice comes out in a croak.

"What has happened to you?" His loud voice seems to shake the chamber and I wince.

"I fell from my horse and took a chill. It seems I do not have much strength these days."

"I heard you were poisoned," he says.

Arnault steps forward hastily. "We do not know that. The Queen has long had an illness in her belly and the chill brought it on again."

But he is too late. The Queen looks at him in horror, and then back to Bothwell.

"Who says this?" she asks.

He shrugs. "Madam, you know how rumors start when a queen is ill. Poison is always the first thing mentioned. I'm sure Arnault is right."

Tears begin to trickle down her cheeks. "Do you know that my husband will not stir himself to come here, though I almost died?"

"Then he is a fool!" Bothwell's voice is raised. "And you are a fool to lie here thus."

La Flamina jumps to her feet. "Lord Bothwell, that is enough. You're upsetting her."

He glares back at her. "She needs to be upset. She needs to be outraged. Look at her. She will lie here and let herself die for no better reason than that idiot of a boy."

He reaches over and pulls the covers back to the Queen's waist. He grabs her limp hand and drags her into a sitting position and puts his face close to hers.

"Listen!" he bellows at her. "You are worth a thousand of any of those fools. You have survived. You have a son—half of Europe is about to come to Scotland for his baptism. How dare you let that prat bring you so low?"

The rest of us are on our feet, Arnault is tugging at Bothwell, and Seton is at the door to call a guard. But there is a stirring on the Queen's face and for the first time since I saw her body lifeless, there is a spark of animation on her features.

"How dare you handle your Queen thus?" she says with a hint of her old steel.

They stare at each other grimly for a moment.

"That's better," Bothwell grunts, and drops her hand. He takes a step backward and sinks down into a chair, his face white. "Madam, I'm too old to take such wounds and then shake sense into you afterward."

He has done what all our soft petting has failed to do. She raises herself up in the bed expectantly.

"I hear you are to ride to meet Lord Hume in a few days," Bothwell says. "I would come with you, but I am confined to a litter until this slice in my leg grows together, and I will not give Hume the satisfaction of seeing me thus. I will come and meet you at Craigmillar when you're finished. There are important things your closest lords must discuss with you. Take heart! You are better away from your husband."

"I do not know that I can ride," she says.

"Of course you can." Bothwell looks at Arnault. "What say you, physician? Shall we give her three days? Four days? How much time to prepare?"

"A week at least," Arnault says.

"You are right. I do not have the leisure of a week." She pushes the covers back. "There are too many urgent matters in the kingdom. I will ride in four days."

Bothwell laughs. "Now you sound like a queen again, Your Grace. Someone call for a meal. A big one, with meat."

We eat in the Queen's chamber. By the end of the meal she has color in her cheeks again and she rises from the bed to walk around.

Bothwell, in contrast, has grown pale and quiet, and finally Arnault orders him to rest and asks me to show him to a room that's been made ready. I take his arm and he leans on me, limping down the hallway, a servant following.

"Jesus, she's taken it out of me," he mutters as we come into the room. He sinks down to the bed and waves at the servant to unlace his boots.

"You had best not tarry." He won't quite meet my eye. "Soon you'll be an unmarried noblewoman with a castle. You don't want any scandal."

I step back from him and move to the door. "Lord Bothwell, what of my father? He was in the grip of melancholy when I left him."

Bothwell sighs. "He made a mistake, letting the prisoners escape, and he can't forgive himself. A soldier can't afford such a luxury as melancholy but he can't get over it."

"He says he's not worthy of the castle, having let you down thus."

"Then he is a fool," Bothwell says. "He's punishing himself far more than I ever would."

"Can't you speak to him? Do what you did with the Queen?"

He grins, leaning his head back on the pillows and closing his eyes. "It worked well, didn't it? I've neglected him, having had a lot on my mind. I'll go back and give him the Queen's talking-to."

"Thank you."

I watch a moment longer as I realize he is falling asleep. His face relaxes and his breathing deepens. In spite of his exhaustion, a sense of vitality still exudes from him.

It is four days, the Queen said, until we ride out to meet Hume. Her promise redeemed at last.

Forty-two

The Queen calls me to meet with her privately the day before we leave Jedburgh.

"This is a matter that must be handled carefully, for Hume will not take kindly to it," she says. "I have thought on this and I will not reveal you to him at first."

"But Lord Hume has seen me at court."

"You are the mistress of disguise. With a different wig and frock, he will not know you, and he will not see you for long. I will send Lord James and Maitland to Wedderburn with Lord Hume, but you and I shall go to Blackadder."

I stare at her. She is afraid, I realize, to strip this powerful family of one of its prize possessions. My heart sinks. She could betray me yet.

"You should choose a different name for the first night," she says thoughtfully. Then she turns to me and smiles. "You will be a spy, only this time you will spy for yourself. Tell me, what name shall you use?"

I take a deep breath. "Alison Douglas. My grandmother's name." If I cannot ride there under my own name, hers is one I may bear with pride, and the Douglas clan is so huge that it should not attract attention.

She frowns. "Very well. The Douglases are not in my favor, but that name should be welcome in the Hume family."

≈　≈　≈

When we set out from Jedburgh, she has fought her way back to sufficient good health to rule again. Lord James, ever the statesman, shows no sign of disappointment. Maitland maintains his usual calm in the face of chaos. Seton still carries the face of a woman reprieved from heartbreak, her smile never far from her lips. The Queen herself rides tall and only her remaining Marys and I know how pale she is under her face powders.

The people of Jedburgh come out to see her off as though it is a great day. Most country people will be lucky to see a monarch once in their lifetimes and many have a relative who escaped the noose because of the Queen's unwillingness to punish them harshly. She rides at the head of a long line of her lords and men-at-arms. She smiles and waves at the people who line the streets of Jedburgh. They wave back and kneel as she passes. For now she is beloved here.

The day is exquisite as only autumn can be. This is my own air, my hills, my earth under the horses' hooves, my eagles circling in the sky, my water trickling in the streams, the land I was born to, the land whose name I carry, my homeland.

It is also the heartland of the Hume family, which holds much of this corner of Scotland: Hume Castle, Wedderburn Castle, Langton Castle, and Blackadder Castle here in the Borders. As we wind our way toward Wedderburn, fear begins to take over my excitement. No Blackadder has walked on these lands and survived unscathed since William was a boy. I am here to avenge them, and even the Queen's party does not feel like enough protection. I wish suddenly that Bothwell was with us.

I see the Hume army from a long way off, his pennants and standards fluttering in the morning breeze, his men mounted in neat rows. Lord Hume himself rides out to meet the Queen, followed by the men of his clan. They are fighters; I can see by the set of their hands on the bridles and their armor. Lord Hume is at the front of his men. To his side, David Hume of Wedderburn, whom I spied talking to the King before Rizzio's murder. I look farther, wondering which is Alexander.

"Your Grace." Lord Hume pulls up his horse, dismounts, sinks down on one knee, and bows his head. "You have brought the sun in its full glory as your worthy companion." Behind him, his men also dismount and kneel.

"Indeed." The Queen inclines her head. "It shows off your realm to great advantage, Lord Hume."

"In truth it is your realm and God's realm; I am but the keeper." Lord Hume smiles and rises to his feet. "We are honored to have you as our guest at Wedderburn."

"You are most hospitable." The Queen nods for them to rise. The men stand and go to mount their horses again.

"There is just one thing. I have long wished to see your castle at Blackadder. I have heard it spoken of in Edinburgh. I would like to stay there if it does not inconvenience you."

I am watching closely and I see one head snap up at the mention of the castle. Alexander.

Lord Hume turns to the man, eyebrows raised in inquiry. Alexander stumbles forward to Lord Hume's side. He is fat, as befits one who was simply born into the lands his family stole, and I can see he is sweating in his ceremonial clothing.

"We have not prepared—" he stammers, looking from the Queen to Lord Hume.

"Your Grace, it is a small castle only and not especially well-favored," Lord Hume says. "I pray you, come and be settled at Wedderburn, and we will ride across to Blackadder tomorrow when my cousin may offer you his full hospitality."

The Queen smiles, and the smile widens into one of her bell-like laughs. Lord Hume, sure of himself, joins in.

"Lord Hume, I have such rich fare when I am in Edinburgh that I have come to long for the plain food that ordinary people eat, and to live a while as ordinary people do," she says. "What I most desire today is to visit your castle as an unexpected friend, not as a royal guest. I will come to Blackadder with just a few of my ladies and the rest of the party will go with you to Wedderburn to feast. We will require only a couple of rooms and a simple meal with your family, as if we are passing travelers."

There is silence, and Lord Hume faces Alexander. I cannot see what passes between them, but Alexander bows to the Queen clumsily. "We would be honored to have you in our home."

"That is settled, then." She smiles. "Lord Hume, I would be

grateful if you would entertain Maitland and my brother this day and see the rest of my party settled at Wedderburn. I will take my two ladies-in-waiting and my guards with me to Blackadder."

There are muttered consultations and bemused expressions. Maitland and Lord James must know nothing of this, for they appear as confused as the Humes. Alexander sends a rider off at a gallop in the direction of the castle. He heaves his bulk back into the saddle and rides forward to join the Queen, his face a mixture of emotions.

Lord Hume is tight-lipped. When the Queen bids him farewell, he bows his head low again, though this time he does not go down to his knee. He gathers the reins in his hands and swings onto his horse lightly.

The parties are rearranged. Lord Hume rides off toward Wedderburn with most of the Queen's train, and our smaller party, with a force of guards, sets out in the direction of Blackadder. As we move out of sight of the main party, the Queen rides across to Alexander.

"It is so slow, traveling with such a large group," she says, smiling at him. "I feel that I have been cooped up for weeks. Shall we go a little faster?"

Without waiting for an answer, she spurs her horse, which leaps into a canter. Alexander must gather his wits, shout to the guards to keep up, and push his own, heavier horse to catch up with them.

I canter behind them and the ground is soft under the horse's hooves. Away from Lord Hume, my fear lessens and when finally we slow to a trot, I ride up close behind the Queen and Alexander. I see him point, and up ahead I can see a stone tower rising above the trees. My heart begins to pound.

We wind around the side of a small hill and drop down to the river. The Blackadder Water. As we reach its banks I turn my eyes to follow it downstream, and see the castle on the far side of the water.

The sight of it at last runs through me in a rush. Built where the bank rises steeply into a cliff, the castle appears to have grown out of the land itself, chiseled from earth and stone.

I have always imagined a fortress, like Tulliallan, but there are windows and walkways opening out to the riverside. Where Tulliallan presents a sheer face of stone to the world, and clear lands all around so that anyone may be seen approaching, the castle of Blackadder is more like the mountain of Arthur's Seat, something from the earth.

"A most unusual setting," the Queen says.

"The river makes a natural moat," Alexander says. "My wife and I like the sound of it rushing past. The front of the castle is more traditional, but I like to show guests this face of it first."

We ride back up the hill and around to the front of the castle, where a group awaits us. From a distance I stare hard at them, trying to pick out William's surviving sister. There are so many women and children waiting to greet us as we ride into the courtyard that I am confused. A younger woman steps forward and curtsies.

"My wife, Catherine," Alexander says.

"Your Grace, we are honored to welcome you into our home," the woman says, and they all kneel or curtsy to the Queen.

As they rise to their feet, I search their faces. An older woman who waits at the back resembles William a little, but she does not have his bitterness carved into her face. She looks intelligent and kindly and she holds a young child by the hand.

I dismount, looking around me as my feet touch the ground. William has only one surviving child, and I could easily reach old age without bearing children myself, but David Hume the elder begat six children from my grandmother Alison in five years, before he died. William knew some of the lines and the names, but the Hume clan has kept itself close and William lost track of the children born. I realize now he would have hated to hear of each new birth.

Catherine and Alexander invite us inside as stableboys take our sweating horses. I follow the Queen, who stops every few steps to exclaim over the castle's construction, its outlook, the tapestries hanging on the wall, allowing me to look around as we enter.

It is too much to take in. All I can feel is my pounding heart, the shortness of my breath, the tightness of my dress around my ribcage. As we walk through the entranceway and into the great hall, the buttresses of the ceiling feel as though they are pressing upon me. I cannot breathe. The cold of the floor seeps up through my feet; the very walls seem to cry out.

I reach out my hand for some support, unnoticed as everyone

crowds around the Queen. The wall feels icy against my hand and at my feet the flagstones are crimson and gleaming. My head spins and I feel myself falling.

Forty-three

The first thing I'm aware of is the press of a hand holding a damp cloth to my forehead. A tender touch; a female touch. I lie still with my eyes closed to savor it.

"Do you feel a little better?"

I open my eyes. The woman I had identified as William's sister is sitting beside me. The softness of her voice brings tears to my eyes.

"There, lass." She puts down the cloth and smoothes my hair back. The feel of her hand fills some old ache.

"Alison?" she says. "I am Beatrice."

She is my aunt, though she does not know it. She wipes my forehead. "You're not the first to be taken over so in that room. Some say it is haunted by the past. Did you see something?"

"Blood, I think."

"I have seen it too," she says softly. "I do not care for that room over much."

"But this castle seems very beautiful."

"I have never known another, so I have nothing to compare it to. I was born here and I have left it no more than half a dozen times in my life."

I look up at her. "I will ask the Queen to invite you to accompany us back to Edinburgh. Holyrood Palace is as magnificent as a French court, and in parts of the city the buildings tower seven or eight stories high!"

"No!" She draws back suddenly.

"But there is much for you to see." I sit up.

She gets up and backs away from me. "Please," she says, putting her hand up. "I have no wish to leave here."

I rest back against the pillows. "It is said you were kept prisoner here as a child," I say.

Her eyes widen. "What?"

"I heard your mother was forced into marriage with David Hume and that you and Margaret were kept prisoner here until you were old enough to be forced into marriage with his brothers," I say, emboldened.

I do not know what to expect, but she laughs. It is not a bitter laugh like William's, but genuine mirth.

"My Lord." She laughs again. "That is the stuff of legend, Alison. Why would we have been imprisoned?"

"Is it not true, then?" My chest begins to hurt.

"Margaret and I were betrothed at a young age, that's true, when our mother married David Hume. But not imprisoned! I wanted nothing more than to stay here and I was glad to marry a man who lived here too."

I take a breath. "What about your brother?"

"Which one? There are many."

"Your full brother. Robert's son."

"William." She looks down at me for a long moment. "Margaret and I were so sad when he died. But our mother had her next son within the year and soon the place was full of children. I have not thought of him these many years." She peers at me more closely. "You seem to know much of our family."

"I am distantly related to your mother, on the Douglas side."

"She was an extraordinary woman," Beatrice says, her eyes softening. "If you are related to her, then you are an honored guest here. What is the lineage?"

I look away. "I do not know exactly. My mother was a Douglas and she told me before she died that she was some kind of cousin to Alison."

"It is hard to lose your mother, is it not? My mother has been dead this past quarter century, but I still miss her dreadfully. Almost more than I missed my husband when he died."

"Did you miss him much?"

"Yes," she replies. "Two of our sons died as babies, Alison. When John died, all I had left was Alexander and I lived in terror that something would happen to him too. But now he is master of this castle and has two children of his own."

309

"What of Margaret?"

Beatrice smiles. "Margaret liked to ride and hunt. Before she even married Robert, she would ride out with him at every chance. They were well-matched, those two. She fell from a horse. Her two sons died in childhood too and Robert never got over the loss. He took a fever and died as well."

"So Alexander is the only one who survives from the Blackadder side?"

She wrinkles her forehead. "Why, yes, I suppose you are right."

There is a loud knock at the door and before I can gather my wits a young woman strides in.

"The Queen sent me to find out if you are all right," she says abruptly, and looks at me with some curiosity.

I stare back. She has a strong stance and a direct gaze. Her hair is the color of burnished copper and her eyes are an unusual green.

"Isobel, you need to wait after you knock," Beatrice says. "This is our guest, Alison. She's related to your grandmother. So you are probably cousins, distantly."

"Half of Scotland is cousin to the other half." She bobs her head impatiently and turns to Beatrice. "The Queen wants to go riding after lunch, and I'm to join the party."

"I will come too," I say.

"Then you'd best get yourself ready," she says. "They are almost finished eating. We'll be leaving from the front courtyard. Do you need a fresh horse?"

"Do you have one that could better my own?"

Her green eyes regard me with interest. "Why, how good is your own?"

"My own is fit for royalty," I say. "Coming from the Queen's own stable. He will hunt all day and still fly over a wall at the end of it. But he does not know this country, and I would not have him injured by a rabbit hole or such like."

"The Queen says she will ride one of our horses astride. Will you?"

"Aye."

"I believe we have just the mount for you, then," she says, with a dangerous smile. She turns and disappears from the room.

"That girl!" Beatrice says, in half annoyance. "She has worse manners than a servant."

"Who is she?"

"She is the daughter of Alison's son David, the Baron of Wedderburn. That family lives at Wedderburn, but Isobel is staying here. Wedderburn is very grand and the boys of the family spend time there, while the girls tend to come here. But Isobel is one of those girls, like Margaret, who cannot abide the staid, indoor life."

I throw back the covers and swing my legs out of the bed.

"Are you fit to ride?" Beatrice asks, coming to my side. "You are still pale."

"I am fit." I get to my feet. "I must find my riding clothes so I may be seated astride."

Beatrice sends for the bags and a servant, who helps me out of my dress and into the breeks and fitted jacket that I wear to ride with the Queen when there are few others to see. It is not male clothing, but masculine enough to raise eyebrows. I sit on the bed while the girl helps me pull on my boots. Beatrice stares.

"You have very unusual fashions in the Queen's court," she says, her expression scandalized. "I have heard that the Queen sometimes goes about dressed as a man, but I dismissed it as gossip."

"It's true, though she does it for fun only," I say. "You should try it sometime."

She shakes her head. "I couldn't, I'm sure." She cannot take her eyes off me.

≋　≋　≋

When I emerge into the courtyard, the Queen comes to my side and takes my hand.

"Are you quite recovered?" she asks softly.

"Yes. I was a little overcome, that is all."

"We have shocked our hosts with our riding attire."

We smile conspiratorially and she releases my hand.

Isobel cannot stop herself staring as I approach. "You are dressed like a man!"

"It is much easier for riding. And for many other things too."

"Like what?"

I take the reins from her and put my face close to the horse. It will not hurt her to know of my standing in court. "When the Queen wishes to mingle with the ordinary citizens of Edinburgh, she and I disguise ourselves and go out into the streets at night."

It seems impossible her eyes could open any wider as she looks at the Queen. "Are men in Edinburgh such fools?"

"We spend more time perfecting our disguise in Edinburgh," I say. "When we are clothed and wigged, I would defy you to pick us as other than a couple of merchants looking for entertainment. Now, what should I know of this fine beast?"

She brings her gaze back from the Queen with difficulty. "He is strong-willed. You must let him know you're in charge. But he is the fastest horse in the stable and, if he respects you, none will try harder."

Our party mounts up. Most of the household wants to ride out with the Queen and there are more than twenty, plus a handful of guards. We move off at a sedate pace and I ride beside the Queen.

The land feels at once familiar and strange. It is soft country, undulating gently, traced by the river and its small tributaries. Sheep and cattle graze, the fields lay bare waiting for next year's crop. There are tiny dwellings scattered around in which the bondsmen and field workers live.

The estate is large—it would take us all day to ride around it, Alexander says with pride. He points out landmarks and evidence of the farm's success. It seems he does not know the game that nobles play, hiding evidence of their wealth and speaking only of how much toil and effort is required to manage it.

I let myself fall behind them a little to try to clear my mind. What did William imagine would happen here, with the generations now born at Blackadder Castle? I am riding among his half-brothers and sisters, half-nieces, nephews, cousins. His mother and his sisters have bred a clan of Humes to share our blood.

"He will be terribly bored if all you do is walk him." Isobel rides up beside me. "There is a stretch coming up where I always let him go fast. Look, he knows already."

Indeed the horse has pricked his ears and raised his head, and he starts to dance a little. I curb him so that his neck arches, and ride up beside the Queen.

"Isobel would take us on a gallop, if you wish," I say.

She smiles at me and reins her horse away from Alexander. "Excellent. I am weary of walking."

Isobel trots forward and as she draws level with us, urges her horse into a gallop. The Queen and I follow suit and in a moment the three of us are pounding down a grassy slope. The wind is cool, the horse beneath me is all fire and muscle, the fields are a blur. Though sidesaddle, Isobel is an excellent rider and she matches us stride for stride.

The rest of the party is far behind when we reach the edge of a woodland and thunder into it. Our hoofbeats are instantly muffled, the sun cut off, the air dank. Up ahead, deer crash away from us, white tails bobbing. We slow down and follow Isobel, twisting and turning between the trees, branches whipping at our clothes, my horse's breath loud in my ears.

At last she slows, pulling her mount into a tight circle, smiling at us triumphantly.

"It's the oldest tree for miles," she says, and the silence of the forest seems to eat her words. "They say it is eight hundred years or more."

The oak is enormous, twisted and gnarled. It would take more than us three to join hands around its girth. I slide down from the horse, walk up to the oak, and lay my hands on its bulk. This tree was here before the land ever carried the name of Blackadder. I am not even an insect on its hide.

The Queen reaches up and runs her fingers through the foliage. "This is a precious thing indeed. There are few such left in Scotland now."

"It is a secret," Isobel says. "Promise you won't speak of it."

The Queen smiles. "I promise."

"We'd better get back." Isobel sniffs the air loudly. "Rain's coming."

I swing up into the saddle again and we walk the slick, blowing horses back along a maze of twisting pathways. I could not retrace our steps but Isobel rides without hesitation, following some set of landmarks I do not perceive. It takes much longer to ride out at walking pace, and near the edge she urges us into a trot.

When we come out of the forest and back into the field, the day has changed. There is a chill in the air and the clouds have rolled in. The rest of our party is waiting anxiously in the open, peering into the gloom to find us. Alexander rides forward to meet us, relief on his face.

"Your Grace, forgive me, we could not keep up with your riding and by the time we reached the forest we could not see which way you had gone." He shoots a furious look at Isobel. "I have sent some of the guards in but they must have become lost, as they have not met you."

"Only I know all the ways through the forest," Isobel says.

"Then I would be pleased if you would go and find them so I may take the Queen back before it rains."

Isobel turns her horse into the forest and we set out at a smart trot back toward the castle. Alexander glances from side to side nervously. There are only three guards with us. The other five are back in the forest and the afternoon feels threatening, the weather pressing in on us from the rear. He is silent, and there is a sheen of sweat on his forehead in spite of the cold wind at our backs.

"I do not believe I have ever seen you at court," the Queen says, reining her horse beside his.

He looks startled. "Lord Hume and David Hume represent our family on such occasions. I am honored you would think of it, but there are far more distinguished men in the family than myself."

"I do not think I have heard Lord Hume speak of you," she persists.

"I am sure he would not, Your Grace. I am but the keeper of this estate, which is small and mean compared to the others in the family."

"It has not been in your family very long, I understand," she says.

He looks confused. "It has been in my family for three generations. My grandfather was married here."

"To its previous owner?"

"Yes," he says. "Alison Douglas, the widow. She had been here with only her daughters for six years, until my grandfather took her into the family and brought children and company into her life again. The castle was a cold and lonely place before that."

"Your own mother would remember those days."

314

"She still speaks of how delighted she was to have so many brothers and sisters, Your Grace." He smiles a little.

"Your mother and your aunt both married into the Hume family too, am I correct?" she asks, guileless.

"Yes. My mother has hardly left the castle in her life and my aunt loved it here too, until she died."

"Do you have brothers and sisters?"

"My mother and her sister were unlucky in that regard and did not inherit Alison's strength for childbearing. I had two brothers who died in infancy, and my aunt's two boys also died as babes."

"So you are now the sole owner of the castle?"

"Yes," he says with pride. "My mother assigned it to me when I was still a boy, in 1543."

"That would be after the last Blackadder heir died?" she asks, her voice not changing tone.

"There were no Blackadder heirs." He frowns. "Just some extended family who had designs on the castle themselves. But they had no rights to it. My mother and her sister were the legitimate heirs."

"Did they not have a Blackadder brother?"

He turns to her. "My mother's brother died as a boy, while they still lived here alone. His headstone lies in our graveyard. You may see it if you wish."

"I would like that," she says, glancing at me.

I take what seems to be my first breath for a long time and find my hands clenched so hard around the reins that my nails are cutting into my palms. The top of the castle is in sight above the trees and we wind alongside the river toward it.

"Do you hunt?" the Queen asks. "We saw a good run of deer in the forest."

He gives an anxious half-smile again. "I do not care much for hunting. Isobel likes it, though. She is a true Wedderburn Hume—a fearless rider and hunter. Myself, I prefer to eat the animal than to chase it."

"Indeed," the Queen says. "Perhaps Isobel would care to join us when we hunt at Wedderburn tomorrow."

"I would not try to keep her away."

The rain begins to spit on the back of my neck and the horses pick up their pace, scenting the stable and the end of their exertions. As we start to climb the hill on the approach to the castle, we come upon a fence surrounding a group of tombstones.

"Our family plot," Alexander says, pulling up. "Alison's son is buried at the back there. It is a little overgrown now. He has been dead—what? More than forty years."

The wind gusts coldly and the horses pull at their reins, impatient at being stopped so close to home. The light is changing rapidly, deepening to a gloom. The Queen lifts her reins and moves off and the rest of the party falls in behind her. I linger, holding the horse back until they are gone.

Forty-four

The grass is unkempt around the graves but I find my aunt Margaret easily enough, flanked by her husband, Robert, and two small headstones for her little sons. Beatrice's husband's grave shows more signs of care. Alison's is the largest and grandest, with the letters deeply chiseled: *Beloved of all who knew her.*

I move away from the main tombstones and into an overgrown area devoid of markers. The rain comes down in a drizzle and the light is failing. At last I come across it. Overgrown and almost out of sight, a child-sized stone: *William Blackadder 1513–1519. Gone to find his heavenly reward.*

I am chilled. The evidence of his death is at my feet, as if he never grew to adulthood and I was never born. I clap my hands to my sides to dispel the feeling and kneel down to trace my fingers across the lettering. It is rough and hastily done.

"You must be very interested in tombs."

I jump. Isobel has ridden up the hill, the rain masking her horse's hoofbeats on the soft grass. She stands outside the fence and her horse touches noses with mine.

I rise to my feet. "I wanted to see your grandmother's grave, being related to her."

"That's not my grandmother's grave," she says. "You should come away from there. They say that part of the graveyard is cursed and all the tombstones were taken away."

"Not all of them," I say. "This one says William Blackadder."

"My grandmother forbade them to touch that one, but all the other tombstones that said Blackadder were destroyed and the ground deconsecrated," she says. "They lie forgotten now."

"Not forgotten by all," I say, before I can stop myself. I make my way out of the yard. As my hand reaches for the gate, the eerie glimmer of the coming storm lights up Isobel's deep green eyes and white face. "Your grandmother was a Blackadder."

She flinches. "That name is cursed. My grandmother was a Douglas, who married a Blackadder. But she died a Hume and that is the line I am descended from. Beatrice and Margaret came from the Blackadder line and look at them. Alexander is the only surviving child between them."

"He is now the master of this castle."

She shrugs. "He is a fat fool. The best the Blackadder line could produce."

"If the name was cursed, why did your family keep it for this estate?"

"They like to remind Alexander of his place. Come, it will rain in earnest in a few minutes and they will be worrying for us."

I mount and we set out toward the castle as dusk rolls in.

"Alexander may not always hold this castle," she says, so quietly I have to lean in to hear her. "And if he does not, the name Blackadder could pass from this land."

"Who else will take it?" I ask.

She says nothing, but looks at me steadily. She must be no more than fourteen years old.

"How could it come to you?" I ask at last. "Alexander has children."

She gives a low laugh. "Alexander is nothing in the Hume family. The offspring of the Blackadder daughters. I come from the noble line. My father is the sixth Baron of Wedderburn and my brother will be the seventh Baron, in line to receive Wedderburn. But I will have something of my own too."

As we clatter into the courtyard on wet cobblestones, she rides close to me. "My grandmother would have wanted me to have the castle. They say I am almost identical to her at the same age. I will show you her portrait."

"I would like that."

She pulls on her horse's reins until he arches his neck and prances like a warhorse. "I will make this place great again. I will not sit frightened inside its walls like Beatrice, or glutting at its table like Alexander."

Stableboys come out and take the horses' heads and bring us blocks to help us dismount. She watches me swing down easily.

"I will learn to ride thus," she says. "And I should like to try the way you wear a man's attire."

≈ ≈ ≈

The storm that hung at our heels on the afternoon ride comes down in earnest, its lightning flashes illuminating the high windows of the dining hall as we enter for dinner.

The Queen sets herself to charming the Hume family. Alexander has had his finest red wine brought up from the cellar and by the time dinner is served, the mood around the table has become congenial.

I listen to every word, toying with my cup, laughing when it is needed, even making the occasional joke to keep the atmosphere merry. I use all my skill to discreetly observe each one of them.

Although she is barely more than a child, Isobel can hold her own in conversation, even attempting some credible French and a discussion about the poetry of Ronsard. She has taken advantage of the education given to children from the more noble line of the Wedderburn Hume family. Alexander, Catherine, Beatrice, and the others who live at Blackadder seem like country yokels in comparison.

The wine continues to flow freely, but I drink little of it. At my side, Beatrice is also quiet and her silence feels strained. I want to speak to her, but I cannot think of anything to say. There is a chill in the room, in spite of the crackling fire in the huge hearth and the lanterns and candles throwing warmth and light into the dark corners. I see no bloody visions this time, but there is still a prickle at the back of my neck.

When the servants begin clearing the dinner dishes, Beatrice stands up and makes a small curtsy to the Queen. "Your Grace, I am an old woman and if you will, I shall retire and leave you to your merriment."

The Queen smiles. "Of course. I am grateful that you have shared your home with us this night. May my lady-in-waiting Alison accompany you to your room?"

Beatrice may not have been to court, but she understands the subtlety of an order from the Queen. She nods and I rise and come to her side.

A servant goes before us with a flickering candle, and the light jumps and dances on the walls. Beatrice leans on my arm as we start up the steps. "Thank you," she says. "The day has tired me."

"It is my pleasure." I hold her more firmly. I wish I could have known her, this quiet woman who does not like to leave her castle.

"Did you enjoy your ride?" she asks.

"Very much. Your lands are very beautiful."

"They are the envy of many, I have heard."

I concentrate on my feet in the dim hallway. When we reach the top of the stairs, she pauses again and takes a deep breath.

"Tell me, is there some reason that the Queen has sought us out, when all the splendor of Wedderburn awaited her? It is not the quality of our food, nor our wine. Alexander does not hunt or play sport, and we do not have the learning of the people she is surrounded by in the capital. What brings her here?"

"The delights of the capital can pall and she has had much care of late." I keep my eyes on the servant leading the way. "She needed to relax away from exalted company for an evening. It is a whim of hers, to change plans unexpectedly."

"She seems to know a great deal about us."

"She is the Queen," I say and shrug.

"I fear that she visits us with some purpose in mind."

We reach the doorway to her chamber and stop. The servant opens the door and begins lighting the candles. Beatrice has let go of my arm and she turns to face me, her countenance in near darkness.

"You are related to my mother. In her memory, I beg you to tell me."

My heart pounds and I can feel the warmth of her body near mine. The silence lengthens between us. At last she sighs and starts to turn away. My hand moves and catches her by the sleeve.

"William lives," I whisper.

She gasps and her hand moves to her throat. "I can show you his tomb."

"I have seen the stone. I do not know what lies under it, but it is not your brother."

She stares and in the silhouette of her face I cannot see her expression. Then she waves the servant away, draws me into the room with her, and closes the door.

"Who are you?" she asks. "Speak the truth if you would make such a claim."

She is William's sister, but she has not seen him for a lifetime and that lifetime has been spent as part of the Hume family. I long to tell her the truth but here in the heart of the Hume holdings, I dare not.

"I am William's emissary."

Her face hardens. "What proof do you have of his claim?"

"I will swear it on the grave of Alison Douglas."

She crosses the room to the window. The lightning is still flashing outside, lighting up her face.

"We have heard of a man claiming to be William Blackadder," she says. "His story was investigated, of course, years ago. Do you know what we discovered? That man was no son of Alison's. He was the bastard child of a lowly Blackadder cleric. He thought to pass himself off as Alison's son and make a claim for these lands. But I tell you, my brother lies dead in the ground yonder."

She turns from the window and I stare back at her in shock. My legs begin to tremble and I sit down heavily in a chair. "I do not believe you," I say.

"You have been deceived. The evidence lies in the church records in Glasgow. A king's charter, no less, proving his lineage." She shakes her head. "Is this why the Queen is visiting us, perchance? If she thinks to somehow champion his claim, the evidence of his bastardry will come out. He will be exposed for what he is."

I shake my head slowly and outside the thunder rolls and crashes. She crosses to my side and puts her hand on my shoulder.

"Who are you, child?"

I shake her hand off and rise to my feet. "I am no one," I say, my voice catching. I cross the room, wrench the door open, and leave her.

Forty-five

I find a servant to take me to my room, high on the top floor. She leaves me candles and a lantern, but I extinguish them and stand by the window to listen to the storm passing.

I lay my hands flat on the window ledge. The rain is so furious that I can feel the fine mist of it against my face. I am trembling. With a few words, Beatrice has ripped the fabric of my world. I cannot believe William would have knowingly lived such a lie. But if a king's charter proclaims him a bastard, our cause is lost.

At last the rain stops. The lightning passes to the west, the wind drops, and the clouds part a little for the moon. It glints on the swollen, rushing river. I take a deep, shuddering breath, and then another. I must go outside. I must trail my fingers in the river and find out if it will speak to me. Surely the truth will be there.

I change back into my riding breeks and wrap my cloak warmly around my body. I make my way through the empty corridors down to the front door, walking quietly past the great hall where the others are still at dinner. But when I step down to the portcullis, the guards refuse to let me through.

"Strict orders," one of them says, looking at my clothes and trying to keep his face expressionless. "The castle is always locked at night. Double the guard with the Queen here."

"Triple the guard, I'd say." Isobel has stepped out of the hall and she comes down the corridor toward us. "The Borders are a dangerous place, Alison, and the Hume family takes no chances of being caught unaware by intruders. The castle is vulnerable, you see. Because of the noise of the river, an army could set upon us in the dark without us hearing. The portcullis is never opened at night."

She turns her face away from the guard, toward me, and in the flickering torchlight I see a quick wink. "Let me take you to your room."

She takes my elbow and walks me along the corridor until we are out of their sight. "I do not like being locked in either," she whispers. "I'm sure even the Queen's great palace must have its secret ways."

I nod. "The Queen escaped the last uprising through a passage in the wine cellar."

"We, too, have such a secret way. Very few know it."

"Will you show me?" I ask. "I am longing to be outside."

"Swear you will keep it secret."

I hesitate only a moment. "I swear."

Isobel leads me down through a maze of stairs to the kitchen, still humming with activity. The cook is preparing the sweet course for the Queen; servants and dogs are snarling over the scraps.

Isobel attracts the attention of the spit turner. When he creeps over to us, she presses something into his hand and he leads us to a store-room.

"Help me with this dress," she says when he leaves us. "I cannot take us there in such finery."

She faces away from me and holds up her hair. I hesitate for a moment and then unlace her. She steps out of the frock and pulls her cloak around her underthings. Then she leads me into a dark corner. Rats skitter past, and together we roll a barrel out of the way. Behind it is an earthen tunnel and she beckons me to crawl inside after her. It is short; at the end she pushes a large stone aside with surprising ease. It must have some clever mechanism to allow it to move so.

As it rolls back, the sudden roar of rushing water is shocking, and the night is black and silver before my eyes. We emerge high up the riverbank, on a narrow shelf above a sheer drop to the rushing water. Through the clouds, the moon lights up the landscape: the hills, the trees, and the river rushing directly toward us before sweeping into a turn at the foot of the castle. There is a mist of very light rain.

She touches my arm and gestures for me to follow her. We scramble down a steep path, clinging to branches and grass.

At the bottom, she steps out in front of me and stands on a rock, her face turned upstream. I make my way to the edge of the water. How long have I waited for this moment? I crouch down in the mud. The reeds pull at my clothes and at last my stretching fingers find the water.

Its touch is so cold I can forget the young woman standing on a rock, gazing upstream with burning intensity. I can forget Beatrice's words cutting into me. I can forget everything except the feel of the water on my fingers, the connection at last, the meeting of elements, water and flesh, flesh and earth, flesh and air. I wait, my fingers dangling in the water, listening. Surely deep in my heart the truth of this matter must lie. Surely my bones know if I come from this land or not.

I wait until I am straining, but there are no words from the river. It rolls past as if it is water that knows nothing but having fallen as rain on the hills, water that has been floating as mist, water insubstantial.

The lightning flashes in the sky far upstream. The clouds cross the moon, plunging me into darkness, then pass, leaving the land silver again. I think of Alison Douglas. She must have known there was a secret escape but she didn't take it. She chose marriage and the castle over freedom; servitude for her and Beatrice and Margaret over the charity of the Tulliallan Blackadders.

William has shackled himself to the castle as firmly as Beatrice. Isobel stands on the rock and plans how she will cast out her cousin and take it for herself. But this castle does not change owners without bloodshed and perhaps I have no more right to be here than David Hume had to take it by force in the first place. If Alison's son in truth lies buried on the hill, then who is William and who am I?

In the patterns of rippling silver moonlight on water, a movement startles me. Isobel has clambered above me on the riverbank and I am crouched on slick mud beside the swollen water. She has only to kick me and I will be in the icy current. I curse my foolishness as I rise to my feet and brace my muscles. I have trusted a Hume and now I will pay.

Isobel leans forward and I steel myself not to recoil, lest the moment unbalances me.

"I'm cold," she shouts, so I can hear her over the river's rush. "There's another storm coming. Let's go back and get some whisky."

I glance back once at the river before we push through the tunnel, closing it behind us and cutting off the water's roar.

≈   ≈   ≈

We creep our way back through the castle, our hair and clothes damp, Isobel carrying her clothes in a bundle. She listens at the door and, when she is certain that the great hall is empty, she pushes the door open and we cross to the hearth. She calls a servant to stir up the fire and bring whisky, and we stand in front of it, our palms facing the flames. Isobel shivers in her underthings. I am shivering too, but it is not from the cold. The whisky burns a path to my stomach but the rest of me feels numb.

"Is it easy to really dress like a man?" she asks.

I shrug. "Dressing is not so hard. Acting like one is harder. You must walk differently, sit differently, speak differently."

"Have you had great adventures playing like this in Edinburgh?"

I put down my cup and the servant tops it up. "It is not always a game. Once I had to kill a man who attacked the Queen, thinking she was a merchant whose pockets he could pick."

"How did you kill him?" she asks, fascinated.

"I shot him," I say, looking her in the eye. "A woman who wants to dress this way must be as good as a man at defending herself."

"I can defend myself," she says. "I am skilled at archery."

I laugh. "That will be useless. You need to be fast with a dagger or a pistol."

"I have used a dagger."

"Can you have it out and at a man's throat before he has reached for his own?"

She stares at me, then composes her features and tosses back her drink. "I want to show you Alison's portrait." She waves to the servant to bring a lantern.

It is a large portrait, hung to good advantage in another chamber on the ground floor. It is one of a pair, and before I look at my grandmother, I stare up at the face of David Hume, fifth Baron of Wedderburn, the man who took the castle with his own hand and compelled Alison to marry him. His eyes are impassive, his jaw strong.

Then I turn to Alison. The painter was a man of skill, for she seems to look at me out of the canvas, as if she would open her mouth and speak to me.

I can see little of myself in her face. She is an older version of Isobel, with her long auburn hair and green eyes and the proud lift of her chin. I wonder that any person, man or woman, could have made her do what she did not want to do.

"Everyone says I look just like her," Isobel says.

"You have the same color hair."

"Is that all?"

I study my grandmother again, looking for William's face. She was a strong woman, who did not let pain show on her countenance. I can see Beatrice, but suddenly all I can recall of William's face is the bitter lines running across his forehead and around his mouth. I cannot picture my own face at all.

"Well?" Isobel says.

I shrug. "You must have inherited your features from the Hume blood."

She turns away from me. "It is late. The servant will take you to your bedchamber."

≈   ≈   ≈

I lie in the dark and retrace every step I've taken since arriving. I have not seen half of the castle yet, only its wide public rooms, one of its winding secret ways and some of the bedchambers. I have glimpsed the bustling kitchen, the great bread ovens, the roasting fire roaring in its pit. I have ridden out into its forest, I have let its water run over my hands.

At the Queen's word this castle will be emptied of people and handed to William and me. My life's dream, here within my grasp. But outside is a gravestone that casts a shadow across everything I have believed in, and down below me the Blackadder Water passes on its way to the sea, indifferent.

326

It is William whose face rises before me. William who has carried the heavy weight of this name and this injustice all his life. William with his pride and his honor, waiting to take his place at last.

I must choose what to do and I wish I knew what God I could pray to for guidance. But when I do lower myself to my knees on the hard stone floor, it is my mother I call upon. The person who knew the depth and breadth of William's desire, the one person who will know what I should do. I kneel with my hands clasped until I am shuddering with cold, my knees aching.

But no answer comes from the castle and no word from the river and no whisper from any waiting ghost.

≈　≈　≈

My sleep is devoid of any dreams to guide me and I wake to the chill of an ordinary autumn morning, the sky leaden, the ground wet, last night's rain hanging heavily off the bare branches outside, the river dark.

The whole family is to ride with us to Wedderburn, even Beatrice, who is pale and dark-eyed and will not look at me when we eat breakfast in the great hall. After the merriment of the night before, we gather grimly in the courtyard in the drizzle. I stay close to the Queen, dressed in the finest frock I own, one I have carried with me all the way from Edinburgh for this day.

We mount and Alexander leads us out of the courtyard, down the hill, and around to the river crossing. Halfway across the bridge, the Queen pulls up her horse and the party comes to a halt behind her. I am by her side, close enough to feel the warmth of her horse near my leg. She turns her head and looks downstream at the castle, wreathed in morning mist, growing out of the rock of the riverbank like something from ancient times.

"It looks so peaceful," she says, into the thick silence.

Alexander laughs without humor. "Don't be deceived, Your Grace. There's nothing peaceful about the Borders. All men sleep close to their weapons here."

They are all staring, not just at the Queen but at both of us. Beatrice's face is as white as the mist, her lips almost colorless. Isobel's hair is even deeper red against the absence of color in the world, and she has chosen a dress the same color as her remarkable eyes. Alexander, after blurting out a laugh, looks like a huge, anxious puppy. I meet their eyes, my chin high, my gaze hard.

The Queen allows the silence to linger long enough for them to feel their fear, before gathering up her reins.

"It was a most enjoyable evening in your home," she says, with a cool smile. "We had best not keep Lord Hume waiting."

We clatter over the wet planks of the bridge. I glimpse the river, the black running water that roars day and night through the dreams of the castle and those who sleep within it.

The Humes ride so close to us that I feel like a prisoner being escorted. But the Queen has dropped a word in the ear of one of her guards who rides between them and the Queen, forcing them to fall back. When we come to a little open ground, the Queen pushes her horse into a canter and, when we pull up, she and I are far enough ahead in the mist to not be overheard.

"I will discuss this with Lord Hume today, with Maitland and Lord James present," she says. "I wish it accomplished with all speed."

I push my horse closer to her so I can speak quietly. "They have cast some doubt on my lineage," I say. "It is a lie, I am certain, but I must go to Glasgow to find out before I take the castle."

She pauses and then shakes her head. "You have waited a long time for this. It is in your reach today and this is your chance, Alison. Take it now, with all the consequences, or see it lost. I cannot come here again."

The mist wreathes around her and a strand of escaped hair falls damply across her face. Beneath me the horse pulls at the reins and snorts. The castle could be mine, but the Humes will be ruthless in destroying the last of William's honor.

I can hear the dull thud of hoofbeats approaching through the mist, the same mist that is swirling around that small tombstone near the foot of the castle walls.

"Well?" Her horse prances, anxious to move.

I take a deep breath, a cold lungful of air rising from the Blackadder Water. I do not know what words I am about to speak until they come out.

"I cannot."

I can see the relief on her face. "If this is your will, then we need not tarry at Wedderburn. I am impatient to reach Craigmillar. But are you sure?"

"Yes," I say.

She smiles. "You are a brave woman, Alison. Once the christening is arranged, we will discuss your future. I will still reward you for your service. You need not live a lowly life."

The guards emerge from the mist and she lifts her reins and rides away from me. Farther back I can hear the softer hoofbeats of the Humes riding in my wake, following the course of the Blackadder Water.

My very sinews resist leaving this place and my heart twists in my chest. To have come so close, to have laid my hands upon its stone and placed my feet upon its earth, and now to leave it is almost more than I can bear. Below me the horse prances in agitation, feeling the urge in my body to gallop after her and tell her I have changed my mind. My breath is harsh in my own ears and I am trembling from some deep place inside.

I wish I were truly alone. I would let loose a terrible keen of my loss into the mist.

≈   ≈   ≈

We ride into Craigmillar. I am riding by the Queen's side, the position of highest honor. Seton has done up my hair this day and I wear the dress in which I would have taken the castle.

The Queen will meet with her most loyal lords and they will discuss the problem of the recalcitrant King and what can be done to bring him into line. But it does not matter to me any longer. I have no birthright to strive for. I am not even a noblewoman entitled to live in the Queen's court and enjoy its privileges. If I stay, the Hume family may now reveal me as an impostor—and thus expose William too. To keep his honor, so hard won, I must leave the Queen.

Bothwell's standard is fluttering on the road ahead of us as we draw near to Craigmillar and the horns blare out the herald for the Queen. In that moment I realize my mother has answered my entreaty and her answer is this: to love William I must bear the weight of this alone. I cannot let the woman he believes to be his sister reveal him as a bastard. I must spare him from the truth and take the failure upon my own shoulders. William will not have his castle but I can make sure he has his honor.

Bothwell is waiting to greet us. He is mounted, though by the ghastly color of his cheeks I can see that his wounds have not yet healed and it has cost him dearly to ride out this day. By his right hand, in the position of honor, is William, his horse pressed close to Bothwell's to bear his weight should he sway. His hair is almost all gray in the sunlight.

There is an expression on his face that I have never seen before. There is something of awe in it, like the way he looked at me when I first rode into Edinburgh dressed as a noblewoman. But it is more than that. I see him straighten himself to sit taller on his horse, his eyes fixed on mine. I see him blinking and I realize he is crying.

It is like I am seeing him properly for the first time in my life and I find tears pricking at the back of my own eyes, while my heart swells in my chest. He is my father, waiting for me by Bothwell's side, whatever name he carries, whatever his lineage may be. I have done this for him. As we ride up to them, my heart blazes with what I can only call love.

Part III
1566

Forty-six

Outside the window the mist reaches into every crack in the stone and fingers it with damp. There might be nothing at all beyond the window of the Queen's chamber in Stirling Castle: no city, no people, no men drinking in taverns, no women trying to warm their children, no spark of love, no joy.

The Queen has hurried her court to Stirling for the baptism of the Prince, for she does not have the heart to hold it in Edinburgh. She has invited the might of France, Spain, England, and the Scottish nobility to attend and has personally borrowed thousands of pounds to pay for days and nights of festivities that Scotland's coffers cannot afford. But the King, who can bring it all down around her if he casts doubt on the Prince's paternity, retreats to his chambers and says he will not come to the christening if she will not give him the crown matrimonial.

"Could you stir up the fire a little?" the Queen asks. "The cold is in my bones."

I move away from the window and cross the room to the hearth. I take up a poker and stoke the fire until it roars and crackles and starts to singe the hairs on my arms. I wish I had a witch's spell to weave this night to keep the darkness back.

Seton tenderly untwists the Queen's braids and La Flamina warms her nightgown. None of us speak. The only sounds are the crackle of the logs and the silken scrape of the comb through the Queen's hair.

"Does something trouble you, beloved?" La Flamina asks.

The Queen sighs. "Lord Bothwell has told me this night there are so many whispered plots that the Privy Council has forbidden any to carry arms in court. Half my lords are in exile. I have taxed the rest of them to help pay for my son's baptism and most of them will refuse to set foot in the church because they cannot abide my religion."

"You have a healthy heir," La Flamina says. "One blessing at least."

"The nobles of Europe are on their way here for the baptism, but what they really wish to see is this marriage of mine. I do not know if my husband will come, or if he does, what disgrace he might cause. He should lighten my cares, but he is the heaviest care of all."

"He is young." La Flamina brings the nightgown to the Queen's side. "Perhaps he will behave better when he sees the nobility gathered. Surely he will be proud to come to the christening of his own son?"

"Do not marry," the Queen says, reaching to grasp La Flamina's wrist. "There is time to change your mind. Maitland is like all the others. He cannot be trusted. Marriage will bring you no happiness."

La Flamina stands still. "Is that truly your wish?" she asks in a small voice.

The Queen rises to her feet. "I wish it but I do not ask it of you. I pray you find more happiness than I have in wedlock."

She steps to the fire and holds out her arms for me to unbutton her sleeves. I start on the left and La Flamina lays aside the nightgown and begins unbuttoning the right hand, her face working.

"I will stay with you, if you ask me," she says.

The Queen stares into the fire. "No," she says at last. "Go with him. You may be like an ambassador, reporting back to me from the country of marriage, giving me hope that my own might one day reach that happy state. I still have Seton and Alison at my side."

I slide off her sleeve.

"Though Alison will soon leave me too." She glances sideways at me. I keep my eyes lowered and move behind her to start unlacing her bodice.

"Everyone leaves," she continues, her voice flat. "I cannot walk away from my charge. I must suffer this marriage and do right for Scotland. They call me Queen but I am more a prisoner than the lowest servant."

"I will never leave you," Seton says softly.

La Flamina casts me a quick, sympathetic glance. I concentrate on the hooks at the back of the Queen's dress, which are stiff and require tugging. When they come apart, I lift the bodice and free her from its clutches. Seton draws the nightgown down over the Queen's head before she can feel the chill of the night air.

The Queen wraps her arms around herself, pressing the warm cloth against her skin. "I need you to watch my husband, Alison. I do not even know if he intends to come to his son's baptism."

"But how?" I ask. "I can't gain his confidence as Alison."

"I have France's leading troupe of actors and costumiers preparing for the masques. They will dress as satyrs. Join them. Be my eyes around Stirling, in the best disguise the French can fashion. You can speak to Anthony Standen about my husband without arousing any suspicion. I will have a word to the guards and they will let you pass anywhere."

I bow my head. "Of course."

She sighs again. "I would that Rizzio were here. He knew just how to handle such difficult situations. His brother does not share his wisdom."

There is a moment's silence. Rizzio did not see the greatest danger of all until it was upon him.

"We will help you," La Flamina says brightly, breaking the silence. "Lord Bothwell is loyal as ever and your brother stands by your side again. You will show the Europeans a spectacle they will never forget. It will be your finest moment."

The Queen shivers. "You are right, my dearest. I will not mope."

She looks at me. "Perhaps you can find a way to keep my husband busy. You have always been so good at that."

She orders me to become a beast and then she asks me to distract him. It is all the permission I need.

≈ ≈ ≈

To make a man into a satyr is not such a difficult thing. The hairy reddish hide of a Scots bull, cut and sewn into legs and a vest. Tottering footwear of leather with a cloven-hoof covering. A beard combed and twisted, two horns attached on a string around the head, hidden in the wig of ringlets so that the appendages appear to have grown there. A leather mask, tight across the eyes. Even I, with my bound breasts, am disguised.

It seems fitting that I shall be a beast in my final service to her.

Perhaps this is the truest expression of what I have become in the past five years. William called me an evil creature and now I believe him.

When I saw him at Craigmillar, my heart full of love, I was willing to withstand his rage. I was protecting him from disgrace and that knowledge made me strong.

He was silent when he heard I had relinquished the castle. I told him we would not be like the others who lived half-lives, driven mad by the desire for it. I told him our honor was greater than if we had driven out our kin who lived there. I almost believed myself that there was no other reason for letting it go.

When he reached out a hand, I went forward into his embrace, the word "Father" on my lips. His arms came around me and for a heartbeat, it seemed that he held me and everything was right.

But then his hands found my throat and the look of disbelief on his face turned to rage and the noise that came from him sounded scarcely human. Bothwell had to drag him off me by force.

"We could never know peace there," I rasped when I could speak. "The Hume family owns all the lands surrounding Blackadder. It would be a life of fear."

William bellowed in rage like an animal, his arms behind his back, tight in Bothwell's grip. "Trust a woman," he snarled.

"I will speak to the Queen and tell her you made a mistake," Bothwell said.

I stared at them, united in their shock. "It's too late. It is done. It was my choice to make."

William stopped struggling, his face twisting. "Get from my sight. You are doubly, triply cursed. I cannot abide you."

Edinburgh itself seemed steeped in William's incredulous rage, for once I returned there with the Queen, the city turned its face against me. When I slipped away from Holyrood in my old disguises and wandered Edinburgh's streets, every cobblestone rose up to bruise me, every fall of slops from its high windows came down unerringly to splash me. The city where I once immersed myself was a foreign place, hard and cold in the midst of the most foul weather, with driving sleet and wind like a sword edge. The loss of our castle was in every cut.

Wandering those streets, I came to feel myself the vile creature that William accused me of being. It felt like every murdered Black-adder had joined their power to his curse. I had longed for a home and now I had none. I had once thought to wed, but I had made myself unmarriageable. I believed myself highborn, but I was the offspring of a bastard. The name of Blackadder hung upon me like a weight, as if every utterance was a curse. I felt like a wraith, as if the coming winter was blowing through my bones and sinews.

I told the Queen I must leave her service but I could give her no reason and no plan for my life afterward. She has never liked being left and she reminds me of her displeasure at every opportunity.

≈　≈　≈

The noble guests have been arriving all morning, with the heralds blaring out for each new party clattering into the courtyard. Now they are gathering in the quadrangle outside the chapel royal. Spurred by the activity, I hurry down the corridor, leading a fellow satyr I have carefully chosen from the French troupe. Anthony Standen is waiting to meet me as arranged.

"The way is clear," he says. "The King is half-dressed, and still drinking."

"This will calm him better than whisky," I say.

We clatter down the empty hall to the King's apartments. Anthony opens the door.

"Who's there?" Darnley lurches into sight. Anthony moves aside and I reach behind me, pull the boy forward by the wrist, and thrust him into the presence chamber. Tottering on his tall hooves, he stumbles and falls to his hands and knees.

It is like watching one of the Queen's lions when a rabbit is tossed to it. Darnley's head swivels as the boy sprawls on the floor and he licks his lips.

"What in the name of God do we have here?" he asks.

"Please, my Lord," the lad stammers, with a coquettish glance from under his fringe of ringlets. He is more of an actor than I gave him credit for. "I'm a satyr."

"A satyr?" Darnley advances and I slip backward into the shadow of the corridor. "One of those that cavort with Bacchus? Do you know, satyr, what Bacchus likes to do with such creatures?"

Anthony closes the door and on that puff of escaping air, I flee.

I wind my way back to the great hall by a longer route, passing Bothwell's chambers. I am hoping for a glimpse of William. I know he has come to Stirling with Bothwell, but it seems he keeps to their rooms. I would try to see, from afar, if he has recovered from losing all hope of the castle. But the chambers are firmly closed.

Forty-seven

She can still command the attention of every man and woman in the room.

The Queen, on the throne at the center of the dais in the great hall, has reached into herself to draw out every shred of charm she possesses and in this she has no equal.

Lord James, Lord Bothwell, and Lord Huntly have been appointed as ceremonial servers for the feast. Lord James and his men dress in green and he kneels to present the cup to the Queen. Huntly, in red, carves the first of the roast meats with a flourish before handing the knife to his man to finish the job. Bothwell, in blue livery, serves each person at the head table before his men take up the job for him. William is not among them.

The King does not appear, the wine flows freely, and streams of servants carry platters of food to the tables. The heat rises, the musicians play, the sound of voices and laughter swells and fills the hall. The young Prince has been christened and, though the King did not come, none has dared deny his paternity. Through it all, the satyrs skip and jump, leaping up onto chairs, twirling our tails, pinching an arm here, tugging a beard there.

In the midst of the laughter and the hands reaching from all sides to fondle us, I see up on the dais some shaking of heads and stern stares from some of the Queen's visitors. But I care not. There is no chance anyone will recognize me and what does it matter if they do? I skip and twirl until I am dizzy. I straddle the laps of men (to scandalized, delighted screams) and threaten to do the same with women. I plant ever more naughty kisses on the lips of my victims and their lips are willing beneath mine.

The older guests and those who are sober begin leaving and the rest settle in for a long night. Servants drag tables out of the way to clear a dance floor and the Queen steps down to take the first dance with Lord Bothwell.

I pass the table where the men of the Hume clan are seated and behind the safety of my disguise I watch them. They do not seem to celebrate. Lord Hume is grim-faced and David Hume scans the room through narrowed eyes. By his side, a young man of his clan looks at me piercingly, and I duck out of his sight.

Seeing them, I suddenly sicken at the whole spectacle. The laughing, greasy faces, the spilt wine, the men who grab at me as I pass, the food and drink smeared on my shaggy hide, the slaps to my rump. I need fear the Hume family no longer, but the sight of them dining at the Queen's banquet reminds me that I have nothing, not even the consolation of my noble bloodline.

The Queen is at the center of the dance floor with Lord Bothwell. She smiles as though every ambassador and dignitary in the room is not assessing her glorious celebration carefully, probing at the situation to find what secrets lie beneath it, what advantage might be found, what gossip might be made of it.

I skip my way to the rear of the great hall and step into the cold December air of the courtyard. I walk away from the revelers spilling out behind me, pull the sweaty mask from my face, and stand still, my breath coming out in clouds. I promised the Queen I would serve her until the christening and now the prospect of my freedom rises up inside of me. Perhaps I might find some contentment in my new life, whatever it is.

At last I clip-clop across the cobblestones of the inner courtyard, the sound of music and voices rising from the hall, the air cold on my face. From the deep shadow beside the chapel royal, a hand shoots out of the dark and pulls me into a hard embrace, a hand over my mouth, the cold scream of steel against my throat.

My captor takes me at a run, around the chapel, out into the garden, his dagger pressing against my skin. When we stop, my heart is thudding and there is a cowardly shaking in my legs. His body is against my back, his mouth close to my ear.

"If you scream, I will cut your throat before the noise escapes."

It is not a man's voice. I nod and my captor frees my mouth and spins me around, the tip of the dagger still at my throat. It is the young man who sat by David Hume.

"You are well disguised tonight, Alison Blackadder."

"Isobel?" I croak. "I did not recognize you."

"As my family did not recognize you when you came to our home, bearing a false name. Queen or no queen, you would not have survived the night if we had known you were one of the Blackadder spawn."

I swallow. I had thought Isobel a striking young noblewoman with pretensions to an estate. I would never have picked her as having the skill for convenient violence.

"My father—" the prick of steel cuts me short.

In the moonlight her eyes are fixed on mine with unwavering intensity. "The ownership of our castle clearly and legally traces back from Alexander, to Beatrice and Margaret, to Alison. Even if the impossible were true and your father was really Alison's son, any right he had to inherit the castle is long gone."

"Then why do you threaten me?"

"We have heard a rumor that the Queen would give you the castle anyway, believing your lies and putting us out, though we are the legitimate owners."

I take a breath. "Did you also find out that I have relinquished my claim? The Queen herself will verify it."

We regard each other in the moonlight. Suddenly she drops her arm and the movement makes me start. She reaches inside her cloak and brings out a folded square of parchment. "This bond is to relinquish your father's unfounded claim to the rightful property of my family. You and your father will sign it, and then you may go about your lives unharmed. If you do not, my brothers will be the ones to visit next time and they are not so merciful as I."

I shrug, forcing myself to appear casual. "If my father is a bastard, as you say, then he has no claim and you have no need of our signatures."

She steps forward again, dagger raised in her other hand, and I feel a pang of fear. Her clansmen are close by, after all.

"Your father has the ear of Lord Bothwell and you have the ear of the Queen," she says. "They are powerful friends. But if you do not sign, even powerful friends will not be enough to protect you. If you have relinquished your claim, as you say, then it matters not to sign."

She thrusts the paper toward me. I reach out to take it and in a flash I seize her wrist instead and twist it up behind her back, snatching the dagger so I have her pinned. Now it is me holding the dagger at her throat from behind, pushing its razor edge against her white skin to stop her outraged struggle.

"Your family has murdered Blackadder men for three generations," I say in her frightened ear. "Even if William is a bastard, he and I are still of the Blackadder line. None of yours has ever died at the hand of a Blackadder. Tell me why I should not begin to even the tally tonight?"

She gasps and I can feel the pounding of her heart against my breastbone and her hair smells of something sweet. For a second I am filled with the desire to kill her. It rises in me like sex, and just as suddenly it's gone again.

I release her with a push so she falls forward to her knees, though I am careful to keep hold of the dagger.

"It seems neither of us has the stomach to kill the other," I say. "But I cannot make William bear this humiliation. Let me sign now, and leave him in peace."

She shakes her head. "It is he who claims to be the heir. It must be signed by him and legally witnessed. You have four days."

"Isobel," I say, my voice softening. "I had to lie to him. He still believes he is Alison's son. Don't make me take that from him."

"Your father is the bastard of Roland Blackadder, Archdean of Glasgow. The records are held in the cathedral in Glasgow for any to see."

A burst of shouting and laughter echoes across the darkness from the square. I shiver. "I need more than four days."

She holds the parchment out to me. "We have lodgings here in Stirling until Christmas Eve. When it is done, bring it to me."

"And walk into such a trap?"

She shrugs. "My brothers would have killed you tonight if that was our intention."

"Why didn't you?"

We regard each other for a long moment. "William is not Alison's son. But Beatrice says even if he is a bastard, he is her distant kin. She begged me not to see either of you harmed. She is an old woman with foolish fancies, but I am fond of her. For her sake I would let you live."

She drops the parchment to the ground and walks away into the shadows.

Forty-eight

The Queen's service has been full of threat, and my life has had its share of fear, but I have not known the icy-spined terror of this night since David Hume's visit to Peebles. For what remains of the dark, I lie awake, having buried myself in the center of a shaggy group of satyrs, an animal blindly seeking safety in its flock. The Hume men are here in this castle, with yet another reason to kill me.

The next morning I rise early and make my way to the King's chambers to retrieve the boy.

"Come, they have just broken the oven seal; the bread is hot." I lead him to the kitchen and we gather servants' fare, trenchers fresh from the oven, and take our breakfast outside, up on the castle wall where the pale sun offers a promise of warmth.

"You must pay me more," he says. "You did not tell me he was diseased."

"Diseased?"

"He is covered in suppurations. The witch in Paris who cures such things is not cheap. But I will go to him again if you pay me properly."

I look at him quizzically. "Knowing he is ill?"

He shrugs. "Double the purse and I will keep him busy as long as you wish."

After we have eaten, I find him the clothes of a page and smuggle him back to Anthony Standen, pushing down my guilt with a payment of three times what I gave him the previous night. Requiring a new disguise, I borrow an outfit of the lad's own clothing myself. A wig and a moustache glued to my upper lip complete the illusion that I am a French actor. When even La Flamina does not recognize me in the corridor, I feel safer.

I must ask the Queen for my reward and tell her I will leave at the end of the baptism celebrations. But she is busy every moment and I cannot catch her alone. By the time evening falls, I am so agitated that I can barely stand still. Knowing that the Queen likes to watch the sunset from the castle wall with only her closest companions, I wait in the garden to meet her.

She emerges from the castle with Seton and La Flamina. They climb the wall to watch the last moments of sunset and then, with the night chill already setting in, they return to the castle. I follow.

They halt at the entrance to the courtyard and the Queen says something. I see Seton frown a little, then bob her head and step into the door, followed by La Flamina. I am about to come closer when the Queen suddenly turns to the side and hurries down the pathway.

I stand still for a moment. It is not my concern, what she does when she thinks herself alone. But I have long had the habit of spying. I follow.

She takes a twisting path into the garden with hurried purpose. When a figure looms out of the dusk, she quickens her step to meet him and I stop.

It is Bothwell. I recognize the timbre of his voice, though not the words as they murmur together. I dare not go closer lest they hear me. I recall, suddenly, walking into Bothwell's sickroom while the Queen was present and the odd expressions on their faces.

It's no use; I must hear them. I inch my way along the grass, keeping in the shadows of the shrubs. When I am close enough to hear their voices, I crouch down.

"You must pardon every one of them," he says. "It is time he was afraid. Then he will not dare to snub you thus!"

"He fears they will kill him." She speaks so softly I can hardly hear.

"Perhaps his behavior will improve if he feels himself threatened."

"They are murderers, my Lord!"

"Your husband refused to come to his own son's baptism. Something must be done about him."

"I do not know what else to do."

"Pardon his enemies," he says. "Let the King feel fear."

"Very well. But not Fawdonside, after he held a pistol to my belly. Nor Ruthven."

"Ruthven is near death. He won't trouble you again."

The plotters who murdered Rizzio and then were betrayed by Darnley and forced to flee. If I am hearing right, they will be brought home to Scotland. More than seventy murderous enemies for our King, set on revenge. He should tremble this night.

As I am trembling now. If it is not enough to have the Hume clan planning my death, now I am hearing words not meant for my ears. I slow my breath until I am scarcely inhaling at all.

"I'm afraid," she whispers. "It all hangs by a thread."

"We shall find a way through this," he says, his voice low.

The bushes rustle. "I must go," she says. "I will be missed."

"Must you?"

Two words and I know that intimate tone in his voice. The hair rises on my neck. Surely not this, not for our married Catholic Queen and her married Protestant nobleman? Are they mad, to court such danger?

They separate without another word, their footsteps leading off in different directions. I wait until the cold has reached right through my bones before I creep back to the castle. I go straight to Bothwell's chambers to speak to William. I must persuade him to flee with me. No good can come of this.

≈　≈　≈

My palms are sweating as I raise my hand to knock.

Edmund Blackadder answers, all black teeth and crushed nose, a thousand fights laid out on his body. I pull off my wig and he looks me up and down.

"You," he says. He pulls open the door and lets me in, closing it quickly behind me.

Edmund's brother Jock is next to William. William looks up and even across the room his rage hits me like a blow, smiting the adult so that I am seven years old again, standing before him as a child.

William leaps to his feet. "Some oaf of Hume's threatened me out in the grounds tonight. Told me if I didn't sign the bond he'd be back to visit again. What's he talking about?"

I drop my eyes. "It is an agreement with the Hume family guaranteeing our safety."

"For what price?" William's voice is low and dangerous.

"Relinquishing our claim." My voice is hardly above a whisper.

"Damn you!" He strides across the room, his hand raised and suddenly I'm no longer a child. My dagger is pointed at him, though I have no memory of drawing it. He stops. Jock and Edmund both draw their dirks.

"The Humes found out the Queen was to give us the castle." I keep the blade steady. "It is lost anyway, William. If we sign a bond relinquishing our claim, we can live without fear."

His face has gone a deep purple. "I would rather die."

"If you will not sign it, then come with me to France. We can ride this very night and sail tomorrow or the next day. I beg you, Father. There is nothing in Scotland but danger. Let's make our life in France, or on the sea again."

"Run away to France," he says, his lip curling. "I will not sell my soul and my birthright for some illusion of safety."

There is a weapon between us, or I do not think I could speak the words. "They say it is not your birthright. They say you are not Alison's son, but the bastard child of one of the Blackadders from the Glasgow church. They say they have proof."

The silence in the room is so profound that I can hear the blood singing in my veins. He attacks me then; dagger or not, he must know I will never use it on him. He strikes me a blow to the side of the head that almost knocks me from my feet and then he has me by the arm, has it wrenched and twisted behind my back, my bones and tendons screaming. My feet scrabble on the floor as he takes me out the door and along the corridor.

"For once in your cursed life, obey me," he hisses. He shoves me so hard out of Bothwell's chambers that I go sprawling on the flagstones and the guards jump and raise their weapons.

He stares down at me from the doorway, his face working. "You are some devil's spawn. You are not my child. Never show me your face again."

Forty-nine

Bothwell is the only one who can compel William to sign the document. I wait until he is breakfasting with the Queen in the great hall, then send in a servant with the promise of an urgent message from Captain Blackadder.

He arrives in the courtyard wiping his mouth. There are deep lines etched around his eyes, as if the wound he took in the Borders has sucked his vitality. I come close to him. "It is I," I say softly. "Alison. William is in grave danger."

He gestures with his head and I follow him around the chapel and into a clear area in the garden. "There are ears everywhere. What is it?"

"He will hate me telling you this. My Lord, I relinquished the castle because the Humes have proof he is not the heir, but only a bastard born to a lowly Blackadder cleric. I did not want to shame him with it, so I told him I had made the decision myself."

Bothwell stares at me, thunderstruck. "Did you see their proof?"

"I saw the grave of Alison's son William in the churchyard," I say. "They swear there is a king's charter in the church records in Glasgow setting out William's lineage. The Queen would not grant me the time to go there. I had a moment only to make my choice."

"I understand a little better now," he says. "But you should seek the proof. Likely it is simply another ploy of Hume's to keep what he has stolen."

"It's too late. Now the Humes are after us again." I draw out the creased parchment from under my jerkin. "I had to tell William that he was a bastard. They want him and me to sign a bond that we are not the heirs and will never seek the castle again. They have given us a week to sign it in front of a legal witness. But he says he would rather die."

"As he should," Bothwell says. "How can he live with honor if he signs such a thing without knowing the truth?"

I spread out my hands. "We have lost the castle. I am leaving for France. With a signature, William may live in safety. You are the only one who can make him. If he will not sign it, then order him to come with me."

"The castle is not lost," Bothwell says.

I stare at him. "What?"

Bothwell walks a few paces and pauses with his back to me. At last he swings around. "This is a matter for men now. Give me the bond. I will take care of it. William is under my protection and I will make sure he is safe. Go to France. You are better off there."

I go to pass the parchment to him, but something in his eyes stops me. I cannot rid myself of the memory of his whispered words to the Queen. I draw my hand back.

"We both must sign. All you need to do is order William. It can be done today in front of a legal witness. Then I must return it."

"You can sign it now, in front of me," he says. "I will arrange for William to sign it and have it returned to Hume."

"Why do you say the castle is not lost?"

He shrugs. "The castle has nothing to do with you any longer."

He reaches out his hand and I step back from him. "Please, Lord Bothwell. William will not live long enough to be of any service to you if this is not signed."

He lunges forward suddenly and grabs for the parchment and in a heartbeat I remember how he trained me in sword fighting on the voyage from France. I dodge him, ducking under his arm, swinging around, and breaking into a run, the parchment crumpled at my breast.

When I am out of his sight, I look around quickly for somewhere to hide. Servants are streaming in and out of the kitchen, ensuring the flow of food and the return of plates from the great hall. I cut across the courtyard and join them carrying plates down the stone steps into the kitchen. In a moment I am hidden in the greasy dark.

≈ ≈ ≈

"You have been having adventures," the Queen says when I come to her chambers and we are alone. "Look at you! You even smell like a servant. How I wish I could run around the castle at will with no one to recognize me."

She is in her bed. With one day of celebrations to go, she is almost at breaking point. She is pale and keeps clutching at her side.

"Your Grace, please release me," I say. "I have fulfilled my promise to serve you until the Prince was baptised. I must urgently attend to family matters. I wish to go to France at once."

"As do I," she says. "Seeing you dressed thus puts me in mind of when you lived as Robert. Do you think, my dearest, we may don a disguise together and ride out to Leith? We could be merchants in search of new markets and set sail for the new world."

She laughs, but there is no humor in it.

"I hope you may be able to arrange my payment so I can sail for France on the next boat," I say, looking at the floor.

"France," she says, and fingers her goblet of ruby red wine. "Do you know, when I sip this, sometimes I think I can taste the sunlight in France striking the grapes? We have so little sunlight here in winter; it seems darkness is all around."

I wait.

"It is hard to get gold at Christmas," she says at last. "Especially after I needed so much for the christening. My coffers are empty."

My heart is pounding and even in the winter cold I am sweating. I make my voice as soft and undemanding as possible. "Perhaps you could give me an authority to get the gold from one of your agents in Edinburgh?"

"Let us be frank," she says. "Bothwell has told me you are afraid of a plot against you and your father, hence your haste to leave for France. You did not think to mention this?"

"I would not add to your worries."

"You are considerate. I have many cares. There are rumors of a plot against me too, and there is nothing I would like more than to sail on the next ship to France, out of harm's way. Being a queen, of course, I may not."

Her hand strays to her side and presses at her waist. "Although I have many cares, I have given some thought to this. It is a most delicate time. I have pardoned the exiled lords and they will return to Scotland. It would be most unwise for me to confront Lord Hume at this time. I need to count on all my lords now."

She sips her wine, winces, and presses her side again. "La Flamina will marry Maitland on Twelfth Night, and another one of my companions is lost to me. My husband and I are estranged, and each day there are whispers of more plots against me. Yet Elizabeth has given a most lavish christening gift to my son and has sent word that she is ready to confer about my succession to the English throne. Scotland has a living male heir who has been the toast of all Europe these past weeks. If I tread my path with great care and wisdom, a new time will come when there is peace among the lords and in the country."

She looks across and gives me a small smile. "You have served me with such loyalty," she says, and her voice is honey. "I cannot send you from my side when there is such danger lurking. The plotters may find you before you sail, or they may follow you to France where I cannot protect you. I will not do it."

She reaches out and puts a hand upon my wrist, her long fingers wrapping around it. "You will be under my highest protection. At my side, no harm will come to you. When it is safe, I shall send you to France myself. Until then, abide with me, Alison."

≈   ≈   ≈

The celebrations finish, the nobles pack up and leave, and still the Queen shows no signs of returning to Edinburgh. The King has not emerged from his chambers since the baptism and Bothwell is ever by the Queen's side.

William believes me evil and I cannot think of anything I can do to protect him. If I stay and share his fate, perhaps he will know in the end that I have loved him as a daughter should.

I count off the days as if they are my last. When Christmas Eve dawns dark and cold, I lie in bed staring at the ceiling. The prospect of my death has been so constant that I am almost at peace with it now. I wonder what the manner of my death will be and how much it will hurt.

The Queen sends a servant for me at first light. Seton and La Flamina are already laying out her clothes and packing her trunk.

"We are spending Christmas at Drummond Castle," she says. "Pray help with my packing. We leave by lunchtime."

I bow at the terse tone of her voice. "Of course, Madam. What about the King?"

She shakes her head angrily. "I told him last night we were going. This morning he has stolen away by himself. He has left a note that he rides to Glasgow!"

"Do not think of him," La Flamina says. "It is Christmas. Let's celebrate."

The Queen strides about in agitation. "There has been enough of celebration. I must think of him. He will be going to join his relatives and I fear they plot against me. There is no clan more powerful in southwest Scotland."

I clear my throat. "There may be another reason. I have heard a rumor that the King has suffered another bout of illness. His body is badly marked."

La Flamina crosses to the Queen's side and takes her hand. "Stop it!" the Queen exclaims. "Do not treat me like a fool. My husband has syphilis, does he not?"

There is silence. She crosses to the window. "Perhaps I shall indeed be delivered from him," she says softly. Then she turns to us.

"My loyal ones, I need your help. I fear I must go myself to retrieve the King from Glasgow and take him to Edinburgh, where I can keep him close by my side. I cannot leave him with the Earl of Lennox and his kin, or they will bring him round to whatever evil plot they are hatching. They will ruin me and try to make their son the only ruler of Scotland."

Seton recoils. "You cannot! The danger!"

"I must ride deep into the enemy's lair and pluck out my husband to halt an even greater danger. I will take every precaution. I shall surround myself with protectors. If I may ask it, I wish you would accompany me." She smiles at La Flamina. "Except you, my love.

For you will be married at last to your Maitland and I would not take you from that."

La Flamina shrugs helplessly. Seton crosses to the Queen and embraces her. "I would not be left behind," she says.

"Of course I will come," I say.

When she dismisses me, I hurry from her presence. At last I have a notion of how to ascertain the truth of William's birth.

≈　≈　≈

The Stag's Rack Inn is busy with men drinking away the cold of Christmas Eve. I arrive in another disguise and so does Isobel, but I pick her as soon as she walks in the door.

"Do you come alone?" I ask as she sits opposite me.

She nods.

"I have armed protectors hidden nearby if you are lying."

"Do you have the bond?" she asks.

I shake my head. "I cannot convince William to sign it without proof of his illegitimacy."

She goes to rise.

"Wait!" I gesture for her to sit again. "The Queen is riding to Glasgow to retrieve her husband in the next few weeks and I shall travel with her. I shall go to the cathedral myself and see the records. If what you say is true, he will sign. I promise it."

"We have run out of patience."

I lean over the table. "Your bond asks William to state he is a bastard. You cannot ask a man to deny who he is without evidence."

"But it will take weeks," she says.

"The Queen will be back in Edinburgh with the King before the Lenten Carnival. Surely your family intends to come to court for that? I give you my word I will have the bond for you then."

She stands. "For Beatrice's sake, because your bastard father is kin to her nevertheless, I will ask them to wait. But there will be no more chances."

She leaves and I wait for several minutes to see if anyone watches. But there is no telltale prickle down my back. She has left her whisky untouched and I pick it up and drain it in a single gulp. If I have seen the proof myself, surely I can make William sign.

I get up to leave. It is not only for William's sake I will go to Glasgow. I would know for myself the truth about my family before I break my ties with it.

Fifty

By the time the Queen brings the Prince back to Edinburgh for safe-keeping and is at last ready to retrieve the King, word has come from Glasgow that Darnley is desperately ill.

We leave the city with four hundred mounted harquebusiers and a litter to carry him home. Lord Bothwell rides at the head of the procession by the Queen's side, but even brave Bothwell does not dare to ride where the Queen will venture. He delivers her to Callendar House, where the Hamiltons are waiting to meet us. Sworn enemies of the Earl of Lennox, they accompany the Queen to the Lennox territory of Glasgow.

When we arrive at the gates of Glasgow, our uniformed harquebusiers and the forty Hamiltons who have swelled their ranks seem a faint defense against the might of the Lennoxes. Should they attack or lay us to siege, we shall never be able to make our way to safety. As we ride toward the Lennox stronghold of Crookstone Castle, looming high above the city, I wish Bothwell was with us. His soldier's instinct would know if we should continue to this place, or demand lodging somewhere less vulnerable to siege.

Seton and I settle the Queen in her lodgings. A message is waiting that the King has begged for her to wait another day before seeing him, so putrid are the eruptions on his face. She shudders, but pens him back a message of love and promises to visit him the following morning. She gives me leave to go out into the city, but insists I take two of the Hamilton men with me.

I am glad she does so. As I ride through Glasgow's winding streets, the faces of its residents are grim, and I do not like the way they stare as we pass and the growing feeling of menace in my wake. My clothes mark me as part of the royal party and I wonder if the whole town is in league with the Lennox clan.

We emerge from a tight street into a broad square and the cathedral rises before me. I dismount and hammer on the door, and the sound echoes into the church. At last a minister answers.

"Your business?"

"Please, sir, we are with the Queen's party," I say. "I have come to look at the church records."

"What is your name?"

"Alison Blackadder."

He stares at me. "Blackadder? Of the great family from Berwickshire?"

I nod, and he opens the door wide. "Do you know where you have come?"

He points toward the right-hand aisle. The late-afternoon sun slants through the stained windows, spilling blood-red on the floor and making me shudder.

"See?" he says, gesturing.

Our name is there, carved on the stone at my feet: *Blackadder Aisle, in honor of Robert Blackadder, Archbishop of Glasgow.*

"A forebear of yours," he says. "What is your lineage?"

"I'm here to find out."

≈　≈　≈

Robert Blackadder, the man I believed to be my great-uncle, rose to become the Catholic Archbishop of Glasgow early in the century. At the peak of his power he officiated at the marriage of King James IV and Margaret Tudor, grandparents to our Queen. The cathedral's archives are bursting with information about him, and the minister enthusiastically shows me record after record.

"I have been told of another," I say. "Not Robert, but Roland."

"Ah yes," the minister says. "There were other members of the family in the church at the time."

He leafs carefully through piles of old documents, raising dust until I sneeze. "Here. Robert's nephew. Roland was the illegitimate son of Robert's brother, Sir Patrick Blackadder of Tulliallan."

He peers at me. "Robert probably did his brother a favor and placed the boy here. He became an Archdean, which was probably as high as he could have risen in the circumstances."

"Did Roland have a child himself?" I ask.

He wrinkles his brow. "Illegitimate too? Now I do recall something about this."

It takes him a long time and I have almost given up when I hear an exclamation from deep in the shelves of the records room.

"Most unusual," he mutters as he brings another parchment out. He lays it down in front of me and we both bend to look at the faint writing.

It is a charter, dated 27 October 1519, declaring William Blackadder an illegitimate child, the natural son of Roland Blackadder, Archdean of Glasgow. It is signed by King James V.

"Strange," he says, drawing back. "I wonder that the King himself would have become involved in such a matter." He looks across at me. "You've gone white. Is this a shock?"

"William is my father. But he believed he came from the Berwickshire line as a legitimate son."

He smiles. "Illegitimacy is a shame some cannot bear, Alison. Do not be too hard on your father."

I lay down the parchment and rise. Yellowed and stiff, its faded writing has struck out my lineage and William's in a few lines of old ink. What Beatrice told me was true. I thought I had accepted the truth of our lineage already, but I feel desolate at the proof of it.

I will leave for France soon and the question of my parentage will not matter. But one question gnaws at me. Did William know that he was the bastard offspring of a cleric who could bear the loneliness no longer? Did he lie all this time, or did someone else lie to him?

Roland, his father, is long dead. The men who made decisions for William as a boy are long dead too. There is only one who might know. John Blackadder of Tulliallan, head of the Blackadder family.

≈   ≈   ≈

When the Queen exerts her charms, there is nothing she cannot win and no will she cannot bend to her own. It takes several days, but she

357

manages to convince the King to leave his father and his paternal heartland of Glasgow and return with her to Edinburgh on a litter.

Our traveling party gathers in the courtyard of Lennox Palace in the morning, mounted up and ready. The King's litter, draped and luxurious, waits by the front entrance.

When at last the Queen appears at the door, gorgeously dressed as though she has not ridden here in fear of her life, a bizarre figure is by her side. At first I think there has been some mistake and by the murmur that rustles through the company I am not the only one. Clinging to her arm is a travesty.

A white mask blocks the King's face from us, but it cannot disguise the small trembling steps and the absurd stick legs that protrude from below the doublet. His hand is a claw on her arm and, when the breeze lifts his hood, a bald skull peeks out, shocking in its nudity. He totters forward to the litter, and with agonizing effort climbs inside. Eight men lift it to their shoulders as though it weighs nothing.

The Queen steps to her block and mounts, and Lord Huntly rides to her side. There is a strained blast from the heralds, harsh on the morning air, and, as if in response, a large raven perched on a nearby building gives a guttural caw.

The Queen glances up for a second, then faces the party with a wide, public smile.

"Let us bring the King safely home," she says, her voice carrying across the square.

There is a ripple as she and Huntly start their horses and the men with the litter move into position behind them. The raven caws again and takes off, flapping heavily in the direction of Edinburgh.

≈   ≈   ≈

It takes four torturous days and nights to bring the King to Edinburgh, with the Glasgow raven accompanying us every step of the way. Even the most hardened soldiers watch it with dread and mutter prayers to ward off this evil omen.

I ride with the Queen's inner circle: with Seton and Bothwell's man French Paris; with Anthony Standen, who never strays far from the King; with Arnault the physician. But I would be happier with the soldiers. The closer I am to the Queen, the greater the risk of breathing in the smell from the King's litter.

It is so foul that the eight men carrying him could be bearing a corpse. Each evening I can scarcely credit that something alive will crawl from the innards of the litter and stand upon two legs. Always the white mask is upon him, but it only increases speculation about the corruption beneath. His very flesh must be rotting to create such a stench.

"It is the mercury," Arnault tells us on the first night. "He is healing quite well, and the odor will pass."

"Pity the Queen," French Paris murmurs so that only I can hear, but there is no one in the party not thinking the same thing. She is married to that rotting corruption in the litter, smelling so much like carrion that a raven will not leave it alone.

There is more than the smell tormenting me. In those four days of riding I recall every boy I sent to the King, the last being the French actor. None of them shall have French physicians and sulfur baths and the quicksilver madness of mercury, not unless they have taken their heavy purses and weighed carefully the needs of the present with the likelihood of the future.

Of all the things I have done in my service to the Queen, these betrayals sicken me the most. What were they for? To bring about a marriage for her that was a living hell. To gain a castle that William and I had no right to. For the rest of my life, those ghosts will come to me in the darkest nights to call me to account.

"Your face is so grim," the Queen says to me on the final morning of our ride, when we trot out together in front of the party for a breath of fresh air. "We have prevailed, Alison. The King is by my side again and all will be well when we are safely back in Edinburgh."

I stare at her, aghast. "You will be a wife to him again?"

"I must," she says. "He is my husband. I am bonded to him."

"But what if he infects you?"

She shivers. "I will not allow him back to Holyrood until Arnault deems it safe. When he does return to my side, this time I will not allow him to stray so far. He is like a young boy, easily influenced. I will keep him close. He will grow up in time, Alison. He could be a good ruler yet."

I have to hold myself still in the saddle so I do not shudder visibly at the prospect.

"Are you still determined to leave me?" she asks.

"I must, Your Grace."

She shakes her head. "I do not understand it. You have no castle to go to, no marriage that I know of. What will you do?"

"I will be free," I say.

She rides by my side in silence for a while. "Very well, if you must. But I do not have gold to pay you just yet. In a month I shall have it. Can you stay with me that long?"

I nod. "Of course, Your Grace. But may I ask a favor? Will you give me leave to ride to my family at Tulliallan? There is a pressing matter I must discuss with them."

"Very well," she says. "But you must be back for the grand masque. Sebastian has asked for you particularly. I shall send a guard with you to make sure you aren't delayed."

I bow my head. Will she ever release me willingly?

≈   ≈   ≈

We bring the King to the Old Provost's House in Kirk O'Field to take his healing baths and treatments. His sickroom is laid with a burning fire and sweet-scented rushes line the floor. When he removes his mask, I see him fully revealed for the first time since he became ill. His face is ravaged. The remains of the suppurating sores are livid on his skin and his head is almost hairless. He looks like a living corpse. I breathe a sigh of relief that we may leave him and return to Holyrood.

We have arrived in Edinburgh in time for the start of the Lenten Carnival. All of the lords will be in Edinburgh, traitorous and loyal alike. The young Prince is here, safe in the castle hold. The Queen has gone to the heart of enemy territory and plucked out the King. She has the upper hand in the country again. She talks about the English succession and perhaps this time it will all be as she says. Perhaps I imagined that tone in Bothwell's voice and there is nothing more between them than should exist between a queen and her most loyal noble. Perhaps the King, stricken by this illness, is truly repentant and they will be reconciled. Perhaps, at last, some small peace will come to Scotland.

I will not be there to see it. I must leave the Queen of my own volition, or she will keep me by her side with another pretext. My only escape is to leave her secretly.

William is lodged in Bothwell's chambers in Holyrood and I must make him sign the bond. Before he does, I will find out from John Blackadder if he knows the truth of William's birth.

Fifty-one

Tulliallan stands in the mist, its sheer face towering above me. I pound hard and after a long wait a servant comes. When I announce my presence, he raises the portcullis. I leave my horse with the Queen's guard who rode with me and go into the great hall.

"Alison," John embraces me formally, touching his cheek to mine. "The Queen must value you highly to send her own guard with you."

We both take a seat near the fire. "I have come about William. There is a question about his lineage I must have resolved."

"Go on."

"In Glasgow I saw the King's charter that declares William is the illegitimate son of Roland Blackadder, Archdean of Glasgow," I say. "The Hume family believes Alison's son died and William has pretended to be him. But a six-year-old boy cannot pretend such a thing."

John stares at me for a long moment and in the gloom his face looks pale. "I had thought this matter long dead." He gets up. "Come with me."

He leads me up the circular stairs to the next level. The library is ringed with musty books and my breath makes clouds on the air. John unlocks a cupboard and draws out a casket. He opens it, flicks through the stack of parchments inside, and withdraws one.

"This?" he asks. It is a copy of the charter I saw in Glasgow.

"You knew of this?"

He holds up his hand to stop me. "William was in great danger, and that brought danger upon us all. When the boy was brought here, my father did not know what Hume believed had happened to him. My father was himself the next in line to Blackadder after William, so he was in danger too.

"Blackadders were high in the church in Glasgow and in the King's favor. My father's illegitimate brother, Roland, was there and it was known that he had a son. My father took William there and he took the place of Roland's son, for his protection. When we heard that the Humes were looking for him, Roland petitioned the King and had this charter signed. We kept a copy here in case it was ever needed for William's protection. I have not beheld it since my father died."

I exhale slowly and John passes the parchment to me. It is stiff with age but the writing is clear.

"What of Roland's real son?"

"He is still a minister in some small parish—Kirconnel, I believe."

"So William really is the heir," I say. "Why did you never tell him of this? I was about to have him sign a bond saying he is illegitimate."

"It was secret and to be used only in extreme need," says John.

There is something in his face that makes me shiver. "So this falsehood can be destroyed now." I stand up and take a step toward a candle, the parchment outstretched.

"No." John stands swiftly and blocks my path. "It is signed by a king. It would be treason to destroy such a thing."

I pause, out of his reach.

"For God's sake, John, tell her and be done with it." I turn as Margaret pushes the heavy door open and steps inside.

John jerks his head at her. "This is Blackadder business, set down before you were born, Margaret. Leave it."

"No, I won't leave it." She crosses the room. "I am married to this name, with its burden of jealousy and revenge. This girl's life has been twisted and ruined because of that castle. Now tell her."

John shakes his head, his jaw set.

"It's all a lie," Margaret says.

He strides to her and grabs her by the throat. "Shut your mouth."

"Tell her," she chokes out. "Tell Alison her father is a bastard."

"Let her go," I say.

He drops her like a dog dropping a rat and sits heavily.

"My father had a plan for this," he says at last. "He was next in line to the castle after Alison's son, and he was avaricious in matters of property. If William ever won the castle himself, my father had the means to prove he was illegitimate and take it himself. I do not know if he would have done so."

"Of course he would have," Margaret snaps. "He would do anything for lands, that man."

"He would have taken the castle from William?" I ask, my fists clenched.

Margaret is rubbing her throat. "It would never have belonged to William. He is indeed the bastard son of Roland Blackadder, just as the charter says. This family kept it secret from him. They were content to let him believe he was heir to a castle, but planned all along to snatch it back if he ever won it."

I stare at her. I cannot speak.

"It was not such an evil thing as it sounds," John says. "I bought William a boat so he had a profession. You were raised with a noble education. He would have had nothing as a cleric's bastard."

"Then what happened to Alison's real son?" I ask.

"Nobody now knows," John says. "It is nearly fifty years ago."

I make my way to the window, my legs trembling. Whatever I had expected, it was not this. Then I swing around as a thought occurs to me.

"You have held the charter," I say to John. "This was not only your father's plan."

"My father passed all the details of his plan to me before he was killed," says John. "Of course, I had no intention of doing anything about it. I have not looked at my father's records in many years."

Margaret laughs bitterly. "Be truthful, John. Your father's desire for lands is not dead in you. William's whole life, and Alison's too, have been crafted so they never knew the truth of their lowly birth."

John stands. "That's enough! I would not have done the things my father planned."

"With all my heart, I would like to believe you," Margaret says. "But the desire for that castle has burned within you, and you never freed William from his false burden. This is a sin, John. I beg you now, put this evil plan aside. It is a secret canker that has eaten at your soul. Do not die with its stain upon you."

He clutches the casket, his face set, and she stares at him as if she will ignite the pile of parchment with the force of her gaze.

≈ ≈ ≈

She comes out with me into the courtyard, where the Queen's guard is waiting with my horse. The sky is pewter and the wind cuts like ice. I want to get away from Tulliallan's tall, blank walls and John's casket with the King's charter locked in it. I mount and look down on Margaret.

"You could have spoken, in all these years."

"You, of anyone, know how the Blackadder men feel about this castle," she says. "I was afraid to speak."

"I thank God for one thing," I say. "When the Queen took me to the castle last year and would have given it to me, I turned it down. I would rather see Lord Hume and his descendants hold it than it go to you and John by such treachery."

I wrench the horse around and break into a gallop across the courtyard, the clatter of hooves drowning out everything. The guard is but a beat behind me as we race in the direction of Edinburgh.

I am sickened by my own clan. The men and women of William's own blood have betrayed him and even now they hold the means to take the castle from him, should he by some miracle win it as a reward from Bothwell. I remember the sound of him weeping and I cannot bear it. I cannot leave him in Scotland believing he owes an allegiance to such people. I must try again, no matter the danger, to convince him he is illegitimate. And I will persuade him to flee to France with me.

A message is waiting for me when I return to Holyrood, penned in a firm hand.

I must speak with you. I shall wait at the White Hart for the next four evenings.

The signature is an "I" with a flourish. I read it twice, fold it, and tuck it into my jerkin. I shall meet Isobel only when William has signed the bond and I have fled the Queen.

≈ ≈ ≈

The Queen's master of pageantry, Sebastian Pages, is devising another grand masque for the evening of his wedding to Margaret Carwood, another of the Queen's favored servants, and Holyrood is crowded with satyrs and nymphs and knights. He has saved me a minor part. I take the role of an elven creature, in green close-fitting hose and doublet, covered with embroidered leaves and branches. The final, perfect touch is a mask fashioned from leather that covers my eyes.

We rehearse for a full day and then the actors leave. I watch carefully as they file through the palace gates. Tomorrow I will be with them and the next day I will sail on a ship leaving Leith for France.

Then I watch until Bothwell leaves his chambers and makes his way to the Queen's rooms. I do not want him there when I speak to William. I take Joseph Rizzio with me to bear legal witness.

Edmund answers my knock. "Funny how whenever there's something to do with the Humes, your daughter turns up," he says, opening the door wider to let me in. Joseph follows and stops inside the door.

Jock has his back to me by the fire and as I cross the room I see he is bandaging William's finger into a splint.

William keeps his head down, but Jock glares at me.

"What happened?" I ask.

"Hume's men," Jock growls. "Said it will be his neck if they don't get their bond."

William's face is ashen. "I will not speak to you. You're no daughter to me."

I stand my ground. "And Robert was no father to you, William. I have the proof."

"That rubbish again," Edmund says.

I swallow. "I have seen the charter in the church in Glasgow. It says you are the bastard son of Roland Blackadder, the Archdean. It's signed by the King. You're not the heir to Blackadder Castle."

My legs are weak. I stare at the floor as the silence lengthens. I am ready to tell him that the Tulliallan Blackadders have lied to him, but the words die in my mouth when I see he is crying.

Edmund comes close and pushes his face into mine. "You're lying. You want him to sign their bond and save your arse."

"I saw it with my own eyes." I step past Edmund toward my father. "They'll kill you. Isn't it worth your life to sign it? If you're not the heir, anyway?"

With his face still turned away, William gestures. I step forward and pull the parchment out of my cloak, creased and crushed from its travels. There is a quill and inkpot on a table nearby. I cross to it, ink the quill, smooth the paper, and hand them to him.

He scribbles with a desolate scratching sound and thrusts it back at me. I blow on the ink to dry it, then lay it down and scratch my name. Joseph crosses the room and quickly scrawls his own signature below William's. It is done.

"You think I betrayed you, but I have only tried to help," I say. "Come to France with me, William."

William raises his face to me. For a moment I think there is a glimmer of hope in his eyes and then he springs from his chair and rushes at me, grasping my shoulders and pushing me halfway across the chamber toward the door.

"Get out of here," he growls. "Take your damned bond and your damned witness and get out." Then he leans close and whispers so no one else can hear, "I beg you."

I stand still in surprise.

Edmund pushes past him and takes my arm. "Go and fawn over your Queen while there's time."

He drags me to the door. Joseph has already crossed the room and walks out in front of me. I twist against Edmund, trying to look back at William, but he has turned away.

"Father!" I call. Edmund gives me a final shove through the door and slams it. I sprawl to the ground.

Joseph helps me to my feet and then leaves me. I cannot let myself weep.

≈ ≈ ≈

To celebrate her safe return from Glasgow with the King, the Queen dines in the great hall with her full household and those of her lords who are loyal.

"Come in disguise," she says to me as I help her dress. "Remind me of happier times so I can believe they will come again."

I draw on some noble finery that I have not worn in a long time and look at myself in the mirror. Although I am growing too old to pass for a lad, my disguise still works. I have spent so much time as a man that I have absorbed the stance and the mannerisms and no one seems to notice how clean-shaven I remain. In France I shall always live as a man, I decide. I will forgo love, even, for the freedom this life gives me.

The Queen does not sit on the dais, but in a show of affection, takes her meal at the head of the long table. The dinner is unusually fine for so late in winter and she smiles warmly on us. She has some of her color back and laughs from time to time at things Bothwell says.

I watch them. Their bodies lean together. She smiles and touches her face. He drinks a lot and eats well. It has always been like this with her favorites. She draws us close to her and binds us with caresses and sweet words. She began with easy targets: her ladies-in-waiting, her poet, her secretary, me. She knew the potency of her charm, and she made us each feel special and needed, as if her life would be so much poorer without us. She has played on the greatest desires of each of us, binding us to her with love and favor.

What is it that Bothwell most desires?

He told me, back when speech flowed freely between us, that it was to serve his Queen with honor. But I do not know what honor means for him now, this man with wife and mistress already, sitting where the King would be seated if he were here. He is a man and a soldier and a noble. If he were any other, I would believe the worst of him, but Bothwell lives by a complex moral code.

"I wish to drink to our new lovers," the Queen says when the plates have been cleared, and the servants are moving around the table topping up the wine.

"My dearest La Flamina and her beloved Maitland, who waited so patiently to be joined. Your happiness is apparent." A cheer rises around the table as we all raise our cups and La Flamina blushes prettily.

"And my master of creation and pageantry, Sebastian Pages, and my loyal Margaret Carwood. If you serve each other with the love and loyalty you have shown to me, it shall be a marriage in heaven indeed."

We lift our cups again and drink to them.

"Now let us dance as though spring were upon us and we were young again and without a care." She claps her hands for the musicians to begin.

For years, to be in the Queen's household meant to dance every night, but that has fallen away since Rizzio's death. Tonight she has made sure the best wine is in our cups and our feet are ready to be merry. She and Bothwell lead us in the pavane.

She dances toward me and it is as if the years suddenly dissolve and there is a young Queen reaching to take my hand, so tall and exquisite that she holds the country in thrall, and I would die for her in a moment.

She leans close to whisper to me privately. "I have missed my handsome Robert. I do not think I can bear for you to leave me."

She has caught me unawares and my heart, traitorous creature, leaps.

"I must do things you can barely imagine," she says, close again. "I have lost so many that I have loved. My mother dead, Francis dead, my uncles dead, my child fostered, and one after another my closest companions leaving me."

"You still have Seton."

"I will always have Seton. But your love is a slippery thing. I believe I have it and I find it gone from my grasp. I mourn its loss, only to find it has returned."

I put my hand to her impossibly small, taut waist as I did that night five years ago. My heart pounds. She has me bound as tight as ever.

369

"I ask you this as a friend," she says as we come face to face again. "Stay with me, my raven. Stay in spite of no reward. Stay because you love me. Stay because you cannot bear to leave."

My breath comes fast. Since the night she first held a sword at my throat, love and danger and desire collided, and those things have been entwined in me ever since.

"I cannot leave you," I say, and it is true.

She smiles, her intimate smile as though we are the only two in the room. As if tonight we will disguise ourselves and run out into Edinburgh's streets, two young men without fear. As if we will race our horses through the park tomorrow and ride high up Arthur's Seat before climbing the summit on foot to see Scotland spread out below us.

Then she spins and advances to the next partner.

I sit the next dance out, taking up a cup of wine and swallowing it to try and gather my wits. How can she turn me to her purpose so easily? How can a handful of sentences bind me again? I have let down the guard on my heart at my own peril.

"Does something ail you?" Bothwell comes up silently behind me and I jump.

"I am quite well, my Lord."

He looks me up and down. "I have not seen you dressed thus for some time."

"The Queen likes it," I say.

He seats himself beside me. "What did you say to your father?"

I swallow. "It's private."

"I have never seen him so despairing, even after he let the Elliots escape from Hermitage."

"I had to make him sign the bond."

Bothwell strikes the table with his fist, making me jump. "I told you to leave it with me! Have you delivered it?"

I hesitate. It's momentary, but he sees it. "You must not give it to them."

I move away from him. "Your protection is not enough. They broke William's finger this night. Next time it will be his neck."

"The castle is not lost to him," he says. "You may walk away from

370

it, being young and a fool, but I intend to restore it to him. I do not want Hume having such a bond."

I jump to my feet. "The promise of a castle is no use to a dead man!"

His hand flashes out and he grabs me by the wrist. We both feel the jolt of physical contact between us. I wrench my arm away and take flight, weaving through the dancers and out of the great hall. He is but a few steps behind me when I reach the corridor. He catches me by the shoulder, turns me, and pins me to the wall.

"Where is it?" he demands. When I refuse to answer, he puts his hand on my chest.

As the parchment starts to crackle I lean forward and kiss him hungrily. I am keeping the bond away from him, I tell myself and then I forget the bond as he presses his body against mine and kisses me as though he is starving. Is it the Queen who has awakened such ravenous appetite in both of us?

At last I pull my mouth away, breathing heavily.

"William is not the heir," I say. "I have seen the proof, under a king's signature. He has no right to the castle and even you cannot change that."

I slip under his arm and run. This time he does not come after me.

The kiss is what seals it. I can trust nothing in this place. My own desires can rise up and take me by the throat, my own heart is treacherous and my body is not to be trusted. I must leave. I must hand the parchment to Isobel and bring the madness to an end.

Fifty-two

We practice for the Queen's masque all day. When at last Sebastian calls the rehearsal at an end, I throw on a heavy cloak against the cold, leave my mask in place, and follow the other elves and faeries and goblins outside. A light snow has fallen during the day and the air smells of more to come later.

We come to the gates laughing and red-cheeked, still playing at being enchanted creatures and teasing the guards. I dawdle and flirt and wink as if I am in no hurry. Dusk is falling and at last we spill out of the palace gates and hurry up the Canongate to enter the city walls before darkness falls. As we pass through Netherbow Port, I allow myself to become separated from the elves, faeries, and goblins and in a moment I am alone in the jostle of Edinburgh's citizens making their way home for the evening.

I stand still for a few moments, savoring my freedom. I am tempted to go straight to Leith tonight and board any ship that is waiting. If the Queen can still stroke my cheek and change my mind, if I can still hunger for Bothwell in spite of it all, then nothing is safe. I cannot trust myself anywhere.

But darkness is coming down fast and the men who broke William's finger in warning are somewhere in the city. While my elven disguise has let me escape the palace, I am not inconspicuous on the street. Already I am attracting glances. I cannot go to Leith discreetly, dressed like this. I must have help.

≈ ≈ ≈

"I never thought you would have the strength to leave," Sophie says, as I warm myself by her fire. "Not with the hold she has over you."

"But I have done it," I say. "I must deliver the bond to the Humes tonight, and then I will sail for France."

Sophie takes a sip of wine. "Have Red deliver it."

"Isobel has asked to see me." I reach inside my jerkin, draw out the note, and hand it to her.

She reads it. "Surely you don't trust her?"

"She's been trustworthy so far. She could have killed me at Stirling, but she did not."

"Let me send Red to get her," Sophie says. "We'll bring her here and give her a taste of being afraid."

She orders dinner and has the servant lay it out on a small table near the fire. It's a rich, meaty stew and the aroma of it makes my mouth water. But she insists we wait until Red returns.

He has found Isobel and he brings her into the chamber, hands bound and mouth gagged. He has frightened her, I can see. She is dressed far too richly for a tavern, in the trappings of a nobleman, her long hair poking out under a wig.

He pushes her down to the floor—not hard—and pulls off the gag. I step forward. She looks up with relief on her face and I remember how young she is.

"Your safe passage was promised. You can trust me," she says, rubbing her wrists.

"But I cannot. Your men broke my father's finger last night. I care to keep my bones in one piece."

She looks around warily. "Where are we?"

"I have been to Glasgow and seen the records," I say. "You were right. William is illegitimate. I have your bond, signed by us both, legally witnessed by the Queen's own secretary."

Isobel starts to rise and Sophie gestures for her to take a chair. She pours her a cup of wine and hands it to her. I can see Isobel shaking.

"I came to tell you something," she says. "Lord Hume let me believe Blackadder Castle would be mine one day. But when I returned from Stirling at Christmas, he had given it to my brother. James has already moved in there with his family and stationed a garrison there. Alexander and Catherine were forced out of their chambers and into the visitors' quarters. Even Beatrice was pushed to a smaller chamber."

"But doesn't the castle belong to Alexander?" I ask.

"Lord Hume controls the property of all his clan."

Her lip trembles slightly and suddenly I feel sorry for her. She is scarcely more than a child and even she has now felt the might of Lord Hume turned against her.

"What has this to do with Alison?" Sophie asks.

Isobel looks down at the floor. "Beatrice was distraught about the move and she wondered why the Blackadder line had suddenly been usurped. She says there is something suspicious in this whole matter and she must speak with you and William."

"You cannot trust her," Sophie says to me. "She has said already she wants the castle for herself."

Isobel raises her head. "Lord Hume removed Alexander from the castle without a second thought. What else might he have done?"

I shake my head. "You walk a dangerous path, Isobel. Do you have any idea what it means to be an enemy to your own blood?"

The color rises in her cheeks. She looks flustered and drops her gaze to the floor again. "Beatrice has begged me to find out what really happened to Alison's son," she says.

"Alison's son is dead."

She gets to her feet. "Then why is my aunt so desperate to speak to William?"

I shrug. "I do not know, or care. It is too late. I am about to leave Scotland. This is all behind me now."

"Beatrice is your kin, even if only distantly," Isobel says. "Do you have any care for her?"

"No," I say. "I have the bond. You will stay here under Sophie's hospitality and, after I sail, you can take the bond and return to your family. I don't give a damn about your aunt Beatrice."

"She says you are so much like her sister Margaret that it is uncanny," Isobel says.

"Stop tormenting me!" I wave to Red. "Take our guest to a chamber and make sure the door is well locked."

Red, taking his cue from my voice, grasps Isobel by the arm and leads her from the room none too gently.

Sophie turns to me. "Stranger and stranger the truth becomes."

"I know the truth, and it is bitter. I don't wish for any further knowledge of the noble Blackadder clan and their plans," I say. "I am sailing on the first ship that leaves."

Fifty-three

The next morning Red accompanies me to Leith to arrange my passage. On the docks the air sings with promise, smelling of fish and salt and spice and adventure. For the first time in weeks my heart lifts. I will go to sea and forget the miseries of land. I will let the wind take me to France, or Ottoman, or Egypt.

But the soonest I can take a passage is three days' time, to Flanders. I pay the captain and, as we step down the gangplank, a man rushes through the crowd toward me. Alert to danger, I drop into a fighting stance, my dagger drawn, and Red does the same. The man comes to a halt. It is Bothwell's servant, French Paris.

He raises his hands. "I mean you no harm, sirs." Then he peers at me more closely. "Robert?"

"Shut your mouth." I straighten and drop my dagger hand to my side. "You've not seen me."

He nods. "You've not seen me either. Pray to God this ship is leaving this afternoon."

I shake my head. "Next week."

He groans out loud. "There's not a single ship leaving this cursed place today," he says and there are tears in his eyes. "Damn them to hell."

I step closer to him. "Why do you run?"

"There is such evil afoot that we shall all be sucked into the maelstrom. Your father is waiting up there on the road. We had one chance today to flee. But if Bothwell misses us, we lose any chance of escaping again. I must go."

"Wait." I grab his arm. "I must speak to my father."

He shakes me off. "There is no time."

"What evil do you speak of? Is my father involved?"

He looks at me despairingly. "Bothwell calls up a storm to break over this kingdom. Run, before it comes."

"Take me to William," I say.

He wrenches himself back. "I've said too much. Get away from me."

He squirms through the crowd and disappears.

"Shall I follow him?" Red asks.

I stare at the crowded dock. "No. We must get back to Sophie's."

≈   ≈   ≈

The Lenten Carnival has arrived, when the back of winter is broken and the season of fasting and atonement and hardship is almost over. The celebrations have already begun, early in the day after mass. Today at court, Sebastian and Margaret will marry and tonight Holyrood will explode with light and color. After the excesses of the Prince's christening, no celebration can again be minor.

Edinburgh is crowded and Red and I must push our way through to Sophie's door.

"Did you find a passage?" she asks.

"I have a berth in three days. But I ran into one of Bothwell's men on the dock. He was trying to get passage for himself and William on a ship. He was terrified, Sophie. He told me there was great evil about to happen and they were trying to outrun it. But there was no ship leaving and he had to return to the palace."

"If it is true and your father is involved, you must hide until you sail," she says.

"Sophie, I must find William," I say. "He and French Paris were trying to flee from Bothwell. If I can offer him a safe hiding place until we sail, he might agree to come with me."

Sophie frowns. "The palace is full of comings and goings for the Lenten Carnival and the wedding tonight. You should be able to get a message to William. I will send Red. Be careful what you commit to paper."

My father, I must speak to you. I saw French Paris today and he told me what you are looking for. The message bearer will tell you where to come to meet me tonight. Alison.

Red is back within two hours of taking my note. William has scrawled a reply on the reverse of the parchment.

Do as you promised and leave for France at once. You are not my child. I never want to see you again.

I stare at the words and my heart twists.

"What is it?" Sophie is watching me. I hand her the note.

"He was leaving Holyrood with three men," Red says. "They carried bags. I followed. They went down on the Cowgate. There are stables there with rooms above them and they went in. They did not come out, at least while I was there."

They both look at me and I straighten. "I will go there. I must speak to him myself."

Sophie shakes her head. "You must wait till darkness. The streets will be busy with the carnival tonight."

"The masque will be on at Holyrood tonight too," I say. "You're right, it will be safer then. But what if they leave?"

"I'll watch," Red says. "I'll take a boy with me and send word back."

"Good," Sophie says. "We shall keep Isobel locked in. Whatever danger is brewing, she is best under our eye."

≈　≈　≈

While I'm waiting for darkness to fall, I make my preparations for leaving Scotland. I will sail in disguise, wearing a beard and the clothes of a merchant in good trade, a man who would go abroad for business interests. I have a forged passport, thanks to Sophie, a purse with a little gold, a small trunk containing clothing and a pistol. When she thinks I will not notice, Sophie slips another purse into the trunk, clinking with silver.

We take our evening sup in her chamber, listening to the sounds of the street outside. I do not know what I should be alert for and so every raised voice makes me jump. French Paris promised evil doings this night, but so far only the sounds of revelry drift up to Sophie's rooms.

Red's message boy comes with the news that William and his men have left the rooms on the Cowgate and disappeared. He says he will keep watch and send for me as soon as they return.

"You should sleep," Sophie says. "It may be a long night."

I stare into the fire. "I cannot sleep," I say and wrap my arms around myself.

She takes up a cup and splashes me a generous dash of whisky. "You could leave him. You owe him nothing."

I stand. "I can't, Sophie. You cannot dissuade me."

She comes across to me and takes both my hands in hers. She looks at me for a long moment, her eyes searching mine. "Do you love only those who are cruel to you?"

I pull away from her. "Of course not."

"Your father, Bothwell, and the Queen," she says. "All have used you for their own ends. All have betrayed you. Yet you cannot let them be. Perhaps it is their very cruelty that draws you?"

"How dare you?"

"I wish you could walk away from them."

"I walked away from the Queen," I say. "Here I sit, out of her service."

She laughs, but it is a sad sound. "Perhaps you are right. I will not believe it till you have sailed."

I stare at her coldly. "You should get some sleep."

She moves away from me. I do not turn around to see her leave, closing the door hard behind her.

I take another mouthful of whisky, for the feeling of it burning down my throat and into my belly. Outside, drunken revelers pass, shouting and laughing in the cold night air.

I am filled with remorse for speaking to Sophie thus and I go to the door, intending to follow her and apologize. But my feet take me in a different direction and I find myself outside the door of Isobel's room.

"Are you there?" I ask softly.

A pause, and then her voice close by. "Alison?"

I slide down to sit with my back against the door so that my mouth is near the level of the keyhole.

"Take me with you," she says. "I would rather flee with you than go home to a family I cannot trust."

I sigh, and it comes from a deep, weary place inside me. "You will bring all the danger of your clan upon me. I cannot."

"Please," she says.

"What would you do in my place?" I ask her.

"Keep me imprisoned, if you must, until we can go together to Leith and sail. None of my family knows where I am. After that, perhaps, you will know you can trust me."

"How can there ever be trust? We have three generations of betrayal between us."

"You think I am still loyal to my family, but I tell you this. I have renounced them. When I leave Scotland with you, I will cast off the name of Hume like a shackle."

I can't help but smile a little. "Names have a way of following you."

"I shall take my grandmother's name, Douglas. You can take it too. Alison Douglas, as you were when I met you."

"And then we are part of another clan with its own feuds and cruelties."

"Then we should take a craftsman's name, a simple name, that does not come laced with blood," she says. "Or we shall make up names that we choose freely ourselves."

"I have already had so many names," I say.

"Don't leave me." I can hear the tears in her voice. "Sophie will try to turn you against me, but I swear to you I am true, Alison."

I let her think I have left, but I do not move. My backside grows cold from the chill in the floor, but I sit there silently, my skin pressed to the door, long after I have heard her stand up and move away.

At last I creep back to the chamber and pull my chair in front of the fire. I stoke it up to try and drive away the cold, and settle down to wait.

It is many hours later and the sounds of night revelry have all but disappeared when the boy comes with word that William is back at the inn on the Cowgate.

Fifty-four

The night is icy and the streets mostly empty now, though I can still hear the sound of festivities drifting up the hill from Holyrood and in the great houses of Edinburgh. A light fall of snow floats down and I pull my cloak closer around my shoulders. The boy leads me down Blackfriar's Wynd, our footprints stretching back into the dark.

Red is waiting in the shadows in the Cowgate. "It's been busy down here," he says softly as we meet. "The Queen's party has gone back to Holyrood after visiting the King at Kirk O'Field. Your father only just came back."

"Where are they?" I ask.

He jerks his head to show me. In the dark it is a small, mean place. "We will go to the door together and when the innkeeper opens it, I will show my pistols. I'll make sure he keeps his mouth shut."

We cross the lane quietly, our steps muffled in the snow. Red knocks softly on the door and a moment later a man wrenches it open. "Who's there?" he grunts.

Red steps forward, both pistols raised. "Not a word," he says quietly. "We have business with the men upstairs."

The innkeeper shrinks back, and Red pushes forward until we are both inside and the door is shut behind us. "Get going," he says to me. "Call if there's trouble."

I climb the stairs to a door at the top. I can hear voices through the wood. I hesitate, raise my hand, and knock. The voices fall silent and a moment later the door opens a crack.

"Jesus!" It is Jock's voice.

"Let me in," I say.

Jock opens the door and admits me, shutting it quickly behind me. William rises from his seat. "What are you doing here?"

"I had to see you," I say, pulling back the hood of my cloak.

"How did you find us?" Jock asks.

"My messenger followed you."

"This is bad." Jock shakes his head. "Who else has followed us so easily?"

"You can't stay," William says, agitated.

"Easy," Edmund says, waving at them to sit down. "It's a freezing night. Give the child a whisky."

Jock pours out a cup and holds it in my direction. I take it and sip. The burn of it gives me courage and I face William. I cannot read his expression, but it is not anger.

"I would speak to my father privately," I say to Edmund.

"You can't!" William says. "I told you. You've got to leave at once."

Edmund laughs. "Calm yourself. We're all family here. Let's hear what she's got to tell us." He pushes William back down on his chair.

"I have passage on a ship in three days," I say. "And a safe place for you to hide. Come with me and escape whatever evil you have been drawn into."

"You shouldn't meddle where you know nothing," Edmund says. "Your father's hour is at hand."

Under my gaze, William shifts in his seat and looks at the floor.

"This is Bothwell's doing?" I ask.

"A favor for Bothwell in return for a pretty reward," Edmund says. "Guaranteed this time, and no woman to ruin the plan. But of course, you are not interested in the castle any more, are you?"

"Bite your tongue," William says.

I swing back to him. "There is more you must know, about the family's treachery. I have ridden to Tulliallan to talk to John. They knew you were lowborn, but they kept it secret from you. They planned to use the proof to take the castle from you if you ever gained it back."

William puts his head in his hands. "Why do you torment me?"

I move in front of him. I would put my hand on his shoulder but I do not dare. "You can never win the castle," I say. "But you have me and you have your life. We could go to France and live without the weight of this upon us."

Jock swigs loudly at his whisky. "Easy for a woman to walk away," he spits. "You just marry another man with a castle."

"I do not believe I will marry." I gesture at myself. "Look at what I've become. Do you think there are landed men who look for a wife such as this?"

"She's right," Edmund says. "No need look for a husband now that she's in league with Hume. I'd say there's a handsome reward from them for her services."

I stare at him in shock and my gut contracts. "You cannot believe that."

"I believe it all right," Edmund says with his nasty grin. "You already have your signed bond saying the Blackadders will never claim what's theirs. Now you come here with some new reason why your father should abandon his castle. You've been in league with them a long time now, have you not? What have they offered you? Marriage to one of their own?"

I shake my head. "You must be mad." I turn to William. "You know I would never do such a thing."

He looks at me mutely and then there is a movement behind me, so fast I don't have time to react. Jock takes me in a sailor's hold from the back, leaving my throat exposed. I struggle for a moment but his grip is iron.

"Father," I plead. William drops his eyes.

"Don't try claiming your kinship now," Edmund says, his voice full of menace. He advances toward me. "Tell us. What pact have you made with the Hume clan?"

"Father," I say again, my voice rising.

Edmund slides his dagger out. "What will make you talk, eh? One less finger?"

I try to struggle but Jock has me in such a hold that I cannot move. Edmund grips my wrist and peels my fingers open. I can feel his blade sharp against my skin.

I must summon Red. I take a deep breath and scream, a high woman's scream. Jock claps his hand across my mouth to stop me doing it again.

"Stop it," William says to Edmund.

"Not this time," Edmund says. "You need to know what unholy alliance she has made to keep the castle away from you so it can be undone."

Edmund presses the knife harder, and the pain shoots up my arm. I look at William, pleading. He reaches to his side and draws out a pistol. He raises it, pointing at the three of us. I stiffen.

The sound of the gunshot is deafening in the small room. The door swings open and Edmund and Jock whirl around.

Red is at the door, holding two pistols like an assassin. One is smoking from where he has shot out the lock. He sizes up the room. If the three of them are against him, he cannot prevail.

William's pistol is still pointing in my direction. "Let her go," he says to Jock.

Jock releases me and steps back, hands up. Edmund lowers his dagger.

"Drop it," Red says, and Edmund lets his weapon fall with a clatter.

My legs are shaking. I meet William's eyes. "Come with me."

He shakes his head. "It's too late."

"Hurry." Red jerks his head. I step through the door and he backs out behind me, his pistol still trained on the three of them. When we are in the hallway, he shoves the smoking pistol in its holster, grabs my arm, and hurries me down the stairs.

We escape onto the street, pull our hoods over our faces, and set off at a run. As we reach the first corner, the whole world splits apart.

Fifty-five

The sound drives into my head, blossoming louder and louder into a roar that obliterates everything else. I clap my hands to my ears and fall to my knees. I am dimly aware of Red beside me, pulling my head down. Then the clatter starts all around us in the dark, like hailstones.

As the frightful noise fades, voices break out from the houses all around us. Babies wailing as they are jerked from their sleep, men calling out, women shrieking. I take my hands from my ears and Red and I stare at each other.

"What in the name of God was that?" he asks.

We stand up and I shake my head to clear the ringing in my ears. We take a step and my boots crunch on a litter of small black shapes on the white snow. The air is thick and choking.

To go back the way we came is to pass William's hiding place. The only way we can move is forward, in the direction of that roar. We feel our way along the wall until we come around a corner into Blackfriar's Wynd. It is so dark that I cannot make out the buildings near Kirk O'Field properly. The Old Provost's House at the south end of the quadrangle is invisible.

I take a step and kick my boot on a massive stone lying in the middle of the street. At the same time a sharp, acrid smell reaches my nostrils. Behind me cries and shouts rise in a cacophony.

"Come away," Red takes my arm. "Some evil has happened here."

I strain my eyes to peer into the darkness. Suddenly I hear footsteps running up behind us. We both swing around.

"Alison!" It's William, a dark shape against the snow. "Get away from here!"

Red pulls me away from the square, but a commotion of voices and lanterns is coming along Blackfriar's Wynd. The night watch.

I can hear voices rising, doors opening. In moments the area will be covered with people.

"Go the other way," William says urgently. He runs toward the light of the lanterns.

"Gentlemen, something has happened!" he cries.

"What brings you here so fast?" One of the watch challenges him.

"I was drinking with friends and the crack shook us from our seats."

"Take him, till we know what mischief has been done here," the leader orders.

Red will not be resisted this time. He pushes me away from the square and back in the direction of the High Street. He has to fight against a tide of people, hastily dressed or still in nightshirts, crying out, holding up lanterns, hurrying past us in the direction of Kirk O'Field.

Sophie is waiting at the door and at the first knock she throws it open and pulls me inside.

"Thank God," she says. "What has happened?"

"There's been an explosion at Kirk O'Field," Red says behind me.

"Where the King is?"

Red nods. "The Queen was there this very night."

Sophie shudders. "See what you can find out."

Red nods and backs away. Sophie shuts the door and bolts it. "Are you hurt?"

"No," I say, but my voice quavers and my legs are shaking.

"It was a near thing, by the look of you. Come and tell me." Sophie puts an arm around my shoulder and helps me to the chamber where the fire is stoked high. She lowers me to a comfortable chair close to its warmth.

"Bring whisky," she says to the maid.

"Bring Isobel," I say.

I do not know what Isobel sees, but she comes straight to me and in her childlike way flings her arms about my neck. She is warm and alive and I cannot help but return her embrace.

≈ ≈ ≈

The King is dead.

By the time Red comes back with the news, the light of Monday is turning the gloom into gray along the dim streets. They found the King lying in an orchard away from the explosion that destroyed the Old Provost's House, near naked, his body unmarked, one of his manservants dead beside him.

I sink into a chair.

"I do not see how he could have been thrown so far, even by that explosion, without a mark upon him," Red says. "This is murder."

Sophie looks grim. "Here is your evil, then. What of the Queen?"

"The Queen's party returned to Holyrood a few hours earlier," he says. "She is safe."

"And the city?"

"There are armed men everywhere and any who try to leave are questioned."

Sophie walks up and down the room, twisting her fingers. "You won't be able to get to Leith. You'll be under suspicion, missing from the Queen's service at such a time."

I shake my head to clear it from the image of Darnley, stinking and corrupt, on the Queen's arm just days ago. "But William is under arrest."

Sophie catches me by the arm. "Listen to yourself! You don't owe him loyalty."

"It was Edmund and Jock who tried to hurt me. William was about to stop them. He came out to warn us and was arrested."

She shakes me. "There will be riots. You must hide until it's safe to leave."

I pace the room, my heart racing. William let me go, when Jock and Edmund would have carved agony into my flesh. He must have known what was to take place, and now they will carve their own agony into his flesh to find it out. I cannot let it happen.

"I'm going to Bothwell," I say. I turn to Isobel. "Go back to your family. Give them the bond."

"No!" Isobel starts up out of her chair, her face working. "I want to sail with you."

"Do you really think, once you step back into those palace gates, you'll be allowed to leave again?" Sophie asks, shaking her head. "You have your moment to escape. Seize it, for God's sake. Break whatever spell the Queen has over you."

"It's not the Queen I go for," I say. "It's my father."

≈   ≈   ≈

By full daylight Edinburgh is alive with raised voices, whispers, knots of people on street corners speaking in urgent tones, women sobbing, the Queen's guards everywhere. Somewhere in a dungeon carved from rock, William waits, incarcerated. They will be keen to question the first man found on the scene, and such questioning, in the midst of Edinburgh's fear, will be harsh.

At Kirk O'Field, searchers move through the rubble and the crowds gather to watch. Bothwell's men are everywhere too, pounding on doors, entering houses, blustering up and down the streets in a show of strength and activity, as though the perpetrator of this deed might still be sitting in a nearby house, waiting for capture. Everyone has a story to tell the soldiers. There are women tugging at their sleeves, arguments breaking out. Everywhere dust and char and shattered stones are covered in a light fall of snow. The sky is lead.

I find Bothwell standing in the square, his face grim as he watches the soldiers carefully.

"My Lord?"

He swings around, startled. "You! What are you doing here?"

"It's William," I say. "The night watch took him."

He reaches out a hand and takes my arm. "When?"

"As soon as it happened. He was here after the explosion. He was the first person they saw."

He leans close. "How do you know this?"

"I was passing," I falter.

"Passing Kirk O'Field at two in the morning just as it blew up?" His grip on my arm tightens. "I told you not to leave the Queen."

"Is she safe?"

I cry out as he crushes muscle and skin against bone. "She is safe, thank God. Now keep your mouth shut."

He calls over a man standing nearby. It is French Paris, his terror plain on his streaked face.

"Take this one straight to the Queen." Bothwell gives one last twist to my arm as he hands me over and I bite down hard to keep from making a sound again.

French Paris hurries me along the street.

"Where is your father?" he hisses in my ear.

"He was taken by the watch," I say.

"Oh Jesus. Oh God." He crosses himself with his other hand.

"Is this the evil you spoke of?"

"Be quiet. I've spoken to you of nothing."

The approach to Holyrood is crowded with people. French Paris and I push through them until we reach the gate. The guard checks us carefully before opening the tall gate a crack so that we can enter the palace grounds. It closes behind me with a sharp clang.

Fifty-six

Seton allows me to take a warm posset into the bedchamber and when the Queen sees me through the gloomy light, she holds out her arms. I embrace her as though I have never left.

"It is a nightmare," she whispers, her voice breaking. "Are you a ghost?"

"I am real, Your Grace." I tighten my arms around her.

She lets go and stares at me with awful eyes. "They meant to kill us both. It's God's will I didn't sleep at Kirk O'Field, or my son would now be an orphan and this country without a ruler."

"But you are safe," I say.

"I cannot bear to be alone." She falls back on her pillows. "Every moment I can hear the sound of assassination."

"No one can harm you here," I say, offering the posset.

She clutches my wrist. "I am too afraid to eat or drink."

I put the posset to my own lips and swallow a mouthful. She stares at me for a long minute and at last, tremblingly, reaches out for it and sips.

"Rizzio was murdered through that very door and I was imprisoned in this room by my own husband. Now he lies murdered too. No one is safe."

"The palace is swarming with guards," I tell her.

She clutches my hand. "You must stay with me. Don't leave me, not for a minute. You and Seton, my two most loyal."

"Of course," I murmur.

She shudders and puts her face in her hands. "He's here. Did you know that? When they have finished laying him out, I must go down and see him. It is so dreadful, I do not know if I can do it."

"They say he is not marked."

She stares at me. "How can that be? The explosion woke all of Edinburgh."

I raise my shoulders in a shrug. "I do not know."

"He had finished his treatment, did you know? He was to come to Holyrood tomorrow and we were to live as husband and wife again."

I remember the stench of him as we brought him from Glasgow and the gorge rises in my throat. Surely she cannot grieve for that prospect?

She looks restlessly around the room. "We must leave here. It's too dangerous. We must go somewhere safer than Holyrood. Dunbar, perhaps? Seton?" Her eyes meet mine again. "Edinburgh Castle," she says. "Where monarchs go in time of need. We shall go there tomorrow. You must stay by my side."

"As you wish," I say.

≈　≈　≈

They hang the Queen's bedchamber with black drapes. We dress her in the royal robes of mourning and braid her hair in tight plaits, severely drawn back from her face.

I do not know what Bothwell says to the night watch, but he returns from the Tolbooth with William before darkness falls. I watch them cross the courtyard from the Queen's window. William doesn't walk like a man who has been tortured and I let my breath out in a trembling exhalation.

Bothwell reports to the Queen's bedchamber. She is seated by the fire, dressed in her mourning clothes.

"Have you seen his body?" he asks.

She nods, her eyes full of tears. "Have you found who has done this?"

"Not yet. But I have men knocking on every door in Edinburgh. They won't stop until they arrest the murderers."

"How can I ever feel safe again?"

"I am sure the plot was not against you, Your Grace. You are safe."

"I am never safe," she says. "I was in my husband's bedroom not two hours before the explosion. They wished to kill us both, I'm sure of it. I thought having an heir would make me safer, but it simply means anyone plotting against me can seize my child and rule in his name."

Bothwell crosses the room to her side. "Hush. The best men in Scotland are guarding you and the Prince. It is a terrible thing your husband has died, but perhaps in time you will consider this a release."

She stares at him. "The murder of a king can never be a good thing."

He bows his head. "Of course not. But while we search for the criminals, we will keep you safe." He glances at me. "You have Seton and Alison by your side, I am pleased to see. I'll make sure they are protected too."

He stands. "I will leave you now, Madam. May I have a word with Alison?"

She waves her hand in dismissal and I follow him from the room. The presence chamber is full but subdued and he walks through it and out into the corridor.

"Come to my chambers a moment," he says, leading the way.

I expect to see William there and my heart is beating, but Bothwell's apartment is empty.

"I see you have brought William back," I say. "What devil's work have you made him do?"

Bothwell grabs me where he hurt my arm earlier in the day, dragging me up on my toes. "I do not know what you were doing at Kirk O'Field, and I do not care to know," he says, his voice hard. "But I tell you this. You will stay with the Queen now, until I tell you. You will comfort her and help her feel safe. If you try to leave, I will send men to get you. Understand?"

I try to pull away from him, but he will not release me.

"You will not speak to your father, nor send him messages," he continues. "You will ask no questions, you will do as you are told by the Queen or myself. Anything otherwise will be at your peril."

I stare up at him. He frightens me. There is something in his demeanor I have not seen before.

"Please don't put my father in danger," I say. "He has been through too much."

"No one is in danger, as long as you do what I say. I know nothing of this, and neither do you. Ask no questions."

I struggle and this time he releases me. "Go back to her," he says.

I cross the room and pause at the door. "Could you tell William I said thank you?"

He turns from me. "No messages, I said."

Fifty-seven

The whirl of the Queen's life swallows me again. I am with her constantly. I hurry to her side in the small hours of the night when she cries out in horror; I help her dress and undress.

I am Bothwell's prisoner, but the Queen needs me, and in this I have never been able to resist her. My worn and battered love rises up like some old soldier on the field of war, alive against all odds. I am her protector now, and in that certainty there is some peace. Perhaps Sophie is right. Perhaps even without Bothwell's compulsion, I would stay with her.

She alternates between wild weeping and eerie calm, between planning to flee and settling herself to take control of her country again. But it has not occurred to her—or any of us—what her country is thinking.

Edinburgh's citizens mourn their twenty-one-year-old King as an innocent. Small shrines to his remembrance spring up in windows, candles burn into the night. I hear that each day people flock to the site of the explosion to weep and pray.

There are as many theories about the murder as there are citizens in the burgh, and word of them finds its way even to Holyrood. There are those who live near Kirk O'Field who say they heard a small army of men run past before the explosion. Two women in Blackfriar's Wynd claim they heard the King's voice begging for mercy, calling, "Pity me, kinsmen." It is sworn that the raven that followed the King from Glasgow croaked on the roof of the Old Provost's House all through the previous day and that supernatural beings swept through the city streets in the night calling out a warning.

Within four days, the first placard is hammered up during the night and it unleashes a torrent of them. Written in different hands, some with drawings, they appear through the city, put up each night afresh for the eyes of the people in the morning. On Saint Giles Kirk, the Tolbooth, the Mercat Cross, on the streets and crossroads. All different, but with one thing common. All accusing Lord Bothwell of the King's murder.

He appears unconcerned. As the Queen falters beneath the horror of the royal assassination, he steps up and assumes her responsibilities. Within a short time he is ruling the country in all but name, while the Queen takes to her chambers for days at a time or rides frantically and without purpose between different strongholds. We move to Edinburgh Castle, then to Seton, then to Holyrood, then Seton again, never more than a few days in each place, each time attended by great trains of servants and guards and advisers. With the greatest effort of will, she attends to urgent meetings with her advisers and reads the flurry of letters pouring into Edinburgh from every corner of Europe, full of horror and outrage, demanding justice, every one carrying the heavy weight of suspicion.

It has been a dark year for our Queen. She is not strong in body and I fear that she will not be able to face this. She falls into a swoon in front of all her court. At night she tosses and turns and cries out in her sleep. Seton and I do everything in our power to comfort her.

"What do the people say?" she asks me one night when we are back at Holyrood and she is unusually calm. "Tell me truly."

"The people read the placards that are pasted around the town at night," I tell her. "Many of them name Bothwell."

"Bothwell," she says. "Without whom the country would have split asunder by now. He rules where I cannot. He is present, when even my brother decides this would be a good time to visit France. He has been ever loyal to me, but there is something about him that others cannot abide. He attracts strife. Why is that?"

"He does not care who likes him." Seton draws a comb through the Queen's hair. "He does not bother to ingratiate himself. He knows he can win any fight, if need be, so he does not bother with pleasantries."

"What think you, Alison?" the Queen asks. "You have had much chance to observe him."

"He is a brute, but he has never wavered in his loyalty to you. There are few lords who could make that claim."

"Few indeed," she says, and her eyes fill with tears. "Even my husband."

"Shh," Seton says.

"No, I must recall it, because around me he becomes more a saint with each new day he is dead," she says, agitated. "They have already forgotten his cruelty, his drunkenness, his rages. They forget he refused to rule, that he barely even signed a document. Now he has become as innocent as a lamb."

It is true. Even I, cloistered with the Queen for most of the hours of each day and night, can feel the tide turning against her.

I hear of the placards denouncing Lord Bothwell as a murderer and I remember William running to warn me only moments after the explosion. When I told Bothwell that William had been arrested, he went at once himself to have William freed, on a day when the whole of Scotland was in chaos and he was needed by the Queen.

I begin to think that while I only ever had the courage to lead the Queen into the snare of marriage with Darnley, Bothwell might have been brave enough to rid her of it. If he is a murderer, perhaps he has in truth been more loyal to her than I.

He comes to see the Queen often and ignores me, apart from the briefest of greetings and farewells. I am dressed as the Queen's lady-in-waiting again, in mourning frocks. Though we are both at Holyrood, William and I never set eyes upon each other and I am too afraid to send any message.

Every night new placards are hammered up around the city and soon the people believe they are supernaturally placed. Bothwell is always named, but other names begin to appear too. One accuses Joseph Rizzio, Sebastian Pages, and Francis de Busso—another of the Queen's foreign servants—as the murderers.

Then one night the first placard appears that dares to accuse the Queen.

Many of the burgh's citizens cannot read, and this message is drawn so that even the lowest will understand it. A bare-breasted and crowned mermaid holding a whip above a hare, protecting it. Two swords, threatening any who would approach them.

The mermaid represents our Queen, as a whore. The hare is the same as the one that Bothwell uses on his heraldic standard.

Edinburgh's citizens are not fools. Even those who cannot read the Latin are in no doubt of the meaning of the words beside the picture. *Destruction awaits the wicked on every side.*

Fifty-eight

When the King's father, raging from Glasgow, at last openly names Bothwell as the agent of his son's murder, Bothwell raises his cup to the tidings.

"An open accusation is better than an anonymous placard," he says to the Queen. "I will go to trial happily to clear my name."

He sends word to his supporters so that on the day of his trial the courtyard at Holyrood is crowded with men on horseback, bearing the colors and standards of their allegiance. The lords who are loyal to Bothwell bring their own men to bolster his two hundred harquebusiers.

The Queen, Seton, and I watch from the window of the presence chamber as Bothwell emerges into the courtyard with Maitland and mounts his horse. A cheer rises from the men assembled and he waves up at the Queen's window. The harquebusiers step into formation around him as he clatters out the palace gates.

It is dark by the time he returns, buoyed by his supporters. He looks up to ensure we are watching for him, sweeps off his cap, and waves it in victory. His men give a cheer that roars across the city.

"I have been acquitted," Bothwell says when he strides into the chamber and kneels before the Queen.

"But I heard word from the King's father that he did not even come to the Tolbooth, as it contained so many armed men," the Queen says.

Bothwell shrugs. "If he had evidence of my involvement, he would have come. It's just an excuse, Your Grace. The court has cleared me of any association with the slaughter of the King."

She gives a small smile. "It is good news that your innocence has been proclaimed." She holds out her hand for him to kiss.

He stands and accepts a cup of wine from a servant. "My men are hammering up placards right now. They say that I shall fight in a single contest against any gentleman who dares to accuse me again of the murder. This will put an end to unjust accusations and evil rumors. Now we must continue all efforts to find the men who perpetrated this foul deed."

≈   ≈   ≈

A mist comes over Edinburgh in the night, pierced by the voice of Bothwell's crier walking the streets proclaiming his innocence. In the morning the fog hangs like a heavy blanket over Holyrood.

"Find me a daffodil, Alison," the Queen says when we have dressed and breakfasted. "I feel as though winter will never end in this chamber. Bring me something with some color."

In mourning, the court has become a place of no color and I am relieved to step outside in the mist, even though it is cold and damp on my skin. I walk around the palace garden, breathing deeply. I cross to the small stone building near the wall. There are stately trees all around it and daffodils usually spring up at the foot of them.

I am in luck. They are blooming and I gather a small bunch to take to her chamber. As I straighten, clutching the flowers, I hear the sound of footsteps coming across the courtyard. I keep still. French Paris emerges from the mist, his eyes wild, clutching something to his chest. When he sees me, he falls back with a cry.

I hold up my hand and he puts his hand on his heart. "Alison. I told your father we should have fled. Now it's too late."

"What's happened?" I lower my voice and step close to him.

"More placards last night," he says. "Bothwell thinks the trial has cleared him, but his enemies are closer than ever. Look."

The placard is lettered in an educated hand. Its author has accused Bothwell of the murder and there follows a list of the names of his devisers and accomplices. Three of them jump off the page at me. Jock Blackadder, Edmund Blackadder, William Blackadder. It finishes with something akin to a poem:

Is it not enough the poor King is dead

But the wicked murderers occupy his stead
And double adultery has all this land shamed?

French Paris clasps his hands together. "We'll be hung."

"Your name isn't there."

"I was seen by the Queen, black as a moor with gunpowder!" he moans.

I step back from him. "Don't say any more. You should burn these at once. Did you find them all?"

He snatches the placards from me. "I must take them to Bothwell. We will all wish we had run before this business is finished."

≈   ≈   ≈

The Queen decides to ride to Seton for the fourth time since the King's death. She is breathless and dizzy, with constant pain in her side. She says the air at Seton gives her some release.

I am as ready to ride as she is. I cannot bear the enclosed chamber of Holyrood, the still mist that hangs in the valley over the palace, the feeling of danger from every side. Seeing my family's name on a public placard, I feel the Queen's cold terror of an unknown enemy waiting.

But she cannot outride the strife of the kingdom. Though we reach Seton by afternoon, before the day closes in, Bothwell, Maitland, and Patrick Bellenden, one of the pardoned conspirators in Rizzio's murder, arrive to discuss urgent matters of state. Seton and I help the Queen into a chair and arrange her hair and clothes before they are shown into her chamber, and she greets them without standing. Bothwell glances at us coolly.

"There are important matters to discuss," he says, as he and Maitland take seats close to the fire.

"I do not see anyone unattended in these wicked days," the Queen says. "My ladies will play chess in the corner."

"Indeed and it is this we must discuss," Maitland says. "Your Grace, every day that the murderers are not apprehended is more dangerous for you."

"What would you have me do?" she snaps, losing her composure. "I have held a trial, which the King's father demanded and then would not attend. I have authorized the fullest investigation by those I trust. I would be pleased to hear your suggestions, as the whole of Europe is holding me responsible."

"Madam, what the country needs is strong leadership," Bothwell says. "I have spoken with your lords on this matter and they are all in agreement. You must marry again at once so there is a powerful man on the throne to enforce discipline."

I must work hard to keep my mouth from dropping open in shock, but the Queen takes no such pains. She stares at him in astonishment.

"My husband is barely cold in his grave." I can see her knuckles whitening on the edge of the chair. "Do my lords have a suggestion what man I shall marry, now that the people are daring to accuse me of involvement in my own husband's murder? Is there some prince that can right this dreadful situation, bring the country back to some stability, and perhaps even salvage my succession to the English throne, which this scandal has almost certainly lost? What savior do they suggest, my Lord?"

Bothwell looks at her steadfastly. "I am honored that they have suggested me."

I wonder if she will rise and leave the room at the outrage of it, but to my surprise, she laughs, a sad and bitter sound.

"Do not play at such a serious matter."

Maitland unrolls a parchment. "Your Grace, with respect, twenty-eight of your lords and bishops have signed this bond supporting the marriage of your good self to Lord Bothwell to unify the realm and bring peace. I urge you to give this your full consideration. Your kingdom needs strong ruling at once, to bind the people together again, and show a united face to those outsiders who would bring you down. Bothwell is all but ruling in your stead now as you recover from this dreadful event—but his abilities will be tenfold greater if you rule together."

She stands and walks away from them and then turns. "Has it escaped your notice, Maitland, that Lord Bothwell is married already, that he is a Protestant, and that he has been under suspicion of the murder of my husband? Do you not think that any one of these factors would disqualify him? Let alone the fact that he is but a subject of mine without royal blood?"

Bothwell does not flinch. "My divorce is underway, Your Grace, and will soon be finalized. I have been cleared of involvement in the King's murder by a legal court. You may be Catholic, but this country is Protestant now. The lords agree that it is time Scotland was ruled by one of its own, a man who has the knowledge of court and country in his blood, not some foreign prince."

"It is of great value to have the support of so many of your lords in this matter," Maitland says.

"It seems most hasty and ill-timed and I cannot agree to it." Her voice rises. "If this is all you have come to discuss, then you must leave me."

"I beg your pardon, Your Grace," Bothwell says calmly. "There are other matters we will speak of instead if this distresses you."

A servant brings spiced wine and Maitland changes the subject. Seton and I pretend to study the chess board. Maitland appears anxious but Bothwell is expressionless and courteous, as though the matter is of no concern.

Now I know what I have seen in him. He has developed Darnley's hunger to be King of this land. When was such a thing born in him? Perhaps it lies dormant in every man, arising when the chance of power is within grasp. I thought William had helped Bothwell rid this land of an unwanted king. But now I see there is much more to it than I had imagined.

As their audience concludes, Maitland makes one more attempt to persuade the Queen to consider Bothwell. She snaps and dismisses them. We take her into the bedchamber and begin to prepare her for bed, but she is agitated as Seton and I fumble over her ribbons and fastenings.

"Am I mad?" she bursts out at last. "Did one of my married lords really just bid me to wed him?"

"It does seem strange," Seton says.

"Strange! My kingdom has fallen to such a state that any man who wishes it thinks he may marry the Queen! That is more than strange. It is treasonous."

"He does much of the ruling at the moment," Seton says.

"Do you think I should accept him, then?" The Queen's color is high. "Do you think, as Maitland does, I have lost control of my kingdom?"

"I think it is a most dangerous time," Seton says. "Perhaps you must take unusual steps to protect yourself and the Prince."

The Queen sighs deeply as Seton draws the comb through her hair. A line of tears starts down her face.

"I thought, once, to marry for love," she says, in a half-whisper. "I have been a fool."

She is silent again and I bring across the heavy armful of her nightgown with its handsome stitching. Seton and I help her out of her dress and, raising her arms, we lower the warm, soft fabric of the nightgown over her head. It has become one of the measuring points of the day, this evening ritual. Another day has passed, the Queen lives, no one has been murdered.

"I will not consider it," she says, as her head emerges. "I will be like my cousin Elizabeth and never marry. I will devote myself only to Scotland's rule and raising my son. That is all that shall lie in my heart now. Scotland and the dear Prince James."

She sits, then stands again restlessly. "I must see him." She takes a few steps, then falters. "We must ride at once, make me ready. He is in danger."

"It is too late to ride tonight," Seton says. She steps to the Queen's side, takes her hand and squeezes it. "We will set out for Stirling tomorrow, if you are well."

"We will leave at first light. I must see him by nightfall."

During my fitful sleep on a pallet on the floor of the Queen's chamber, I dream of Bothwell's painful hold on my arm. I try to cry out, but no sound will come.

Fifty-nine

It is not an auspicious meeting between the Queen and her son. She snatches him from the arms of the Countess of Mar and holds him so tightly that he squirms and begins to cry. The Queen tries to restrain his struggles but he becomes more frantic and opens his mouth in a wide wail. The Countess takes him back from his mother's hands and calms him.

The Queen cannot see that she frightens him. Until lately no one, except perhaps Seton, would have dared to speak of such things to her. But I see her lip tremble and I take her arm and lean in close so none can hear my words.

"Do not clutch him so, let him have time to accustom to you again," I whisper, and when the Countess brings the babe to her lap a second time, the Queen is more controlled and he tolerates her affections.

The Earl and Countess of Mar have ordered a fine feast for the Queen, but she stamps and paces and fidgets, gets up and down, and asks her son to be brought again to her, no matter that he has been bedded for the night. He comes, sleepy and irritable, hitting her on the face with his small fists, and I pity the nurse who takes him away to bed afterward.

"Do you wish to stay here with him a little while?" the Earl of Mar asks as we dine. "It is a terrible time and perhaps he will bring you some comfort."

"I wish to raise him myself so that he does not reach for his nurse rather than his mother," the Queen says.

Silence greets the remark. She looks up at the cautious faces of the Earl and Countess and forces a smile.

"It is a foolish fancy, of course. I speak out of grief. A few months ago I had a family. Now I feel so alone."

"You are not alone," Maitland says, patting her hand. "Your son is safe here, your loyal subjects dine with you in the best-defended royal stronghold in the country, and your personal guard is ever alert to your well-being. We shall spend a few days here with your son and perhaps you can forget these dreadful events for a time."

"The murder of my husband is not something to be forgotten or put aside."

"Of course not," Maitland says, sitting back, but he is undaunted. "I mean only that you can take comfort in your beloved son, until you are ready to take the comfort of a husband once more."

"Know you of this, Mar?" she asks, turning to him. "I am told by Maitland that my lords and bishops are for once in agreement that I should marry from within their own ranks, a man not of royal blood, who is indeed already married. A man cleared of involvement in my husband's murder, who is yet the subject of gossip about the same. What think you?"

Everyone drops their eyes and Mar quickly swallows his mouthful of food as he gathers his wits.

"I am certain Your Grace will make the wisest decision," he says at last, and dabs his mouth with a napkin.

"What of you, Lord Huntly?" She turns her attention to his down-cast eyes. "Bothwell is married to your own sister. What do you make of this?"

Huntly puts down his goblet with care. "My sister is divorcing Lord Bothwell, Your Grace."

"For what cause?"

"He was adulterous with a serving girl." I can almost see him squirm.

"I see." She takes a dainty mouthful. "He is an adulterer as well as a heretic, according to my religion."

Maitland steps in with his customary smoothness. "Your Grace, these are desperate times and Lord Bothwell may not be your husband of choice. With the greatest respect, a man's hand is needed to bring the country back under control. You are, quite rightly, stricken with fear and grief and desperately worried about your son. No one expects you to manage the business of ruling in such a dreadful time.

But consider your lords. Who else can you trust the way you can trust Lord Bothwell?"

She glares at him until he drops his gaze.

"Bring me my son," she says at last, laying down her fork. "I wish to see him before I retire."

$$\approx \quad \approx \quad \approx$$

We spend three nights at Stirling, a breathing space before the Queen must be moving again. The Prince tolerates being on her knee but does not show her any special affection. I leave him strictly alone lest he remember our former closeness. I do not think she could bear to have him favor someone else.

The days are lengthening, the weather warming, the cycle of the year turning as though spring has every right to appear as usual. There are flowers everywhere and a babe to dandle. There are no angry mobs in Stirling; the people go quietly about their business. We can almost forget the strife of the country here and the Queen becomes a little calmer.

On the fourth day we set out for Edinburgh with the Queen's retinue of guards. Thirty armed and mounted men, plus Huntly, Maitland, the courtier James Melville, and a small party of servants. The Queen leaves her son with reluctance, holding him in the courtyard until he squirms and struggles.

At last she hands him back to Mar. "Guard him well and I order you, yield him to no one except myself, no matter what happens."

He bows low. "I shall guard him with my life, Your Grace."

We wind down the steep streets of Stirling. The people come out to watch, but their cheering is ragged and falls silent quickly behind us.

The Queen rides tall, but after some hours on the road she begins to sway in the saddle and clutch at her side. Her pain becomes so bad that we must stop in a small cottage and take comfort from a wide-eyed landholder and his family before she can ride again.

We spend the night at Linlithgow and the following morning is sunny again. I wish to let the horse run as we did in days of old, to let my imprisoned body stretch and be free. But there is no galloping over the hills in these days, not when an armed guard accompanies her at all times.

We ride through the day and by the afternoon we have all been lulled into a peaceful state. The sun is warm and the horses are plodding, half asleep, heads down. We cross the New Bridge at Cramond and come round a bend to see them.

Our horses throw up their heads and our party halts. Row upon row of horsemen, in ranks, face us in silence. We are outnumbered tenfold, nay twentyfold at least.

Then I see Bothwell at the head of this army and my breathing begins again. For a moment I thought we were being attacked. He brings his horse forward at a slow canter, his face grim. He rides straight to the Queen, dismounts, and puts his hand on her bridle.

"Your Grace, there is a citizens' uprising in Edinburgh. I come to convey you to Dunbar for safety."

She stares down at him. "I thank you, Lord Bothwell, but if there is an uprising I must go to Edinburgh and face it down. I cannot flee."

Maitland and Huntly both ride up to her side and our guards jostle and press in closer.

"With your protection we can reach Holyrood in safety," Huntly says.

Bothwell ignores him. "Your Grace, the whole of your party will accompany us to Dunbar."

There is something in his voice that chills me. The way he has his hand on the bridle of the Queen's mount is heavy with menace. There is silence for a few moments and then Huntly draws his sword with a loud clang.

"Do you think to stop us?" he asks.

Bothwell glances back and his men raise their swords. The effect is a ripple of steel.

"Hold, Lord Huntly." The Queen puts up her hand. "We shall go with Bothwell, for I do not want bloodshed in this matter." She looks around at our guards. "Stand aside," she says. Then she turns back to Bothwell. "I trust you will allow my men to return to the city."

"Your retinue shall come to Dunbar and from there we shall assess the situation." He turns to the men in the front row. "Bring the Queen's party."

It's then I see William. He rides forward, shoulder to shoulder with the others, and grasps the bridle of Maitland's horse. In a moment we have all been similarly seized.

"One escapes," a man calls out. James Borthwick, a horseman of the Queen's who was riding at the rear of our party, has managed to slip away and has pressed his horse into a gallop in the direction of the city.

"Leave him," Bothwell says.

We set out at an uncomfortable trot. To reach Dunbar, we must skirt Edinburgh to the south of the Flodden Wall. As the city comes into sight, the boom of cannon fire from the castle echoes down from the battlements.

Bothwell gives the Queen a triumphant look and she stares up at the castle, her face afraid. What has happened in the city?

≈ ≈ ≈

Darkness falls and still we ride, shivering in our day clothes, pressing on toward the sea. I am close behind Maitland, watching William's back, but he never turns to meet my gaze.

We ride up to the fortress of Dunbar close on midnight, the moon obscured by scudding clouds and the wind tasting of salt. I am shivering and my legs ache from so many hours in the saddle. Seton has been sagging and sobbing occasionally in front of me. How much worse will the Queen be?

As our party is led into the courtyard, the wind moans over the battlements and the soldiers make fast the great gates behind us. Maitland did not speak the truth when he called Stirling the greatest royal stronghold in Scotland. Dunbar, with its stout defenses and armaments, gifted to Bothwell by the Queen, could vie for that title.

Bothwell tries to help her dismount but she refuses to take his hand and climbs down herself, her spine erect, her head high, her mouth set. Seton and I dismount and in moments we have been hustled away from the rest of the party. They take the three of us inside the castle, hurrying us down the stone corridors and into a chamber in which a fire crackles fitfully.

"We have much to discuss," Bothwell says, leading the Queen to a chair.

"Then I am sure you will not want me to faint away from cold and lack of sustenance," she says.

He bows his head, but it is only a shallow bow. "Indeed, my apologies, Madam. I shall call for food and drink at once. I have a chamber where your ladies will be comfortable."

"I insist they remain with me." I can hear the fear in her voice.

A servant brings food and drink and heavy cloaks that go some way to staving off the cold. Seton and I are still shivering but the Queen has herself under tight control and it is only the bluish tinge at her lips that shows how she suffers.

Bothwell lays a parchment down on the small table in front of her.

"We have discussed this matter," she says.

"You don't understand the danger you're in. The country is on the brink of rebellion. All of Europe is in an uproar. Your own safety and that of the throne is threatened."

"Indeed, Lord Bothwell, I have had fear for my safety this day."

"I have brought you here for safety, I swear, but also out of love," he says. "I have been bold to you today because the strength of my love has forced aside the reverence I naturally bear you. I live only to serve you, Madam, and the best way I might serve you at this time is as your husband."

"I do not wish to discuss it any further tonight," she says. "I order you to send my guards to Edinburgh to find out what has happened there, and to return with an adequate force to escort me back."

"It is too dangerous to return to Edinburgh."

The Queen is defied all the time by omission and deceit, but rarely to her face and I watch him, fascinated. Something has happened to Lord Bothwell. Since the King's murder perhaps he has seen that a monarch is only flesh and blood, vulnerable like any other person. It seems the monarchy holds no fear for him now.

The Queen is white-faced with exhaustion but he continues trying to persuade her. She remains firm, periodically asking for Maitland or Huntly or for messages to be sent, all of which he refuses.

At last she gets to her feet. Seton and I stand too.

"Lord Bothwell, you have put your case most forcefully and I shall give it consideration and discuss it with my advisers," she says. "We have ridden more than forty miles this day, much of it in the dark, and I am weary. I wish to retire for the night."

He stands too and bows. "Allow me to escort you." He holds out his arm to her. She stares at him a long moment before taking it coldly.

There are guards ahead of us and behind us as we walk down the corridor.

"What about our belongings?" asks Seton, as we hurry to keep up with Bothwell and the Queen. "The Queen requires her trunk."

"They have been sent up," says Bothwell, not looking back. "Here we are, Madam."

It happens in a flash. At one moment he is bowing by the open door of a bedchamber, allowing the Queen to step past him. The next moment the guards have blocked our way and Bothwell has stepped into the room behind her.

Seton's scream of "No!" comes a heartbeat before the door crashes shut and the sound of the bolts sliding home echoes down the corridor.

Seton rushes to the door and pounds on it, but a guard drags her off.

"You ladies will sleep elsewhere," he says roughly.

When Seton struggles he twists her arm until she stops. Another guard behind us pushes me away. From inside the room, muffled by the door, I hear the Queen's cry of fear.

Sixty

When we are allowed to see her the following morning, her lip trembles and her gaze slides away from me. I can see the beginning of a bruise where her nightgown comes down to show her cleavage.

She whispers that I must try to send secret word to the Governor in the town of Dunbar to come and rescue her. I whisper back that James Borthwick will have arrived in Edinburgh and will even now be gathering forces. Today, surely, rescue will come.

Bothwell comes into the chamber and he has the walk of a man who would be King. The Queen flinches at the sound of his step. When he crosses the room and lays his hand on her bare flesh where neck meets shoulder, she shudders.

"Your men, Huntly and Melville, return to Edinburgh today with the rest of your guard," he says. "Maitland shall stay here with you and me."

She does not lift her eyes. "How long do you intend to keep me here?"

"Just until it is safe to return to the capital." He squeezes her shoulder. "Enough time that you are reconciled to me. You are still Queen here. This is your house, you are free to command as you please."

"I would speak to Huntly and Melville before they leave."

He bows. "Of course, my dear. I shall bring them directly." He leaves and I hate the swing in his step.

"Make me presentable," she says.

Seton and I do our best, draping her with a light cloak to cover the bruise on her clavicle and the rip in the edge of her nightgown. I lay my finger on it as I cover her. Without looking up she says, "Don't."

When Melville and Huntly are led into the chamber by guards, they both fall to their knees. Huntly sports a bruise under one eye.

"I do not know where to turn for help," she says to them and my heart aches to hear her voice.

"We shall raise assistance, Your Grace," says Huntly.

"I fear you may be too late." She gives a ghastly smile. "My brother is tarrying in France, my most trusted lord has abducted me against my will. Maitland has advised me I must marry Bothwell. A document says that the majority of my lords and bishops agree with him. You can see the manner of Bothwell's persuasion. What do you advise?"

Melville gets to his feet. "Those who advise you to marry him have betrayed your honor for their own ends. He is commonly judged to have murdered your husband and the people will never forgive you if you join with him."

She is silent a long moment. "Yet I find myself in a situation where marrying him may be the only choice. If my lords truly believe this is the best way forward, I may have to succumb to it."

"We will send men to free you," Huntly says. "Do not give in, Your Grace. You are the Queen."

≈   ≈   ≈

But Scotland has abandoned its Queen.

Two more days and nights pass and no assistance comes from any quarter and no word comes from lord or bishop. Bothwell rarely leaves the Queen's side and each night he locks himself into her bedchamber. There are armed guards with us always. At night they wait outside the door of the bedchamber where Bothwell lies with the Queen.

I have nothing to do but help the Queen with her dressing and remain in her presence, a prisoner. Though we are but twenty-five miles from Edinburgh, we could be at the other end of the earth.

"I shall marry him," she says, when we come to dress her on the third morning, her hair in wild disarray, the bedclothes looking as if a battle has been fought within them.

Seton lowers her head and I see a tear fall, shining, through the air to the flagstones. The Queen sees it also, and reaches out to take her hand.

"I have no other choice. No one has come to take me from here. My lords obviously agree that such a rough wooing is acceptable. The country must have a ruler and while ever I am trapped here, rebellion threatens. If anyone may keep this unruly land under control, it is Bothwell."

She holds her other hand out. I take it. "He has lain with me. I could be with child, and if I do not marry him I would bear a bastard out of wedlock. What could be worse than that?"

I squeeze her hand. "He is a brute."

"Yes," she says. "But you must not speak of him thus if he is to be my consort."

We dress her finely, for she says they will walk outside for the first time since we have been imprisoned and perhaps play croquet. When Bothwell comes into the chamber he strides across the room. Instead of bowing, he bends down and kisses her cheek.

"How does my love this morning?"

"I am adequate," she says.

"Why, more than adequate, beloved." He draws back to look at her. "Have you told your ladies that you have reconciled yourself to my affections?" He looks from Seton to me. "That is good news, is it not? We must bring your mistress to Edinburgh, so that all the preparations may be made for our marriage."

"I trust you have sufficient funds to pay for such a swift divorce," I say before I can stop myself.

Bothwell stiffens and straightens, his cold gaze on me. He comes around to my side and takes my arm.

"I would speak to you a moment." With a jerk which makes me stumble he pulls me to the door.

"James," I hear the Queen say as he takes me into the corridor.

It is only a few steps to the chamber where Seton and I sleep. As he closes the door behind him, he gives me a shove that sends me sprawling to the floor. I remember I am dealing with the man who has ravished a queen.

"Listen well," he says. "The country is on the brink of ruin while

413

the Queen weeps and laments and rides around at her pleasure. Is that what you want to see? The nobles slaughtering each other's armies for a chance at the throne? Or Elizabeth invading and grasping the throne herself?"

"The people are loyal to her," I say.

He shakes his head. "Accusations that she is a murderer are posted on Edinburgh's walls in the dead of night. She has lost their respect."

"Do you truly think this will win it again?"

"I have taken the only chance to save Scotland," he says. "The people know she was kidnapped and forced. They will think less of me, but that matters not. There is no one else who can take control. I compelled the lords to agree. I can pull the country out of disaster once the Queen is with me."

"It's one thing to force the lords, but you cannot force the Queen," I blurt.

He reaches down, grabs me under the armpit, and pulls me to my feet in a single motion. He presses me to the wall, his face close to mine. "I hold your life and your father's life in my palm and I could crush you. I can have you imprisoned in a moment and you will spend your days in a rock cell under Edinburgh Castle. Do you understand?"

I nod.

He gives one last wrench to my arm that makes me gasp. "It's time you were not so close to my wife."

He pulls me to the door and thrusts it open. I stumble by his side back into the Queen's chamber. He lets go of me so I enter the room freely and walk unsupported across the floor to the Queen and Seton. All three of us adopt blank expressions.

"It is sunny. Are you ready for croquet, my love?" he asks.

"It will be most pleasant for all of us to have fresh air." The Queen smiles at him, ignoring me.

"Indeed," he says. "And you shall have some more company to enliven your court. My sister comes to join us this day, with Lady Margaret Reres and Janet Beaton. They are all three good riders and, if it pleases you, tomorrow we will take some exercise on horseback."

Janet Beaton was Bothwell's mistress years ago and rumored to be a witch. Perhaps he has called her to bind the Queen to him with charms and witchcraft.

Seton finishes dressing the Queen's hair while Bothwell waits, tapping his foot.

"My sister knows the latest French fashion for the fixing of a woman's hair," he says.

"Seton has done my hair since I came to Scotland, my Lord."

"Then it is high time for a change. Lady Reres and my sister shall attend to you from tomorrow." He watches me, lacing up her dress with trembling hands.

"I do not like the way you touch the Queen," he says. "It is too familiar."

"Whatever do you mean?" the Queen asks.

He laughs. "It has pleased you to keep a companion who is thought to be an androgyne or hermaphrodite or worse." He crouches in front of her. "You allow her to be overly familiar with you. It is not good for your reputation. She shall not dress you any longer. Lady Reres and my sister shall attend upon you from now on."

My hands fall to my side. "You shall dress as a boy again, to remind you not to touch the Queen in such a manner," he says to me. "You are not to be with her alone; it is not seemly."

I cannot bring myself to bow to him but I bob my head and step back from her.

The Queen smiles up at him. "My dear, I have some womanly matters that I must attend to in finishing my dressing. We will come out to the croquet field shortly."

He turns without bowing and leaves the room. The Queen holds out her hand. I go forward and take it.

"Sometimes a prince must do dreadful things for the good of the people," she whispers, lacing her fingers into mine. "Nothing is safe or certain."

"I don't want to leave you," I whisper back.

"You see what's become of my power."

Seton's eyes are filling with tears. "He is evil," she says.

"Hush," the Queen chides her. She squeezes my fingers. "I will miss you, dear one."

"I will still be close by."

"I think not," her voice is trembling. "You are a true soul, Alison. I bless you." She pulls me into a quick embrace and then drops her arms and adjusts her necklace.

"Come, Seton. I'd best not keep Lord Bothwell waiting," she says.

Sixty-one

Twelve days after the Queen's kidnap, when Bothwell is assured of his success, he brings her back to Edinburgh.

Perhaps Mistress Beaton has used witchcraft to help him, for by the time he leads the Queen into the city by the bridle of her horse, to the sound of the castle's cannons booming out in salute, he has won her. She no longer shudders from his touch. She no longer resists her bedchamber. She sends instructions before her to Edinburgh to speed the divorce so that she may marry him.

Banished from her side, I do not know how he has brought such a thing about. Has he truly won her heart somehow, or does she make the best of an evil situation? I cannot get near her to ask such a thing. When Seton catches my eye during the long ride, she shakes her head sorrowfully at me.

Reduced to a lowly page, I ride toward the rear of the Queen's entourage. Although I am far back I can hear the cheers that greet the Queen as she rides through Netherbow Port. But I also hear how the cheers fall away as she passes. By the time I ride under the port, there is no cheering. The crowd scowls at us.

As we come up the High Street, there is a commotion in the crowd behind me and I turn to see what it is. The street is narrow, the crowd pressed close, the guards ahead are slow to look back. A hand grasps my ankle and Isobel's ocean eyes are looking up at me urgently from the crowd.

"Come," she says, and in a heartbeat I slither from the horse, duck under her arm, and squirm away through the crush of bodies. A yell rises up behind me from the guards as I make the side street. Isobel pushes me into an open doorway, bolts it behind us, and urges me up the stairs into the tenement. The guards run up the street and pound on a few doors, but it is their job to ride with the Queen, not chase her servants, and soon they return to the procession.

Standing next to Isobel at an upper window, peering down, my breathing slows to normal. Isobel has improved her ability to disguise herself and I see she has cut her hair short. She is dressed like a merchant and no one would pick her otherwise.

Her face is alight with mischief. "Smoothly done, aye? You must trust me, for all you protest."

I turn back to the street, instantly angry. "I'm not a fool. If I need an escape route, I'll take whatever's on offer. *Trust no one* is what you'll learn by the time you reach my age."

She stands next to me and peers out too. "Pity you didn't teach the Queen that lesson. Is it true he ravished her?"

"Yes."

"The talk in Edinburgh is that she colluded in her own kidnap, to make it appear she is forced into this marriage when really she has planned it."

"Since when do you know the talk in Edinburgh?"

"You overwhelm me with your gratitude." She draws back. "I have had overmuch time waiting around in Edinburgh for you to reappear."

I shrug. "I did not ask you to wait, or to rescue me."

She scowls. "You do not know what is happening here. Sophie and I planned this with great care when we knew the Queen's party would return."

"Last I knew, Sophie was keeping you under lock in her house."

"There's much to tell you," she says. "It's not safe here—let's get back to Sophie's and we will talk there."

She has brought a servant's garb for me and thus disguised I follow her through the wynds and closes. There is a cold shiver of fear between my shoulder blades. If the news has reached Bothwell that I have escaped, I am certain he will send men to find me. I know too much.

My fear eases slightly when I step over Sophie's threshold. It has always been a safe haven, this house: unbreachable. Sophie is waiting in the main chamber, with the fire crackling and food and drink laid out. She stands and comes toward me and presses my cheek with hers, then smiles at Isobel. "Well done."

I look from one of them to the other. "What have you brought me here for?"

"You've not told her?" Sophie says.

Isobel shakes her head. "Alexander made contact with me. The lords have signed a bond that they will bring Bothwell down."

I wave my hand. "You are wrong. Bothwell has a bond with twenty-eight signatures of support for the union."

"Either the lords were coerced into signing Bothwell's bond, or they meant all along to use this marriage to bring down Bothwell and the Queen too," Sophie says.

"Lord Hume has signed the new bond, and all the Hume men have armed themselves and come to fight, as have the other lords and their men," Isobel says. "We do not think Bothwell can stand against them."

"But what of the Queen?" I ask.

"She is beyond help," Sophie says. "The lords are a wolf pack with the scent of blood in their nostrils. They made their bond at Stirling. I do not think even a soldier such as Bothwell can prevail."

I stare at them. "None of the lords came to Dunbar when they could indeed have saved her. The Queen believes they want this marriage."

Sophie sits by me and puts a hand on my knee. "Listen to me. They have taken her son from Stirling and they plan to rule in his name. You cannot save them this time. Not the Queen, nor William. I do not know what will happen to the Queen, but this time you must flee in earnest."

"I must send word to them at least," I say.

"William already tried to protect you so you could escape," Sophie says. "He would wish you to get away safely now, I am certain of it."

"Even if I wanted to, how could I get away? The city is full of soldiers. Bothwell will have men searching for me."

She shakes her head. "Bothwell will just now be discovering the trouble that awaits him. I do not think he will be worried about you. We have horses waiting in a stable in the Pleasance ready to leave at once. Red will come too and we shall ride south at speed."

They are both silent for a moment.

"There are no ships leaving Leith in such an uprising," Sophie says. "Many are fleeing to Glasgow to sail from there, but that is dangerous country for you. We think it best to ride for Berwick and try to board a ship from there."

They still won't look at me. "Is there something else?"

"Beatrice is desperately ill," Isobel says at last. "She sent a sealed letter for me. In it she said she has information about William. But she may not live long and she says her soul will be in peace only if she can give it to him before she dies."

I shake my head and raise my drink to them both. "Sophie, I can see you have quite lost your mind. Has Isobel bewitched you somehow, that you would agree to such a plan?" I drain my cup. "I must return to the Queen. If what you say is true, she needs me more than ever."

Sophie puts her hand on my arm. "If the lords rise up against the Queen in open rebellion, many will die. The dangers you have faced before are nothing compared to this. Our plan sounds dangerous, but no one will expect you to ride to Blackadder. All Hume's men are gathering, bent on bringing Lord Bothwell down, and none will be at the castle. They will not be thinking of you or William."

I feel helpless. "Do you really believe this is what I should do?"

"This is all you can do for William now," Sophie says. "We will travel in disguise and Isobel carries the bond you and William signed in case any do discover you. It is dangerous, but what choice do you have? Danger is everywhere. It may be none of us can escape it. Red and I will sail with you and stay away from Edinburgh until this uprising is over."

Isobel comes to my other side. "What will you do?" I ask her.

She smiles as if she has not a care. "Leave the bond at Blackadder, bid my aunt farewell, and come with you to France, of course."

I stand and cross to the window. On the street below, men and women go about their business. Edinburgh has its own life in which its citizens trade, barter, fight, wed, seduce, befriend, and betray each other. But our lives are inextricably entwined with the life of Scotland's sovereign. There is not a person on the street, down to its lowest beggar, who is untouched by the Queen. She has been ravished and they believe she has colluded with her ravisher and that he has murdered her husband. Bothwell imprisons her in the very heart of her own kingdom in her own castle. Under such a rule, where can truth or safety be found?

Leaving Edinburgh this time is a physical pain in my body. The thought of the Queen in thrall to Bothwell, not knowing that her lords are to rebel again, twists in my gut as we slip through Netherbow Port and Cowgate Port and into the Pleasance to retrieve the horses. She makes men love her, but it seems that nothing she does can make them loyal to her.

It is not only the Queen I am abandoning. I am riding away from William and in such an uprising what hope does he have of surviving?

I speak little to my companions as we wind through back tracks and byways, through the Lammermuir Hills and into the Borders region. At last we come through the hills to a place where we can look south. A small stream rises there, a slender vein of water running through the grass.

"It's the Blackadder Water," Isobel says, dismounting. "They say the water from here can give you prophetic dreams."

Red helps Sophie down and I dismount too, stiff from the long hours of riding.

"If it can prophesize how I am to enter Blackadder Castle and escape again without detection, then I will drink it," I say. I kneel on the bank and cup the water in my hands. It is cold and sweet in my mouth, as innocent as I remembered.

"You will arrive at Blackadder as a physician from the Queen's household, sent as a favor to our family," Isobel says. She is rummaging through a saddlebag and she draws out a richly embroidered doublet. "Wear this. It's smart enough to fool them."

"What about you?" I ask.

"I will wear a woman's riding habit, like the Queen does, and a wig so they do not see I have cut my hair," she says.

I look at Sophie, who is smiling. "Did you know she was such a plotter?" I ask. "I must remember to stop thinking of her as a child."

"You were in the Queen's service yourself at sixteen and plotting constantly, I recall," she says.

"How do you and Red fit into this scheme?"

"It will take persuasion and gold to get us a passage, even from Berwick. While you are at Blackadder, Red and I will ride on to Berwick to arrange it. We will come back and collect you from Allanton."

I stand up, and wipe the water from my mouth with the back of my hand. "I am the last to know the plans, once again."

"Be pleased we had the wit to work out a plan while you were imprisoned with the Queen," Sophie says.

"Let's go," Isobel says. "It's not far. If we ride hard, we will be at Blackadder by nightfall."

≈　≈　≈

Isobel and I ride across the bridge, the river tumbling and tossing below us. I am afraid to see the castle again and when at last I do, it is as I remember, an ancient creation of stone rising out of the river-bank. My breath catches in my throat to see it.

We ride around to its formal front and into the courtyard. Last time I came here at the Queen's side and no one could touch me. This time I feel small and vulnerable. Beside me, Isobel keeps a jaunty demeanor but there is a tightness in her jaw. Her red wig falls in ringlets around her face.

The stable master comes out and greets her.

"Does my aunt yet live?" she asks him as she steps down to the mounting block.

"Aye, though it's said not for long."

"Keep our horses ready to leave at short notice. There is a war brewing in Edinburgh; who knows what will happen?"

"Very good." He bows his head and leads my horse to the block so I may dismount.

Isobel jumps down nimbly. It is possible she has all along intended some evil in bringing me here, and I will gasp my final breath inside these walls this day. Every Blackadder who has trusted a Hume has died for it. How could I have agreed to this?

Alexander's wife, Catherine, comes to greet us and Isobel embraces her. "Cousin, I have brought Arnault, the Queen's own physician, to see Beatrice."

I bow and take Catherine's hand. "*Bonjour, Madame.*"

She looks at me uncertainly. "Does he speak Scots?"

"No," says Isobel. "He came from France with the Queen. How is my aunt?"

Catherine's eyes fill with tears. "She has not long to go, I fear. Do you think he can help her?"

"Perhaps," Isobel says.

Catherine reaches out and clasps her hand. "I don't understand what has happened. Why did they take the castle from Alexander? Why did they move us from the rooms we've always lived in? Alex has been sent to fight and he barely knows how to hold a sword. If Beatrice dies and something happens to him, I am alone in the world with my children, owning nothing."

"Lord Hume decides what is best for the family and we must accept that," Isobel says. "I'm sorry to rush, but Arnault should see Beatrice at once. Afterward we shall join you for dinner."

Beatrice has been moved from her generous chamber into one that is mean and dark and on the northern side of the castle. A fire flickers in the corner but does little to reduce the cold. Isobel crosses the stone floor to the bed.

"Beatrice?" she asks, taking her hand. Beatrice opens her eyes. There is a sickly pallor to her skin.

"William?" she asks.

"I could not bring him, dear Aunt," Isobel says, her voice tender. "But I have brought William's daughter."

Death is not far from Beatrice. I can see its shadow on her face as I come close by the bed.

"Beatrice? Do you remember me?"

Her eyes flicker and roam over my face; her mouth works. "Alison Douglas."

"Yes, though it's really Alison Blackadder."

She reaches out a hand and takes mine, her fingers cold. "I must see William," she whimpers.

I squeeze her hand. "He is protecting the Queen. But he has sent me in his stead. Isobel tells me you have something for him."

She draws her hand away. "I can give it only to him." She pulls the covers up to her chin and begins to shiver.

Isobel's face is hard in the candlelight. "This room is not good for you. I shall see if I can have you moved back to your own room."

Beatrice shakes her head restlessly. "Do not trouble yourself. The room matters little now."

Isobel strokes her forehead until she calms. "Is there anything I can get you?"

"*Vise a la fine*," Beatrice says. "A dram of whisky will help." For a second I can see the ghost of a smile.

"What do you mean?" Isobel asks.

"Don't you know?" I say. "The Blackadder credo. See it through to the end."

"I will leave you with Alison a little while and come back with the whisky," Isobel says, stepping back. Before she leaves she calls a servant to build up the fire and light some more candles.

I take Beatrice's hand. She turns her head and for a moment I see a younger woman's face under her creased skin.

"Lord Hume took the castle from Alexander with a snap of his fingers, as though he had no right to it," she whispers. "I looked in my mother's papers for the old documents of ownership when Isobel told me about the bond you and William were to sign. I found a casket, well hidden. It contains a letter addressed to William."

"Did you read it?"

She shakes her head. "I could not. I have thought William dead for most of my life. But why would my mother have written to a son who lies buried just outside? I can think only that her son must have lived." She squeezes my hand tightly. "It must go to William and no other."

"I am his only child. Can you not give it to me?"

She tosses her head. "I do not know who to trust! It cannot fall into the wrong hands. Whatever she has written must be dangerous for her to have hidden it thus." She stares at me again, wild-eyed, and her voice rises. "I myself signed the Blackadders' ownership of this castle over to the Hume family. What if I was wrong to do so?"

"Hush," I try to calm her. "It is done now."

Her face collapses and she begins to weep. "What injustice have I done my brother, if he lives?"

I take both her hands. "Beatrice, you cannot change it. But I swear to you, I will take the casket to William. You can do that for him at least."

The door opens and Isobel hurries across the room to the bedside. She holds the whisky to Beatrice's lips. Beatrice sips at it and closes her eyes.

Isobel takes me by the arm and draws me away from the bed. "A rider has been sent to Wedderburn to report that I've returned," she says quietly.

I straighten up, my heart thudding. "What will we do?"

"They will come for me and you will be discovered," she says. "We must leave at once."

"Who can you trust?"

"There is a lad in the kitchen who got the warning to me. I have sent word for the stableboy to take the horses outside and wait for us at the graveyard. I can trust him. We'll take the secret way out of the castle."

"I must bring the casket for William," I say. I step back to the bedside. Beatrice has sunk down into the pillow, her eyes closed. I shake her shoulder gently, but she doesn't stir. I shake it again, harder, and her eyes open suddenly.

"Alex, my boy?" she cries.

"It's me, Alison." I lean close. "Where is the box for William?"

"Under the bed." She tosses her head, agitated.

I bend down and draw out a small wooden casket, well carved, bound with iron and fronted by a stout lock. The key is inside it.

Isobel kisses her on the brow. "We must flee. Goodbye, Aunt."

I come to the side of the bed, bend low, and kiss Beatrice's cheek. "God be with you, Aunt."

"And you, my dear," she says, in a second of lucidity before her eyes close again.

≈ ≈ ≈

The boy is waiting for us near the heat and bustle of the kitchen. He leads us round through the bakery and into the storeroom where the passage begins.

"I thank you," Isobel says to him, and I hear the clink of coin. "We may owe you our lives this night."

The three of us tug the stone out of the way. Isobel and I crawl into the tunnel and there is a loud grating as the boy slides it back into place behind us. It is dark at the other end and I put my hand on my dagger. The roar of the water rises up like a live thing as we emerge.

They set upon us as I crawl from the tunnel. One grapples with me and I can hear Isobel's exclamation cut off as another takes her. The casket slips out of my hands, clattering over the rocks as I struggle. The bank is steep and slippery and it is dark, but I have a dagger in my hand. Over the roar of the water I hear a human cry of pain as I find my mark and the dagger sinks home into flesh. The hands loosen their grip on me and I throw myself toward the only safety I can imagine.

The Blackadder Water rises up to take me with its icy touch. I hit the water and scrape over a rock. The current pulls me into the main body of the river where the water is fast and cold. I let her take me. I can hear nothing of Isobel. Just the roar of water in my ears.

≈ ≈ ≈

My eyes adjust to the darkness and I can make out the high banks rushing by as the river carries me. This is my own river, is it not? She will surely carry me to safety. I must only keep my head above the water and not allow the weight of my clothing to drag me down.

Above me, stars wink in and out of the clouds. It is a relief for once to have only water to struggle against. There is no human hand here, my life is a matter for the Blackadder Water and me to work out between us.

But as she carries me, and the cold water embraces my body, I realize something. The Blackadder Water is not water carrying my name; it is water holding nothing but itself. One day the castle will fall. Its stones will tumble and lie on the earth again, its timbers will rot, and there will be no more footsteps and voices. But the river will still run, even if our name is forgotten.

The rush of the water is loud and I surrender myself to the flow. I smell the clean scent of water and soil and grass and at last I understand. In sweeping me away, the Blackadder Water has given me a gift, washing me clean of my longing for the castle. It has even swept away William's casket with its weight of human concerns. The castle's spell is truly broken.

The cold begins to creep up my limbs and the weight of my cloak drags at me. My arms and legs feel heavy. I must leave the river's embrace and make my way to shore.

But it turns out she wants something in return. I start to paddle toward the southern bank but she drags me ever more swiftly, keeping me in the fastest part of the current. The river that gave me my name now wants to take me back to her bosom.

A roar rises out of the dark ahead of me and I frantically try to recall the course she takes. Is there a waterfall in these parts? I kick harder to try and reach the shore and now I am truly afraid. There is nothing inviting about the river's embrace. Now she has her claws locked into me and she will not let me go.

Suddenly I am tumbling and tossing through foaming water. My head goes under and the fight to bring it to the surface again is exhausting. I break through and take a great gasp of air, and I remember. It is the confluence of two rivers—the Blackadder and the Whiteadder, above the village of Allanton. From here, the combined river runs swift and full down to the sea.

I discover an unexpected passion to live. My leaden limbs come to life, I kick out and stroke. At last the water is shallow enough so I can get a grip and drag myself from one rock to the next, my numb fingers slipping and clawing, my feet scrabbling on the slippery river bed. The current tries to drag me back and twice she almost succeeds, pulling me from my feet and slamming me against hidden rocks.

"Let me go!" I beg.

In answer she flings me against a last rock and my head meets it with sickening force. I cry out with the pain of it and feel myself go limp. She has won.

But now that she has me, she relinquishes me. The current takes me into a quieter eddy of water behind a rock. I spin for a moment and come to a halt.

The world is weirdly slanting and whirling around me as I crawl on hands and knees out of the water and onto a patch of stones. I collapse, coughing, and it is some moments before I can see where she has flung me.

It is too dark to pick out any kind of landmark, only that the bank runs high above my head. I can see stars, scudded by clouds, and a glimmer of light low down in the sky—the moon has risen, though as yet it casts little light. I am shivering so hard I can barely stand, but I force myself to crawl up the bank, then walk back and forth, slapping my arms against my sides and stamping my feet.

By the time the moon clears the clouds and sends out a gleam of light, my legs have given way. I huddle under my sodden cloak in a crevice between two rocks. A cold wind blows up, cutting around the rocks. I pull the cloak tight around me and force my head up each time it nods onto my chest. I cannot feel my hands and feet.

They say that in order to die, salmon come back to the very river where they were born. On this dark night, I think of William. I could die on any lonely hill in Scotland or in some stinking wynd at a murderer's hand. Or in a bed of my own, soft and old, like Beatrice. He would be pleased, I think, that if I am to die in such a manner it is here, by the Blackadder Water. Whether or not we are noble, we share the name of this river and I have returned to it at last.

It hurts to leave this life. The cold is knife cuts all over my body. Beatrice lies dying too, this night. She is my closest blood kin except for William. We will make this last journey together and find out if it is the priests or the reformers who are right about the judgement that awaits us. Witches believe in a great female spirit that takes us all back to her breasts to begin the cycle of life again. It is a heretical thought, but one that brings me a little comfort at this hour.

Praying seems like a mockery to a God who knows my treacherous heart in matters of religion. I cannot ask for my life to be spared now. But I find myself asking for William's forgiveness. The running water sounds like laughter.

Sixty-three

I awake from a dream of my mother's arms, to hear my name being called, faint over the roar of the water. With great effort I raise my head. But my response comes out only as a whisper.

The call comes again, closer. "Alison!"

This time it cuts through the warmth of my sleep. I am curled between the rocks, my arms and legs so cold I cannot unfold them. The moon is high in the sky now.

I raise my head and with my remaining strength I call, "Help me!"

My voice sounds like a croak, but there is an answering call close by and then someone comes scrabbling over the rocks and I feel hands on me.

"Alison," she says and I realize she is weeping. "I thought you had drowned."

"I'm the daughter of a sailor; I won't drown," I try to tell her but having made one cry I cannot will my voice to work again. With a great jerk, I start shuddering with the cold. The pain of it is so terrible that an animal noise issues from me.

Isobel disappears for some time I cannot measure. She returns and somehow makes a fire. She wraps her own cloak around me, forces brandy between my icy lips, and at last sits close to me, pressing her body against mine.

The brandy burns a path to my belly, but no farther, and it seems I can feel ice moving toward my chest. I know I will die if it reaches there.

"Don't leave me," she says, and that is the last I remember.

≈ ≈ ≈

Trying to wake is like coming up from deep underwater. I try and try and at last the weight lifts a little and my head breaks the surface.

I am warm. There is a fire in the room and I'm in a bed. My body is still oddly distant—I ask my hand to move and it does, but reluctantly.

"Alison?"

Sophie comes into my field of vision and bends down, putting a hand on my forehead. I stare up at her mutely.

"Can you speak?"

I open my mouth, but only a croak issues forth.

"Don't try," she says. "Wait a moment."

She brings a bowl and lifts me up a little so she can tip the liquid into my mouth. I have never tasted anything so wondrous and I suck at it eagerly.

"Easy, easy," she says. "That's good, you're hungry." When it's finished she lowers me.

She pulls the covers up again, and presses my forehead. "I would wake Isobel, but she has not left your side these two days and she is exhausted. Could you sleep again? It's sleep that will heal you now."

I could not fight away sleep if I tried. Its embrace is as inexorable as the river's current.

The next time I surface, Isobel is close by. This time she cradles me and feeds me more broth and I lie in her arms at rest. For once it seems that I am not searching, I have nothing to do, no place to be. I fall back into the river of sleep.

When I wake next, sunlight is coming into the room and Isobel and Sophie are both there. I sit up unassisted. My body is my own again. Isobel approaches with broth. I reach for it and down it in a few swallows.

"Where are we?" I ask when it's finished.

"Allanton," says Isobel.

"It's been a week," Sophie says. "The cold nearly took you. That and the blow on your head."

"A week!" I sit up.

They both nod. I look at Isobel. "What happened that night?"

"There were two servants, loyal to my brother, waiting for us," she says. "I heard you go into the river. I could not get my dagger out, but

432

I kicked my attacker in his manhood and got away. I had to wait till the moon came up. The stableboy was loyal and was waiting for me with the horses. I watched for a long time, till I was sure no one was there. Then I went searching for you. Thank God you were washed up on the south bank."

I look down. "I am in your debt."

"Not only that." She is grinning. "I heard you drop the casket on the rocks. I went back and found it."

She crosses the room, comes back with the casket, and puts it down on the bed. "You will have to break it open. The key is lost."

I take it in my hands and shake it a little. There's a scuffle of papers and something rattles. I rest it down again.

"It is William's to open, while ever he lives," I say. "He must see that I have not tampered with it."

Isobel looks downcast. "Surely you want to see what's in there?"

I shake my head. The effort of conversation is suddenly exhausting. "What now?" I ask.

They look at each other. "The Queen and Bothwell are married," Sophie says. "The lords are raising their armies. The country goes to war against its sovereign."

I stare at her in shock. "Does any lord stand by her?"

"A few," she says. "But the rest now call themselves the Confederate Lords and they go to take the Queen from Bothwell, who they say is a murderer, adulterer, and ravisher. There are still some in the Borders loyal to Bothwell. But most have turned against him."

I run my hands over the dark wood of the casket. "Are we still to leave from Berwick?"

"I have ridden there to find us passage, but the English are interested in this rebellion and they have their own armies gathering," says Sophie. "Berwick is watched even more closely than Leith."

"Then what?" I ask.

She stands, shaking her head. "I do not know. Men are rising to arms all through the Borders, for the Queen or against her. Every road to Edinburgh is crowded. I do not know if they will fight in the capital, or where else a battle might take place, but the common talk is it will be south of Edinburgh. Perhaps we should try to make our way to Leith, after all. Anyone riding away from Edinburgh is likely to be questioned, whereas anyone riding toward it is presumed to be summoned to arms."

The casket is warm under my hands. If we return to Edinburgh, there is a chance I can give it to William.

Isobel is grinning. "Another disguise."

"What this time?" I ask.

"There is only one that is safe," Sophie says. "We go north as soldiers of Lord Hume."

≈ ≈ ≈

It is some days before I can mount a horse again and, even after we set out, the weakness in my body persists and I cannot bear to be cold. Red rides close by my side.

We ride as men going to war, in the colors of the Hume clan. The country is full of men like us, carrying weapons and wearing what armor they can fashion. Some are barefoot, carrying only sharpened spikes lashed to sticks. They say they go to save the Queen from the ravening clutches of Lord Bothwell but there is no love in their eyes.

As we near Edinburgh, the word comes along the road. Balfour, appointed by the Queen to hold Edinburgh Castle safe, turned upon her. Barred from her own stronghold, the Queen fled the capital with Bothwell and made for Borthwick Castle, there to try to raise more men.

The taverns in the villages surrounding the capital are crammed, but we beg lodging from a family loyal to the Confederate Lords and they bring us more news as we eat our dinner. The first forces of Hume, Morton, and Mar have met up south of Edinburgh to march on Borthwick. Bothwell fled out a window and left the Queen, and the lords did not know what to do next. They rode on to Edinburgh, leaving a guard stationed at Borthwick. But the Queen outwitted them. She dressed as a man, escaped the castle, and rode off on Bothwell's trail.

My heart lifts at the news. She will triumph. She always does, in such adversity, when she can rise to her daring best.

After dinner, Red settles himself on the floor and Isobel, Sophie, and I crawl into the bed. I do not mind so much being in the center. I crave warmth and cannot have enough of it.

"If Bothwell did ravish the Queen and force her to marry, then surely she would be glad of the lords' rescue," Isobel whispers, mindful of listening ears at doors, as we try to sleep. "Why has she gone to be with Lord Bothwell now?"

Sophie, on the other side of me, shakes her head. "She has a woman's heart, our Queen. Now she is wedded to him, she may have fallen in love."

"More likely she has fallen with child," I say. "Her worst fear is an illegitimate babe. To avoid that, she will do anything."

Sophie and Isobel fall silent and after a time their breathing deepens. Red snores. We are packed tight as herrings in the bed, but I feel alone. I lie staring into the dark. The night is full of noise, of hooves and footsteps in the street, men's voices. It is the feel of a pack of hunting dogs before they catch the scent of their quarry, every muscle straining, seeking. The very air thrums with it.

It is Bothwell being named over and over: Bothwell who is still accused of having murdered the King, Bothwell whose name has been written on placards night after night in Edinburgh. But what shall happen to the Queen if they bring Bothwell down? What mercy will there be for her if she is with child?

William, who has been Bothwell's right hand all these years, will be on this battlefield. I do not know how I will get the casket to him, but I keep it close at all times.

Isobel sighs and shifts in her sleep and her body presses closer to mine. I stiffen, but with Sophie against my other side, there is no way to move away from her.

She is a child, younger than I was when I fell in love with the Queen, and even less able to hide her feelings. It is in her eyes. I ignore it; I give no answer to the question there.

But one thing has changed since the night in the river. I make no more jibes about her untrustworthiness. I settle back in our rough soldier's bed and force myself to sleep.

Sixty-four

We have thought ourselves safe in the colors of Hume, but danger comes from a new quarter. As we ride out of the stable yard where we have been lodged, a man canters up.

"Hume men?" he snaps. "Hurry up; they'll leave without you."

There is no chance to slip away. He rides behind us up the street until we join the rear of a huge group of fighting men.

"The battle is at hand," a man who seems to be a leader calls out. "We ride to Carberry Hill. Make speed."

I catch a glimpse of Isobel's frightened face as the mob presses forward into a canter. Red rides close to Sophie and I know he will not leave her side. We surge up the roadway, a mass of moving horseflesh, men, and arms. The noise is deafening and around us men yell and wave their weapons as though we are already in the charge of battle. The air reeks of sweat and horse and rage.

At last we sweep around a hill and come into view of the battlefield. Even I, who have seen battles before, gasp. The Queen's forces are arrayed on the opposite hill, with Bothwell's standard fluttering in the sunshine. On our side, with far greater numbers, are the armies of Hume, Mar, Morton, and the other lords. Over them all, a massive standard with a kneeling child and the words *Avenge my cause, o Lord.*

As we slow down, I look frantically from side to side until I catch sight of the others. I ride close to them, our horses jostling.

"Keep with me, at the back. When the fighting starts, we will flee. If we are lost, we must try to meet at Sophie's."

I have never ridden into a battle before. We had thought to leave Scotland's danger, and now I find myself in the middle of it—on the side opposing my Queen, with only a dagger to defend myself.

≈   ≈   ≈

The easiest way to beat a Scottish fighter is not to let him fight.

There are thousands of men on the field ready for battle, but this is a battle with the Queen and, faced with the reality of it, her lords would rather parley than fight against their anointed sovereign.

The messengers ride back and forth across the field and the sun grows hotter and hotter. Even the horses are dozing, rocking on their legs, their heads hanging low. The battle rage, which roared at the start of the day, fades as the lords continue talking. Most of these men are farmers, not soldiers, and their battle-lust cools with the inactivity. Men on both sides melt away like snow, though it is the Queen's army that dissolves the fastest.

At last it appears some agreement is made. There is a stir up and down the field. The horses stop dozing and prick up their ears. Men who have been lying in the shade get to their feet. We crane our heads to see what is happening.

From our vantage point, I see the Queen ride out to meet James Douglas, the Earl of Morton, at the center of the field. Oddly, for a man who is opposing her in battle, he bows to her. Then he takes her horse by the bridle and begins to lead her across to our side.

The men around me turn to each other, confused. "What's happening? Are we to fight?"

Across the hill, Bothwell leaves the battlefield at a gallop. He flees through the ranks of his own men. Swift as a fox he crests the hill and disappears.

"They will not fight now," I say, as we press forward to see the Queen led to the waiting lords.

The men around us move to see too and we are carried on a wave. I am waiting for a cheer in celebration that the Queen has been taken from Bothwell's clutches, but what rises in the throats of the men around me is an angry jeer. I look around, shocked. Every face is hostile. There are fists raised, and the words yelled at her make me cringe. "Whore! Murderess!"

"My God, they will attack her!" I say to Isobel and, hardly knowing what I do, I push my horse into the throng of snarling men. Their leaders shout to restore order, but without conviction in their voices. The blood-lust of the battlefield has turned upon her.

I ride close enough to see her face. She stares around her at the swarm of soldiers in horror as they roar and bellow insults at her. They jostle against her and she must grab at her saddle to keep her balance.

Morton mounts up and the other lords ride to flank her, but this is not a victory march. They surround her and raise the standard about her head, the piteous lament of the fatherless Prince. They march off with her in the middle and with a roar the soldiers follow, calling for the Queen's blood.

≈ ≈ ≈

The lookouts stationed along the road race ahead of us to the city to spread the news, and even from a distance I hear raised voices. For a moment my heart lifts. This is the city that has never turned its back on the Queen. She will ride through it as of old, up to Edinburgh Castle, the fortress, where our sovereign can always find safety, and the people will weep with joy that she has returned to them.

We come up the Canongate to Netherbow Port and as she passes through, I hear the muffled roar of voices. But it is not till I pass through the port myself that the noise hits me like a blow.

I have never heard such hatred. There is not a face that isn't twisted in rage, no mouth not shouting an obscenity. The Queen is far ahead of me now, but the shouting does not die down in her wake.

The street rises in front of me, and I can follow her progress by the position of the standard. It stops, well short of the castle, and my gut twists. Will they put her in the Tolbooth like a criminal?

I push harder, forcing my horse through the crowd. I am in time to see them lead her into Black Turnpike, the house of the Lord Provost. She turns her head at the door and I glimpse her last disbelieving look before they sweep her inside.

"Burn her!" a man next to me yells. I look down from the horse. He is shaking his fist and his face is so contorted I doubt his own wife would recognize him. "Whore!"

"They will kill her, I fear," I say.

Sophie nods. "But there is nothing you can do."

I sit, then stand again. I rub my arms. Even on a June evening the cold of the Blackadder Water is deep in my bones and nothing will relieve it.

"Should I go and look for Isobel?" I say restlessly.

Sophie shakes her head. "She knows to come here."

"Then where is she?" I walk across to the window. The street is still thronged with people. "Do you think they mean to take the Queen to the castle? Why is she in Black Turnpike?"

Sophie is watching me with a pitying look.

"Stop it," I say.

"Then don't be a fool."

She takes the heated wine from the servant and brings it over to me herself. "I doubt they will execute her, not without more evidence she was involved in the murder. But I think it likely our Queen will meet with an unfortunate accident before long. It is most convenient, is it not, that she has left a babe as an heir?"

I take the cup, but the spicy taste of it is the taste of nights in the Queen's chamber.

Sophie puts her arm around my shoulder. "You must say goodbye to her. It is over. While confusion is everywhere, we shall leave, properly this time. Not your loyalty, or your love, or your life will help her now."

She is still holding me when a loud knock comes at the door and a moment later Isobel strides in.

Sophie makes to draw away from me, but I tighten my grip to hold us in embrace a little longer. Whatever the question is in Isobel's eye, let this be an answer to it. She does not know of love between women, but neither is she a fool. If she sees this, surely she will understand something and have the sense to put her heart out of my reach.

When I do draw back from Sophie, Isobel has stopped inside the doorway and her color is high. Sophie shoots me a hard look. She knows what I have just done.

"We were worried," she says to Isobel. "But you're safe."

Isobel's hand drops from the door handle and she takes a breath. Was I so transparent in my adoration of the Queen, at the start?

"I tried to find news," she says. "I saw Alexander in Hume's army. I followed him, but it was a long time before I could catch his eye and speak with him discreetly."

Her lips start quivering. "Beatrice died the night you fell in the river."

I am sorry at once for that embrace. I approach her but she turns her body away, takes a few breaths and squares her shoulders.

"I have hot wine here," Sophie says. "What more have you heard?"

Isobel has herself under control. "Bothwell is on the run. They have given him a day to leave Scotland but he is riding for Dunbar to raise more men and come for the Queen."

"He has little chance," says Sophie.

"They will send a force the day after tomorrow to hunt for Bothwell, but it was the Queen they really wanted. In the streets there is talk of executing her for murder. I heard not one word spoken in love for her."

"At first light we will go to Leith," Sophie says. She looks at Isobel. "Is your family still seeking Alison?"

"Alexander says all men have been called in for this battle, but there is a standing order that anyone who comes across William or Alison should murder them."

It is only what I expect, but the news sends a surge of fear through me, nevertheless.

"There is also a standing order that I am to be apprehended and brought to Lord Hume himself. They are busy with this rebellion, but it is best we do not tarry. We should climb the Flodden Wall and leave tonight."

"No," I break in. "It's better to leave openly. Disguise works best when people see what they expect to see. We ride out of Netherbow Port tomorrow in daylight. If anyone asks, we are merchants going to Leith to collect a valuable cargo. We travel light, as if for a day or two."

"Then I shall go to my bed," Isobel says. At the door she stops. "What will you do with William's casket?"

William, with the rest of Bothwell's army, is fleeing somewhere through the countryside, and Hume has a death warrant upon him. This has been his life for almost fifty years.

"I will take it with me," I say. Isobel nods and leaves the room.

Sophie looks at me coolly after Isobel leaves. "That was cruel."

"You warned me in the first place that her feelings would be trouble."

"Her feelings kept her searching that riverbank in the dark for hours, with only the smallest chance she would find you."

"Then they have been useful," I say. "But I must cut them off now. Isn't it kinder for her to think I love another?"

"Kinder than what?" Sophie's eyes flash. "That you cannot love because the Queen has taken your heart and twisted it into a bitter, black thing and you are content to let her keep doing so?"

I step back in shock, as if she has struck me.

"You wish only to love the Queen, and it's always been so," she says.

"But Angi—"

"You have never really loved anyone but the Queen."

In a moment I realize it is true. The Queen had Angi hanged and still I did not leave her. There is no love that has ever come close to my passion for her.

I walk away to hide my confusion. I stand with my back to her, looking out the window. Foodsellers are lighting their lanterns over the doors. Up the hill I can still see a crowd gathered out the front of Black Turnpike.

"It's not my concern, Alison," Sophie says sadly. "But I say this to you. When we leave tomorrow, leave your past here in Edinburgh and cut yourself finally free of whatever hold the Queen has on you. If you do not leave her behind this time, she will drag you to your ruin, along with her own."

She walks to the door. "I bid you good night," she says, and closes it behind her.

Sixty-five

In the morning light, the port at Leith is like another battlefield. The dock teems with men, pushing and shoving their bundles, carts, goods. Mercenary soldiers hoping for a side to join, foreigners trying to flee, and not enough ships for all of them.

We thread through the rabble in single file, despairing.

"There!" Isobel points to a ship lowering its gangplank. The crowd surges toward it until a man on the ship pulls out his pistol and fires into the air. The echo of the shot reverberates through the sudden silence and the crowd backs away.

But a small group is hurrying up the gangplank and I would know the walk of one of them anywhere. It's William, followed by Jock. I start to push my way through the crowd.

When I make it to the foot of the gangplank, William and the ship's captain are standing on the deck above, looking intently behind me. I turn my head. Soldiers are coming down the road toward the dock, moving fast and wearing Hume colors.

I hurry up the gangplank and find myself facing the mouth of the pistol.

"It's all right," William says, waving at the captain. "I'll deal with this one."

"William," I say.

"Get away from me," he says curtly.

I hold out the casket. "Take this. It's from Beatrice."

"Get away!" he yells.

The violence of it makes me jump. The boys start to pull up the gangplank and I have to run to get off it or be thrown in the water. On the dock I turn, thinking to throw the casket onboard, but it is too late. The crewmen hoist sails as if their lives depend on it and the

442

boat eases away from the dock. The wind snaps at the sails and I can see it lifting William's hair. He is on the sea, where anything can happen. I am bound to land, unsafe.

He has left me to their mercy and escaped without me.

The pain of it keeps me rooted to the spot. Leave the past behind me, Sophie said, and it seems I have no choice. William has cut me adrift and soon there will be oceans between us and no way to find him again.

The commotion on the dock rises. The crowd jostles me and I look around. Sophie and Isobel have reached my side.

"Come away," Sophie says.

I turn, and over her shoulder I see the Hume soldiers advancing. A rush of dread goes through me, but then I realize it is the ship nearest to me on the dock they are making for.

There is a force of them, some fifty men, and the ship is large and fast. The man leading them marches up the gangplank and the captain comes down to meet him. They talk. The next minute the crew is making her ready to sail. Other activity on the dock ceases as everyone stops to watch.

The ship that carries William is sailing down the firth with the wind at her back. The second ship sets out with a great flapping and it is like seeing a wolf set out on the trail of a rabbit. When the sudden boom of a cannon rings out and the puff of white smoke rises from the larger ship, I groan out loud. Sophie clasps my arm.

The larger ship comes alongside the smaller and after a few minutes they both turn back toward the port. The large ship docks first. I am staring at the smaller ship trying to make out William, when the man leading the soldiers comes to the top of the gangplank as it crashes down onto the port. He raises his voice, and silence falls so that it carries across the docks.

"I have here under arrest four men charged with being art and part of the murder of our lamented King," he calls. "Jock Blackadder, William Blackadder, James Edmonstoun, and Mynard Fraser. Make way. They are bound for the Tolbooth."

I clutch Sophie's arm so hard that she gasps. A jeer rises from the crowd, swelling as they bring the four men, hands bound behind their backs, to the edge of the gangplank.

"Murderers!" a voice yells, and there is a volley of shouts.

A stone is flung, and another. William and Jock stand impassively, barely flinching as the stones rain around them. One strikes Jock and blood trickles down his face.

The soldiers manage to hold the crowd back while the second ship docks and the rest of them come to shore, but all four men are cut and bleeding and the sight of it threatens to drive the crowd to a frenzy. Sophie has an iron grip on my arm lest I run forward. The soldiers fire shots into the air to clear a passage and they push the prisoners along, stumbling, battered by stones and words, up the hill to Edinburgh.

The three of us stand, staring after them until the mob calms down. It takes all my will to not break into abandoned sobs. I stare hard at the outline of Edinburgh up on the hill so I do not have to see the dark mass of soldiers taking William to the Tolbooth.

Sixty-six

The cells deep in the entrails of the Tolbooth are carved from solid rock so no one outside can hear the shrieks that issue from within. It is a place more terrible than even Edinburgh Castle's dungeons. The men in the Tolbooth take pleasure in their work, and they know every way in which to make waiting unbearable, and then every way to make their captors long to only be waiting again.

It is likely they will hold William a while. It softens a man wonderfully, being made to wait for his own torture.

Sophie knows a lawyer, a powerful man, and she calls him urgently to meet us in her chambers. He accepts a drink, but his face is grim.

"It's not an ordinary arrest," he says. "He is to be tried by the Lords of the Secret Council."

"I do not know of them," Sophie says.

"No one does. It is a new coalition and your man is doubly wanted by them. They seek the King's murderers and they also know he was trying to take the ship to Dunbar for Bothwell to make another stand for the Queen."

For a moment my heart lifts. At least he was not fleeing the country without me.

"The Confederate Lords must have someone to punish," the lawyer continues. "Those on the ship were not the only ones arrested—Sebastian Pages from the Queen's household, and two others, Black John Spens and Francis de Busso, are being held too. But Edinburgh calls for a hanging, and swiftly."

"I must see him," I say.

"Can you afford it?"

Sophie calls for Red and money changes hands. When the lawyer leaves, she takes me by the shoulders.

"You mustn't expect that he can save William. The lords have this country in their grip now."

"What of the Queen?" I ask.

"They say she is losing her mind," Sophie says. "She was seen at the window of Black Turnpike with her breasts exposed! I thought it was tavern gossip, but my lawyer heard two men tell of it who had seen it with their own eyes. She does little to help her own cause."

"Do you think we'll ever get out?" I ask.

Sophie and Isobel are silent. I pick up the untouched whisky and gulp it. The sound of raised voices, rough and frightening, drifts up to the windows.

"Why don't you open the casket?" Isobel says. "There may be something in there you can tell William that will bring him comfort."

Sophie sends for a chisel and mallet, and when it comes I lay the casket on its side on the stone hearth. It is a well-crafted thing and I do not wish to damage it, but in the end I must strike the lock with force until it cracks.

I pick it up reverently and sit with it on my lap to ease the broken lid back.

A carved toy soldier lies on top, limp as a dead body. Next, a curl of a child's auburn hair, bound in a ribbon. Then a pile of parchment. I unfold the first piece. It is a family tree, showing Alison's son, William, beside Beatrice and Margaret.

I stare at it and my hand begins to shake. "I do not think I can bear this."

Sophie squeezes my shoulder.

I lift out the second parchment. It is a deed setting down the lines of inheritance for the castle. Under William's name is a note, added in 1527, that Beatrice and Margaret have signed over their ownership to John and Robert Hume, their husbands.

At the bottom, thicker than the others, is a letter to William, sealed with wax so old that it crumbles when I break it. The handwriting is close and tight. I get up and walk closer to the lantern, away from Sophie's and Isobel's curious eyes.

My dear William

I do not know if this shall ever find you, or even if you still live. But there are matters I must set down here, even if you do not ever read this letter.

I have done some great evil in the name of protecting you, and now I would confess it, not only to my God, but to you too, whose whole life has been affected.

Two things I did, and you may judge which of them turned out to be the most evil.

I knew the girls would be bound to marriage and you would be killed if you remained at the castle. But I needed to explain to David Hume where you had gone, William—and it needed to be convincing. These were not men to be turned aside with some careless lies.

There was a child, a boy, in the kitchens. His mother was a maid who had died birthing him, and another maid had taken him as her own. He was sickly himself. I had him brought up from the kitchen.

I killed him. I suffocated him with a pillow and the weight of my body, while my girls were in the next room. I had two of the men in the garrison go out in the dark and bury him at once in the grave-yard. I told Hume my son had died of an illness of the lungs a few weeks earlier. I believed once it was underground, any child's body would suffice, even if it was dug up.

I have never forgotten how he struggled and I have thought of him and prayed for him every day of my life since then. I know my priest, when he hears this, will believe it is a great evil and perhaps my soul will never recover from it. But perhaps it is what I did afterward that was the greater evil.

At first I thought such an injustice as the Humes carried out could not last long and Hume would be forced to relinquish what he had stolen, in weeks or perhaps a few months. I believed you would be safe at Tulliallan and before long you would be back with us again.

But I was wrong. I underestimated the Hume clan's power and their determination to keep the castle. I was married to David

447

Hume within a day and with child in a matter of weeks. By then I knew enough of him to realize he would never relinquish what he had gained.

I discovered too that he knew of you and knew of my subterfuge. He knew I had murdered to try to keep the castle and in this I was no better than he. He threatened to reveal it and have me hanged.

I could not protect you myself and that was when I decided what to do. I found a way to send word to Glasgow to Robert Blackadder the Archbishop and, with his royal connections, he arranged the charter that wiped you of your birthright. I made it as public as I could, having it lodged in the church records, sending it to Tulliallan, and making sure that David knew it existed. "The child is nothing but a bastard. Leave him be," I told him. In reply he said, "Let us hope he never needs reminding of it."

I sent money to Tulliallan for you and asked your uncle to make sure you had an honorable living. I preferred you alive, even as a bastard, to being dead with some idea of honor.

William, I have learned something about this castle. The desire to possess it drives men mad. My own actions to keep it have brought great suffering, and I wonder if that is the reason the Blackadders have never been able to regain it. A punishment for my sins, perhaps? I knew what a burden it would be upon you to carry the family's expectation. I knew that after Hume children and their children were born here, it would never be possible for the Blackadder family to regain it and I did not wish to see your life sacrificed for such a thing.

I hope you understand that I gave you freedom to make what honorable life you could. I wanted you to marry and have children without fearing they would be lost to you, as you were lost to me. It is too great a price to pay.

Now David Hume has been dead for many years and I do not have long to live myself. Beatrice's son Alexander is the next owner of Blackadder Castle. Do not regret its loss—in the end it is just stone. I traded your birthright for your life and in my mind it was

a fair trade. It has brought me some comfort, in the nights when the
loss of you was a hole inside me.
  With love, my son.
  This Thursday 17 March 1541, at Blackadder.
  Alison Douglas

I stagger at the end of the letter and I put my hand out to take hold
of something steady in this crumbling world.

Fifty-seven

I fold up the parchment with shaking hands. Someone brings whisky and I raise it to my lips, but the stench of it makes me gag, and I put the cup down again. Damn Beatrice for having told me that such a letter exists.

"Leave me," I say to them, and I turn my back.

My voice brooks no argument. Even Isobel dares not speak to me. They leave the room quietly and close the door behind them.

I look out into the High Street, at Edinburgh, the pride of Scotland, seething with hatred, and I let my heart join it. The black running water is inside me. If William had seen such a letter earlier, he could have carved out a life as a ship's captain with quiet honor and I would never have had to know the depths of the Blackadder family's treachery.

It is an evil thing, that castle, extending its long shadow over our lives. It has driven men and women to deceit, betrayal, and murder for the chance to own it. I thought we had a sacred bond with the land and the water, but perhaps the bond my family made was nothing more than greed.

I stay still and the roar of the evening gradually dies down into the silence of the night, broken by scattered yells. Sophie and Isobel have long since retired, the household has bedded down and still I sit here.

Up on the High Street, the Queen awaits her fate, and down below its surface this same night my father is in a cell, imagining what awaits him.

I rise from my seat, find my cloak and slip out into the night. I will keep vigil with them. I do not care any more what befalls me.

≋ ≋ ≋

It is a summer night in Edinburgh and her wynds and closes stink like carcasses. But her High Street, the pathway of lords and kings, runs broad and open down the spine of the hill, connecting the castle to Holyrood Palace, passing through Saint Giles and the Tolbooth. All the instruments of power in this land—the monarchy, the nobility, the church, and the law—all strung out along the city's backbone.

I creep like a spy to a shadowed corner where I can watch Black Turnpike. There is a light burning in the front room upstairs. The Queen will be keeping her own vigil tonight, on her knees praying to her Catholic God to release her from the grip of her Protestant lords.

If I leave her, what shall I have left?

She has been everything. She has been the light that shone on my days, and the shadow cast over them. Like Alison Douglas, I have murdered, sending boy after boy to Darnley, for the good of the Queen and for my own gain.

What deluded creatures we are. God, Protestant or Catholic, must laugh bitterly when He watches our furious machinations, our arrogant belief that we hold our own fates in our hands. What hope do the ordinary men and women hold, if even our Queen cannot rule her own destiny?

Sophie says I can't help the Queen any longer, but a queen is not overthrown so easily. There will be those gathering even now to support her. There will be plans and counterplots, diplomats sent and communiqués written from church and state all over Europe. The Confederate Lords have struck a decisive blow in the battle, but they have not yet won it.

And the Queen, our brave Queen, will even now be planning some daring escape. She has triumphed before, against great peril. I could stay by her side, help her, comfort her.

There is a movement in the shadows nearby and I freeze. Someone else watches. I hear a muffled sob that I recognize.

"Seton?" I whisper, and cross to her side.

"While she is awake, I shall stay awake," she says.

"But why out here?"

"They will not let me in with her. They know I am no danger. They do not even bother to confine me. So I shall pray for her out here, where at least I can watch for her light."

I crouch beside her. "Will you go back to your family?"

She shakes her head in the dark. "Why do you ask? You know I will never leave her."

I lean back against the rough stone, and Seton bows her head in prayer again. After a moment I stand and touch her shoulder in farewell.

I creep farther up the street and come into the market square. It is easy to press into a shadow against the walls of Saint Giles and watch the Tolbooth. A lantern burns at the door and two guards yawn and scratch.

There will be lords still plotting now how to free the Queen, but there is no one planning how to free William. The only one who might, Bothwell, is a fugitive himself.

My father sits deep in the Tolbooth, under my very feet. I crouch down, then kneel. Then I prostrate myself on the ground and press my ear to the stones, as if I could hear him. I strain to listen. The cold rises into me.

Edinburgh is a city of stone, and stone is too old to care what human hands touch it and press it, what human blood is spilt upon it, what tears rain into its cracks. The stones do not speak of William. They do not speak of kings or queens. They do not speak names. They speak of stretches of time I can hardly imagine. They speak of sea and earth and heaven. They speak of stars tracing their mysterious lines through the sky. They speak of human lives forgotten and human lives unborn.

I press my hands to them, as if some trace of warmth might make its way through them and find William. I press my hands to them as though I could become part of them. My heart is a stone already. If I lie there against the stone long enough, my whole body will harden.

It is close to dawn by the time I make my way back, shadow to shadow, down the High Street. A breeze has sprung up, whispering of a summer day, and there is a slight chill in the air.

Isobel is waiting, sitting outside the door, a cloak wrapped around her. I do not see her and I jump when she speaks softly.

"I read it," she says, getting to her feet.

My hand is on my dagger. "You had no right."

"She was my grandmother."

"And mine, for all the good it has done me," I say bitterly. "You should have let me die in the river. It would have been kinder than knowing what I know of this family."

She steps forward and grabs my shoulders with both hands, taking me by surprise, and before I can fight her off she shakes me. I do not expect such strength from her. My teeth knock together, my head snaps back, my bones seem to loosen in their sockets.

"You're always so angry," she says.

Were I a man, I would stab her, but I am a woman and instead I start to cry. She accuses me of just what I see in William: a life burned up in useless rage.

When she stops, my bones have turned to water and I stagger against her. I put a hand out, I grip the fabric of her cloak. She brings me close slowly, as though I am a wild animal that might turn on her and, in truth, I am trembling with the fear of what I will do to her. Don't unleash the river, I want to beg. Not the black running water, not the danger of such feeling, not the risk of drowning, not that.

Then I am against her and she is at once river and land, ocean and earth, solidity and melting. How could all that be contained in one body?

She knows nothing of love between women, but she brings her lips to mine and my blood thunders in my ears. She does not know the art of kissing, she is no experienced courtier, but her lips are raw feeling, rushing into me, her lips are waterfalls and rapids beating on the rock of my heart. It is not stone after all, in the face of such a deluge. It does care what human touches it.

At the end she draws back a little to look at me. The light is changing. I can see her face as everything moves from black to gray and she looks at me. She touches my cheek again with a trembling hand.

"Alison Blackadder," she says.

Sixty-eight

This will be the manner of his death if he does not confess.

For murdering the King, a man is drawn backward on a cart through the city to the Mercat Cross. There he is hanged by the neck until the life is almost choked from him. But his neck is not allowed to snap and he is cut down while the flame of life still flickers. Then a sword is drawn across his belly and his insides dragged out with a hook, while he yet lives. At last he is quartered like the carcass of some beast.

Once it is done, not even his bones will lie in peace: arms, legs, body, and head will be separated in death, nailed up like carrion at the entrances of four towns—Glasgow, Stirling, Perth, and Dundee—with his head left on a pike here in Edinburgh, food for the kites and ravens.

"They won't torture him to death," Sophie says. "They need a public execution for this. They will offer him a chance to confess and be killed by hanging only. But such a promise cannot be trusted."

≈   ≈   ≈

The stench, of vomit and excrement and urine, is like a solid thing in the air, and the dark is full of groans and whimpers and the scuttling of rats. If the priests ever wanted to show us hell, they need only step a few feet away from Saint Giles into the Tolbooth.

Prisoners are not allowed visitors, but Sophie's gold in the hands of the lawyer has bought me a little time with William before his trial, and one of his gaolers leads me down the corridor, hewn out of bedrock, past rows of cells from which the sounds of agony and madness emanate as we pass. Once I hear a cry, a familiar voice as we pass a set of bars, a scuffle. "It is Jock here," a voice calls. "I beg you, help us.

Help us!" The last rises to a near shriek and I shudder, but I do not turn around.

William is on the floor and, at first, as the lantern light slants across him, I think he is dead. His eyes are half-closed, only the whites showing, and all his limbs are splayed unnaturally. The gaoler enters the cell and shoves his foot against William, who stirs and moans.

"I'll be back for you shortly," he says to me with a leer.

"Will you at least leave me the lantern?" I ask, trying to keep my voice steady.

"No lights allowed here," he says. "You're breaking the rules anyway. Have to sit with him in the dark. You'll be ready to leave when I get back."

He clangs the door behind him and his footsteps retreat and in the silence that's left I hear the steady sound of dripping. I get down to my hands and knees and start to crawl in William's direction.

"William?" I say, resisting the urge to whisper. When there's no answer, I try again, louder. "Father?"

The sound of him stirring, the ragged catch of his breath. "Alison?"

I feel something soft against my fingertips and find my way to his chest. "I'm here."

He makes a sound of such agony that I recoil in horror, thinking it is my touch that hurts him.

His breath is ragged, coming in great sobs. "No, no, not my daughter. God no."

I reach forward again. "It's all right, Father. I'm not imprisoned here. I've come to see you, that's all."

His breathing eases a little, but I realize he's weeping. I cannot bear the sound of it.

"I don't want to hurt you," I say, leaning close. "Where can I touch you?"

"Head," he says.

I move around the strange shapes of his limbs on the floor until I find his head. I put my hand on his hair and then bend down and kiss him on the brow, and there is a sound like a broken sigh. I feel around his neck and shoulders but they are shaped all wrong and I dare not lift his head to lie in my lap.

I bring my own body down flat and put my face close to his, so close our cheeks are touching in the dark and I cannot tell where the wetness comes from. I rest my hand on his chest again and I can feel the rise and fall of his breathing and the thudding of his heart against my fingers.

"I have something to tell you," I say.

"And I you," he says, labored.

"I'll stay with you." My voice breaks. "I'll be waiting and watching over you, Father."

"No," he says. "Promise me. Leave Edinburgh. Promise me, do not watch when they bring me out. Wherever you were going to sail, go."

"For once, let me be with you!"

His face moves and, although his voice is ragged, it is tender. "You are with me, my girl. They can never take you out of me."

I bring my other arm around until I am holding him.

"I was so afraid they'd hurt you," he whispers. "I tried to make you run away. Why didn't you go?"

I am glad of the dark. The cold of the stone presses my belly and my heart cracks a little. "I couldn't leave you."

"Go to France, find your mother's family. Go anywhere. The castle is nothing."

"You're right," I say. "But you must know. I saw Beatrice. She gave me a letter from your mother."

"Good," he says.

"Shall I tell you what it said?"

"No," he says. "It doesn't matter now."

"I never meant to hurt you," I whisper.

He is silent a long time. "I would have liked to see the river," he says at last, so faint.

"Here it is," I whisper, my face close. "I have carried it to you." I hold him and weep silently, as if tears could wash him away.

Up in the corridor I hear the clang of the gate, and see a glimmer of light. "I will have to go, Father."

He whispers softly, "There's money, behind a stone, near the fireplace. Take it."

I press my lips to his cheek. "I don't want to leave you."

"You must," he says. "My love."

≈　≈　≈

It takes a sizeable number of William's coins to buy our passage on a ship to Denmark. It pulls out of Leith with the tide on the morning of the summer solstice, a clear day when the sky and the sea are both blue and the wind smells of nothing except empty ocean. Sophie, Red, Isobel, and I, bound for a new life.

It is less than six years since I sailed into this port with the Queen and the promise of life and color and joy was enough for me to pledge my heart to her. Now she waits, imprisoned in Loch Leven on an island where none can reach her easily, for a change in her fortunes. She promised light and wonder, and along with them came murder and betrayal.

She stood here on the deck of the ship with her four Marys around her, five pretty maidens against the might of Scotland. If I had not been so young myself, I could have foreseen her fate that day. She had no hope against the nobles of this country, who would never in truth tolerate a woman ruling over them. It is an ancient, blood-soaked country and six years in the hands of a woman has not been enough to change it.

Isobel is beside me, staring back at the land. I expect her face to be somber as she walks away from a noble lineage and all its privileges, but a smile creeps around the corners of her mouth. She leans close, the wind rushing around us. "Sophie has told me that in Sweden there is a whole army of women dressed as soldiers," she says. "Shall we go and find them?"

I look at the shoreline as it draws away from us, and then back at Isobel again. Her red hair blows across her forehead and her eyes are the exact green of the ocean. I shrug, and spread out my hands.

Can I love her?

My heart struggles and beats like a trapped bird as the space between me and the soil of Scotland widens. I have left the Queen to her fate, I have left William to his death. I have left the Blackadder Water to

457

flow from the heather of the Lammermuir Hills, down, down, past a castle that will one day again be a collection of stone, past the villages, into the waters of the Whiteadder and down into the sea. The Hume clan will live and die, babies will be born, men will grow old, women will dance and plow fields, the stars turn in the sky, the rocks crumble and fall, and still that river will run, no matter who claims it.

Black running water, water with no history, water that does not know its name. I turn my face away from Scotland and into the wind.

Postscript

The identity of the King's murderer has never been solved, though many were accused, including the Queen herself and some of Scotland's leading nobles.

On 27 June 1567, Captain William Blackadder was tried by the Lords of the Secret Council. Although he insisted he was innocent, he was found guilty of being art and part of Darnley's murder. He was hanged, drawn, and quartered at the Mercat Cross in Edinburgh. John Blackadder was also executed.

The same month, the Queen was imprisoned by her lords in Loch Leven Castle on an island in Loch Leven. In such harsh conditions, she miscarried Bothwell's twin babies. Taking advantage of her weakened condition, the lords forced her to abdicate in favor of her infant son, who became King James VI of Scotland. She was forced to name her half-brother, Lord James Stewart the Earl of Moray, as regent.

Mary was held captive for a year until she disguised herself as a servant and escaped. She raised an army to regain her throne but was overpowered and fled across the border into England, throwing herself on the mercy of her cousin Queen Elizabeth. Elizabeth ordered that Mary be kept under house arrest at a series of castles in northern England. Her confinement lasted some twenty years, until she was found guilty of plotting against Elizabeth and sentenced to death. She was beheaded on the third blow of the ax on 8 February 1587.

Mary Seton stayed with the Queen until 1583, when ill health forced her to move to a convent in France. She never married.

Bothwell fled to the isles of Orkney and Shetland, where he tried to raise more men to return to Scotland to fight for the Queen. He was pursued by his enemies and narrowly escaped to Norway, where he was imprisoned in harsh conditions for years. He died in 1578, insane from his confinement.

In January 1570, three years after he became regent, Lord James was assassinated by a member of the Hamilton family after many of the nobles had become disaffected with his rule and believed he was plotting to seize the throne for himself.

Lord Hume became a supporter of Mary's after she fled to England. With Maitland and Kircaldy of Grange, he held Edinburgh Castle in the hope of her eventual return. In May 1575 the English army brought siege guns and after thirteen days of bombardment that almost reduced the castle to ruins, it fell to James Douglas, the Earl of Morton. Hume and Maitland both died in prison later that year.

On Queen Elizabeth's death in 1603, Mary's son became King James I of England.

Tulliallan Castle was lost to the Blackadder family by John Blackadder's grandson less than one hundred years later, when he impoverished his estate and retired to America.

Blackadder Castle was never again held by the Blackadder family. Its ruins still stand on the banks of Blackadder Water in Berwickshire.

Author's note

Brought to fame (or infamy) through the *Blackadder* television series written by Ben Elton and Richard Curtis and starring Rowan Atkinson, the name "Blackadder" originally comes from the Cambro-British word *awedur,* meaning a running stream. Blackadder Water rises in the Lammermuir Hills, flows down through the village of Allanton in Berwickshire on the Scottish-English border, and joins the Whiteadder Water before flowing to the sea. The Blackadder family took its name from the river and built Blackadder Castle on the river-bank sometime in the fourteenth or fifteenth century. The estate was broken up and sold in the 1920s, but many of its buildings and farms still carry the Blackadder name.

I am indebted to the following books for my research:

Bingham, Madeleine. *Scotland Under Mary Stuart: An Account of Everyday Life.* New York: St. Martins Press, 1971.

Dunn, Jane. *Elizabeth & Mary: Cousins, Rivals, Queens.* London: Harper Perennial, 2003.

Fraser, Antonia. *Mary Queen of Scots.* 1969. Reprint. Great Britain: Phoenix Press, 2003.

Guy, John. *My Heart Is My Own: The Life of Mary Queen of Scots.* London: Harper Perennial, 2004.

Weir, Alison. *Mary Queen of Scots and the Murder of Lord Darnley.* London: Pimlico, 2004.

Acknowledgments

In Scotland, thanks to Blair and Patricia Harrower of Blackadder Mount, who invited me in for tea, shared their information about the history of Blackadder Castle and allowed me to visit the ruins of Blackadder House on their property. I'm grateful to John Russell, caretaker of Old Tulliallan Castle, for taking a descendant of the dastardly Blackadders on a tour of Tulliallan and its grounds. VisitScotland arranged personal tours of the Palace of Holyroodhouse and Stirling Castle, which were most useful. Christa Wynn-Williams made me welcome at her home in Edinburgh while I was researching the book. Astrid Turner and Rob McConnell put me up in Saint Andrews for weeks on end and helped point me in the direction of Blackadder Castle in the first place.

In Alaska, thanks to Carolyn Servid and Dorik Mechau of the Island Institute for a much needed one-month writer's residency in a house facing the ocean and surrounded by forest. The residents of the picturesque town of Sitka on Baranof Island made me very welcome, particularly Richard Nelson (Nels), Liz McKenzie and the good people of the Back Door Café.

In Australia, Varuna, the Writers' House awarded me a Litlink residency to work on this novel. *The Raven's Heart* was later selected for the Varuna HarperCollins Manuscript Development Award, which involved a ten-day residency at Varuna. Thanks to Varuna's staff, creative director Peter Bishop and award judge Katherine Howell for their enthusiastic support and to the other winners that year who were great company during the residency—Jessie Cole, Damean Posner, Brad McCann and Maryanne Khan.

Linda Funnell from HarperCollins gave me detailed and wise editorial suggestions as part of the award and was very generous with her time. Thanks also to Jo Butler, Kate O'Donnell, Kate Burnitt and other editorial staff at HarperCollins for their advice in murdering my darlings and bringing the manuscript down to a manageable size.

The Northern Rivers Writers' Centre in Byron Bay has been an ongoing support since I moved to Byron Shire more than a decade ago and I thank previous directors Jill Eddington and Jeni Caffin, and the centre's staff, particularly Susie Warwick.

Many friends and family members, including Helena Bernard, Roe Ritchie, Jude Berg, Suzy Manigian, Sue Fick, Niki Georgallis, Dee Verrall and others, gave help of different kinds. Thanks to all of you.

I'm grateful to the many people interested in the history of the Blackadders who generously continue to share their research, including those who contribute to "Blackadder: The Real Damn Dynasty" family history website and email list.

My writing group went well beyond the call of duty in reading several drafts. Heartfelt thanks to Hayley Katzen, Sarah Armstrong and Emma Hardman for their stamina, constructive critique, humor and title ideas.

And thanks to my partner, Andi Davey, who never wavered and kept me fuelled with love, kisses and the world's best coffee while I wrote *The Raven's Heart*.

Jesse Blackadder

Passionate about words, Jesse Blackadder is an Australian novelist and award-winning freelance journalist.

Jesse has won several writing awards, most recently the Guy Morrison Prize for Literary Journalism, the Varuna HarperCollins Manuscript Development Award, and the Gay and Lesbian Mardi Gras Short Story Award. She was awarded the 2011-12 Australian Antarctic Arts Fellowship by the Australian Antarctic Division and traveled to Antarctica to research the first woman to reach the frozen continent.

Jesse has also been a writer in residence in Sitka Alaska, in the outback of Australia, Byron Bay, and at Varuna, the Writers' House in the Blue Mountains.

She lives in Byron Bay, Australia.

For more information about Jesse Blackadder
and her writing please visit her website:
www.jesseblackadder.com

For more information about Bywater Books
and the annual *Bywater Prize for Fiction,*
please visit our website:
www.bywaterbooks.com

CPSIA information can be obtained
at www.ICGtesting.com
Printed in the USA
JSHW022236280621
16390JS00003B/10